The
Sapphire
Child

ALSO BY
JANET MACLEOD TROTTER:

The Raj Hotel Series

The India Tea Series

HISTORICAL

The Jarrow Trilogy

The Durham Trilogy

The Tyneside Sagas

A Handful of Stars

Chasing the Dream

For Love & Glory

The Great War Sagas

No Greater Love (formerly The Suffragette)

A Crimson Dawn

Scottish Historical Romance

The Jacobite Lass

The Beltane Fires

Highlander in Muscovy

MYSTERY/CRIME

The Vanishing of Ruth

The Haunting of Kulah

TEENAGE

Love Games

NON-FICTION

Beatles & Chiefs

The Sapphire Child

Book 2 of the Raj Hotel Series

JANET MACLEOD TROTTER

LAKE UNION
PUBLISHING

Text copyright © 2020 by Janet MacLeod Trotter
All rights reserved.

No part of this book may be reproduced, or stored in a retrieval system, or transmitted in any form or by any means, electronic, mechanical, photocopying, recording, or otherwise, without express written permission of the publisher.

Published by Lake Union Publishing, Seattle

www.apub.com

Amazon, the Amazon logo, and Lake Union Publishing are trademarks of Amazon.com, Inc., or its affiliates.

ISBN-13: 9781542092609
ISBN-10: 1542092604

Cover design by Plum5 Limited

Printed in the United States of America

To Connie, Timothy, Yumna, Delilah, Ajooni,
Mollie and April – our young ones who bring us
joy and hope for the future.

Prologue

'Coward!'

Andrew thought he'd misheard. He stood, bat in hand, ready to face the bowler.

'Cowardly, cowardly, Lomax,' George Gotley hissed at him from behind the stumps. 'Just like your father.'

Andrew attempted to ignore him and concentrate on the bowler.

'Lily-livered Lomax,' George needled him again. 'Can't see why they chose you for the First Eleven. You'll let them down just like your father did the regiment.'

Andrew felt a slight sweat break out on his brow. He gripped his bat harder and, still facing forward, said through gritted teeth, 'Shut up, Gotley. You're jealous 'cause my dad is a Great War veteran and yours isn't.'

The bowler was now starting his run up.

'I'd be ashamed if he was my father,' George retorted. 'He was a disgrace to the Rifles.'

Andrew clenched his teeth even harder to stop himself retaliating. Gotley resented him being chosen for the school cricket team and was using this house match to taunt him, he told himself.

'Do you know why your father left the army, Lomax?' George persisted. 'Court-martialled for cowardice – should have been shot – that's what my papa said. Now your father's just a box-wallah with a couple of second-rate hotels for half-halfs.'

He could stand it no longer. Turning to glare at his classmate, Andrew shouted, 'Shut up!'

A moment later, the cricket ball came hurtling at him and caught him on his shin pad.

'Owzat!' bellowed George, and the umpire's finger went up into the air.

Andrew didn't protest, but as he walked back to the pavilion, bat under his arm, he was overcome with anger. Behind the cricket pitch, the Himalayan foothills rose in a jagged line that pierced the blue sky. That way lay Kashmir, where his father and stepmother lived. He longed to be back there. How dare Gotley say such things about his dad!

When George and the other fielders trooped into the changing room, Andrew was waiting.

'Not such a great batsman after all, are you, Lomax?' George crowed. 'Out for a duck.'

'What you said out there was unforgiveable, Gotley.' Andrew advanced on him. 'I demand an apology.'

George sneered, 'I'm not going to apologise for anything. It's all true. Papa told me all about your father disgracing the Peshawar Rifles. Don't know why they allowed you into this school, Lomax. It's supposed to be for the sons of the army's elite.'

Andrew towered over George, clenching his fists. For an instant he saw alarm on the other boy's face. 'My father was a hero in Mesopotamia and before that he served on the North West Frontier for years. He was soldiering when your father was a puking baby in nappies.'

George flushed. 'My papa's a major – which is more than your father ever was. And mine hasn't been drummed out of the regiment for cowardice.'

'That's a lie!' Andrew glanced around at his teammates; no one was meeting his look. 'Donaldson?' he appealed to his friend. 'You know my father; he's no coward.'

Donaldson seemed wary. 'Leave him be, Gotley.' Then, pulling Andrew away, he added, 'Come on, Lomax; ignore him.'

Despite being riled, Andrew made a supreme effort and stepped away. Gotley was known for baiting other boys and boasting about his father being a major, yet he had never picked on him before. At thirteen, Andrew was tall and muscular for his age, which perhaps had kept him from being a focus of George's bullying.

'And that's not all.' George followed Andrew and prodded him in the back. 'Your father's a double disgrace. Carrying on with that woman you pretend is your stepmother. What's it you call her? Meemee?' He repeated the name in a whining, babyish tone. 'Meemee! Meemee!'

Andrew spun round, anger flaring again. 'Don't you dare talk about my stepmother like that!'

'But she's not your stepmother – not according to my papa – because your father never married her. She's just his whore—' George said with glee.

'Steady on, Gotley,' Donaldson said, trying to intervene.

Andrew brushed his friend aside and pushed George back in the chest. 'You rat, Gotley.'

George laughed in his face. 'Funny; that's what my papa said about your father and his mistress – they're like a couple of sewer rats copulating. And she's not even pretty. Got breasts like pancakes—'

Andrew could no longer hear a word of what Gotley or anyone else was saying. Anger coursed through his whole body, making his head and ears pound with noise. He sprang forward at George, giving off a great roar of rage, and tackled him to the ground, and with Gotley immobilised he let his fists fly. George screamed and struggled. Andrew saw blood spurt from George's nose, but he didn't stop.

Suddenly, a voice barked, 'What in God's name is going on?'

Someone grabbed Andrew round the neck and pulled him back. Choking, he resisted, still trying to swing at George. Captain Rae, their games master, had seized him by the collar and hauled him to his feet. George was still writhing on the floor, hands over his face, moaning in pain.

'Explain yourself,' Captain Rae ordered.

Andrew stood panting. He wasn't going to tell tales.

'Lomax savagely attacked Gotley, sir,' one of George's friends piped up.

'Gotley provoked him,' Donaldson defended Andrew.

'Enough!' bawled Rae, bending over George. At the sight of blood, he said, 'Help him up, boys, and take him to Matron.'

When Andrew moved to lend a hand, Rae grabbed his arm. 'Not you, Lomax. You've done enough harm already.'

'But, sir—'

'Don't "but, sir" me,' he snapped. 'You're in big trouble, Lomax. Now, get out of my sight!'

Chapter 1

Twenty-year-old Stella Dubois quickly brushed her honey-blonde hair and sprayed on eau de cologne – a gift from her friend Baroness Cussack – before rushing out of the manager's bungalow and across the servants' compound. Frisky, her ageing dog, ambled out of the shade of a jacaranda tree and wagged his curly tail in welcome.

'Hello, old boy!' She bent and hugged him round the neck, receiving licks to her pink cheeks. It wasn't even seven o'clock in the morning, yet the air was already hot and oppressive.

'Stella!' her mother called from the bungalow steps. 'Don't get distracted. Mrs Shankley will be waiting for you. Chop chop!'

Stella gave Frisky a final pat and leapt up.

As she hurried across the hotel courtyard, she exchanged grins with Sunil the porter, who was sprinkling water from a bucket to dampen down the dust.

In the foyer, beneath the noisy whir of overhead fans her father was hovering behind the polished reception table, waiting to greet his guests for breakfast. Charlie Dubois, electric light glinting off his bald head, was dressed immaculately in a dark suit and faded lilac cravat. No matter how high the temperatures climbed, he refused to wear lightweight white suits, dismissing them as too casual for the honoured position of manager of The Raj Hotel. Catching sight of his daughter, his round moustachioed face creased in a broad smile.

'Good morning, Sweet Pea!'

'Morning, Pa!'

Threading her way through the profusion of potted ferns and jumble of cane tables and chairs, Stella hurried past the dark teak staircase and down the corridor. She knocked on Mrs Shankley's bedroom door and then entered, knowing the old woman wouldn't have heard.

'Morning, Mrs S,' she shouted. 'Did you sleep well?'

Once stout and robust, the former missionary had shrunk to a frail and forgetful elderly lady who constantly misplaced her new electrical hearing aid, her reading glasses and on occasion even her false teeth. Myrtle, Stella's mother, was of the opinion that their long-time guest should be placed in a nursing home, but Stella couldn't bear the thought.

Winifred Shankley was kind and gentle and had been a resident of The Raj Hotel for as long as Stella could remember. Mrs Shankley was half-dressed and peering under the bedside table.

Catching sight of Stella, she smiled. 'My dear, I seem to have mislaid . . .' She gave an apologetic shrug. 'Well, I'm not sure quite what. Do you think you can help? Sorry, I'm such a nuisance.'

'No, you're not,' said Stella, getting down on all fours and searching. 'Here it is – your ear trumpet.' She stood up and handed over the ancient brass device. 'You don't need it any more, Mrs S. You use an electrical hearing aid now, remember? The one with the battery that goes inside your handbag.'

Stella quickly retrieved the slim headset from the bedside table and fitted it over the woman's head. 'That better?'

Winifred's face lit up in a smile. 'Stella, you are an angel. What would I do without you?'

As she helped the resident dress, Stella chatted about their mutual friend, Baroness Cussack.

'The baroness is already in Kashmir staying on the *Queen of the Lake*. I had a postcard from her last week.'

'Postcard from the queen?' Winifred marvelled.

'No, from Baroness Hester.' Stella laughed.

The missionary gave a girlish giggle. 'Ah, silly of me. Well, dear Hester is the nearest we have to royalty at the Raj, isn't she?'

'She is! I can't wait to see her. I'll be travelling through Srinagar next week on my way up to Gulmarg and will spend a couple of nights with her.'

'Gulmarg?'

'Remember, that's where Pa's bosses, the Lomaxes, live now? They run The Raj-in-the-Hills Hotel – open it every hot season and I go up there to help.'

'Ah, yes, Kashmir.' Winifred nodded. 'How are Captain Tom and dear Esmie?'

Stella reached for a hairbrush and began to tidy and fluff up the woman's thin white hair. Only the most long-standing residents still called the hotel owner 'Captain'. It was a throwback to when the dashing Tom Lomax had been an officer in the Peshawar Rifles before the Kaiser's war. But Tom didn't like to be referred to as such and never talked about his time in the army or that part of his life before he married his third wife, Esmie. To do so could precipitate one of his dark moods – 'black monsoons', as Esmie called them.

Stella adored them both. Tom had saved The Raj Hotel from bankruptcy and kept on the Dubois family to manage it, for which her parents would be forever grateful.

Stella also had a soft spot for their thirteen-year-old son, Andrew. Despite his age he was generous and kind and made her laugh. She hadn't seen him since Christmas, even though he was at school in the hill station of Murree, which was only two hours away.

'I'm longing to see the Lomaxes,' said Stella. 'They haven't been down here for months. I love Kashmir, but I wouldn't want to spend the winter there – it's far too cold and there's nothing to do once the holidaymakers leave – and I'd miss my family and the hotel and all my friends here.'

Winifred gave her an expectant look. 'Am I going with you to Gulmarg?'

'Sorry, Mrs S, not this time. I'll be working. My cousin Ada is going to come in and help you like she did last year. You like her.'

The old woman looked unsure. 'Ah, Ada. That's kind of her. But I'll miss you, Stella. No one can take your place.'

Stella kissed her soft cheek. 'I should hope not,' she said, smiling. 'Because I'll be back before you know it.'

Stella kept busy all day. After helping Mrs Shankley to the breakfast table, she took a turn at the reception desk while her father chatted to the guests. She supervised the replenishing of flowers in the hallway and the lounge and helped her mother draw up menus for the week ahead. In the afternoon she played cards with Mr Ansom and Mr Fritwell, two of the other residents who had lived in the hotel for as long as Stella could remember. Ansom was a stooped, craggy-faced retired engineer with sparse hair who walked with the aid of a stick; Fritwell was a portly former army quartermaster with a trim white moustache and a penchant for pink gin. They spent most of their days sitting in their favourite cane chairs in the foyer, where they could gossip and keep an eye on the comings and goings in the hotel. They dozed under copies of the *Civil and Military Gazette* or sat in the fug of Ansom's cigarettes and played cards.

'Are you courting yet, Stella?' asked Fritwell.

'No.' Stella gave a smile of amusement as she shuffled the cards.

'Charlie Dubois would send them packing, eh, Stella?' Ansom gave a throaty laugh.

'Your brother must have suitable friends,' persisted Fritwell.

'I'm not interested in Jimmy's friends,' said Stella. 'All they talk about is cricket or cars. The man I marry will be interested in the things I like. I believe what the baroness told me: marry for love or not at all.'

'Bravo, Stella!' Ansom grinned. 'That's you told, Fritters. Now deal the cards and stop trying to put Stella off her game.'

That evening, Ada came to the Dubois' bungalow to discuss the duties she would take over from Stella. Her cousin was plumply pretty with wavy dark hair and an infectious laugh. They sat on the veranda steps trying to catch any lick of evening breeze.

'Watch out for Fritters,' Stella warned. 'He'll quiz you about your love life and try to marry you off before the summer's out.'

'Well, if he can introduce me to some charming army officers,' Ada said with a grin, 'then I'll not complain.'

Stella nudged her. 'They'll be over seventy and probably incontinent.'

Ada laughed. 'It's all right for you – you're going to the hills where there'll be heaps of young officers on leave looking for girls to flirt with.'

'I'm going there to work, not flirt,' Stella reminded her.

Ada arched her brows. 'I'm sure there'll be time for both.'

'Anyway,' said Stella, 'I've written out instructions for you . . .'

'Yes, yes, I know all that.' Ada waved an impatient hand. 'Is it true Jimmy is courting that girl from Lovell's haberdashery – Yvonne Harvey?'

Stella shrugged. 'I can't keep up with my brother's girlfriends.'

'I saw them doing the quickstep at the railway dance last Saturday,' said Ada. 'She was flirting with him all evening.'

'I didn't know your dad let you go. Pa wouldn't like me going to the railway dance.'

Ada huffed. 'There's nothing wrong with railwaymen. Uncle Charlie is too fussy – just because you're fair-skinned and mix with the likes of the Lomaxes, he thinks you can marry above us Anglo-Indians.'

Stella defended her father. 'Pa doesn't look down on anyone and neither do I. It's just that he doesn't want me marrying anyone till I'm older – and when I do, the choice will be mine.' She held up her list of jobs. 'Come on, we're supposed to be going over this.'

Before she could begin, though, Stella was interrupted by her father hurrying across the hotel courtyard, his look agitated.

'There you are!' He stopped and mopped his brow with a lilac-coloured handkerchief. 'Sorry to spoil your evening, young ladies.' He gave Ada a distracted look.

'What's wrong, Pa?' Stella said, getting quickly to her feet.

'It's the Lomaxes – I've just had a telephone call.'

'What's happened? Is Mr Lomax all right?'

'Yes, yes, I spoke to him. They're coming to Pindi. They'll be here in a couple of hours so we must prepare their rooms at once.'

Stella brightened. 'That's good news, isn't it? Are they coming to shop?'

'No, it's not shopping that brings them down from Kashmir.' Charlie's brow furrowed. 'It's Master Andrew.'

'Andrew?' Stella felt a moment's anxiety.

Her father dabbed his upper lip with his handkerchief. 'There's been some sort of trouble in Murree.'

Chapter 2

Andrew sat outside the headmaster's study, squirming in his seat. He couldn't sit still. He jiggled his leg and rubbed at his sore knuckles. He pulled at his constricting tie and gnawed at a calloused finger, noticing his palm was still engrained with soil from scrambling up the ravine behind the school. He sat on his hands and tried to calm his racing pulse. Was it only four days ago that life had been normal?

Today, he should have been playing cricket but here he was, like a condemned man, sitting in disgrace, awaiting his fate. None of his friends had spoken to him since the incident; instead they were avoiding him as if he could infect them with his sudden unpopularity. He had put another boy in the school sanatorium with a broken cheekbone and a bloody nose.

'You could have damaged his sight!' Mr Bishop, the headmaster, had fulminated. 'We won't tolerate bullying at Nicholson.'

Andrew had refused to say why he had attacked George Gotley. He was prepared to take his punishment and he forced himself not to cry out when Bishop had given him ten strikes of the cane on his backside. His skin still smarted from the beating. He'd thought that would be the end of it, but Gotley's father was a major in the

Peshawar Rifles and had arrived at the school demanding further retribution.

'If you don't expel that Lomax boy,' Major Gotley had thundered, 'I shall take the matter to the police.'

Now, two days after the major's interference, it was his father's voice that Andrew could hear remonstrating with the headmaster beyond the door of the study.

'Surely a suspension for the rest of term would be punishment enough?'

'Major Gotley thinks not,' said Mr Bishop in his whining nasal voice. 'I'm sorry, Mr Lomax, but I'd rather the police weren't involved.'

'Then let me speak to the major – man to man – and see if we can sort out the misunderstanding.'

'I fear it's too late for that. If Andrew had shown any remorse for his actions, Major Gotley might have been mollified. But your son refuses to apologise.'

'I'll damn well make him apologise!'

Andrew cringed to hear the anger in his father's voice. Of all the people in the world, it was his father whom he wanted to please the most. When his parents had arrived twenty minutes ago, his father had given his shoulder an encouraging squeeze and said, 'We'll get this sorted.' Esmie, his stepmother, had hugged him and kissed his cheek, but there had been no time for him to explain anything as Mr Bishop, with a nervous twitch of his billowing black gown, had ushered the adults into his study.

Andrew strained to listen.

'Perhaps he should be allowed to explain for himself.' It was Esmie's voice speaking calmly over those of the men. 'Andy is a caring boy. We don't understand why he should have attacked George Gotley. We're not excusing what he's done, but there must be a reason.'

Andrew's insides twisted at Esmie's familiar endearment; at home he was always called Andy.

He heard his headmaster sigh. 'He's refused any attempt to explain himself. It's obviously jealousy, pure and simple. The Gotley boy said it was unprovoked. He said that Andrew has always resented that George's father is a serving officer in the Rifles.'

Andrew was furious. What a lie! George had goaded him until he could bear no more of his poisonous words. It was his father who had been a hero in the last war, not Gotley's. Major Gotley had still been in training in 1918, whereas his father was a veteran of Mesopotamia and had been at the relief of Baghdad. Old Fritwell, the portly ex-soldier at The Raj Hotel, had told him so on many occasions.

The study door opened and Andrew quickly stood up. Mr Bishop, his round face sweating, wagged a plump finger at him.

'Come in, Lomax,' he ordered.

Andrew followed. His father was standing in front of the headmaster's vast untidy desk, hands plunged in his pockets, jiggling coins. Esmie, seated, gave him an anxious smile.

'This is your last chance to explain why you punched George Gotley,' said Mr Bishop.

Andrew's palms sweated. He felt breathless. 'I'd rather not say.'

His father lost his patience. 'For God's sake, Andrew! I know boys fall out about things. Just take your punishment and say you're sorry.'

'I've been punished,' said Andrew, meeting his father's look.

'Don't be insolent, Lomax,' Mr Bishop rebuked. 'You're on very thin ice here. If you don't explain your behaviour, I'll have no choice but to expel you. Nicholson's will not tolerate wild and savage behaviour.'

Andrew gritted his teeth. His jaw was aching with the strain of not shouting at his hateful headmaster.

Esmie touched him gently on the arm. 'I can tell you've been upset by something, so this is your chance to say what happened. Please, Andy.'

Andrew looked into Esmie's kind face. Her pretty grey eyes were full of compassion and she was smiling with encouragement. She was smartly dressed in a summer frock and blue hat – he knew she was trying to impress baldy Bishop – but her flyaway brown hair was still escaping its pins and curling around her slim cheeks. His eyes stung with tears he had managed to hold back for days. She was his 'Meemee', the one he thought of as his real mother – not the remote woman in Scotland who sent him extravagant and useless presents on his birthday.

'We can keep it between ourselves,' she said softly. 'Just tell your dad and Mr Bishop what you got so angry about.'

Andrew longed to confide in them but he couldn't tell them the truth – especially couldn't tell *her* the full truth – and would rather face expulsion than repeat the vile words.

Mr Bishop pulled on his gown and puffed out his red cheeks. 'Out with it, Lomax. This is your final warning. Apologise!'

Andrew's head throbbed with anger. 'I won't apologise, sir. Not for the lies Gotley said about . . . about—'

'About what?' Tom Lomax cried in bewilderment. 'For God's sake, Andrew, spit it out.'

Andrew could not bear his father's pained look. 'He called you a coward!' he blurted out. 'Said you were a traitor to the Peshawar Rifles – that you'd been court-martialled and left the regiment in disgrace – that you should have been shot for cowardice and that the Lomaxes are lily-livered.'

Andrew expected his father to shout with indignation, but he didn't. His lean face went rigid as he clenched his jaw. His blue eyes looked sad, not angry. Esmie brushed Tom's hand and they exchanged knowing looks.

Andrew felt his insides knot with anxiety. 'I told you it was lies, Dad,' he said. 'He made them up because you were a hero in the war and his father wasn't.'

'Well,' huffed Bishop, 'why didn't you say any of this before? I'll have to speak to Major Gotley—'

'No,' Tom said forcefully, 'I won't have my son interrogated further by the major or anyone else.'

'Don't you want to clear your name?' Bishop asked.

It was the very question Andrew wanted answered too, but the look his father gave the headmaster was withering.

'I have nothing to explain to you or anyone else,' Tom said. 'Least of all to a puffed-up man like Major Gotley who drips poison into the ears of his impressionable son.' His look softened as he glanced at Andrew. 'This whole episode has been blown out of all proportion. It's a spat between boys. George should not have provoked Andrew, but neither should my son have resorted to violence to settle their quarrel. You should have got to the bottom of it sooner and not allowed yourself to be swayed by the major's threats.'

'Now look here, Lomax,' Bishop blustered. 'I find your tone most offensive. We've only Andrew's word on this – he could be making it up and trying to get poor Gotley into trouble.'

'Why are you so quick to believe George?' Tom demanded. 'Is it because he's the son of a major and not a mere box-wallah like me?'

Bishop went puce. 'Of course not.'

'Well, my son's word is good enough for me,' Tom said hotly. 'As far as I'm concerned, the matter has been dealt with. Andrew has explained the provocation and taken his punishment.'

Andrew watched the sweat break out on Bishop's head. 'It most certainly has not been dealt with,' he said, his voice rising. 'I have a boy in the san' with a broken cheekbone and a father demanding the police be called. Nicholson School is in danger of being brought into disrepute by the actions of Lomax Junior. Despite what George might or might not have said, your son must apologise for his savage attack.'

Andrew saw sudden fury flash in his father's eyes. 'I would have thought that ten strokes of the cane was payment enough for the punch that Andrew threw.'

'Not in my book,' snapped Bishop. He turned and glared at Andrew. 'One last time: are you prepared to say sorry to young Gotley?'

Andrew stared back, unblinkingly. 'I'm sorry I broke his cheekbone – but I'm not sorry I hit him, sir. And if he said those lies again, I'd hit him again.'

Bishop wagged a finger in his face. 'Then I have no choice but to send you home, boy!' He turned to Tom. 'Lomax is suspended for the rest of term. I should expel him on the spot but I'm a reasonable man and hope that a period of reflection at home and some discipline from his parents will lead him to see the error of his ways. If he sends a written apology, I shall allow him back next term.'

Andrew looked between the adults, wondering if this was good news or not. He would get a whole summer to roam around Gulmarg free from lessons – yet he would miss out on all the cricket matches, sports day and the summer camp at Ghora Gali.

He saw Esmie put a restraining hand on his father's arm, to no avail.

'That won't be happening,' Tom said in a clipped tone. 'I don't wish my son to be sent to a school where the headmaster finds it more convenient to believe the word of a bully rather than the bullied. Andrew will not be returning next term. No doubt that will be a relief to you, Mr Bishop.'

With that, he took Esmie by the elbow and placed a hand on Andrew's back, steering them both out of the door.

Andrew's pulse drummed. He was dizzy with the speed and turn of events. He tried to catch Esmie's eye, but she was looking worriedly at his father. He had seldom seen his dad so furious, his jaw set and his dark eyebrows gathered in a frown. Andrew felt a surge of euphoria; his father had stood up for him in front of sweaty Bishop.

He couldn't wait for word to get back to the spiteful George of heroic Tom Lomax who wouldn't let his son be intimidated by Major Gotley or humiliated by badger-breath Bishop. He was leaving Nicholson's. He felt defiant and vindicated – and he hadn't had to utter the other foul words that George had said that he knew would have wounded his father far more than being called a coward.

While his father made a phone call to Rawalpindi to alert the Duboises of their staying overnight, Esmie helped Andrew pack. He felt suddenly awkward with his stepmother and threw his clothes hastily into his trunk. Half an hour later, all three were driving out of the school gates in their lumbering van with its fading lettering proclaiming 'The Raj Hotels: Rawalpindi and Gulmarg' on the side.

Andrew sat between his parents, unnerved by their silence. His father chain-smoked as the vehicle jostled along the Mall.

He forced himself to ask the question that was preying on his mind. 'Dad . . . none of it's true, is it? About the court-martial and having to leave the army under a cloud?'

His father's expression tightened. 'Now's not the time to talk about this,' he replied.

Andrew's alarm grew. He longed to hear his father deny the accusations. Why couldn't he just tell him?

Esmie gave him a reassuring look. 'Your father is one of the bravest men I know – and he certainly wasn't forced to leave the army – he chose to go.'

Andrew watched his father, expecting him to confirm her words. But he stared rigidly ahead, gripping the steering wheel, and said nothing. An hour ago, Andrew had been triumphant that he had stood up for him, but now he wondered if his father was regretting it. He seemed very cross with him.

Andrew decided he might gain his approval by talking about the future rather than dwelling on the past.

'Where do you think I should go to school, Dad?' he asked. 'Can I go to Biscoe's in Srinagar? They do mountaineering and trekking, as well as lots of swimming.'

'It's too soon,' his father muttered. 'Let's just see.'

'If I went there,' Andrew enthused, 'I could be a weekly boarder and come home to Gulmarg at weekends. And in the summer term I could lodge with Baroness Cussack on her houseboat so that I don't miss out on weekend cricket matches.'

'Andy!' his father protested. 'You can't just expect to walk into whatever school you fancy. They'll want to know why you've left Nicholson's.'

Andrew's stomach tightened. 'They won't ask Mr Bishop, will they?'

'Even if they don't, word travels fast.' His look softened. 'Don't worry about it. Meemee and I will have to discuss it first.'

'But Biscoe's might be just the place for you,' Esmie said with a pat on his arm.

Andrew stiffened at her touch. George's loathsome words wormed their way back into his thoughts.

As they descended to the plain, Andrew grew sleepy and his head began to nod.

'Put your head on my lap,' Esmie offered.

Andrew forced himself to stay awake. 'I'm fine, thank you.'

He turned away from her puzzled look and stared rigidly ahead.

Chapter 3

The Raj Hotel, Rawalpindi, 1933

By the time the Lomaxes arrived at the hotel – having stopped to eat on the way – it was late and they went hurriedly to bed, assuring the Duboises that everything was fine. Stella was struck by how much Andrew had grown, and he gave her a bashful smile as he made for the stairs.

'Look. I'm much taller than you now!' He patted the top of her head the way she used to do to him. His voice was deeper, too.

'Stop that.' Stella batted his hand away and laughed. 'I bet I can still beat you at backgammon.'

'Bet you can't.'

Esmie interrupted. 'Plenty time for challenges tomorrow. Bed now, Andy.'

He didn't seem to know what to do with his gangling limbs and clumsily knocked into a table, scattering a pile of newspapers. Stella bent to help him pick them up and he ruffled her hair again.

Stella laughed and pushed him off. 'I'd forgotten how annoying you can be.'

Andrew smiled and thrust his untidy pile of newspapers back on the table. ''Night, Stella,' he said, leaping up the stairs two at a time.

Early the next morning, Stella found Tom smoking in the courtyard and talking to her father. Frisky was snuffling around Tom's feet.

'Ah, Stella!' Tom looked pleased to see her. 'I've just been telling your father our reason for being in Murree. I'm sorry if we caused concern. There's nothing to worry about. It's just we're not happy with the school and have decided to take Andy away from it.'

'Oh dear,' said Stella. 'I'm sorry to hear that. I thought Andy was happy—'

'Not for us to comment, Sweet Pea,' her father interrupted.

Tom drew hard on his cigarette and continued. 'Anyway, there was no point paying to stay in Murree when we were so near Pindi – and we thought we could take you back with us, Stella – save you the cost of the journey next week.'

Stella brightened. 'Oh, yes please!' Then she looked quickly at her father. 'If that's all right with you, Pa?'

Charlie smiled. 'Of course it is. Whatever is most convenient and beneficial for Mr and Mrs Lomax will gladden my heart too.'

Tom nodded, his smile tight. 'Thank you, Charlie.'

Stella bent to pet Frisky. 'Aren't we lucky, old boy? We'll be in Kashmir earlier than expected and your friend Andy will be there too.'

Tom ground out his cigarette. 'I'd appreciate it if you kept the news about Andy leaving Nicholson's to yourselves for the moment. We don't want him being the subject of gossip around Pindi.'

Stella gave him a look of surprise. 'Of course, we won't say a word, Mr Lomax.'

By the time Stella had Winifred Shankley ready for breakfast, Andrew had been sent off with Jimmy on some errand. Apart from a quick hello the previous evening, she'd had no chance to speak to him and she suspected the Lomaxes were trying to keep their son out of the way of the inquisitive residents.

While Tom took the van to the garage to have the tyres pumped and the oil changed, Esmie asked Stella to accompany her to Saddar Bazaar to choose curtain material for The Raj-in-the-Hills. Esmie seemed a little subdued, so Stella did most of the talking as they walked in the shade of Esmie's parasol and hunted the stalls of the busy bazaar. Stella picked out a bolt of bright yellow with a pattern of blue birds and Esmie arranged to have it delivered to the hotel.

Esmie seemed in no hurry to get back to the hotel and steered Stella out of the bazaar and towards the Mall and its shady trees. Stella marvelled at how girlish Esmie still looked even though she must be approaching forty. She moved with a quick gracefulness and looked so elegant even in the plain practical dresses she preferred to wear. But Stella could see she was preoccupied, her delicate face strained.

'You're worrying about Andy, aren't you?' Stella finally asked.

Esmie looked at Stella with a sad but knowing expression on her face.

'Mr Lomax told me how you've taken him away from Nicholson's. Was he very unhappy there?'

'Is that what Tom said?'

'No, he didn't give a reason, but I just assumed . . .'

Esmie stopped and looked around to make sure they were alone. 'I want to be honest with you, Stella. You're like one of the family and you're close to Andy. It wasn't really our decision to take Andy away from Nicholson's; we did it before he was expelled.'

'Expelled?' Stella gasped. 'Whatever for?'

'He attacked another boy – the boy had been saying cruel things about Tom – but that was no excuse for what Andy did. George Gotley has a broken cheekbone and his father was threatening to go to the police.'

Stella was indignant. 'Andy would never start a fight. That boy must have said or done something really bad.'

'It was silly gossip about Tom's time in the army, which George must have got from his pompous father, Major Gotley.'

'If George provoked Andy then they should both be punished equally. Is the Gotley boy being sent home too?'

Esmie shook her head.

'Tom's made up his mind that Andy shouldn't go back there. If the headmaster won't deal with bullies – or bullying fathers – then he'd rather he went elsewhere.'

'Has he another school in mind?'

'Not really. Andy would like to go to Biscoe's in Srinagar.'

'That would be nice,' Stella said in approval, 'and he'd be closer to home.'

'Yes, I'd like that too. It's just . . .' Esmie's brow furrowed.

'Tell me,' said Stella.

Esmie sighed. 'I worry about his mother's reaction when she gets to hear of Andy's removal. Lydia will have to be told before the gossip reaches her.'

'But she'll want the best for Andy, won't she?'

'Oh, Stella, I don't know,' Esmie fretted. 'It might be just the excuse she's looking for to insist that Andy goes back to Scotland to be educated.'

'To Scotland?' Stella was dismayed. 'But Andy wouldn't want that, would he?'

'I don't think so,' said Esmie, 'but I suppose we've never given him the choice. Tom's always resisted it, even when Lydia promised—' She stopped abruptly. 'Anyway, Tom would hate it if Andy went so far away. And Lydia's never really shown much interest in her son, so I'd worry for him.'

Stella still remembered the forceful Lydia, though she hadn't seen her since childhood when Lydia had returned to Scotland when her marriage to Tom broke down. To Stella she had seemed as beautiful as a princess with her pale gold hair and her large blue eyes. But she also remembered her changeable moods: one moment spoiling her with presents and the next shouting rudely at Stella's parents. While she had enjoyed being fussed over, Stella had never quite trusted Lydia, who had always seemed to cause upset and tension among the grown-ups.

She remembered the relief among the residents when Lydia left, but also her mother's disgust at her sending baby Andrew back to India for Tom to bring up. *'Imagine giving up your son like that? That woman has a heart of stone.'*

Esmie, on the other hand, could not have been a more caring mother to Andy.

Stella touched her arm in reassurance. 'I'm sure there's no need to worry. Andy has a mind of his own – his mother can't force him back to Scotland against his will.'

As they turned back towards the hotel, Esmie was still pensive. 'I can't help feeling that there's something else upsetting Andy.'

'Such as?'

'I'm not sure – it's just an instinct.' Esmie looked uncomfortable. 'He's been a bit distant with me since this happened.'

'Do you want me to try and find out what's bothering him?' asked Stella.

Esmie hesitated. 'I shouldn't really ask you – but you've always been so good with Andy – if he'll tell anyone, it'll be you. Would you mind?'

'Of course not,' Stella said. 'He's probably embarrassed that he's caused such a fuss – he might feel that he's let you down. I'm sure it won't be anything more than that.'

Esmie smiled at last. 'Thank you, Stella. You're such a kind lassie.'

'Don't worry about it,' Stella said. 'I'm sure once Andy's back at Gulmarg he'll be his usual self.'

At dawn, two days later, Stella and the Lomaxes left for Kashmir with Myrtle Dubois insisting on them taking enough food for a journey twice as long.

'In case there are landslides,' she said, as she supervised the loading of the van with baskets of sandwiches and curry puffs, oranges, bananas, tinned cheese, tinned biscuits, a thermos of tea and one of coffee, bottles of soda water and bars of chocolate.

Andrew chose to sit in the back of the van with Frisky, so Stella sat up front with Esmie while Tom drove. As they left the plain and took the twisting hill road up through the pine trees, the conversation petered out. Stella wound down the window and breathed in the fresh air, excited for her first glimpse of the snow-capped mountains. No one spoke as they trundled through Murree and past the driveway to Nicholson's School.

Then they were plunging down the road to Kohala and the suspension bridge over the roaring Jhelum River, leaving British India and crossing into Kashmir. Stella's spirits soared as she gazed on the distant Himalayan peaks – they seemed to be welcoming her back.

Chapter 4

It was after dark by the time the log cabins of Gulmarg came into view. Abandoning the van at the end of the cart road, they walked up through the settlement. A full moon was bathing the turf of the golf course and polo ground in a ghostly silver, while the spire of the stone-built church thrust towards a myriad of stars. Most of the chalets were still shuttered from the cold season but soft lamplight shone from one or two.

A welcome breeze blew off the hill, bringing the scent of thyme and marjoram from the high meadows. Sounds were amplified: the bleat of a sheep and whinny of a horse. Laughter drifted down from the veranda of a sprawling low-lying building.

Panting, Stella stopped to take a breath. 'I see Nedous Hotel is already open.'

'Last week,' said Tom. 'We should have been opening this week too . . .'

The Raj-in-the-Hills lay beyond the main settlement and behind a belt of trees, nestling close to a secluded meadow. Word must have reached the staff that the Lomaxes were approaching, because Bijal, Tom's bearer, came hurrying down the path with a pony. Beside him, Maseed the assistant cook held up a kerosene lamp to light their way.

'Hello, Bijal!' Andrew called out as he rushed forward, setting Frisky barking.

'Andrew-sahib!' Bijal grinned in surprise. 'Back so soon?'

'Yes, and Stella's with us too.' Andrew turned around and pointed into the dark.

Stella had stopped to marvel at the sight of the mountains looming over the meadows, their peaks glinting in the moonlight.

'Come on, Stella!' Andrew shouted.

She waved, forcing her tired legs on. As she greeted Bijal he offered her the pony.

'Thanks, but let Esmie ride her,' said Stella, heaving for breath in the thin air.

'Meemee is much fitter than you, Stella,' Andrew teased her.

'Yes, but I want to walk across the meadow.' She pulled off her sandals and plunged her feet into the chill grass, breathing in the honey-sweetness of wild flowers. 'I've been dreaming of this moment. Come on, Frisky!'

The dog scrambled from Andrew's arms and followed at her heels.

'Wait for me!' cried Esmie, kicking off her shoes too and catching her up.

Laughing, they set off, arm-in-arm. Ahead, at the top of the meadow, lay the green-roofed hotel – no bigger than a large bungalow – its wide front door thrown open in welcome. Stella relished the whiff of woodsmoke on the clear air. Was it only that morning that they had left the furnace of Rawalpindi for this mountainous scented heaven? Esmie squeezed her arm and whispered, 'I'm so glad you're here, lassie.'

'It's the high point of my year.' Stella gave a grateful smile.

By the time they reached the hotel, their legs and the hems of their dresses were damp with dew, but neither cared. They went around the back to the annex where the Lomaxes lived. Bijal laid on tea, whisky and samosas by the sitting room fire and dispatched Maseed with two mules to bring up the luggage from the van.

Tom arched his aching back and downed a large whisky.

'You should have let me do some of the driving, darling,' Esmie said, sinking into a comfortable armchair.

'You know I make a terrible passenger,' Tom said with a wry smile. 'Always wanting to grab the wheel.' He poured himself another drink and lit a cigarette.

Stella sat by the hearth, drying her dress and sipping tea. Andrew played with Frisky, and as their play grew more boisterous the dog knocked over a side table.

'Bed, Andy,' his father said abruptly. 'You're making the dog too excitable.'

'He likes it,' said Andrew, continuing to tickle the dog and ignore the order.

Tom drained his drink and marched over, grabbing his son's arm. 'Now!'

'Tom, not so roughly,' Esmie cautioned.

Tom snapped at Andrew, 'You may not be at school but you're not on holiday either. Your mother and I will set you lessons and you'll stick to lights-out at nine. Don't think you're going to run wild all summer.'

Stella took hold of a barking Frisky and calmed him down. She saw Andrew flush with humiliation as he slunk from the room.

'I'm ready for my bed too,' Stella said, exchanging looks with Esmie. 'Unless there's anything I can do?'

'No, thanks, lassie. You must be exhausted. We're all exhausted.' She gave Tom a look. He was already pouring a third whisky.

Whisky was sometimes a precursor to one of Tom's bouts of melancholia. He was obviously upset by Andrew being forced out of Nicholson's and it had all happened at the start of the busiest time of year, when the Lomaxes were getting the hotel ready for the hot season.

Settling into her tiny bedroom at the back of the hotel, Stella determined to be optimistic. She would do all she could to help smooth things between Andrew and his parents, as well as carrying out her duties around the hotel.

Stella pulled the cool sheet up to her chin and lay back with a contented sigh. From the open window she could gaze at the stars and hear the call of a jackal in the forest beyond. She was asleep in minutes.

Chapter 5

Sometime in the night, Stella woke to the sound of footsteps in the compound. Sleepily she thought it must be the chowkidar carrying out his nightwatchman duties, but then she smelt the familiar aroma of Tom's cigarettes. Shining her torch on the bedside clock she saw it was two in the morning. What was he doing up at this hour? Sitting up in her narrow single bed, she peered out of the window.

The moon had dipped, but there was just enough light in the starlit sky to make out the tall dark-headed figure gazing upwards and blowing smoke rings. As if sensing he was being watched, he turned and looked towards the hotel. Stella almost gasped. It was Andrew, not Tom!

But then she couldn't help being amused; Andrew was experimenting with one of his father's cigarettes. If Tom caught him, he'd be in even bigger trouble than he already was. But then Tom was probably deep in a whisky-induced sleep. Esmie would be more forgiving of her stepson and chase him back to bed. Should she go out there and do so herself? Was there something else worrying him – as Esmie suspected – apart from the upset over the Gotley boy?

Stella had promised to try and find out, but was this the right moment to question Andrew? She could imagine him teasing her: *'You're not my ayah, so stop nannying me.'*

Not for the first time, Stella began to think about her relationship with the Lomaxes. She was part-employee, part-friend. She'd grown up with Andrew and was probably fonder of him than her own brother, Jimmy. For the past three years, she had come to The Raj-in-the-Hills to help out wherever she was needed. She was allowed in the kitchen by Felix, the flamboyant Goan chef, to make custard tarts and choux buns. She played piano for the guests after dinner or on wet days, and she helped the ayahs entertain the children while their parents went golfing or riding.

She was also a confidante to Esmie. Stella knew that her helping out at the Gulmarg hotel allowed Tom the leeway to either be the hospitable host or to retreat to his painting studio and be alone. Esmie encouraged her husband in his art, telling Stella, *'He's a fine artist and it's good for his mental health.'*

She was on the point of climbing out of bed to go and join Andrew outside when she saw him lick his finger and thumb and extinguish the cigarette stub. He retreated to the hotel annex, dropping the stub into a plant pot as he went. The moment had gone. She lay awake until it was almost dawn, puzzling over what was causing the boy to be so restless.

The next few days were hectic. Stella spent hours helping Karo, the Pathan sewing woman, make bedroom curtains out of the bolts of cloth from Saddar bazaar. She went over menus and checklists with Esmie and helped Tom paint some old bedside cabinets white. Bijal oversaw a top-to-bottom spring clean of all the rooms, made sure the mali had the gardens looking neat and that the syce had the ponies and mules ready for the guests arriving.

All the while, Andrew was confined to Tom's office where he sweated over maths problems and science questions that Esmie had set him. On the fourth day, when Stella took him a glass of milk and a biscuit, he looked up hopefully.

'Can you help me with this?'

Tom put his head around the door. 'No, she can't. Stella is helping Esmie.'

Andrew put his head in his hands. He had blue ink on his fingers from fiddling with his pen. 'These are too difficult,' he complained. 'Can't I read a book instead?'

'Certainly not,' said Tom.

Stella retreated with a smile of sympathy. Outside the door, she said to Tom, 'Would you like me to take him for a walk? He'd be doing games if he was at school and maybe some exercise might help him concentrate better on his lessons.'

Tom grunted. 'You sound like Esmie. Do you think I'm being too hard on him as well?'

Stella side-stepped the question and smiled. 'He's thirteen. His lessons are important but he also needs to let off steam. Give him an incentive to finish his equations.'

Tom sighed. He turned back and opened the office door. 'Andy, we'll go for a ride after tiffin,' he said.

Stella heard Andrew yelp, 'Yes!'

'As long as you finish those questions now.'

An hour later, a message was brought up to the hotel to say that the chef, Felix Dias, had arrived in Srinagar a day early.

'I'll fetch him in the van,' said Tom, 'and I'll pick up those oil paints I've ordered from the chemist while I'm in town.'

After a while, Andrew tracked the women to the linen room where they were counting sheets. He waved his ink-spattered jotter in triumph. 'Finished! Time for riding. Where's Dad?'

Stella and Esmie exchanged looks.

'I'm sorry, Andy,' said Esmie, 'but he's gone to collect Felix.'

Andrew's face sagged in disappointment. 'What? But he *promised*.'

Esmie smiled. 'You can go out once he's back.'

Andrew rolled his eyes. 'You know he won't be back till after dark.'

'He might be.'

'No, he won't,' Andrew retorted. 'Here are your stupid answers!' He threw the exercise book at her.

'Don't speak to me like that,' Esmie chided. Andrew turned and ran from the room. Esmie hurried to the door. 'Where are you going?' she called after him.

He didn't answer as he bolted down the stairs. They heard him clatter across the hall and the front door bang shut. The two women looked at each other in concern.

'He seems so angry with me,' Esmie said helplessly. 'I really don't know what I've done.'

'Let me go after him,' said Stella.

Esmie put a hand on her shoulder. 'Thank you, lassie.'

Even though Stella went up the hill by pony, it took nearly an hour to catch up with Andrew. She'd known where he would go: the high marg where the Gujjar shepherds kept their flocks of sheep and herds of cows and buffaloes. Trotting through the pine forest she was nervous of encountering a bear, but pressed on towards the grassy meadow that was dotted with the Gujjars' makeshift log cabins. She skirted the settlement, not wanting to encounter any of the fierce dogs that helped guard the flocks.

Eventually, she found Andrew sitting by a wild indigo bush on the edge of the wide meadow where pines gave way to juniper and birch. He was smoking again, but hurriedly stubbed out his cigarette as Stella approached. She made no comment as she dismounted and sank onto the grass beside him.

'What a view,' she gasped, gazing across at the majestic wall of Himalayan mountains to the north with its highest snow-clad peak, Nanga Parbat, towering king-like over them all. Far below, to the east, she could see distant Srinagar nestling in its green valley and Dal Lake glinting in the sunshine.

'What took you so long?' he asked, his look guarded.

'Gave you a good head start.' She nudged him. 'I wanted to give you time to calm down after your little tantrum.' Stella winked.

'I suppose Meemee's sent you to do her dirty work and drag me back.' He gave her a mutinous look. 'Well, I'd rather spend the night in a Gujjar's hut than do any more of her silly sums.'

Stella sat back and eyed him. 'Would you rather be at Nicholson's? Are you regretting what you've done? Esmie thinks it's not too late. If you wrote an apology you could still go back – if that's what you want.'

'Never!' Andrew said hotly. 'Meemee doesn't understand.'

'She knows you're upset but she doesn't understand why you're taking it out on her.'

'I'm not taking it out on her,' Andrew protested.

Stella put a hand on his shoulder. 'Andy, you haven't been nice to her since they picked you up from Murree. What's she done to upset you?'

Andrew hung his head and said nothing. Stella withdrew her hand. Idly, she began to pick wild flowers, twisting a long grass around them to create a small posy. She waited.

Quietly, Andrew said, 'I can't get Gotley's stinking words out of my head. They keep buzzing round and round . . .'

'Oh, Andy,' Stella said gently, 'you know they aren't true. Your dad's never been a coward about anything. Soldiers like Major Gotley don't like him because he turned his back on the army for a peaceful occupation – they look down their noses at box-wallahs like my father and yours. But our dads couldn't care less what snobs like Gotley think.'

Andrew gave her a look of despair. 'It's not just that,' he mumbled.

'Then what?'

He shook his head.

'Andy, you can tell me. I won't repeat anything to your parents that you don't want me to.'

He eyed her. 'You promise?'

'Of course.'

He dropped his voice to a whisper. 'George Gotley said terrible things about Meemee – disgusting things.'

'About Esmie?' Stella was baffled. 'What things?'

Andrew's head drooped further, his cheeks turning puce. 'He called her a . . . a . . . whore.'

Stella gasped. 'Why on earth would he say that?'

'Said she wasn't properly married to my dad – that she's just his mistress – and not even a pretty one 'cause she has pancakes instead of breasts. He went on and on saying these vile things in front of the other boys—'

'How dare he! No wonder you thumped him. I'd have done the same.'

Andrew looked back at her with tears welling in his large blue eyes. 'But why would he say that? I can't help worrying that he knows something I don't know . . .'

'Oh, Andy!' Stella threw an arm around him. 'Of course he doesn't. He was just being cruel.'

'I feel horrible for thinking badly of Meemee, but I couldn't stop hearing those words—' Abruptly he dissolved into tears.

Stella pulled him close and wrapped her arms around him, stroking his tangled hair as he cried into her shoulder.

'I'm glad you've told me,' she said softly. 'It must have been terrible keeping that bottled up. But they're just spiteful words from an unkind boy. None of it's true.'

Andrew drew back and wiped his tears on the back of his hand. 'I hate George for what he said – and the other boys too. They didn't stand up for me, so I'll never go back.'

Stella could see how unhappy he was. Perhaps the betrayal by the other boys was harder to bear than George's taunting? They had believed the bully rather than Andrew.

'Well, the best thing now,' said Stella, 'is to look forward and not back. By next term you'll be at a new school and starting again, making new friends where the Gotleys can't spoil things.'

Andrew tore up a handful of grass. 'What if there're army children at Biscoe's? Sons of officers in the Peshawar Rifles? Like Dad said, word can spread. Perhaps I should go to school much further away . . .'

Stella tried to be reassuring. 'They were lies made up by George, why should anyone else care?'

'George said his father told him,' Andrew mumbled. 'Kept saying it was all true.'

'Well, who would you rather believe – your dad or the Gotleys?'

Andrew gave her a cautious smile. 'Dad, of course.'

Stella stood up. 'Come on; let's go home. You've missed tiffin and must be ravenous. And it's time you made it up with Esmie.'

Nodding, Andrew got to his feet. 'Do I have to tell her what George said?'

'Not if you don't want to,' said Stella.

'I don't,' said Andrew forcefully.

For a moment, it struck Stella how like his father he looked with his hands plunged in his pockets, unruly dark hair falling into his eyes and his look stubborn.

Then he smiled, and the stern look vanished. 'Thanks, Stella. I always feel better after talking to you.'

'That's what friends are for, Andy,' she answered, smiling affectionately.

They set off down the marg, leading the pony between them, and Andrew began to talk about playing cricket.

Stella was relieved that his unhappy mood seemed to have passed.

Back at the hotel, Andrew apologised to Esmie and gave her an awkward hug. Esmie looked pleased, but quizzical. Stella slipped off to finish some sewing before Esmie could question her.

Chapter 6

The next day, cheered by the arrival of the ebullient hotel chef, Stella threw herself into helping Felix do an inventory of kitchen equipment and order ingredients for the following week. The first guests were due in a week's time.

It was late in the afternoon as the Lomaxes and Stella were gathering for tea on the veranda that a chaprassy came running up the path.

'But we've already had the dak for the day,' Esmie said in surprise.

'Looks like he's got a telegram,' said Tom, crossing to the steps.

Andrew was quicker and leapt down the stairs ahead of his father. Conversing with the Muslim chaprassy in Urdu, he returned, waving the brown envelope at Tom.

'It's for you, Dad.' He handed it over and resumed throwing a cricket ball in the air and catching it.

The women looked at Tom a little anxiously. Tom tore open the envelope and read the message. His frown deepened.

'Who's it from?' Esmie asked, going to his side.

Tom quickly stuffed it back in the envelope. 'We'll talk about it later.'

'Tom!' Esmie protested. 'Is it bad news?'

Andrew stopped his ball-catching and looked suddenly afraid. 'Nobody's died, have they?'

'No, nothing like that,' Tom said quickly.

'Then what?' Esmie pressed him. 'You're making us worried.'

Tom swallowed. 'It's from Lydia.'

'My mother?' Andrew asked. 'Is she all right?'

'Yes. Well, she's concerned. She's heard about you leaving Nicholson's – Bishop must have wired her.'

Andrew's face reddened. 'Is she very cross?' he mumbled.

Tom sighed. 'Probably cross with me for not telling her myself.' He handed the telegram to Esmie, who read it.

Stella couldn't read her expression: was it fear or anger?

'What does she say?' Andrew turned the ball in his hands in agitation. 'Am I allowed to read it?'

Esmie handed it back to Tom and said quietly, 'Tell him, Tom.'

Tom's jaw clenched as he stood, undecided. Finally, he said, 'Your mother would like you to visit her for the summer.'

Andrew looked astonished. 'In Scotland?'

His father nodded. 'Yes, in Ebbsmouth.'

A look of relief crossed the boy's face. 'Well, that's not bad news, is it?'

Tom and Esmie exchanged looks. 'It's not practicable,' said Tom. 'There's the expense of the boat trips – even if you'd get a berth at this short notice.'

'Wouldn't Mother pay?'

'Even if she did, you'd have to be back here by September to start school somewhere – and we couldn't take you – the hotel's just about to open.'

'We couldn't send you unaccompanied, Andy,' said Esmie.

'Stella could take me,' he suggested, looking at her expectantly. 'You've never been to Scotland, have you? We could go together.'

Stella felt a flutter of excitement at the idea, but she also felt caught in the middle. 'I certainly couldn't afford the voyage.'

'But what if Mother paid? She's got bags of money,' Andrew persisted.

'I'm needed here, Andy,' said Stella.

Andy looked hopefully at his stepmother.

Esmie floundered. 'Maybe another year, when you're older.'

'But I'll never have another summer off school like this one,' Andrew pointed out, adding quickly, 'I could do lessons on the boat and with Mother.'

Tom gave a huff of disbelief. 'Your mother's shown no interest in your schooling up to now – she's the last person who'll make you buckle down to studying.'

Stella knew at once it was the wrong thing to say; Andrew's eyes lit up with delight.

'Please can I go?'

'Why the sudden interest in Scotland?' Tom asked.

Andrew glanced at Stella and she wondered if he was thinking of their conversation on the marg. He shrugged. 'I suppose because Mother's never asked me before – and you've always said it's too far away. Though it can't be that far, because other boys from school have been to Britain on furlough with their parents. Donaldson said it's hardly more than two weeks' journey if you get off the boat in Marseille and take the train.'

Tom ran a hand through his greying hair. 'Esmie and I will have to discuss it.' He turned and signalled to Bijal. 'We'll have tea now, thank you.'

'So you're not saying no, Dad?' Andrew persisted.

'We'll talk about it later.' Tom stuffed the telegram in his trouser pocket.

Over the next few days, Andrew badgered his father about going to Scotland. Stella knew that part of the boy's sudden enthusiasm must be his desire to get away from the upset he had caused his parents and leave behind the shame of expulsion from school. In Scotland, no boys would taunt him with gossip about his father or Esmie. She also wondered if he was flattered by Lydia's unexpected invitation – the mother who had always shown scant interest in him – and secretly craved attention from her.

Tom, though, resisted his pleas. 'Your mother's telegram was sent in anger over you leaving Nicholson's – it was a spur-of-the-moment suggestion which she obviously hasn't thought through.'

Then two airmail letters came from Lydia: one for Tom and one for Andrew. The chaprassy delivered them as they were having breakfast on the veranda. Andrew tore his open in excitement.

He was triumphant. 'Listen to this! Mother really does want me to visit. *It's high time I got to see you. Are you as tall as your father yet? We'll have such fun this summer. We can play tennis and go sailing and I'm sure we can drum up some other boys if you get bored with the grown-ups.*"

'And is she going to send a magic carpet to fetch you?' Tom said with a grunt of disbelief.

Andrew's eyes shone as he read aloud. ' *"I've booked you onto the SS* Rajputana *– it leaves Bombay on the 12th June. I've paid for two tickets so your ayah can come with you. You can return at the end of August when your grandmother and I go on holiday to Capri."* Ayah?' Andrew laughed. 'Doesn't she know I haven't had an ayah since I was a small boy?'

Tom looked shocked. Esmie gave him a worried look.

'What does your letter say, Dad?'

'I'll read it later,' Tom said, leaving it on the table unopened as he finished his half-eaten toast.

'But you will let me go, won't you? Mother's bought tickets—'

'We'll discuss it later,' his father said, slurping down tea and standing up. 'I've got a lot to see to today.'

Stella was picking flowers at the far end of the garden when she overheard Tom's raised voice coming from his studio.

'. . . the gall of it! Lecturing me on neglecting our son when she's not shown the slightest bit of interest in him since he was born. Now I'm getting blamed for Andy's wild behaviour.'

'It's not your fault, darling.' Esmie's voice was placating.

Stella hesitated. She wanted to move away but if they heard her, they would know she had been listening. She held her breath, wondering if she could creep away without being noticed.

Tom let out an anguished sigh. 'But perhaps it is? All that talk of me being an unfit soldier – the court-martial – all they say about me is true.'

'Don't be ridiculous – of course it's not true. You don't have one cowardly bone in your body. Tom, what you did was brave beyond words.'

'That's not how half the regiment saw it.'

'They were wrong. You have nothing to be ashamed of. In fact, isn't it time you were straight with Andy and told him what happened to you in the war? He's old enough to understand. And perhaps you should tell him about your loss of Mary and the baby—'

'No, not that!'

A silence followed. Stella knew she was the only person that Esmie had confided in about Tom losing his first wife in childbirth. *'The baby died too,'* Esmie had confided. *'Sometimes the memory overwhelms him. The bad things he saw during the war made it all worse.'*

Esmie continued. 'I hate keeping secrets from Andy – I'm not sure I can carry on pretending . . . Don't you think we should also be honest with him about us, Tom? He's not a child any more.'

'You're not serious?' Tom said sharply. 'I refuse to let the gossips have a field day or drag your name through the mud. I couldn't bear it – and it would make things ten times worse for Andy.'

Esmie sighed heavily. 'Oh, Tom! What are we going to do with him?'

'I don't know.' Tom groaned. 'He's set his heart on going to Scotland – and maybe it's cruel to try and stop him. He hasn't been since he was a baby and I know Lydia's mother must be longing to see him. And maybe Lydia does now too. Perhaps I'm being unfair to her?'

'Unfair to Lydia?' Esmie exclaimed. 'She's the one who's been unfair to us!'

'I know,' Tom said in agitation. 'But maybe if we let Andy visit she might change her mind about things . . .'

'Oh, darling,' Esmie said, her voice anxious, 'can we trust Lydia not to poison Andy against us?'

'Perhaps he could stay at The Anchorage with my sister?' Tom suggested. 'Tibby could chaperone Andy and keep Lydia at bay.'

'You know Lydia wouldn't settle for that – she'll want to show off Templeton Hall to him – and him to the county set.'

'Well, I could still ask Tibby to keep an eye on him,' said Tom. 'And maybe his suggestion of Stella going with him is a good one. She's sensible and Lydia always liked her. I'm sure if I asked Charlie he wouldn't stand in the way of Stella having such an opportunity.'

'I agree about Stella but . . .' Esmie sounded torn. 'Aren't you afraid Lydia won't let Andy leave once she's got him in Ebbsmouth?'

'Lydia will tire of him after a week,' he said derisively. 'She can't bear children and she's never been motherly towards him. Andy will be far too boisterous for her. She'll show him off for a few days and then realise that he doesn't fit in with her social engagements and abandon him to her mother or Tibby.'

There was a pause and then his voice softened. 'Come here, my sweet one, and stop worrying. Andy will be chomping at the bit to come back to us after a couple of weeks. By the time he comes home, he'll be ready for a fresh start at a new school. Besides, Lydia could never take your place in Andy's affections – you're all the mother he needs.'

'I thought I was,' Esmie said, 'but after these past two weeks, I'm not so sure.'

Stella was caught by a sudden dilemma. Should she tell Esmie what Andrew had told her? But he had made her promise that she wouldn't and she knew if she betrayed his confidence, he would never trust her again.

She crept around the back of the studio as swiftly and silently as possible and headed back to the hotel.

Chapter 7

Stella had a restless night pondering the Lomaxes' conversation and particularly Esmie's puzzling words about wanting to confess something to Andrew. What secrets were they keeping from him? Yet, the possibility of travelling abroad thrilled her. She imagined herself on the boat and then seeing Britain, where both her parents' families had come from generations ago.

What an adventure it would be! She had heard so much about the country from Esmie. Then there was Ebbsmouth, where the Lomaxes came from: a fishing town on the east coast of Scotland with beautiful sandy beaches and a castle where Tom's sister Tibby lived. She had never seen the sea.

Stella eventually fell asleep imagining herself high up in a castle tower listening to the sound of the waves pounding the rocks below.

The following day, Tom took Stella aside. 'I've decided to let Andrew go and see his mother for the summer and wondered how you felt about going with him?'

'To Scotland?' Stella was thrilled.

Tom nodded. 'I can trust you to look after Andy,' he said, 'and you'll know how to handle Lydia. She can be difficult at times, but she was always fond of you and I'm sure she'll give you a good time. And Mrs Templeton is a kindly soul; Lydia's mother will make you feel at home. I'm sorry Mr Templeton has passed away – I always got on with Lydia's father. But I don't want to force you to go, Stella, if you don't want to. I know Esmie will miss you terribly.'

'I love being here, Mr Lomax,' Stella replied, 'but I've always dreamt of visiting Britain. If my father agrees – and you can spare me here – then I'd really like to go. Thank you!'

They went outside to break the news to Andrew, who was throwing a ball with Frisky on the hotel lawn. He gaped at his father as the news sank in. Stella had expected him to whoop for joy, but he just stood staring at them.

'You're letting me go to Ebbsmouth?'

'Yes,' Tom said. 'It is what you want, isn't it?'

Andrew looked at Stella. 'Are you coming too?'

Stella grinned. 'Someone has to keep an eye on you,' she teased.

He gave a faltering smile. 'Great. Yes. Of course I want to go.'

'That's settled then,' said Tom.

Over the next few days, messages came and went between Gulmarg and the Duboises in Rawalpindi.

Charlie wrote, *Mrs Dubois and I are most grateful for the opportunity that you are offering our daughter out of the bountifulness of your heart. We do, however, have a concern that she is not yet a fully fledged grown-up – although she becomes of age in August – and so would wish for her to be chaperoned on the voyage to the homeland. Perhaps it could be ascertained if a missionary lady or someone of good repute could be prevailed upon to keep a motherly eye on Stella. We know our daughter is of very good character, but we hear tales of romances at sea and would not want her to be the subject of unwanted attention.'*

Stella coloured with embarrassment when she was told by Esmie of her father's worries over her reputation.

'I'm perfectly capable of fending off any advances from bored young men,' she said in amusement.

'I'm sure you are.' Esmie laughed. 'But I think it's best if we do as your father asks. There are usually one or two older women who advertise as chaperones on these journeys. We can look at the ads in the newspapers.'

Passports were quickly applied for, and Tom asked the superintendent of police to sign a declaration that Andrew was his son, and to vouch for Stella as a 'fit and proper person' to receive a British Indian passport. They would pick up the documents in Lahore on their way to Bombay.

As the time grew nearer, Stella could hardly contain her excitement, but Andrew seemed strangely subdued. He would take himself off on long walks across the high margs with Frisky at his heels. One afternoon, she waylaid him on his return.

'Penny for your thoughts,' she said casually, while greeting Frisky with enthusiastic patting.

Andrew shrugged.

'I can tell something's bothering you,' Stella persisted. 'Are you worried about the long journey? Going so far away?'

Andrew shook his head.

'Are you still dwelling on what Gotley said?'

'Not really.'

'What, then? Are you having second thoughts about wanting to go to Scotland?'

When he didn't answer, Stella steered him towards a garden bench and sat down next to him.

'It's not too late to call it all off,' she said gently.

He gave her a wry look. 'But you're looking forward to it so much.'

'That doesn't matter. This trip is for you. I'm sure your parents would be delighted if you didn't go. They're going to miss you terribly.'

Andrew eyed her, his look forlorn. 'Meemee maybe – but I think Dad wants me to go. He's been so cross with me over this Gotley business and he won't answer my questions about why he left the army. They both treat me like I'm still a kid, but I'm not.'

Stella was silent, sensing he had more on his mind. He gnawed at his thumbnail. 'Part of me wants to go to Scotland and part of me . . .'

'Are you worried about meeting your mother?' Stella asked. She saw from the troubled look in his blue eyes that she was right. She touched his shoulder. 'It's bound to be a bit nerve-wracking at first but she might be feeling a little anxious too, don't you think?'

'I hadn't thought of that.'

'And it won't just be the two of you all the time. You'll meet your grandmother and Auntie Tibby too. I'm sure they'll all welcome you with open arms.'

At last, Andrew smiled. A little bashfully, he said, 'Thanks, Stella.'

Then he reached for Frisky and began fussing over the dog. 'Come on, boy. Let's race Stella back to the hotel.'

Jumping to his feet, Andrew sped off with Frisky chasing him and Stella following along behind.

It was arranged that Ada would come up to Gulmarg and help out in her place, while their cousin Lucy would take over Ada's duties with Mrs Shankley at the Raj.

Ada arrived two days before Stella and Andrew were due to depart. The cousins hugged in delight.

'I'm so envious of you visiting Britain,' said Ada. 'My dad hasn't stopped going on about what a privilege it is – keeps saying you're taking a trip home.' Ada laughed. 'It's not as if our family even came from Scotland. I think the Dixons were from Yorkshire.'

'Dear Uncle Toby,' said Stella in amusement. 'I'll bring him back something special from home.'

'Just think of it,' said Ada with a dreamy look. 'In a few days you'll be at sea and mixing with all those young officers and businessmen. Bet you come back engaged.'

'I certainly won't,' Stella said with a roll of her eyes. 'I want to see a bit of life before getting married. Don't you?'

'I suppose so. You will come back?' Ada looked suddenly anxious.

'Of course I will.' Stella took her cousin by the hand. 'Come on; let me introduce you to the handsome Felix. He'll teach you how to make pastry that melts in the mouth.'

The day before leaving Gulmarg, Stella received an airmail letter from Lydia saying how delighted she was to hear from Tom that it was Stella who would be accompanying Andrew and *'not some timid little ayah'.*

Yet Stella was uncomfortable at the words that followed.

> *It will be lovely to see if you are still as pretty and engaging as the child I remember. We'll keep quiet about your being Anglo-Indian. Not that it bothers me but some of the county set can be a bit stuffy. It helps that you don't look at all native. Mummy is dying to meet you again.*

She showed it to Esmie.

'Typical Lydia,' Esmie said with a look of irritation. 'She just says what's in her mind without thinking. She doesn't mean to cause offence.' She put her arm around Stella. 'If she gets too overbearing and you want to escape, you must go and stay with Tibby at The Anchorage. Promise me you will? Tom's written to his sister and told her to befriend you.'

Stella nodded in thanks. 'What's Tibby like?'

Esmie smiled. 'She's great fun. A bit eccentric in her tastes but she's one of the kindest people I know. I've no idea how she keeps the old castle going – her father died leaving her with hardly a penny – but she's made it a haven for struggling young artists and they earn their keep by helping around the house and gardens.'

'Sounds an interesting place,' said Stella. 'I wouldn't mind doing my bit if she needs a hand.'

Esmie squeezed her shoulders. 'I know you wouldn't, kind girl. But this is a holiday for you. Tibby will just be happy if you visit her.'

Stella said, 'You and Mr Lomax are so kind to let me go. I feel a bit bad that it's not you taking Andrew for a visit to Scotland. I know how you miss it.'

Esmie stiffened. 'It's best if I don't. It would be awkward. Lydia and I don't see eye to eye any more.'

'Can I ask why, Mrs Lomax?'

Esmie hesitated before saying, 'I say this in confidence, Stella. It was Lydia's decision to part with Tom but even so, I think she resents me being with him.' She gave a pained look. 'Adults can be very complicated.' She forced a smile. 'But I don't want my estrangement with Lydia to overshadow your trip. I'm sure you're going to have a wonderful time.'

Stella remembered anew how difficult Lydia had sometimes been as Tom's wife and how she'd lorded it over the staff and guests at the Raj. It left Stella with a twinge of apprehension.

'Oh, and there's one other thing you should know,' said Esmie, with an uncomfortable look. 'Lydia still goes by her married name. Despite not having been with Tom for years, she likes to be called Mrs Lomax.'

They left at dawn on the 11th June, a sleepy Ada and a smiling Felix waving them off from the hotel steps. Esmie and Bijal (and Frisky the dog) were going as far as Rawalpindi; Tom was travelling with them to Bombay and seeing them onto the ship.

At the Raj, Charlie and Myrtle fussed over their daughter, nervous and proud that she had been chosen to escort Andrew to Scotland. Charlie had been reassured that Stella was to be chaperoned by a middle-aged governess who was returning to England.

At the station, as Stella hugged and kissed her family, she noticed Esmie giving Andrew an emotional goodbye.

'Take care of yourself, my darling boy,' she said, her eyes welling with tears.

Andrew grabbed his stepmother in a tight hug. 'I'll miss you, Meemee.'

Esmie's face crumpled. Neither of them could say any more. Tom guided Andrew quickly on board. Stella hugged Esmie and said, 'I'll look after him, I promise.'

Esmie gave a tearful smile. 'I know you will. Just bring him back safely.'

After stopping briefly in hot and hectic Lahore to collect their pass-ports, two days after leaving Rawalpindi they were standing in the broiling heat on the Bombay quayside amid the chaotic jostling of porters and travellers. The great hulk of the SS *Rajputana* loomed above them. Coolies ran up gangplanks, sweating under the burden of heavy trunks, while cargo was being winched over the ship's side. Their luggage had already been taken on board. Stella saw a topee-wearing young man with a bandaged leg being stretchered on. He was putting on a brave face and winked at her as he went by.

Stella was suddenly nervous, her brow perspiring under her summer hat. They were to have met their chaperone, Miss Jessop, in the embarkation hall, but she'd left a note to say she would meet them on the ship.

Tom was fretting. 'I really would like to have met her before you leave. Esmie will want to know – and what shall I tell Charlie?'

'I'm sure she'll be as proper and upstanding as her advert described her,' said Stella. 'Being old, she probably wants to get out of the heat.'

'I suppose so,' Tom said, running a finger under his collar.

'Stella will look after me,' said Andrew. 'We don't need some battleaxe governess to tell us what to do.'

A flicker of a smile crossed Tom's face. 'I know Stella's perfectly capable – but I just wanted to keep Charlie and Myrtle happy. We parents worry about our children whatever age you are.'

The three stood together watching people embark, Andrew biting on his fingernails. Stella knew both father and son were reluctant to say their goodbyes.

'I think we'd better get on board,' she suggested gently. 'Thank you for bringing us, Mr Lomax – thank you for everything.'

Tom nodded. He turned to his son and cleared his throat. 'Andy, I want you to know that I don't blame you for what hap-pened at Nicholson's and I'm sorry you've ended up having to leave because of it. I feel responsible – given that you were defending my reputation.' He put a hand on Andrew's shoulder. 'Someday we'll talk about it – when you're older – there are things I should explain . . .'

Stella saw Andrew's anxious expression. 'I wish you would tell me now, Dad—'

'When you come back, I promise . . .' Tom's voice wavered as he struggled to keep his emotions in check. His eyes shone with tears. He stuck out his hand to Andrew. 'Be good for Stella and write to Esmie,' he instructed.

Awkwardly, Andrew shook his hand. Then, spontaneously, they both gripped each other in a hug. For a few seconds, they clung on fiercely.

'Just come back. That's all I ask,' Tom said, his voice cracking.

Andrew's voice wobbled. 'Of course I will, Dad.' Then tears began to spill down his cheeks.

Tom kissed his forehead and pulled away, almost pushing Andrew towards the gangplank. 'Off you go with Stella and find the elusive Miss Jessop. Make sure your mother wires to let us know when you arrive in Ebbsmouth.'

Stella steered Andrew by the arm but he disengaged and wiped his eyes on his sleeve. 'I'm fine.'

At the top, it was a struggle to look over the throng of other passengers making their way on board. They moved along the deck to find a space to wave.

'We can look for our cabins later,' said Stella, knowing Andrew would want to watch his father till the final moment.

She could easily pick out Tom in his crumpled white suit, standing a head taller than anyone else around him, holding his hat aloft as he waved. He continued to stand there as the gangplank was removed and the crew made ready for departure. Stella was startled by three deafening blasts from the ship's hooter. With a judder, the liner pulled away from the quay. Her heart hammered with excitement and nervousness. There was no going back.

Slowly the shimmering buildings and the Gate of India receded; the din and smells of the dockside lessened. Bombay became a hazy patch of brown at the edge of sparkling sea. But the image of Tom waving and straining for a last glimpse of Andrew was imprinted on her mind like a photograph. How very much he loved his son.

Andrew stood gripping the rail and staring back. 'Goodbye, India! Goodbye, Dad! Goodbye, Meemee! Goodbye, Frisky . . . !' he shouted, seemingly mentioning everyone he could think of that he would miss.

Eventually, Stella put a hand on his arm. 'Come on, Andy. Let's go and find our geriatric governess and see if they're serving afternoon tea.'

At the mention of food, Andrew's tear-swollen eyes lit up. He smiled and nodded, and together they went below deck.

Chapter 8

Andrew was sprawled in a deckchair flicking through an out-of-date copy of *Wisden* that someone had left behind. Its pages curled in the fierce sun. The heat was furnace-like as they sailed up the Red Sea, and no one had the energy for daytime deck games. Further along the row of deckchairs he could hear Miss Jessop giggling over a game of cards with one of her admirers.

Andrew smiled. What a surprise their chaperone had turned out to be, he thought. Moira Jessop was only three years older than Stella and not particularly pretty – a bit mousy in Andrew's opinion – but she was gregarious and laughed a lot, so the young men on board were happy to flirt with her.

He'd heard some of the burra memsahibs tutting about her too. 'Look at that Jessop girl – she's with a different man every day – she won't have any reputation left by the time she gets off this boat.'

'Well, it's her last chance to catch a man, isn't it?'

'What was she doing in India? Does she have family there?'

'No, I heard she came out with the fishing fleet but blotted her copybook in Calcutta. Hired as a governess but she was quite useless.' The matronly woman had dropped her voice to an excited whisper. 'Apparently she was caught in a dalliance with the master of the house and was sent packing.'

'That's what you get when you employ young girls from the lower-middle class.'

Andrew thought they were being unnecessarily unkind. He liked Moira and her unstuffy attitudes, and he especially liked her complete disinterest in what he or Stella got up to on the voyage.

'I didn't want to show my face to your father,' Moira had told Andrew on first meeting, 'as I knew he'd think me too young to chaperone either of you. Which I am. So, I'm not even going to try.' She'd let out a peel of laughter. 'You're free to do what you want – as long as you don't tell tales to your parents and I still get paid.'

Andrew had relished the thought of this journey with Stella and the chance to see her every day. He now felt special receiving so much attention from her, proud to be seen with the prettiest girl on board. In his mind she far outshone all the other young women on the ship in every way, from her lustrous fair hair to the curve of her pink lips. He loved the way her cheeks dimpled when she laughed and the sensual movement of her hips when she walked.

Lately, he'd been unable to get her out of his thoughts even when they weren't together. Every morning he was filled with anticipation at seeing her and now every evening he lay in his bunk thinking about her. This growing interest was exciting, yet a little confusing for him. He had always loved Stella, always thought they were friends and he could tell her anything, but he had never experienced such a physical reaction to being in her presence. He wanted her to himself now too, and he felt a little jealous of the young men who seemed to shower her with attention, particularly his new cabin-mate.

Andrew was sharing with the man on crutches that they'd seen being stretchered on board at Bombay. His name was Hugh Keating, and he seemed a genial enough young Irishman. He worked for the Agriculture Department in Quetta, a mountainous outpost in semi-desert. He'd been shot in the leg by a wild tribesman while out riding just before going on furlough, but was determined not to miss out on a trip home. Andrew had been so impressed that he'd asked to see the bullet wound, but the Irishman's kneecap had been shattered and was well bound up.

Hugh had asked a lot of questions about Stella.

'Her family works for my father,' Andrew had told him. 'Dad has two hotels – one in Rawalpindi and one in Kashmir – the Duboises run the Raj in Pindi. But Stella's more like a friend of the family, really.'

'And a very pretty one too,' Hugh had said with a wink.

Andrew had blushed. 'I suppose she is.'

He might have felt resentful at his prying into Stella's life but Hugh was so good-natured and easy to talk to. Besides, he had told eye-popping stories about living among the savage tribes of Baluchistan. They were just the sort of tales that he wished his father would tell him about his army life on the wild North West Frontier.

'She's quite elusive, your friend Stella,' Hugh had said after the first five days at sea.

'She's been very seasick,' Andrew had explained. 'Never been on a boat before.'

When they'd docked at Aden to take on coal, Stella had emerged from her cabin, and Andrew had introduced her properly to Hugh.

'It'll be much calmer all the way up to Port Said,' Hugh had reassured her.

'I'm glad to hear that,' Stella had said with a wan smile.

She had soon revived. For the past two days, Stella and Moira had entered into the evening revelry of deck quoits and dancing. They were never short of suitors from among the young men who had spent the last couple of years in remote postings in the mofussil where the only European women were either married or missionaries.

Hugh, despite being on crutches, took part in the quoit-throwing with great gusto, but couldn't compete on the dance floor for Stella's attention. Instead, for the past two nights he'd kept Andrew company on deck. Last night Hugh had offered him sips of whisky from a hip flask and cigarettes, and he had accepted both.

Sitting on deck now, trying to keep in the shade, Andrew's temples throbbed and his throat was parched. Was that what whisky did to you? Why on earth was it so popular? He thought of his father's erratic moods after drinking liquor and wondered why he bothered. It just seemed to be something that all the British in India did – or at least the men. He'd never seen Esmie drink more than a glass of sherry on special occasions.

Andrew went in search of lemonade. Sauntering along deck he saw that Moira was playing cards with Hugh and felt a twinge of jealousy on Stella's behalf.

He flopped down beside them and asked, 'Where's Stella?'

'Probably writing up that diary of hers,' said Moira, fanning herself with her cards. 'She won't let me read any of it which just makes me all the more curious. Your go, Hughie.'

He picked up a card and eyed Andrew in amusement. 'How're you feeling today, young man?'

'Felt better.' He grimaced.

'So, what were you two up to last night?' Moira asked, raising an eyebrow.

'Man talk over a few nightcaps,' said Hugh with a wink.

Andrew hardly remembered their conversation. Had he told Hugh about Nicholson's or just wittered on about The Raj-in-the-Hills and Kashmir? He hoped he hadn't opened up about his surge of feelings towards Stella.

To his relief, Stella appeared and diverted the conversation. She was looking fresh and pink-cheeked under a straw hat, wearing a yellow frock with a heart-shaped neckline that he was pretty sure belonged to Moira. It suited Stella better, showing off her fuller figure. Andrew felt himself blushing and looked away.

Stella smiled. 'Playing cards without me?'

'Join us,' Hugh insisted at once, using a crutch to pull a deck-chair into position beside him.

She ignored this and sat down beside Andrew. 'Are you okay? You look a bit feverish.' She put a hand to his forehead. It was deliciously cool against his hot skin.

'Nothing an aspirin and some baking soda won't cure,' Moira said with a laugh.

'Meaning?'

'Too many chota pegs with Mr Keating last night,' Moira explained, a tease in her voice. 'Hurry up and play, Hugh.'

Stella sat back in shock. 'Andy? Tell me you haven't been drinking alcohol.'

Andrew's flush deepened. 'Just a few sips.'

'Mr Keating!' Stella rebuked. 'What were you thinking? He's only thirteen.'

'Is he?' Hugh looked aghast. 'He doesn't look it. I thought he was sixteen—'

'Oops,' said Moira, pulling a mock-serious face. 'Everyone's in trouble. And I'm supposed to be the chaperone. Naughty me.'

Stella gave Andrew a stern look. 'From now on I'm watching you like a hawk.'

'Don't be too hard on the lad,' said Hugh. 'And we don't want to keep you off the dance floor, Miss Dubois. I promise you it won't happen again. Will it, Andrew?'

Andrew shook his head. He felt utterly humiliated. He itched to be on land again playing cricket or out riding. He experienced a stab of homesickness for Gulmarg. He hadn't been gone a fortnight and he was missing home.

Stella brushed his hand as if guessing his state of mind. 'How about we sit inside and write letters home while it's too hot to do anything else? Then perhaps Mr Keating will give you a game of quoits later.'

Andrew saw a look pass between Stella and Hugh and wondered what it meant. Was she challenging the Irishman to behave more responsibly?

Andrew stood up, eager to leave and just be with Stella.

'See you for a sundowner,' Moira called as they walked away.

Stella found it hard to concentrate on writing a letter home. What would she tell her parents or the Lomaxes about the first week at sea? That it was as if they were travelling unchaperoned? That by the time she'd recovered from horrendous seasickness Andrew was under the influence of a handsome, irresponsible cabin-mate who encouraged him to drink whisky? That she, Stella, had spent the past couple of days neglecting Andrew in favour of the dance floor and keeping company with Moira Jessop, a failed governess with a racy reputation? Least of all could she tell them she was drawn like a magnet to that same cabin-mate, a charming, fun Irishman with a broad smile and dark-blue eyes. Any of these things would send her mother and father rushing for the vapours, and the Lomaxes regretting having sent her at all.

So she wrote a subtly censored version about playing deck quoits and reading in the library; of how friendly their chaperone was, and that Andrew was well and eating heartily.

She looked across the table at Andrew labouring over a single page of the ship's headed writing paper. He'd hardly written more than two sentences. Was he really as okay as she hoped or had he drunk too much last night to mask his unhappiness? Since he'd unburdened himself to her about his anxiety that his father was somehow rejecting him – as well as his fears of meeting his formidable mother – Andrew had appeared to be in good spirits. But perhaps he was still troubled. She would have to keep a closer eye on him; after all, that was what the Lomaxes had entrusted her with.

Andrew chewed his pen and glanced at her with bloodshot eyes.

Stella laughed. 'You look terrible. Shall we go and find some lime juice and leave the writing till later?'

Andrew grinned at her in relief, already half out of his chair. 'Oh, yes please, Stella!'

She gathered up their half-hearted attempts at correspondence and followed him out.

Hugh took Stella aside after dinner. 'Will you come on deck with me, Miss Dubois? I feel I owe you an explanation.' When Stella hesitated and glanced over at Andrew, Hugh persisted. 'The lad's going to get an early night. Please, come with me – just for a few minutes.'

Stella nodded. 'Just a few minutes then.'

Her heart thumped as she walked with him and tried not to keep glancing at his face; the straight nose, the dimpled chin and the sweep of wavy brown hair that made her want to run her fingers over its undulations. He'd become adept at going up and down stairs with only one crutch, so Stella carried the other one until they were out on deck. He led her towards the rail and leaned against it.

'Look at those stars,' he said, gazing up in wonder. 'Have you ever seen such a sight?'

'Yes, loads of times,' she said. 'The night sky over the Himalayas can be even brighter.'

Hugh laughed. 'Oh, Miss Dubois, I love your candour. It's so refreshing. Too many women just agree with men out of politeness.'

Stella blushed. She didn't think she'd said anything out of the ordinary. The way he was looking at her keenly made her pulse start to race.

'I'm feeling bad about leading Andrew astray last night,' he said, 'and I can tell you're still cross with me.'

Stella half-turned away and gazed out across the dark sea. 'As I said, I feel guilty for neglecting Andrew. I'm as cross with myself as with you, Mr Keating.'

'Well, don't be,' he said. 'I think what happened was probably a good thing.'

Stella looked at him in astonishment. 'Why on earth do you say that?'

'Because he won't do it again in a hurry. It might have put him off liquor for life – or at least for a few years. And isn't it better that he experienced his first taste of whisky in the company of someone who cares about his welfare and wouldn't let him have too much – and certainly won't be telling his parents?'

She felt wrong-footed by his argument, as if somehow the whole thing had indeed been a good thing.

'I'm not sure about that,' she answered.

'Stella,' he said, 'may I call you Stella?' She nodded and he continued, 'The other good thing was that the whisky loosened his tongue. Andrew started confiding in me about things that are worrying him.'

Stella felt alarmed. 'What did he say?'

'How he's nervous about meeting his mother. He doesn't know her and is frightened he won't like her – especially as his father and stepmother have never really spoken about her.'

Stella sighed. 'Well, I'm concerned about it too. I remember Andrew's mother as quite a difficult woman – moody and demanding. But at other times she could be charm itself.'

'Well, perhaps you'd better not tell that to Andrew. The more you encourage him that it'll be all right the better, don't you think?'

'Yes,' Stella agreed. 'Thank you for telling me. Andy hasn't said any of this to me recently. I'll try and think of some nice things to say about his overbearing mother.'

Hugh smiled. 'That's all I wanted to say. Now, I won't keep you if you want to join Moira and the others.'

Stella turned back to stare out to sea. 'It's so lovely out on deck; I think I'll stay a little longer.'

'You don't mind if I keep you company?' he asked.

'I'd be happy if you did.'

They stood very close at the railing, their arms touching. Stella's heart drummed so hard she thought he must be able to feel the vibration through their arms. Her throat was tight with nervous excitement at being so close.

Hugh said in a low voice, 'Last night we also talked a lot about you, Stella.'

Her heart lurched. 'Did you?'

'Andrew is very fond of you, and . . .' He stammered slightly for a moment and she turned her head to look at him. 'I find I am falling under your spell too.'

'My spell?' Stella laughed gently. 'You make me sound like a witch.'

Hugh shifted his weight to be sideways on. He ran a finger down her bare arm that made her tingle all over. 'Perhaps you are. I'm certainly quite bewitched by you. I could drown in those gorgeous green eyes of yours.'

Stella shivered. No man had ever made such bold comments to her before. Monty Gibson had once held her hand and called her pretty and his twin brother Clive had kissed her at a Boxing Day party and said she had sweet lips. But none of the young men of her community had ever made her feel as desirable as Hugh Keating did by merely touching her arm and gazing into her eyes.

'Maybe it's the beautiful night that's gone to my head,' he murmured, 'but I've never felt this way about a girl before. You know what I really want to do, Stella?'

She swallowed, unable to speak, and shook her head.

'I want to kiss you so much. Will you allow me to kiss you, Stella?'

She glanced around in case they were being overheard, but there was no one close by and they stood in the shadows.

'Yes,' she said, breathlessly.

They leaned towards each other and he kissed her gently on the lips. It felt like butterflies and set her whole body tingling again. He ran a hand across her hair and then kissed her again, this time more firmly. She wasn't sure how he managed it but somehow, he was able to prop himself against the railing and slip his arms around her. He ran his fingers through her hair again and down her back, pressing her body against his as they continued to kiss.

When they broke away, Stella felt wobbly at the knees and had to hold onto the rail.

'God, Stella, you're beautiful,' he murmured. 'I can't believe how lucky I am that you're on the same ship as me. The stars above must have decreed it.'

Trembling, Stella laughed.

'I'm serious,' said Hugh. 'Don't you believe in fate, Stella? I think we were destined to meet.'

'I don't know if I believe in fate,' she replied, 'but I'm very glad that we've met.'

He brushed her cheek with his hand and ran his thumb over her lips, which made her yearn for him to kiss her again.

'Are you courting anyone in Pindi, Stella?' he asked. 'I asked Andrew but he wasn't sure.'

'No, I'm not,' she whispered.

'That's hard to believe,' he said, his full mouth twitching in a smile. 'The boys in Pindi must be mighty slow off the mark.'

Stella gave a soft laugh. 'My father's very protective – he doesn't encourage boyfriends.'

'Well, I'm glad he's not chaperoning you now.' Hugh gave a roguish grin.

'So am I,' she said.

He trailed a finger down her neck and traced it across the bare flesh at her heart-shaped neckline. Stella thought she would faint at the ecstatic sensation it sent right down to her toes. They kissed again and this time she opened her mouth as he did and tasted him on her tongue.

'Hughie! Is that you over there?'

Moira's cry had them breaking apart. Stella moved away from him as her friend approached a little unsteadily along the deck towards them.

'Stella, there you are. I've been looking for you everywhere.' Moira looked between them. 'Oh, have I interrupted something? Stella, you look very pink in the face. Is everything all right?'

'Yes, I'm fine,' Stella answered.

'We were trying to work out what stars we're looking at,' said Hugh.

Moira thought this was funny. 'Goodness, don't ask me! Anyway, if you've finished being astronomers then they're organising a game of charades downstairs. You love charades, Stella, don't you?'

'Yes, but—'

'Good, I thought so.' Moira turned to Hugh. 'And I bet you can manage with your sticks. It'll be such a hoot. Come on, you two; they're picking teams. Let's be on the same side.'

Stella knew it was useless trying to resist Moira when she'd set her mind on something. With a longing look at Hugh, she fell into step behind Moira and they made their way below.

Chapter 9

By the time they reached Port Said, Andrew had made friends with an American boy, Bob Werner, a couple of years his senior, who was travelling with his parents. His father was an engineer with an oil company in Assam and the Werners were using a spell of leave to tour Europe. Bob was athletic and happy to play deck cricket – he'd been taught cricket by the sons of tea planters – and in turn he explained baseball to Andrew.

Stella seemed happy that he'd made friends with the polite American boy and stopped watching him so vigilantly. Andrew had noticed that she spent an increasing amount of time on deck with Hugh rather than on the dance floor with Moira. Andrew and Bob would come across them playing backgammon – Stella always seemed to be winning – or helping each other over a game of patience.

Hugh would greet them enthusiastically, but never invite the boys to join them. If Stella suggested it, Hugh would laugh and say, 'The lads don't want to sit around when there are more active games to be played.'

Out of earshot, Bob said, 'I bet you a dollar Mr Keating will propose to Miss Stella before we get to Marseille.'

Andrew was aghast at the idea. 'Don't be ridiculous! She hardly knows him.'

Bob looked earnest. 'Mom says the India ships are famous for whirlwind romance and quick engagements. The men on leave don't have much time. And Miss Stella looks mighty taken with your cabin-mate.'

'Stella's much too sensible for that,' said Andrew.

But the thought troubled him. What if Stella did lose her head over the Irishman? What if she went off with him? Andrew dismissed the idea. Stella would never leave him to face his mother and Ebbsmouth on his own. She'd promised his parents that she'd look after him and Stella always kept her word.

The voyage began to pass more swiftly and they were soon on the final stretch through the Mediterranean. The nearer they drew to Marseille and the train journey through France, the more Andrew's thoughts turned with expectation to arriving in Scotland. What was his mother really like? He thought of her as some distant deity or the Snow Queen from Hans Christian Andersen's tale – beautiful and remote – but not at all motherly. Recently, Stella had been trying to reassure him by telling him little anecdotes of how his mother had been kind to her as a small girl at the Raj. But what would his mother be like with him?

His father kept no pictures of his mother and the only photograph Andrew possessed was one that Esmie had given him out of her battered album. It showed Esmie and his mother standing arm in arm, smiling broadly on the steps of a bungalow. Esmie looked much younger. From what he could see of the tiny black-and-white picture, his mother was pretty and Esmie had told him she was fair-haired. On the back it read, 'Buchanan Road, Pindi, January 1st 1920.' So Esmie had still been good friends with his mother in those days – before he was born.

He wondered what had happened to break up their friendship. Was it just Esmie being loyal to his father or was there another reason? George's poisonous words about Esmie resurfaced. *'Your father never married her. She's just his whore . . . they're like a couple of sewer rats copulating!'*

How could anyone speak about his beloved Meemee like that? To stop himself dwelling on it, he thought of Stella again. She must come with him and not go off with the Irishman, however amiable he was.

The next time Andrew was talking to Moira he asked, 'What do you think of Mr Keating?'

'He's very charming – a bit of a ladies' man, I'd say.' She smiled. 'Why do you ask?'

'He likes you too,' said Andrew. 'He told me.'

Moira looked surprised. 'Really? Did he say so? I got the distinct impression he's keen on Stella.'

'Well, he's nice to Stella but I think he prefers someone a bit – er – more mature.'

'Goodness, you must have some very grown-up conversations for your age in the Keating cabin,' Moira said in amusement.

Andrew reddened. He wasn't lying when he said that Hugh liked Moira, but he was pretty sure if Stella gave him any romantic encouragement, Hugh would press his suit with her rather than the failed governess. It worried Andrew that Stella might already have done things with Hugh, such as kissing, for they'd started calling each other by their first names and he'd witnessed them touching hands under the table and sharing secret smiles.

Moira tweaked his nose playfully. 'Will you be my little cupid and tell Mr Keating I'll meet him on the upper deck at cocktail hour?'

'Of course,' said Andrew.

Later, when cocktail hour came around and Stella seemed disappointed not to find Hugh in his usual deckchair ready to play backgammon, Andrew felt guilty. She ended up playing dominoes with Andrew and the Werners instead. The next day was suddenly stormy and Stella kept to her cabin trying not to be sick. The day after that was their last at sea and Stella was kept busy packing Andrew's trunk and her suitcase and marking them for disembarkation.

To Andrew's relief, Hugh was staying aboard until Tilbury, London. Moira surprised them by saying that she was too.

'But you're coming with us on the train, aren't you?' Andrew queried.

'You don't need me for that,' said Moira breezily. 'I've decided to stay on the ship and look after poor Hugh with his bad leg.' She gave a coquettish smile.

Stella flushed at the news but gave her friend a hug. 'Good luck, Moira. You've been a hopeless chaperone but a lot of fun.'

'We have had fun, haven't we?' Moira giggled. 'Made those snooty memsahibs choke on their cutlets! Perhaps we'll meet again. I hope so.'

Hugh came to wave them off, propped up on his crutches.

'All the best with meeting your ma,' Hugh said, with an encouraging smile at Andrew. 'I'm sure you'll have a high old time in Scotland.'

'Thanks, Mr Keating. I've enjoyed being your cabin-mate.' They shook hands.

Hugh took Stella by the hand. 'Goodbye, Stella. I'll have to work on my backgammon before we next meet.'

'Are we likely to meet again?' she asked a little stiffly, pulling away from him.

'I very much hope so,' he said. 'One of these days, I'll come and stay at one of the Raj hotels – escape the heat of Baluchistan.'

'I'm sure the Lomaxes would be delighted to have you,' Stella replied.

'It's you I would rather be seeing,' he said, giving her a direct look.

Briefly she nodded at him. 'Goodbye, Hugh. I've enjoyed meeting you.'

As she turned away, Andrew noticed her eyes were brimming with tears.

Feeling guilty at Stella's unhappiness, Andrew dashed after the Werners to say farewell. The Americans were leaving the ship at Marseille too, but were staying on the French Riviera.

When Andrew and Stella finally got onto the quayside, Andrew looked back to see Moira and Hugh standing close together, watching them go.

'They're waving at us,' he said.

Stella hesitated a moment and then, putting on a broad smile, turned and waved back.

Andrew thought Stella seemed subdued on the train north. She was probably growing nervous at the thought of meeting his mother in two days' time. He experienced a fresh stab of guilt that she could be missing Hugh – and that he might have spoilt her final days with the young Irishman. Andrew suddenly regretted that he had encouraged Moira to go after Hugh. He shouldn't have interfered. Stella was so seldom sad and he hated to see her like that now.

By the time they got to Paris, she seemed more her usual self. Andrew was consoled by the thought that once Stella got to Scotland, she would forget all about Hugh Keating.

Chapter 10

After their long journey, Stella was entranced by the sight of the neat harbour town and the sea beyond, as the train made its way along the estuary.

'The cottages are made out of pink stone,' she marvelled. 'So pretty!'

Andrew was infected by the same nervous excitement. 'And look at that huge tower on the cliff edge,' he said. 'Looks like it's about to topple into the sea! Do you think that's The Anchorage?'

'Where your Auntie Tibby lives?' Stella asked.

'Yes, Dad said it was more of a tower house than a real castle.'

As the train slowed to a halt, Stella adjusted her hat and licked her dry lips. She straightened Andrew's tie – she'd insisted he wore one for meeting his mother – and reached up to smooth down his tufts of dark hair with her fingers.

'You've got a smut on your cheek,' she said, licking a finger.

Andrew pulled away. 'Don't! I'm not five years old.' He rubbed his face with the sleeve of his jumper.

Stella laughed. 'Sorry, Andy. I'm just a bit nervous.'

He looked at her with large blue eyes. 'So am I. Come on, let's go and get this over with.'

The platform was busy, as the train was full of holidaymakers. Stella peered at the expectant faces, wondering if Lydia would be as she remembered her from her patchy memories of thirteen years ago.

A well-dressed woman in a navy frock and large-brimmed hat was standing at the barrier, peering down the platform. Beside her an older, stouter woman was waving a handkerchief.

'Is that them?' Andrew asked. 'Is that my mother and grandmother?'

'I think you might be right. I don't really remember what old Mrs Templeton looks like – but I'm pretty sure that's your mother. Go on,' Stella encouraged, 'give them a wave.'

Andrew did so, and the woman in navy responded by raising a hand and beckoning him to her.

'You go ahead,' said Stella, 'while I see to the luggage in the guard's van.'

Andrew seemed panicked. 'Please don't leave me now, Stella.'

'Okay,' Stella agreed, placing an encouraging hand on his back and steering him forward.

As soon as they got to the barrier, Stella recognised Lydia. She was plumper in the face but still beautiful. She had the same large blue eyes as Andrew and wore her blonde hair in neat waves to her chin.

'Hello, Mother,' Andrew said, holding out his hand.

Lydia was gaping at her tall son. 'My little boy – you're so big – I didn't expect . . .' She seemed suddenly overcome and clutched at his hand. Quickly she recovered. 'My goodness, you're the image of your father!' She touched his cheek with a white-gloved hand.

Andrew smiled nervously. 'He joked that I might be as tall as him by the time I return to India.'

Lydia cried, 'For goodness' sake, you've just arrived! I'll not have you talking about going back already.'

'Sorry.' Andrew flushed.

Lydia turned her attention to Stella. 'My, my, you've grown into a beauty. Your parents must be very proud to have such a fair daughter. I know how much pale skin means among your people.'

Stella dipped her head, trying to hide her immediate annoyance at Lydia's patronising words. But this was Andrew's holiday and she'd do everything to help it go well.

Lydia introduced them to her mother. Minnie Templeton kissed Andrew on the cheek. 'Call me Granny.'

'Certainly not!' Lydia protested. 'He'll call you Grandmamma. Granny sounds so parochial, don't you think? And while we're on the subject, Andrew, you will call me Mamma.'

Minnie didn't seem put out by her daughter's rebuke and smiled at Stella. 'Welcome, dear. You won't remember me but I visited The Raj Hotel when my dear husband was still alive.'

'I do remember,' said Stella, shaking her hand. 'You were both very kind and gave me money to buy a bell for my bicycle.'

'Fancy you remembering that,' Minnie exclaimed.

Lydia was issuing orders to a station porter about luggage when a tall woman dressed in men's plus twos and waistcoat pushed her way through to them. She wore a battered plum-coloured hat on top of a mop of unruly brown hair.

'Andrew!' She lunged at the boy, kissing his cheek and hugging him. 'I'm your Auntie Tibby. Welcome to Ebbsmouth. Sorry I'm late. Bicycle got a puncture. And you must be Stella?' She had a smoker's husky voice and gave Stella a hearty handshake with tobacco-stained fingers. 'Tom and Esmie are always singing your praises.'

'Very pleased to meet you, Miss Lomax,' said Stella.

'Call me Tibby. Miss Lomax makes me sound like a frightening old spinster.'

'That's what you are,' Lydia murmured out of Aunt Tibby's hearing, putting a possessive hand on Andrew's arm.

'Hello, Lydia – and Mrs T,' Tibby said amiably. 'I hope you'll bring Andrew and Stella to The Anchorage soon.'

'We'll see,' said Lydia. 'They need to settle in at Templeton Hall first.'

'Perhaps you'd like to come up to the Hall, Tibby dear?' Minnie suggested.

Lydia frowned at her mother. 'Not today. Andrew and Stella need to rest after their long journey.'

'Of course,' said Tibby. 'You can ring and let me know when's convenient.' She smiled at Andrew. 'Do you play golf?'

'I've tried,' said Andrew, 'but I'm not very good.'

'Well, you can come and hack around my rough-and-ready course anytime you want. Some of the boys like to play.'

'The boys?' he queried.

'The artists who live with me.'

Lydia took her son by the arm. 'Come on, let's get you home. Car's parked at the entrance. Goodbye, Tibby.' She swept Andrew forward, leaving her mother and Stella to follow.

Tibby fell into step with Stella. 'I hope you'll call in at The Anchorage whenever you please. You'll be very welcome, dearie.'

'Thank you,' Stella replied. 'I look forward to visiting.'

Tibby gave a wide smile that made her hazel eyes crinkle in her weather-beaten face. She looked nothing like her twin brother, but Stella took to her at once. She sensed that Tom's sister would be an ally against the forceful Lydia, if one should be needed.

Stella, sitting in the back of the car with Minnie, gazed in wonder as they drove up a tree-lined gravel drive bordered by lush green lawns and flowerbeds packed with colourful flowers and shrubs. Ahead lay a beautiful whitewashed mansion, its casement windows partially hidden beneath creeping honeysuckle and climbing roses. The whole vista was a riot of colour, and heady floral scents wafted in through the car windows. Andrew had been right when he'd said his mother had bags of money.

Lydia, who was driving, had not stopped talking since the station, her stream of conversation almost solely addressed to Andrew who was sitting in the passenger seat beside her. Stella tried to listen in at the same time as showing an interest in Minnie's obvious pride at her garden.

'. . . and I got Lily, the maid, to lay out the lead soldiers on the nursery table,' said Lydia. 'They belonged to your grandfather Archibald – Tibby thought you might like to play with them. Looking at you, I'd say you're already too old for that. Mind you, old Archibald used to stage mock battles in his library till the day he died. Keeled over in the middle of re-enacting Waterloo, by all accounts. But he was a strange old bird. Cantankerous wasn't the word.'

'Dad said he was a bully,' Andrew commented.

Lydia huffed. 'Your father was too soft – let himself be pushed around when what he should have done was stand up to the old boy. I tried to smooth things over between them but it was a waste of time and energy. Both as stubborn as each other in their own way.'

'Lydia, dear,' Minnie murmured from the back seat, 'Tom's not here to defend himself, so don't be unkind.'

'Oh, Mummy, you just think the best of everyone. Daddy knew what Tom was like – he always took my side . . .' Lydia's voice wobbled.

Minnie sat forward and flapped a handkerchief at her daughter. 'There, there. Don't get upset in front of Andrew.'

Lydia took one hand off the wheel and dabbed at her eyes. 'I'm sorry, it's just I get emotional every time I think about Daddy.' She glanced at Andrew. 'Your Templeton grandfather was the most wonderful man in the world – the epitome of a true gentleman – and I miss him every day, even though he passed away over five years ago. You would have got on so well with him.'

'I'm sorry not to have met him,' Andrew said.

Lydia sniffed and balled the handkerchief in her fist. 'Yes, well, you've your father to blame for that. He wouldn't bring you for a visit when you were younger, even though I begged him to—'

'Lydia!' Minnie chided. She put a hand on Andrew's shoulder. 'Do you like tennis, dear? We still keep the court in good shape even though your mother doesn't play much these days.'

'Yes, I do,' Andrew said with enthusiasm. 'There are courts at Gulmarg and I play with Dad—' Abruptly he stopped, giving his mother an anxious glance.

'Your father was quite good at tennis,' Lydia conceded. 'That's how we met. My dear friend Harold brought him over to make up a game of doubles with me and Esmie. Did you know that?'

'No,' said Andrew. 'Does Harold still come and play tennis here?'

Lydia gasped and brought the car skidding to a halt just short of the portico. She heaved on the brake and turned to Andrew in astonishment. 'Harold's dead! Surely Esmie's told you about him? He was her husband before she went off with mine.'

Andrew turned red and stammered, 'I – I knew she was married to a Dr Guthrie and worked with him as a nurse in the North West Frontier.'

'Well, that's Harold,' said Lydia. 'He was your father's best friend. Does he not speak about him?'

'Not really,' Andrew mumbled.

'I find that astonishing,' Lydia cried.

Minnie intervened. 'Best not to open up that can of worms, dear.'

Lydia gave her mother a sharp look and seemed to bite back a retort. She tapped Andrew on the knee. 'Come on, let me show you around your new home.'

Stella had to make an effort not to gawp in wonder at the interior of Templeton Hall. The light streamed in from stained-glass windows and threw vivid colours across the tiled hall floor and up the curving wrought-iron staircase. At the base of the bannisters, life-size statues of half-naked nymphs held aloft electric lights. She caught Andrew looking transfixed at the bare metal breasts and hid a smile.

'Lily!' Lydia called out, and a stout woman in a black uniform and starched white cap came bustling through a swing door.

'Ma'am.' She bobbed.

'This is my son, Andrew.'

Lily gave another bob and smiled, showing crooked teeth. 'Welcome tae Templeton Hall, Master Andrew.'

'And this is Stella, Andrew's nanny – or sort-of nanny. She knows all about running a large establishment, so will be a great help.'

Stella looked in confusion at Andrew and saw him raise his eyebrows.

'Fetch the luggage in, please, Lily,' Lydia ordered. She turned to Stella. 'Perhaps you could help her with the trunk? We used to have a butler for these sorts of things but staff are much harder to find these days. I hope you don't mind?'

Stella hid her astonishment. At home it would have been the job of male servants to fetch and carry – she would certainly never have been expected to haul a trunk around – a fact Lydia must have known. But she didn't want to embarrass Lily by mentioning this. 'No, of course not.'

'Then Lily can show you to your room.'

'I'll go and talk to Cook about lunch,' said Minnie. 'It's nice enough to sit out on the terrace.'

Stella put down her handbag and followed the maid back outside.

'Old Mr Baxter used to do all the carrying,' muttered Lily. 'It's me does everything the now.'

'You can't be the only servant?' Stella was astonished. In India, a house that size would have had a dozen servants at the very least.

'Aye, since old Baxter went tae his maker. There's Hector comes in tae dee the garden twice a week – and there's Miss MacAlpine, the cook. But it's me does everything else. Aye, I've been here twenty year – since I was fourteen.'

Stella thought she looked much older than thirty-four, but nodded. 'The Templetons must be grateful for your loyalty.'

Lily let out a burst of laughter. 'I dinnae have much choice. Ma family's all gone and I'm too ugly tae marry!'

'No, you're not,' said Stella. 'You have very pretty eyes.'

Lily laughed again. 'Well, maybe you and me can gae on the hunt together, eh?'

They struggled inside with the heavy trunk, Lily puffing and wheezing.

'Would you like to rest for a minute?' Stella asked her as they re-entered the hallway.

Lily glanced up the stairs where they could hear Lydia talking excitedly to Andrew. 'Better no,' she said.

They laboured on, pausing on the turn of the stairs and then again on the landing. Finally, they reached the far end of the corridor and entered a large airy bedroom.

'Put it on there.' Lydia pointed at a toy chest.

Lily gave a grunt of relief. Stella looked around. It was still a nursery for a small boy, with a fireguard over a tiled fireplace and an array of pristine teddy bears on a single bed. Andrew was standing at a table in the window peering awkwardly at neat rows of toy soldiers.

'Stella, these belonged to my grandfather Archibald,' he said with a guarded look.

'You're allowed to touch them,' Lydia said brusquely.

'Ma'am,' Lily interrupted. 'Shall I unpack the trunk?'

Lydia waved a hand at her. 'No, you can go and get on with your work. Stella can put Andrew's things away.'

'I can do that,' Andrew said quickly.

'Certainly not,' said Lydia. 'You and I will join Mummy on the terrace for lunch. I want to hear all about your time on the ship.'

'And Stella can join us too?'

'Later, perhaps.' Lydia gave Stella a forthright look. 'Once you've hung up Andrew's clothes, get Lily to show you to your room. I thought you'd be more comfortable taking your meals with the staff.'

'But Stella eats with us at Gulmarg,' Andrew protested.

'Darling, this isn't Gulmarg,' Lydia said firmly. 'Your father never did know where to draw the line between us and the Duboises. Nothing personal, Stella. It's just we've never eaten with staff at Templeton Hall. Even my own dear nanny always ate in the kitchen.'

Stella said quickly, 'Whatever you say, Mrs Lomax.'

She gave a worried-looking Andrew a reassuring smile and took over from Lily. Lydia was making it quite plain that she viewed her as no more than Andrew's ayah and certainly not as a friend of the family. Stella refused to be downhearted. She was lucky to be there and Lydia had been generous in paying for her voyage over. It suited

Stella to keep busy so she would do whatever the Templetons asked of her; it was all a great adventure.

Later, she lugged her own suitcase to the top floor. Lily showed her to a small attic room with a narrow bed and a chest of drawers and a thin rug on the bare wooden floor.

'I'm next door,' said Lily. 'It gets stuffy up here in the summer, so I always leave ma windy open.'

As soon as she'd gone, Stella closed her skylight. To her it didn't seem warm at all, and she put on an extra cardigan.

Miss MacAlpine was a smallish woman with red hair who darted around the kitchen like a restless bird, lifting pot lids, stirring, sniffing, sipping and making suggestions to herself.

She welcomed Stella with a quick smile. 'You don't look very Indian, lassie.'

'I'm not,' said Stella.

The cook cocked her head. 'Are you no? The mistress said you were.'

'I'm Anglo-Indian,' she explained. 'I'm British through my mother, and French and British through my father. Both families have lived in India for several generations but we still think of Britain as our home. That's why it's so exciting to be here. I'm the first one to come back in four generations.'

'An-glo-Ind-ian.' Miss MacAlpine enunciated the words as she ladled out the soup into delicate china bowls. 'A wee bitty of everything in your blood, aye?'

'Well . . .' Stella was unsure.

'Makes for a rich soup,' said the cook, nodding sagely. 'Take these out to the terrace, Lily.'

'I like to cook,' Stella said as she watched Miss MacAlpine skin a large blanched tomato and slice it. 'The chef at The Raj-in-the-Hills has taught me quite a few recipes – curries and how to make Portuguese pastries.'

Miss MacAlpine looked startled. 'The mistress doesnae like curry – doesnae like anything that reminds her of India. But she has a sweet tooth and will eat pastries and tarts at any time of the day.'

'*Pasteis de nata* are like custard tarts,' said Stella. 'They're delicious. I'd love to help you with the cooking if you'd let me.'

The cook eyed her. 'I dinnae ken if the mistress would allow it. I was telt you were to be in charge of Master Andrew.'

'I think Mrs Lomax wants to spend time with Andy herself. So when I'm not needed perhaps I can help you out?'

The cook considered this while placing the sliced tomato next to pieces of ham and potato salad on three plates. 'That's kind of you to offer, lassie. Let's just see whit the mistress says.'

After Lily went back out with a tray load of the ham salad, Cook distributed the leftover soup into three tin bowls. 'Sit yoursel' doon, lassie, and have your broth – and you can tell me all about these Indian custard tarts.'

Chapter 11

For the first week, the good weather held and Lydia made the most of showing off the area to Andrew, buying him a new bicycle and organising a picnic to the sheltered cove below The Anchorage. Stiff knees prevented Minnie from joining them, but Stella was brought along to carry the picnic and supervise Andrew swimming in the sea while Lydia stretched out on a rug and flicked through a magazine.

Stella had brought her swimming costume – excited by Esmie's reminiscences of dips in the sea – and got changed in an old boathouse. Andrew was already up to his waist when Stella ran into the water.

She shrieked. 'It's freezing!'

'I told you it was,' Lydia called out. 'That's why I never swim – unless I'm in the south of France.'

'Come on!' Andrew grinned. He thrashed towards her and splashed her.

Stella was so shocked by the icy spray that she couldn't even scream. She chased Andrew in the shallows and pushed him into the sea. He pulled her with him and her head went under. She came up gasping and choking.

He looked panicked. 'Are you all right?'

She had never experienced such cold or the taste of salt water in her mouth but her whole body tingled.

'That was horrible!' Suddenly she was laughing. 'You're horrible.'

Andrew sighed with relief and started laughing too. 'I'll race you to that rock over there.'

'That's enough for me,' she said, wringing out her wet hair and shuddering with the cold.

'Stay in, Stella,' Andrew urged.

But she was already running up the beach.

Stella wrapped herself in a towel and watched Andrew swim to a rock and back. Lydia had already made it plain that she was there as a servant and nothing more.

Andrew came out of the sea and while he towelled himself down, Stella made an effort to engage a bored-looking Lydia in conversation. 'What an interesting home The Anchorage must be, Mrs Lomax. Looks like it grows straight out of the rock, doesn't it?'

'It's a bleak old place,' said Lydia. 'Terribly damp and cold, no matter what the time of year. I couldn't bear to live there, but Tibby doesn't seem to mind the lack of modern comforts.'

'I think it's rather romantic,' said Stella. 'Like the tower in Rapunzel.' She pictured herself letting out a coil of fair hair and Hugh – a dashing knight – scaling the cliff and climbing up to meet her.

Andrew laughed. 'Imagine if the only way in was Auntie Tibby leaning out the top window and letting down her hair.'

Lydia huffed. 'It's just the sort of mad thing Tibby would do.'

Stella had thought about Hugh every day since leaving the ship. She'd been hurt and confused at his sudden switch of interest from herself to Moira in the final few days of the voyage. One minute they'd been spending all day in each other's company – and the evenings tucked away in dark corners of the deck, kissing – and then she'd been felled by another bout of seasickness and by the time she'd emerged from her cabin, Moira had been monopolising Hugh and he didn't seem to care. Stella hadn't said anything to either of them and she'd left the ship without being able to get Hugh alone and discover what had caused his change of heart. Yet, as they'd said goodbye, he'd said how he'd like to visit her at The Raj Hotel and she'd been left not knowing what to think.

Stella resolved to try and put him out of her mind. Craning her neck to look up at the forbidding-looking castle keep, she was filled with curiosity; she was keen to see inside The Anchorage. She wanted to learn more about Tom's early life there, yet knew she couldn't ask Lydia. The woman seemed jealous whenever Andrew mentioned his father – or Esmie – so it was best to avoid speaking about either of them.

Lydia spent the rest of the week taking Andrew out for drives around the county to introduce her son to various friends and acquaintances. Minnie accompanied them but Stella was left behind.

'Make yourself useful and help Lily with the laundry,' Lydia ordered.

Stella struggled to hide her irritation at her high-handed manner but did as she was asked.

Stella also offered to help Miss MacAlpine in the kitchen, but on the third day of looking for things to do, the cook chased her out.

'It's a braw day – you dinnae wanna spend it in a hot kitchen. Away you go and breathe in God's fresh air, lassie. Take some shortbread from the tin.'

At a loose end, Stella went to the garage where Lydia had said there was a spare bicycle that she could use if Andrew wanted to cycle around the town. Finding it, she dusted it down, pumped up the tyres and decided she would visit The Anchorage. Tibby had said to call whenever she wanted. Cook gave her a tin of her deliciously buttery shortbread to take as a present and Stella set off into a blustery headwind.

Twenty minutes later, she arrived at a set of rusty iron gates and stopped to catch her breath. One gate was ajar, so she wheeled her bicycle through. Large trees swayed above, sighing in the wind. A grassy track twisted ahead through overgrown lawns dotted with daisies and buttercups, and she was assailed by the honey scent of warm grass and wild flowers that reminded her fleetingly of Gulmarg.

But this was nothing like Kashmir. Ahead lay the castle, its ancient stone looking pinkish in the sunshine. The building was a hotchpotch of pepper-pot towers, crenulations, narrow windows high up and large casement windows down below. Half of the front wall was covered in dark creeping ivy.

Stella hesitated. Perhaps she shouldn't be coming here on her own?

'Hello! Can I help you?'

Stella was startled by a voice in the trees. She stood clutching her bicycle as a slim dark-haired man in white emerged from the long grass. She gaped at him; he was wearing tight churidar pyjamas and a loose-fitting kurta.

He pressed his palms together and bowed in greeting. 'Namaste.'

'You're Indian?' she gasped in delight.

'I am Indian by birth and a citizen of the world.' He gave her a grave smile and extended his hand. 'Dawan Lal from Lahore.' He had a soft cultured voice and an intense look in his dark eyes.

'Fancy that!' Stella shook his hand, delighted to find someone from so near home. 'I'm Stella Dubois from Rawalpindi.'

'Ah, Tibby has told me about you – she's been hoping you would visit.'

Stella smiled. 'Oh, good. I've been at a bit of a loose end – Andrew has gone out with his mother again. I hope Miss Lomax won't mind me coming without him?'

'I'm sure she won't,' he reassured her. 'Please, allow me to escort you to the house. You can leave your bicycle by the wall – it'll be quite safe.'

'Thank you,' said Stella, taking the tin of shortbread she'd brought as a gift from the bicycle basket. They fell into step together. 'So, you're one of the artists who live in the castle?'

'Some might call me an artist.' He gave a deprecating smile.

'What would you call yourself?'

'A sadhu – a disciple – of Art.' He made a sweeping gesture with his hands. 'Art cannot be contained in mere paintings or confined to the sketchbook. Art is all around us – it is in the glory of nature and in the exquisite architecture of a beautiful building.'

She let him chatter on as they skirted round the side of the castle, through a kitchen garden with neat rows of lettuce, onions and potatoes, and a glasshouse filled with ripening tomatoes. Dawan led Stella in through a back door, its paint blistered and peeling, and down a dark corridor. Faintly, she could hear a piano being played somewhere deep in the house.

'We'll try the kitchen first,' said Dawan. 'Tibby was going to make soup – we've a mountain of marrows to get through.'

They found Tibby in the barrel-roofed kitchen, down on all fours and peering into a cupboard. Dawan called her name.

She replied without looking up. 'The mice have been into the oatmeal – droppings everywhere. Have you been removing the traps again, Dawan?'

He ignored her question and announced, 'Tibby, we have a visitor. Miss Stella Dubois of Rawalpindi.'

Tibby leaned around and looked up. She was still wearing the same shapeless purple hat she'd worn at the railway station.

Her face creased in a smile. 'Stella, how delightful! Have you brought Andrew to see me?'

'No, I'm sorry,' said Stella. 'He's out with Mrs Lomax. He'll be annoyed I've come without him – I should have waited, shouldn't I?'

'Not at all,' said Tibby, standing up. Wearing a man's riding jacket over a flowing scarlet dress embroidered with flowers, she padded barefoot across the flagstones.

Stella handed over the tin. 'Miss MacAlpine made you some shortbread.'

'Delicious! My favourite, thank you. We'll make sandwiches – I think there's jam, and some boiled eggs left over from breakfast. Let's eat al fresco. I'm ravenous. Do you eat eggs, Stella? Or you can have cheese – if Dawan hasn't fed it all to the mice. We've gone vegetarian since Dawan arrived. He's Hindu.'

'I have no religion except Art,' said Dawan gravely. 'Shall I make some tea?'

'That would be kind,' said Tibby, peering into a large bread bin. 'Oh dear. The boys must have used all the bread for toast this morning. Shall we have oatcakes instead?'

Stella thought of the mouse droppings in the oatmeal.

'Why don't we make a salad with the egg?' she suggested. 'I see you're growing tomatoes and lettuce. Perhaps we could spice it up with some onion and herbs and a bit of ginger. Do you have ginger?'

'What a good idea,' Tibby enthused. 'Do you hear that, Dawan? Someone else who likes ginger. A woman after your own heart.'

'Of course she eats ginger,' said Dawan. 'She was raised in the Punjab.'

'We might steal you away from the Templetons,' said Tibby, lighting up a cigarette. 'I have absolutely no artistic flair in the kitchen.'

'You do us proud, Tibby,' said Dawan. 'We eat simply but well – and you have an amazing talent for growing marrows.'

Tibby blew out smoke and roared with laughter. 'Oh dear, I was supposed to be making soup, wasn't I? I got distracted by the mice.'

Stella went with Dawan to pick some lettuce and tomatoes, and came back with cucumber, red onion, parsley and thyme too. She set about making the egg salad while Tibby, cigarette bobbing up and down at the corner of her mouth, hunted out an old wicker picnic basket and Dawan boiled up a pan of tea, milk and sugar to fill a thermos.

'That's how my brother Jimmy likes his tea,' said Stella. 'The Indian way.' Breathing in the aroma, she had a sudden pang of longing for home; it was over a month since she'd left Rawalpindi and she was missing her family.

Tibby must have sensed her homesickness. 'Come on; let's find a sheltered spot in the grounds and you can tell me all the news from India.'

Tibby led them to a tumbledown cottage overlooking the cliff – a former lookout – and Dawan spread out a rug on springy grass in the lee of the gable end.

Eating and chatting with Tibby and Dawan, Stella relaxed. She realised how tense Lydia made her feel, never quite knowing what mood she would be in or whether some casual remark that Stella made would offend her. Most of all, she enjoyed being able to speak about her home and family – subjects that Lydia also objected to – and talk of Tom and Esmie. Tibby wanted to hear all about her brother – whom she affectionately referred to as Tommy – and how things were going in Gulmarg. She made Stella feel she could say anything without it being taken the wrong way, and so found herself talking frankly about the upset over Andrew's dismissal from school in Murree.

Tibby shook her head. 'It seems very silly of the school to let a spat between the boys get out of hand like that.'

'Gotley's father – a major in the Peshawar Rifles – threatened to report Andrew to the police for hitting his son. Esmie thinks it was the major who filled George's head with the lies.'

'How unfair,' Tibby exclaimed, stubbing out her cigarette. 'Tom was a hero in the war and no coward. He did his bit for the Rifles. What a pity Andrew rose to the bait – he should just have ignored the wretched Gotley.'

Stella sighed.

'Is there something else to this incident?' Tibby asked, her hazel eyes full of concern. 'There is, isn't there?'

Stella hesitated, glancing at the Indian.

'Anything you want to tell me you can say in front of Dawan,' Tibby said. 'He is very discreet – and I tell him everything anyway.'

Dawan smiled and stood up. 'I have work to do,' he said. 'I'll leave you ladies to talk in peace.'

As he went, Tibby said, 'Tell me what is troubling you.'

'Andrew confided in me about something else Gotley said, but made me promise that I wouldn't tell his parents. He knew his father would be very hurt by it, but it preyed on his mind. It was about Esmie, you see.'

'Esmie?' Tibby queried.

Stella nodded.

Tibby touched her arm. 'You wouldn't be breaking your promise if you confided in me – but I shan't force you if you'd rather not.'

Suddenly Stella longed to unburden herself to this kind woman.

'It's all been so upsetting for the Lomaxes,' she said. 'First Andrew being thrown out of school and then his mother blaming them for neglecting him and demanding that Andrew be sent to her for the summer.' When Tibby gave her a nod to continue, Stella said, 'I overheard them arguing about it – whether to allow Andrew to come to Ebbsmouth at all. I don't think they trust Andrew's mother not to turn him against them. For some reason they think she'll say things that they don't want Andrew to find out about.'

'What sort of things?' asked Tibby.

'Something about their relationship.' Stella shrugged.

After a pause, Tibby asked gently, 'What was said about Esmie that made Andrew so upset?'

Stella sighed. 'Awful things. Gotley called her a . . . a terrible name. The worst name you can give a woman.' She dropped her voice to a whisper. 'He called her a whore.'

'How distressing,' said Tibby. 'Why would he say such a thing?'

Stella blushed as she repeated the words. 'He said Esmie was Mr Lomax's mistress – that they weren't properly married and were living a sinful life. But I told Andy that was nonsense and that of course they were married.'

Tibby said nothing. She opened her cigarette case but then closed it again.

Stella went on. 'I remember them coming back married after a trip to Delhi about the time he started school in Murree. Then they went back to Kashmir to start running The Raj-in-the-Hills.'

Tibby was staring out to sea. Stella waited for her to agree. Tibby cleared her throat and met Stella's questioning look. Her eyes were full of sadness.

'Tom and Esmie may live as man and wife,' she said quietly, 'but they aren't married. They can't be. Tom is still tied to Lydia.'

Stella gaped at her. 'What do you mean, tied to Lydia?'

'She won't give him a divorce. I don't want to speak ill of my sister-in-law but she has been very cruel to Tommy. I think it's because she still wants to have a hold over him and deny him what he wants most of all – to be married to Esmie.'

Stella was shocked. 'How awful,' she said.

Tibby nodded. 'And so unkind to her friend Esmie too. They used to be as close as sisters – went to school together. Did you know that Esmie saved Lydia's life when she was kidnapped by Pathans?'

'I don't know all the details,' said Stella, 'but years ago the baroness – one of the residents at the Raj – showed me a newspaper article about Esmie being a heroine in the rescue.'

'She certainly was. Esmie risked everything to lead an expedition into tribal territory to find Lydia and bring her to safety. And on top of that, my brother had to put up with Lydia's philandering with a cavalry officer. She was trying to run off with him when she got kidnapped – left baby Andrew behind without a second thought.' She grew more heated. 'I wouldn't be at all surprised if Lydia was behind the rumours about Tommy and Esmie not being married. From what I gather, she's still in touch with the gossips of Pindi. If she knows that Esmie is living openly with my brother and posing as his wife, and she almost certainly does, then she'll be terribly jealous.'

Tibby pulled up a handful of grass in agitation; her cheeks were red with indignation.

Stella was appalled by Lydia's callous behaviour. 'I should have told Esmie what Gotley had said about her to Andy – given her the chance to explain things properly to him before he left.' She looked at Tibby in distress. 'What if Andrew hears about it from Lydia?'

Tibby grabbed Stella's hand. 'None of this is your fault. You kept your word to Andrew. I can understand my brother's frustration at not being able to marry Esmie – but by not being honest about their true relationship he's landed himself and Esmie in an awkward situation. I suppose appearances matter more in the colonies. I wouldn't give two figs what people said about me – but no doubt it's different for Esmie trying to carry out the duties of a respectable hotelier's wife.'

'What do we do about Andy?' Stella asked.

Tibby squeezed Stella's hand. 'Nothing for the moment. Wait and see if Lydia brings up the subject. If she does, then we can let Andrew know the full picture. After all, it's only from Lydia's meanness that Tommy and Esmie aren't properly married. My guess is that she won't want to be seen in a bad light and won't mention it.'

She let go of Stella's hand and sighed. 'What's so damnable is that it was Lydia who couldn't wait to leave India and Tommy – she didn't even want Andrew. She came rushing back here and immediately took up with a rich wine merchant. He was called Colin Fleming, as I recall, and she knew him from way back. He had always been sweet on her apparently. But she tried to have her cake and eat it – avoid a scandalous divorce with Tommy and have Colin as an escort.'

'So what happened?' asked Stella.

'Colin surprised everyone by proposing to a much younger Frenchwoman he'd met on the Riviera. They had a swift wedding in Nice and Lydia was left with no one. After that, the best Tommy could get from her was a formal separation.'

Tibby began packing up the picnic basket. Stella took in deep breaths of salty air to try and quell the anger she felt inside. The thought of going back to Templeton Hall and being civil to Lydia filled her with distaste.

Yet pretending to Andrew that everything was fine would be a harder task. Her heart ached for him. He was the innocent in all this, caught up in his parents' wrangling. Subdued, the two women returned to the castle.

To delay her return to Templeton Hall, Stella asked Tibby to show her Dawan's artwork. Brightening, Tibby took her into a large room on the ground floor with tall windows that flooded the room with afternoon light. Paintings were propped against the walls and the parquet floor was covered in paint splashes. A long table was strewn with brushes, paints and jars of coloured water, and the room smelt of turpentine. Dawan, wearing an enveloping apron, was standing at an easel at the far window, absorbed in his work.

Tibby waved across the room at him. 'You don't mind if Stella looks at your paintings, do you?'

He gave a distracted smile and put down his brush, wiping his hands on a rag.

'Please don't stop on my account,' said Stella. 'I'll be very quiet.'

'But Tibby won't be,' he replied, crossing the room.

Together, the three of them toured the room looking at the paintings in turn. Stella found them startling. Two or three were of white women dressing or bathing but most were of Indian people – striking faces and bold colours – done with a simplicity of style that seemed very modern and European.

'May I see what you're working on at the moment?' Stella asked.

He seemed pleased and led them back to his easel.

'It's Manjusri – the goddess of beauty and learning.'

Stella was transfixed by the depiction of a half-naked woman with four arms, wearing a scarlet skirt similar to the dress Tibby had on. Her face was still a blank but Stella had the unsettling thought that Tibby might have posed for the artist.

In one of the upper hands the goddess held a book of Scottish poetry and in the other a large white flower.

'She should be holding a sacred book full of wisdom,' explained Dawan, 'but my goddess is a lover of literature.' He paused. 'The flower is the lotus – a symbol of beauty.'

'It's very . . .' Stella searched for the right word. 'It gets your attention.'

Both Tibby and Dawan laughed.

'Thank you for showing me your work,' said Stella. 'Perhaps you'll let me see Manjusri when she's finished?'

He bowed in agreement and picked up his brush again.

The women returned to the kitchen, retrieved Miss MacAlpine's tin and then walked to where Stella had left her bicycle.

'I'm so grateful to you and Dawan for giving up your day to entertain me,' said Stella.

'You must come whenever you want.' Tibby smiled, her eyes full of understanding. 'I'm sorry that what I've told you about Tommy still being married to Lydia has come as a shock. It was bound to come out sooner or later that he's not properly married to Esmie – and I think it's best to know these things. Secrets can lead to so much heartache once they're found out.' She put a hand on Stella's shoulder. 'You must see The Anchorage as a safe haven. If you ever need to escape from Lydia, promise me you'll come here.'

Stella felt a pang of gratitude. 'Thank you.'

Clouds were rolling in off the sea as she pedalled away. In minutes, a chilly sea fret had settled over the town and hidden the old castle from view. Stella's dread mounted the closer she got to Templeton Hall.

Chapter 12

Andrew slipped off to the garden with his cricket ball. A damp mist hung over the trees and it had begun to drizzle but he was happy to be outside. He'd been cooped up all day playing board games with an eleven-year-old girl called Flis or Tish or some silly name, while their mothers lingered over a long lunch and gossiped about people he didn't know. The girl had a cold and was forbidden to go outdoors.

Andrew put his head back and let the soft rain dampen his face and hair. He didn't know rain could come as a fine spray and smell of the sea, so different from the violent deluges of a monsoon. Restlessly, he paced around the garden, throwing and catching his ball and practising bowling. When would Stella come back? Lily said she'd cycled over to The Anchorage hours ago. How he wished he'd gone too.

These visits to his mother's friends, to have lunch or tea, were a trial. He was constantly on edge, trying to anticipate his mother's mood. One minute she was patting his back and introducing him to her friends as her 'darling boy' and the next she was scolding him for being clumsy and ordering him to 'run along and play'. He would much rather his family had all gone together with Stella to see his aunt. He longed to explore the old castle.

Just then, a woman on a too-large bicycle emerged out of the mist, straining to pedal up the drive. He ran towards her. 'Stella!'

As he reached her, she slowed and came to a halt with a wobble.

'Hello, Andy,' she said, out of breath. 'Have you had a good day out?'

'Yes, thanks. Well, not that good. Quite boring actually. I wish I'd been with you at The Anchorage. I can't believe you went to see Auntie Tibby without me. What's she like? Did you meet the artists?'

'Let's get out of the rain,' she said, 'and I'll tell you.'

'I'll push the bike for you,' he offered. 'You look tired out.'

The rain came on harder as they reached the shelter of the garage. Inside, Andrew propped the heavy old bicycle against the wall and Stella flopped onto a dusty mattress that looked like it had once belonged to a swing seat. She pulled off her wet cardigan and shook her damp blouse to try and dry it. He squatted down beside her, shaking rain out of his hair.

'Is Auntie Tibby as mad as Mamma says she is?'

'No, she's lovely. A bit disorganised but really friendly. We went for a picnic on the cliffs with one of the artists – he's Indian and from Lahore, would you believe?'

'Lahore! Can I meet him too? Does he paint or sculpt?'

'He paints. He's very serious about his art – calls it his religion. His pictures are really interesting – one or two are quite racy.'

'What do you mean, racy?'

He saw a blush creep up Stella's face.

She pushed a strand of wet hair behind her ear. 'Well . . . some of the women he paints are half-naked.'

Andrew felt himself reddening too. 'Oh, what does Auntie Tibby say? Is she shocked?'

'Not in the least.' Stella grinned. 'In fact, I think she might be his muse.'

'What's a muse?' Andrew studied her green eyes.

'A woman who models for an artist so he can be accurate in drawing the body.'

He gaped at her. 'You mean Auntie Tibby takes her clothes off in front of the Indian artist?'

Stella smothered a laugh. 'Judging by his latest painting, I think she might.'

Andrew realised how much he'd been missing their casual conversations. She was the only person he could tell how he was feeling without fear of being patronised.

'I can't work out what my mother wants,' Andrew said quietly. 'She says she's waited thirteen years to spend every minute of every day with me, but . . .'

'Go on,' Stella encouraged.

'I think she likes the idea of me more than the real me.' He shrugged. 'I can't seem to do the right thing – I just annoy her. She tells off Grandmamma too, but she's too good-natured to take offence. And I hate the way she's always saying snide things about Dad. I wish she wouldn't. I really want to please Mamma – she's paid for this holiday and she's really generous—' He broke off with a sigh.

Stella rubbed his arm comfortingly. 'She's not the easiest person to please, is she?'

Andrew nodded, feeling a twinge of guilt that he was being so critical of his mother.

'Can't she find some boys your own age among her friends' families?' Stella suggested.

'Not so far.' Andrew rolled his eyes. 'Just girls with dolls.'

Stella gave a sympathetic smile. 'Well, perhaps you should ask her – or suggest it to your grandmother? I'm sure Mrs Templeton would understand.'

Andrew nodded, encouraged.

Stella reached for her wet cardigan and got to her feet. 'I need a hot bath. Come on, let's go.'

He watched her walk on ahead, her wet skirt sticking to her shapely legs, which were splashed with mud.

He wished she was allowed to join them for meals – that his mother would treat her like family in the way his father did – but Stella never complained. He should just be glad she was on the trip with him and enjoy the moments he could spend with her. It was impossible to imagine a summer when Stella would not be around, though he supposed if she fell in love and got married then that time might come.

What if Irishman Hugh tracked Stella down to the Raj and proposed to her? She would go off to Baluchistan or maybe further away – back to Ireland even – and he might never see her again. Andrew felt an ache in his chest at the idea.

Quickly dismissing it, he headed after her, and as she walked towards the back of the house, he walked into the front and took the polished stairs up to his room two at a time.

Chapter 13

After dinner, Stella joined the family in the drawing room. She sat mending clothes and sewing on buttons for the household while Andrew played cards with his grandmother and Lydia worked her way through half a decanter of sherry. Stella felt a tension in the air. She knew Lydia was ruminating on something; she'd been frosty with her all evening. Andrew kept exchanging anxious glances with Stella, which made her think he'd probably been the object of his mother's waspish tongue at dinner.

Lydia drained off her fourth sherry and finally addressed her. 'So, Andrew tells me you went to The Anchorage today, Stella. I thought you were spending the day helping the servants.'

'Miss MacAlpine said she didn't need me and told me to go out. I hope you don't mind, but I borrowed an old bike from the garage.'

'The bicycle's the least of my worries.' Lydia waved a dismissive hand. 'I'm more concerned about your rash behaviour. Did Tibby send you an invitation to call?'

'Not specifically,' Stella admitted. 'But when we first arrived, Miss Lomax said to visit anytime.'

Lydia regarded her with cold blue eyes. 'I'm sure she only meant with Andrew. I must say I think it rather presumptuous of you to call on Tibby – you're just the nanny – and you went without my son and with no prior arrangement – and without my permission.'

'I didn't know I needed your permission, Mrs Lomax.' Stella tried to steady her thumping heart.

'Of course you do,' Lydia snapped. 'I'm responsible for you while you're over here. But as soon as my back is turned, you're gallivanting off on your own to a place with a dubious reputation.'

'Dearest,' interjected Minnie, putting down her cards, 'The Anchorage is perfectly respectable. Tibby may be a little eccentric but I'm sure she didn't mind Stella calling. There's no harm done.'

'We don't know what she got up to!' Lydia exclaimed, her face florid with indignation. 'Tibby fills that place with odd men. Stella took a great risk going there alone.'

'I'm sorry,' said Stella, trying to defuse the situation. 'I didn't mean to make you worry. It was thoughtless of me and I won't do it again.'

Lydia seemed mollified. 'I should think not. I'm just thinking of your own well-being, Stella, that's all.' Abruptly, her mood lightened. 'Is the house still falling to pieces?' she asked. 'I haven't been in such a long time.'

'Not that I could see—'

'I bet it is. Everyone knows the awful Archibald left the place heavily in debt. Poor old Tibby – that's why she has to take in those waifs and strays,' Lydia declared. 'Is she still wearing Tom's clothes?'

'She was in a dress,' said Stella.

Andrew piped up. 'Stella says there's an Indian artist living there from Lahore.'

'She's taken in an Indian?' Lydia's tone was disdainful. 'Whatever next?'

'I'd like to go and see his paintings. Could I, Mamma?'

'Whatever for?' asked Lydia. 'I've always found Indian art rather vulgar.'

'I liked his bold paintings,' said Stella. 'They were bright and colourful – a bit like Mr Lomax's.'

'Like Tom's?' Lydia gave a derisive laugh. 'Well, this Indian isn't going to win any prizes then, is he? That's typical of Tibby – she can't help taking in lame ducks.'

'Mr Lal isn't a lame—'

'Never mind what he is. Let's listen to some music. Stella, be a good girl and put something on the gramophone. Something we can dance to. Andrew, move the card table and roll up the rug.'

Lydia's sudden whims still surprised Stella, but she was thankful at her change in temper. She put down her sewing and went over to the wind-up gramophone that was kept in the alcove beside the inglenook fireplace. On a shelf above was an array of records in their paper sleeves.

'What would you like to dance to?' she asked.

'Ragtime,' Lydia ordered, getting a little unsteadily to her feet. 'Anything by Scott Joplin. We'll do the Turkey Trot and the Grizzly Bear.'

Minnie, sighing at having to abandon the card game and move, said, 'Dearest, these young ones won't know what they are.'

'Then I'll teach them,' said Lydia. 'Come on, Andrew, on your feet and shift the table.'

'But I can't dance,' he protested.

'Then it's time you learnt,' insisted his mother. 'I taught your father to dance to ragtime – or tried to. I brought records back from America during the war.'

'You were in America during the war?' Andrew asked in amazement as he shunted chairs out of the way.

'I certainly was – dodged German U-boats to go and fundraise for the war effort. Did your father never tell you?'

'No,' said Andrew. 'He never talks about the war.'

'Typical of Tom not to give me any credit. I bet you know all about how the wonderful Esmie was nursing in Serbia.'

Stella's insides fluttered at the mention of Esmie. Lydia's mood was so volatile when she'd drunk a lot of alcohol that she might say anything.

Andrew shook his head as he rolled the Persian rug out of the way.

'Well, I did my bit too,' said Lydia. 'I was the personal driver of a brigadier-general. Esmie was a mere nurse.'

'I've found one,' said Stella, quickly winding up the gramophone and putting on the record.

Lydia was diverted from her brooding train of thought by the jaunty music. She pulled off her shoes. 'Watch me, Andrew!'

Lydia's face lit up as she kicked up her heels and waved her arms, dancing enthusiastically to the old-fashioned tune. Stella could just imagine a younger, thinner, vivacious Lydia captivating Tom with her energetic dancing and forceful personality. She watched Lydia pull her son into the dance, shouting instructions and encouragement. When the record finished, Lydia cried, 'Put it on again, Stella!'

Stella was eager to take part – she picked up dance steps quickly – but hesitated without being asked by Lydia. Andrew was heavy-footed and struggled to keep up. She watched, hoping his lack of skill wouldn't annoy his mother.

When the record finished again, Lydia – puce-faced – collapsed into a chair.

Minnie clapped. 'Oh, well done, dearest! You can still do it.'

'Mummy, you make me sound ancient.' Lydia rolled her eyes. 'Gosh, I need a drink. Stella, pour me a whisky, will you?'

Stella glanced at Minnie for permission; the older woman was always fretting that Lydia drank too much after dinner.

'Don't look at her,' Lydia snapped. 'Drown it in soda if you must. I'm just thirsty.'

'I'll get it, Mamma,' said Andrew, rushing to the drinks tray. 'I know what to do.'

Lydia huffed. 'I bet you do. A hotel is no place to bring up a young boy – all those old soaks drinking chota pegs from dawn to dusk. Is your father still drinking too much?'

'Lydia,' Minnie admonished.

Stella saw the indecision on Andrew's face; he didn't know how to answer. He wanted to please his mother without being disloyal to his father.

'Would you like me to put on another record?' Stella intervened. 'You could teach Andy to waltz or quickstep.'

'Why do you insist on calling him Andy?' Lydia said sharply. 'His name's Andrew.'

'Sorry.' Stella blushed.

'I don't mind her calling me that,' said Andrew.

'Well, I do,' said Lydia. 'It makes you sound common. And Stella should be calling you Master Andrew – she is staff, after all.'

Stella exchanged looks with Andrew. She thought he was going to laugh and knew that that would only rile Lydia further. She hurried across.

'Let me do that,' she said. 'You sit down.'

He nodded and went to sit with Minnie. Stella poured a small whisky from the decanter and filled the glass to the top with soda. She wondered how soon she might be able to escape to her room. She thought of Tibby and Dawan and how they had instantly made her feel at home. How she wished that she and Andrew were staying there. Now she was unsure whether she'd be able to visit again.

To her relief, Lydia downed her drink and declared that they should all go to bed early.

She addressed her son. 'Tomorrow, your grandmamma and I are going to take you shopping and get you some decent clothes.'

Andrew's face fell. 'Do I need new clothes?'

'None of them fit you – you're like a runner bean – trousers halfway up your shins. Your father might let you run around like a savage but you can't here. We'll go to Edinburgh on the train – have lunch at Jenner's or the Royal Over-Seas Club. We'll have a fun day out together.'

'Can Stella come?' Andrew asked.

'That won't be necessary,' Lydia said curtly. 'I'm sure Stella can make herself useful in the kitchen or helping Lily.'

'Of course,' said Stella, packing up her sewing.

'And Stella,' Lydia added. 'Just remember, I don't want you sneaking off to The Anchorage on your own – not with the odd characters that lodge with Tibby; people might talk. You're my responsibility and I know your parents wouldn't approve of you mixing with those bohemian types or making friends with an Indian man. Don't you agree?'

Stella hid her dismay and nodded. She said her goodnights and hurried from the room. Mounting the stairs to the attic, she had a surge of homesickness. She had only been at Templeton Hall a week, yet it seemed an age – and another five weeks stretched ahead of enduring Lydia's disparaging remarks and living in fear of the truth coming out about Tom and Esmie's sham marriage.

This was nothing like the fairy-tale holiday to her homeland that she had imagined. How naive of her to think that Lydia would treat her as anything other than a servant – and one who thought herself above her station. She knew the woman saw her as an upstart Anglo-Indian who mixed too freely with Andrew. It came back to her vividly how, when the Lomaxes had lived at the Raj, Lydia had often been rude to the Duboises – especially to Stella's parents – for being Anglo-Indian. She'd overheard Lydia in her haughty voice calling them 'half-halfs', the derogatory term used by many British for those who were of mixed blood.

Stella had hoped that being pale-skinned and fair-haired would have helped her be better accepted as British in the land of her forefathers. On the ship, she had mixed freely with other young non-Indians – Hugh had never asked her awkward questions about her background – and she thought it would be the same here.

It was true that the servants and Tibby had treated her kindly, but Lydia was determined to keep her firmly in her place. Perhaps that was the real reason why she didn't want to take her with Andrew to the houses of her friends; she didn't want them treating her as if she were British. Lydia might only have lived in India for a short time but she had quickly picked up the racial prejudices of some of her countrymen and women. Tom and Esmie were unusual in their easy acceptance of the Duboises as their friends.

Lydia, she feared, would do everything she could to isolate her at Templeton Hall and disrupt her friendship with Andrew. It struck Stella that Lydia was jealous of their close relationship. No doubt she would see it as her duty to make her son see the world as she did – and instil in him the idea that Stella was his social and racial inferior.

Sadness gripped Stella. She curled up on her narrow bed and squeezed her eyes shut to stem her tears. She should never have agreed to come. This was not her country – and however friendly and loving Andrew was, the Lomaxes would never be her family. She'd been a fool to think that it could ever have been so.

Chapter 14

The following week, Stella was heartened when Lydia invited round a boy of Andrew's age to play tennis with him. Whether this was because Andrew had asked her to or, more likely, because Lydia was tiring of his constant company, Stella didn't know. Noel Langley was on holiday with his grandparents who were renting a cottage in Ebbsmouth.

'Noel is a dear boy,' Lydia declared, 'and his grandfather was a business friend of your Templeton grandfather. You'll get on like a house on fire.'

Andrew seemed to quickly make friends with the smaller, stockier boy who was soon coming round every day. His grandparents were just as keen as Lydia to let the two boys entertain each other.

When the weather was fine, they played tennis or went out on bicycles. Stella was sent to supervise them on the beach, where she joined in games of beach cricket and made sure they didn't climb the cliffs.

It amused Stella to overhear snatches of conversations about their shared love of cricket and Noel's enthusiasm for Andrew's military heritage.

'Both your father, grandfather *and* great-grandfather were in the Peshawar Rifles?' he asked.

'Yes,' said Andrew proudly. 'My great-grandfather survived the Indian Mutiny and Grandpapa was a colonel and fought against the Afghans.'

Stella listened to Noel talk animatedly about his home and school in Durham – a city over the border in England – where he played lots of cricket and rowed on the river.

'Perhaps you could come and stay with us before your holiday ends?' Noel suggested.

Andrew was quick to agree. 'I'd like that – as long as Mamma says I can.'

'And do you think I could visit your aunt's castle?' Noel asked. 'See all the swords and portraits of your ancestors?'

Andrew gave Stella an enquiring look. She knew he was wondering how to make such an arrangement without upsetting Lydia.

'Perhaps your grandmother could ask Tibby to lay on tea for the Langleys,' she suggested. If anyone could win Lydia round, it was Minnie Templeton.

Andrew gave her a grateful smile. 'Yes, I'll ask Grandmamma.'

A few days later, it was arranged that Minnie and the boys would go to The Anchorage for a round of golf and afternoon tea – and to Stella's delight, she was allowed to go too.

Lydia found an excuse not to join them. 'I'm meeting an old friend in Newcastle for the day, so I'm afraid I can't be there,' she said. 'You will be good for your grandmamma, won't you, Andrew?'

'Of course he will,' said Minnie with a smile of affection. 'And I've taken the liberty of asking the Langley grandparents along too. I think they're just as curious to see the old castle as Noel is.'

Lydia shuddered. 'Rather them than me.'

On the day of the visit, Lydia left for an early train and the Langleys came for lunch before going round to The Anchorage. Stella, at Minnie's invitation, joined them for the meal too, and afterwards, they all piled into the Langleys' large Hillman Fourteen and drove to the castle.

The visit was a huge success. They were greeted by Tibby in full Highland dress – accompanied by her gardener on his bagpipes – and given a tour of the ancient tower. While Noel enthused about the muskets and moth-eaten flags, Stella was touched to see Andrew's eyes fill with tears at being led into his father's old bedroom in the highest castle turret.

'Did my father paint this?' Andrew asked his aunt, peering at a framed picture of a beach below pink cliffs and a boathouse in shadow. Stella recognised it as the beach where she'd swum with Andrew.

'Yes,' said Tibby, 'and the one over there is of St Ebba's Church and its graveyard. They were special places for him. I should really take them downstairs because the damp will spoil them sooner or later, but . . . somehow they belong in here.'

Stella saw Andrew swallow and turn to stare out of the window. She knew in that moment how much he was missing his father and had to resist putting her arms around him in comfort.

Soon, Tibby was leading them outside for golf followed by tea in the summerhouse: huge floury scones with gooseberry jam and tea served in cracked china cups. Finally, before they left, Dawan showed them around his studio and talked animatedly with Mrs Langley about surrealism.

Stella observed the boys staring with interest at the paintings.

'Does it make you want to be an artist too?' Stella asked Andrew.

'Andrew's going to be a soldier like his pater,' Noel said at once.

Andrew shrugged. 'Maybe a soldier and an artist,' he answered with a bashful smile.

Chapter 15

Stella saw Lydia looking out for them as the Langleys' car pulled up under the portico. She waved and came out to meet them.

'How was tea with Tibby? Not too much of a trial, I hope. Come in for a drink – it's the cocktail hour.'

'We won't stay,' said Mr Langley through the open window.

'Oh do!' Lydia insisted. 'I've had a rather dreary day with a friend who could only talk about her cats.'

'Just for one, then,' Mr Langley agreed.

The boys sprang out of the car and began gabbling about their visit.

'Goodness,' said Lydia, interrupting their flow. 'Run along now and wash your hands – they look rather grubby. And, Stella' – Lydia turned to her – 'a letter came for you. I gave it to Lily to put in your room. The postmark was Dublin. I didn't know you had Irish relations.'

'I don't,' Stella said in bemusement.

Andrew gave her a strange look. 'It might be that Irishman from the ship.'

'What Irishman?' demanded Lydia.

Stella flushed. She shot Andrew a pleading look.

'I shared a cabin with him,' said Andrew hastily. 'He was a good sort. He was on crutches because of a bullet wound to his knee, so I helped him out.'

'So why is he writing to Stella and not you?' Lydia asked.

Andrew shrugged.

Stella recovered her surprise. 'It's much more likely to be from our chaperone, Miss Jessop. She was going to do some travelling.'

Lydia lost interest. 'Well, go and keep an eye on the boys, will you? Make sure they don't do any damage to Mummy's flowers.'

Stella hid her frustration. All she wanted to do was rush up to her attic room and see if the letter really was from Hugh. How had he got this address? He must have remembered Andrew telling him where his mother lived. She was filled with excitement, but she had to curb her impatience as she followed the boys outside.

It was another hour before the Langleys left and Stella was able to run up to her room. She seized the envelope on her bedside cabinet and tore it open. Glancing quickly at the end, her heart drummed to see that it was from Hugh.

Stella sank onto the bed, lay on her back and read it with shaking hands.

> *My dear Stella,*
>
> *How are you? I hope you are well and that you are enjoying your first trip 'home' to Britain. Is it as good as you expected? What is Andrew's mother like? I hope she's not the dragon you remembered from your childhood! The important thing is that she's kind to her son so I hope he is having a jolly time of it too.*

I am having a pleasant time in good old Ireland. I can't tell you what a relief it is to be able to walk outside without being scorched by the sun or drenched in sweat in two minutes. Now I just get drenched in rain! But I'm happy to swap the heat of India for the rain of Ireland for a few months.

My leg is healing well and I'm getting about now with a stick instead of crutches. I hope to be riding soon and by the time I return to India maybe I'll be able to play polo again. I'm visiting lots of relations and enjoying drinking a decent stout – one of the things I miss in India.

I must confess that it won't be so hard returning east now that I know there's a pretty green-eyed girl living in Pindi. I have every intention of visiting The Raj Hotel someday and hope you will be there.

I think of you often, Stella, and wish we could have had another week on board the Rajputana *together. The final days dragged after you'd gone. I missed our games of backgammon and chats on deck – and especially kissing those sensuous lips of yours. To tell the truth, I spend every day pining for you and your beautiful green eyes.*

Do you miss me too? I have to know. Because if you do, Stella, then would you consider being my girl? But perhaps you've met some handsome Scotchman and haven't given me another thought. If that is so, then please ignore this letter. Give my best wishes to Andrew.

With fond regards,
Hugh Keating

*P.S. I'm staying with my sister in Dublin for a while,
Mrs Henry French, so if you want to write back then
send the letter to the above address.*

Stella crushed the letter to her chest and let out a squeal. Hugh still liked her! More than that, he pined for her. She read the letter again, savouring the words. He thought her pretty and missed her. And all this time she'd thought that it was Moira who had caught his interest. But he made no mention of the chaperone. She must have been mistaken in thinking there had ever been anything between Hugh and Moira. Stella berated herself for turning cool towards him and wasting the final couple of days avoiding his company because Moira was always around him.

She closed her eyes and conjured up Hugh's broad smile, wavy brown hair and the way his dark-blue eyes creased when he laughed, which was frequently. Once, when he'd got soaked by a water game on deck, he'd pulled off his shirt and she'd seen his sinewy body, the skin pale in contrast to his sunburnt neck and forearms. She'd experienced a delicious frisson at the sudden exposure of bare skin and the way his firm muscles had stretched as he'd shed his wet shirt.

So, he didn't have a sweetheart waiting for him in Ireland. It struck her that she didn't really know much about Hugh, and Andrew hadn't been able to tell her many details either. He'd mentioned that he came from farming stock and that's why he'd applied for the Agricultural Service in India. He'd called his family Anglo-Irish, which she'd gathered meant they were Protestant and had links to England.

She hadn't mentioned that she was Anglo-Indian because she knew he wouldn't see that as the same thing at all; she was not equivalent to him socially. Yet he hadn't struck her as a man who would mind that she might have a trace of Indian blood far back in her lineage. But should she be frank and tell him before they embarked on a friendship?

She dismissed the unsettling thought. He liked her for who she was – and she liked him. They could write to each other and see what happened when they both got back to India. There was nothing improper in that. She felt a thrill at the thought of striking up a courtship by letter with the handsome Hugh Keating.

Stella could hardly eat that evening. All she wanted to do was go to her room, compose a letter to Hugh and write up her diary for this momentous day. She was hopeful she might be able to slip away after supper and not join the others in the drawing room. Thursday was the evening that Minnie went out to visit a widowed friend, Mrs Guthrie, so perhaps Lydia would be content to play a quiet game of cards with her son. Stella found it increasingly difficult to sit in the same room as Lydia and listen to her litany of woes or waspish comments about anyone who wasn't a Templeton.

The bell rang, summoning her to the drawing room, and her heart sank.

Stella could tell straight away that Lydia was drunk. Her face was flushed, her eyes unfocused and her voice was loud. Stella went to a corner chair and opened the sewing box she'd brought with her.

'Put that away and sit down here,' Lydia ordered, pointing at the chair opposite her.

Stella hesitated. Andrew glanced at her over his game of patience and she saw the tension in his face. Her pulse quickened as she forced a smile and perched on the sofa.

'So, tell me,' said Lydia, 'who's been writing to you from Dublin?'

Stella quelled her annoyance. It was none of her business. But if Lydia knew it was from a young unmarried Irishman from the ship then she might make things awkward for her. No doubt Lydia would write to Tom or even her parents about it and prevent her writing back to Hugh.

'It was from a Mrs French,' said Stella. 'We met on the boat but I forgot she came from Dublin.'

She caught a disbelieving look from Andrew. Well, it was only a half-lie. The letter had come from Mrs French's Dublin home and that's to whom she would reply.

Lydia seemed disappointed and gave a wave of her hand. 'I always find the Irish rather garrulous, don't you?'

'Friendly people, I'd say,' Stella replied.

Lydia picked up her empty sherry glass and handed it to her. 'Be a dear and fill this up again.'

Stella took her time going to the table with the decanter and half-filling the glass. There was no Minnie there to try and restrain Lydia's drinking. Handing back the glass, she asked, 'Would you like me to put on some music, Mrs Lomax?'

'Not tonight,' Lydia said. 'You've had enough stimulation for one day, according to my son.'

Stella looked across at Andrew and saw the heat creep into his cheeks.

'Oh yes.' Lydia gave a drunken laugh. She was slurring her words. 'He's told me all about you playing golf and the vulgar paintings that Indian man hangs in the dining room. I hope the old colonel's spinning in his grave.'

Stella thought it best to say nothing.

'I must say, I think it quite extraordinary of Tibby to have you all trooping around the old tower and poking into bedrooms as if she were showing off some grand country house. I can't think what the Langleys must really have thought of it. They were impeccably polite but it doesn't exactly show the Lomaxes in a good light, does it? The place is so down-at-heel and yet Tibby behaves as if her family are still of high standing. I bet she boasted to the Langleys that the Lomaxes are descended from Robert the Bruce. Did she, Andrew?'

He looked up in interest. 'Are we descended from Robert the Bruce?'

Lydia swigged her sherry and huffed. 'I doubt it. But the Lomaxes always looked down their noses at us Templetons – even though we could have bought them out lock, stock and barrel.'

'I'm proud to be a Lomax,' Andrew said, with an intense look in his eyes that reminded Stella of Tom. 'We're a family of warriors and I want to be one too. Noel was really impressed – he wishes he was one of us.'

Lydia's expression darkened. She polished off her drink. 'Warriors?'

'Yes.' Andrew grew animated. 'My great-grandfather helped put down the Indian Mutiny and my grandfather fought the Afghans – he was a friend of General Roberts of Kandahar. Even Dad told me that.'

'Did he now? And what else did *Dad* say?'

Stella was uneasy at the icy tone.

'Not much,' Andrew admitted, 'but I know Dad was a hero in Mesopotamia – Mr Fritwell at the Raj told me so.'

'Fritters?' Lydia said with derision. 'What does he know about the Peshawar Rifles? He was a mere quartermaster for some inferior infantry regiment.'

116

'Well, I suppose Dad must have told him. Dad hasn't explained everything to me yet because it was probably too gory, but he's promised to tell me when I go home.'

'Home?' Lydia said, a sudden tremble in her voice. 'Don't you feel at home here with me and Grandmamma?'

'Of course,' Andrew said. 'I didn't mean . . .'

Tears sprang to Lydia's eyes. 'That pains me so much, Andrew. I adore having you here and yet all you can think about is your father who doesn't deserve your devotion – no, not in the least bit.'

Stella was suddenly incredibly anxious. Where was this leading? She wondered whether she should intervene, but Andrew was speaking again.

'What do you mean, doesn't deserve?' Andrew frowned. 'I wish you wouldn't speak badly about him all the time.'

'Oh, you've no idea what I had to put up with,' said Lydia. She reached for a handkerchief and dabbed her eyes. 'And now you're being cruel to me too – I can't bear it.' She began to sob.

'Mamma?' Andrew sprang up and went to comfort her. 'I'm sorry. Please don't cry.'

'I sh-shouldn't let myself get emotional about your father and what he's done. But it's just too much to hear you speak of him as a hero. I was taken in by all that heroism nonsense too, but it's not true.'

Andrew looked at her in bewilderment. 'Don't say that, Mamma.'

'Darling, I know things you don't. I have friends in army circles. But let's not spoil the evening by talking about it.'

Stella saw Andrew's agitation grow. 'What things don't I know?'

'I don't want to be the one to tell you,' Lydia said, sniffing into her handkerchief.

'Tell me what? Please, Mamma, what do you know that I don't? You're as bad as Dad for thinking I'm too young to be told things.'

'Oh dear, if I must,' Lydia said. 'Come and sit beside me.'

Stella felt now that she had to say something. Standing up, she said, 'Isn't it time Master Andrew went to bed? It's been a tiring day and perhaps this could wait—'

'I'll decide that.' Lydia gave her a hostile look and Stella sat back down.

Andrew perched beside his mother and began biting a fingernail.

Lydia put a hand on his knee. 'I'm distressed to say this,' she began, her tone dramatic, 'but your father was court-martialled in Mesopotamia for some cowardly act. He should have been shot, but his good friend Harold Guthrie intervened on his behalf and his sentence was commuted on grounds of . . . of . . . mental instability.'

Andrew looked like he had been slapped across the face. He gasped in shock. 'No! I don't believe it!'

Lydia withdrew her hand. 'I knew you wouldn't. I shouldn't have said anything . . . You're too young to cope with the truth.'

Tears welled in his eyes.

'That's why your father left the regiment – he didn't choose to; he was forced out. That's the only reason he doesn't want to talk about it.'

Abruptly, Andrew's shoulders sagged as he struggled not to cry. Stella rose to go to him, but Lydia put an arm around her son and patted his hair.

Andrew's voice wobbled. 'Th-that's what G-Gotley said . . . that Dad was a coward. I thought he was lying.'

'My darling boy,' Lydia said in dismay. 'Is that why you got expelled? For defending your father?'

Andrew nodded. 'Gotley was *hateful*.'

'But what he said was true,' Lydia said brutally.

Stella looked on in distress. Lydia was the hateful one for denigrating Tom in his son's eyes.

She spoke up. 'Even if Mr Lomax was court-martialled, it doesn't mean he wasn't a hero. Think of all the years of war he went through – all he had to endure – and he was a brave Rifleman on the North West Frontier for years before that. It's not true that he was a coward.'

Andrew looked up, hope flickering across his face.

'You always did stick up for Tom, didn't you, Stella?' Lydia said in a cold voice. 'Such misplaced loyalty. We were all taken in by him. I would never have married him if I'd known the truth about his character. I was duped into marriage and promised a glamorous life in India – but that all turned out to be make-believe too.'

Unable to stand this twisting of the truth, Stella blurted out, 'You just weren't suited to India! That wasn't Mr Lomax's fault.'

'Don't be impertinent,' Lydia snapped. 'You were a little girl and had no idea what was going on at the Raj.'

Stella seethed at her condescending tone. 'I could see you were both unhappy – until baby Andrew came along. Mr Lomax adored Andrew from the moment he was born and would have done anything for you both. You could have had a good life in India but you chose not to.'

'How dare you!' Lydia went puce with anger. 'You jumped-up little half-half! You had no idea what I had to put up with – a cheating husband and a best friend, the saintly Esmie, who stabbed me in the back.'

'That's a lie!' Stella glared back. 'Esmie saved your life.'

Lydia stood up unsteadily and stabbed a finger at her. 'She ruined my life! Pretending to be loyal to me when all the time she was plotting to take my husband away from me.'

'That's not true,' said Stella, furious. 'Don't say such things in front of Andrew.'

'Why shouldn't he know?' she said shrilly. 'That woman has usurped my place – I'm his mother, not her.'

Andrew sat open-mouthed, stunned by their arguing.

Lydia looked at him, wild-eyed. 'For years I've put up with Esmie posturing as your mother,' she said. 'But not any more. I want you to live with me. It would break my heart for you to go away again. You must stay!'

Andrew's expression was riven. Stella wanted to shout out that it was Lydia who was the cheating partner in his parents' marriage and that it was his mother who had rejected him and left Tom to bring him up. But he had suffered enough being subjected to Lydia's vile outpouring.

Swaying, Lydia held out her arms to her son. He hesitated. Lydia let out a sob. 'I can't bear it if you leave me . . .'

In alarm, Andrew stood up and hugged her. 'Please don't cry again, Mamma.'

Lydia wept into his shoulder and pawed at his hair. Stella looked on, appalled.

'Don't desert me,' Lydia wailed. 'Stay with me . . . and Mummy . . . and then your father might come back . . . We can be a family again . . . here in Ebbsmouth.'

Andrew drew back. He looked confused and a little scared. 'But Dad's got Meemee now. His life's in India.'

She clawed at his arm. 'It doesn't have to be – he could still choose us.'

'I don't understand . . . Dad loves Meemee.'

Lydia shook her head. 'He doesn't! He can't do. If he did, he wouldn't still be married to me!'

Andrew leaned back. 'How can he be? He's married to Meemee.'

'No, my darling, he's not. I can see what a shock that is to you but Esmie is nothing more than a mistress to him. I'm still his wife. They've both been living a lie.'

'No!' Andrew shook his head as if he could throw off the words he didn't want to hear.

Stella could take no more. She didn't care what Lydia said to her, she would not see Andrew subjected to any more of his mother's vitriol.

'You're right, Andy. Your father does love Esmie – and she him – so much so that they've both been forced into a pretend marriage for appearances' sake. But only because your mother won't give your father a divorce – out of spite; she can't bear to see them happy—'

Lydia lurched at Stella and slapped her hard on the cheek. 'Shut up you chee-chee bitch and go to your room!'

'Mamma!' Andrew sprang between them, balling his fists. 'Don't!' he shouted.

Lydia's expression crumpled at once. 'I can't believe you'd defend this treacherous girl instead of your own mother,' she sobbed. 'Can't you see how they've all been keeping secrets from you?'

Andrew's look faltered. 'Stella? You knew they weren't properly married?'

'Only since coming to Ebbsmouth.' She tried to explain. 'Tibby . . .'

'Auntie Tibby knows? Why didn't you tell me?'

'I hoped it would never come out,' Stella said with a despairing look.

Lydia reached for Andrew. 'She can't be trusted – none of them can; only me. I'm the only one who truly cares about you.'

He shook her off. 'Why wouldn't you divorce Dad?' he accused.

Lydia's head drooped. She crumpled onto the sofa. 'Because I still love him!'

Stella stared at her in disgust. How could she profess love for a man she had just said such cruel and wicked things about? She was beneath contempt.

For a moment, Andrew looked undecided too. His hand hovered over her shoulder. Then abruptly, he turned and strode from the room. Stella followed him out.

He was too fast for her, taking the stairs two at a time. She chased after him. 'Andrew, wait!'

He thundered up the corridor. As he reached his bedroom, he turned on her.

'You knew and you never told me,' he said, his look stormy.

Stella stopped short. 'I'm sorry, Andrew. But your mother should never have said those horrible things about your father and Esmie – she's had too much to drink.'

'Don't blame Mamma! At least she's told me the truth.'

'Only part of it. She's the one to blame for denying your father a divorce and forcing him and Esmie into an impossible situation. What else could they have done?'

Andrew's eyes glistened. 'They could have been honest with me – and so could you. I put Gotley in the san' with a broken cheekbone because of their lies.'

Stella swallowed. 'I'm so sorry – I know it's been a terrible shock – but when we get back to India, they'll be able to explain—'

'Stop it,' he hissed. 'I don't want to hear any more. Just go, Stella!'

He threw open the door to his bedroom, rushed inside and slammed it shut behind him.

Stella stood there shaking. She put out a hand to knock – she wanted to comfort him – but hesitated. Nothing she said would make any difference while he was so distressed. She would try and make amends in the morning – and perhaps Lydia might wake up feeling a little contrite for having created such upset.

She leaned her head against the door in despair. Guilt overwhelmed her that she had added to Andrew's misery by not being frank with him about what Tibby had told her. Didn't he have a right to know? They were all covering up the truth to save him being hurt and humiliated, believing he was too young to cope with the situation. Yet all Andrew wanted was for them to be honest with him. She of all people should have known that.

Chapter 16

Stella got no sleep that night. The terrible row played in her head over and over. Lydia's spiteful words had been relentless. In a few short minutes she had dismantled Andrew's adoration of his father. *'Court-martialled . . . cowardly act . . . should have been shot . . . mental instability . . .'* And then Lydia had confirmed George Gotley's gossip that Esmie was not properly married to Tom. Andrew's beloved Meemee – the woman he thought of as his stepmother – had been living a lie.

Stella lay tortured by thoughts of her own part in this. She would have to write to the Lomaxes and warn them of what had happened. Given how word travelled so quickly around British circles in India, it was surprising that they'd been able to keep up the pretence for so long. Was that why they'd chosen to live a more reclusive life in Kashmir rather than in the army town of Rawalpindi?

Tom's mental well-being must also have been a factor when they opted for a quieter life in Gulmarg – a place that was cut off in winter. She knew that Esmie shielded him from the outside world to some extent. Stella was one of the few people who knew that Tom's bouts of depression were caused not only by shell shock but also his grief over the deaths of his first wife and baby daughter. It made Stella realise that another reason why Esmie would risk the shame of living outside of marriage with Tom was so that she could nurse him and take care of him during the bad days.

Stella gave up trying to sleep. She switched on the light and fetched her writing case. She began writing a letter to Hugh, but soon gave up. How could she write to him of love and happiness when her feelings were in turmoil? All was now overshadowed by the awful confrontation with Lydia.

Instead, she pulled out a fresh piece of blue airmail paper and began to write to Esmie.

Stella overslept. She'd fallen asleep at dawn and now woke groggy and exhausted. Splashing water on her face and dressing hurriedly she went below. The clock in the kitchen showed it was already mid-morning. Cook had left out some oatcakes and honey for her breakfast and a note saying she had gone shopping. Unable to face more than a nibble of oatcake, she went looking for Andrew. Today, the Langleys were due to return to Durham and she knew he would want to spend his final hours with Noel, no matter what state of mind he was in.

Stella dreaded bumping into Lydia, so began by searching outside in the hope that the boys were playing in the garden. There was no sign of them and she noticed that Lydia's car was gone. At least she could avoid seeing Andrew's mother for a little longer. She returned inside and went upstairs to check if Andrew was still in the house. His bedroom door was wide open.

To her surprise, she found Lily stripping the sheets off his bed. 'Hello, Lily.'

'Morning, sleepy-head.' Lily grinned. 'I couldnae wake you.'

'Sorry, I slept badly. Has Andrew gone out?'

'Aye. Gone doon to the Langleys.'

'I thought he might. I suppose he'll be away till after lunch?'

Lily scooped up the pile of linen. 'He'll naw be back for a while.'

'What do you mean?'

'He's awa' to stay wi' Master Noel in Durham. Dinnae ken for how lang.'

Stella's spirits plunged. 'Did you see him this morning?'

'Aye, he was naw his cheery self. Off his food too. Mrs Templeton couldnae get him tae eat and was feart he was sickenin' for some'at.'

'Did he ask for me before he went or leave a message?'

Lily shook her head. 'Naebody was sayin' much at all. The mistress had a sore heed. It was Master Andrew who asked if he could gang wi' the Langleys. His mither was straight on the telephone to ask Noel's granddad. She's dropping him off there the now.'

Stella felt miserable at the thought of how unhappy Andrew must be after the previous night's row.

'Is Mrs Templeton in the house?'

'Aye, I think she's in the conservatory.'

Stella returned downstairs and found Minnie dead-heading plants.

Minnie looked up with a worried frown. 'Ah, Stella, perhaps you can tell me what's been going on? I hardly got a word out of Andrew this morning and now he's rushing off to stay with the Langleys. Did you know he was going?'

Stella swallowed. 'I knew Noel was keen for him to visit Durham but I didn't know it would be today. I wish I'd been able to say goodbye.'

'Well, he'll probably just be gone a few days. Lydia was very keen for him to join Noel. I suppose there'll be more for them to do together in Durham than here – other boys to play with . . .'

126

She gave a distracted look. 'Did anything happen last night while I was out? Lydia was a bit tearful this morning.'

Perhaps Lydia was feeling contrite, Stella wondered. How much should she tell Minnie of the terrible scene in the drawing room?

'Things were said in the heat of the moment,' Stella began, 'about Mr Lomax . . . and about Esmie. Andrew got a bit upset.'

'Oh dear.' Minnie sighed. 'I could see from the decanter that there'd been a lot of sherry drunk.'

Just then, a car appeared on the driveway. It was Lydia returning.

'Oh, well, she's back now and can tell me herself.' Minnie put down her secateurs.

Slow minutes went by. A car door slammed and the front door opened. Lydia's heels tapped noisily across the tiled hall floor. 'Mummy?' she called.

'In here, dearest!' Minnie called.

Lydia came in and stopped short at the sight of Stella. She looked at her coldly, then, ignoring her, spoke to her mother. 'The Langleys have left. They send you their best wishes.'

'That's kind,' said Minnie. 'And how was Andrew?'

'Absolutely fine. He was excited to be going to Durham. The change will do him a power of good.'

'Yes.' Minnie eyed her. 'I hear he was upset last night.'

Lydia looked suspiciously at Stella. 'What have you been saying to my mother?'

'Don't be hard on Stella,' Minnie chided. 'She's said very little. She was just worried about Andrew—'

'Well, there's no need,' Lydia said, putting on a smile. 'I'm glad you're here, Stella. I was wanting to have a quiet word. Come with me.'

Stella glanced anxiously at Minnie.

'Lydia,' Minnie said, baffled. 'What is this all about?'

'I'll tell you later, Mummy.'

Stella followed Lydia out of the conservatory, through the hall and into the drawing room. As soon as they were out of earshot of Minnie, Lydia's pretence at friendliness evaporated.

She rounded on Stella. 'It's your fault that Andrew's gone away. To think how I've taken you into my home and treated you more like family than staff, but what thanks do I get? None! I get betrayal. Well, I've had enough of your interference. You've tried to set my son against me in favour of Esmie but it hasn't worked. He's ashamed of her now he knows the truth. He doesn't even want to talk about her – or Tom.'

Stella dug her fingernails in her palms to try and stay calm. 'I think it was Mr Lomax being called a coward that really upset—'

'Shut up! I'm not asking for your opinion,' Lydia hissed. 'I think it's best that you leave Templeton Hall. There's nothing for you to do here while Andrew's away and I don't want you around when he's not. You can go and stay with Tibby or I'll pay for you to lodge in the town – but I don't want you under my roof, not after the hurtful things you've said about me. You've made Andrew very upset and I'll never forgive you for that.'

Stella flushed with anger. How dare she accuse her of upsetting Andrew! Her eyes stung with tears but she refused to cry in front of the hateful woman.

'I'll ring Tibby now and see if she'll have you.' Lydia said with an icy look. 'Go and pack your case.'

128

Within the hour, Stella had packed, said hasty goodbyes to a dismayed Lily and a baffled Minnie and had been driven round to The Anchorage by Lydia.

Andrew's mother dropped her at the gate. Gripping the steering wheel, Lydia said in a voice full of loathing, 'You've been such a disappointment to me, Stella. I remember you as an amenable girl who was eager to please, but you've turned into someone who thinks they're above their station. I blame Tom and Esmie for encouraging a half-half like you to think you could be the equal of my son. You're not to contact him. If I had my way, you'd never see him again.'

Stella opened the back door and quickly climbed out, unable to bear any more.

'And don't try and come round to see my mother as she won't be there,' Lydia added. 'I'm going to take her away for a holiday while Andrew's gone. Is that clear?'

Stella ignored the question. 'Thank you for the lift, Mrs Lomax.' Heaving out her suitcase, she shut the car door firmly and walked away.

But she couldn't keep up a brave face for long. Willie the gardener found her struggling with her case up the drive.

'Let me take that, Miss Dubois,' he said, quickly shouldering the case.

'Thank you,' Stella said, on the verge of tears.

Then she caught sight of Tibby striding down the overgrown track and waving.

Stella ran towards her. 'I'm so sorry, Miss Lomax . . .' She broke down crying.

Tibby pulled her into a hug. 'Don't be sorry. It's wonderful to have you to stay. I'm surprised you've stuck it out so long with Lydia – she can be quite impossible.'

Stella buried her face in Tibby's shoulder – she smelt of cigarette smoke and cooking – and was comforted by her words.

'Last night was terrible,' Stella sobbed. 'I've let Andy down and now he's gone away.'

Tibby steered her towards the castle. 'Come on. We'll have some of Dawan's chai tea and you can tell me everything.'

Chapter 17

The final two and a half weeks in Scotland dragged by. Stella did her best to keep busy at the castle, helping in the kitchen with meals using food grown in the garden, and ordering supplies from the village shops. Tibby, whose housekeeping was erratic, was lavish in her praise of Stella's attention to detail.

'You are amazing, dear girl. No wonder my brother is so admiring of you and your family – no doubt you keep his hotels shipshape.'

There were only three artists in residence over the summer: Dawan, a young bearded man called Mac, and Walter, a student from Glasgow who hammered away making furniture in one of the outhouses. Stella enjoyed their company at mealtimes but each was absorbed in their work during the day. Time hung heavily and Stella worried about Andrew. She had heard nothing from him and neither had Tibby.

'I'm sure it means he's having a lovely time in Durham,' Tibby assured her. 'I wouldn't expect a thirteen-year-old boy to waste a moment of his holiday writing letters to his aged aunt.'

Stella had sent the airmail letter to Esmie that she had written in the small hours of what had turned out to be her last night at

Templeton Hall. Now she wondered whether that had been wise. What could Esmie do at such a distance? It would probably have been better just to wait till their return – or write from the boat to give warning – rather than let Esmie and Tom stew over the revelations.

After a week at The Anchorage, Stella decided to write to Hugh. She had tried to push him to the back of her mind while she dealt with her new surroundings and situation, but he had lingered at the edge of her thoughts. It would give her something pleasurable to do and she began to indulge in daydreams about how they might meet up in India after his furlough.

One evening, she took out her writing case and settled down at the table in her bedroom window. She couldn't find his letter. Panic seized her. She took everything out of the small attaché case, but the letter wasn't there.

Overcome by a sickening feeling, Stella realised she must have left it in the attic bedroom at Templeton Hall. She had slept with it under her pillow but had been so tired the morning she had left and had had to pack up so quickly that she'd forgotten to retrieve it. How could she have been so careless?

Stella determined to go round to Templeton Hall and get Lily to let her into the house to search her room. Hopefully, Lydia and her mother would still be away on holiday.

Borrowing a bicycle from Tibby, Stella cycled over the next morning, buffeted in a strong wind coming off the sea. The sky looked laden with rain clouds. To her relief, there was no car under the portico and the blinds in the conservatory were pulled down. She wheeled the bike round to the back entrance.

The kitchen door was locked. Perhaps the servants had been given leave while Lydia and her mother were gone. Stella knocked but no one came. In frustration, she turned to go, and then remembered that Miss MacAlpine kept a spare key tucked under a stone behind a rain barrel. Stella retrieved the rusty key and triumphantly let herself into the house.

The range was still lit so someone was keeping an eye on the house. Stella crept up the back stairs and into her room. To her dismay, her bed had been stripped and the blankets bundled into the mothball-smelling chest; a sure sign that she wasn't expected back.

Quickly, she searched under the bed and moved the chest of drawers in case it had slipped out of sight. Nothing. Perhaps Lily had found it while clearing the room and had hung onto it for safekeeping.

Hesitating for only a moment, Stella went into Lily's room. Just as she was beginning to search, she heard a creak on the stairs. Dashing out of the room she came face to face with a startled Lily.

Lily screamed. She clutched her chest. 'Whit a fright you gave me!'

'Sorry!' Stella cried, turning pink with embarrassment. 'I didn't mean to.'

'You been in ma room?' Lily accused.

'I was just having a quick look. I've lost a letter – the one that came for me the other day. It's special. I thought you might have found it and kept it for me.'

Lily leaned up against the wall to catch her breath. 'So it was you that left the door unlocked – I was afraid we had burglars.'

'Oh, Lily, I'm so sorry. Come and sit down.' Stella steered the maid into her bedroom.

'I'm glad it was just you, lassie,' Lily said, calming down. 'I hate been in the hoos all by ma sel'. Cook's away for the coming week, seeing as the mistress and Mrs Templeton aren't coming back for another fortnight.'

'Where have they gone?' Stella asked.

'Durham. Staying near Andrew.'

Stella's insides twisted. 'Have you heard how he is?'

Lily shrugged. 'When the mistress last spoke tae Cook, she said Andrew was having the time o' his life. Likely he'll be there till the end of his holidays.'

Stella felt resigned. 'That's good, if he's happy.'

Lily eyed her. 'So what did you dae to mak' the mistress tak' against you, Stella? She was in a bad fettle when she left.'

Stella sighed. 'I was sticking up for Mr Lomax and Esmie.'

Lily nodded. 'I mind when they were friends – the mistress and Miss Esmie. She was a kind sort, Miss Esmie – and Captain Lomax was a handsome man. We all liked him too and the mistress was happy in those days.'

Rain spattered against the skylight and Stella knew if she delayed any longer, she'd get a soaking cycling back.

'Lily, did you find my letter from Dublin?'

'Aye, I did. It fell oot the linen when I stripped the bed.'

'So where is it?'

'I asked the mistress if I should tak' it round to The Anchorage for you but she said she would dee it . . .'

'She never did.'

Lily said, 'Well, she's been awa' since. I'm sure you'll get it when she's back.'

Stella had no such confidence. It was far more likely Lydia had simply thrown it away. She could hardly bear the thought that she might have read it first. For Lily's sake, she tried not to show how upset she was at the maid not passing on the letter herself.

Seeing how the sky was now completely grey, Stella declined a cup of tea.

'I better get back before the rain gets worse.'

Cycling back, the wind had strengthened and Stella found it hard to stay upright. By the time she reached The Anchorage, she was soaked to the skin. Tibby sent her off to have a hot bath. That night, Stella couldn't get warm and lay shivering while she berated herself for being so careless in losing Hugh's lovely letter.

Two days later, Stella came down with a chill and a heavy cold that went to her chest and kept her in bed. Tibby, having banished her to bed, was not a diligent nurse. It was Elsie, the gardener's wife, who came up with cups of tea and bowls of broth. Despite her kindness, Stella lay feeling utterly homesick and longing for her time in Ebbsmouth to end.

It wasn't until the last week of the holiday that Stella had shaken off her cold and was feeling like her old self again. Only then did she finally write an affectionate letter back to Hugh, telling him about the early part of the holiday and not the rift with Lydia. She said she would like it if they carried on writing to each other and that there was no one else courting her.

Unable to remember the exact postal address of his sister in Dublin, she hoped that the letter would eventually get to him. She didn't know the size of the Irish city, but surely there could only be one Mrs Henry French? Stella consoled herself with the thought that she could always write to him in Baluchistan once she was back in India.

Unexpectedly, Tibby got a note from Lydia, summoning her round to Templeton Hall.

'Am I to come too?' Stella asked. 'Is Andrew back home with her?'

Tibby said, 'I'm not sure. Perhaps it's best if I go alone and see how the land lies.'

Stella spent an anxious two hours waiting for Tibby to return. Desperate to keep busy, she went to help Willie and Mac in the garden picking runner beans and the last of the raspberries.

When she heard Tibby's ancient car rattling down the track, Stella rushed to meet her. Tibby climbed out and adjusted her purple hat in a nervous gesture.

'Is Andrew home?' asked Stella.

'Yes. I saw him. He seemed in fine fettle.'

'Oh, good, I'm so glad,' Stella said in relief. 'Am I to be allowed back to Templeton Hall before we leave?'

Tibby took Stella gently by the elbow. 'Let's sit on the steps for a minute while I explain.'

'Explain what?' Stella's heart began to pound.

Tibby said nothing until they were both perched on the third step leading up to the castle doorway.

'A lot seems to have happened in the past couple of weeks in Durham,' Tibby said. 'I suppose Noel Langley might have something to do with it – the boys appear to be the firmest of friends.'

'Meaning?' Stella prompted, anxiety curdling inside.

'Well, Andrew has chosen to stay here and go to school in Durham.'

Stella gaped at her in shock. 'You mean, his mother has chosen?'

Tibby gave her a pitying look. 'Not just Lydia – it seems it's Andrew's decision too. He's taken the entrance exam for Dunelm School and has been accepted. He seems quite thrilled at the idea.'

'I don't believe it,' Stella cried. 'He must come back to India. Mr Lomax won't allow him to stay here.'

Tibby's face fell. 'I do feel badly for Tommy – I know how devoted he is to Andrew – but that's something he will have to sort out with Lydia. Maybe it's time she was allowed to have Andrew for a bit – before he's grown up. It certainly seems to be Andrew's choice.'

'I want to see him.' Stella was adamant. 'When am I allowed to?'

Tibby put a hand on her arm. 'It seems you're persona non grata at Templeton Hall so I'll invite him round here, I promise. Lydia can't deny me that; I'm his aunt, after all.'

Stella was stunned. She couldn't believe that Andrew didn't want to return to India and his parents. Lydia was behind this. Stella was full of anger at the thought of the damage Andrew's mother had done.

Three days before Stella was due to begin her journey back to India, Lydia and Andrew came over to The Anchorage for afternoon tea to say goodbye. Stella rushed to hug him but he stuck out his hand instead, glancing at his mother as he did so.

Stella reddened and shook his hand.

It was raining, so Tibby showed them into the library where a fire had been hastily lit. The conversation was stilted – Lydia hardly acknowledging Stella – and Tibby tried to keep it going by asking Andrew about Durham. He was soon chatting about playing cricket with Noel and several other boys who lived near the Langleys.

'Isn't it wonderful?' said Lydia with a triumphant look. 'It's a dream come true for me to know that Andrew will be nearby and can spend his holidays here in Ebbsmouth. His grandmamma is thrilled too.'

Andrew said quickly, 'But I can also spend some of the summer holidays back in India, can't I, Mamma? You said so.'

Lydia gave an indulgent smile. 'If that's what you want, darling.'

'Yes, it is.' He looked at Stella. 'Mamma says there are flights with Imperial Airways now that can cut down the travel to a few days, not weeks. Think of that! I could spend the summer at Gulmarg and maybe Noel could come too.'

Stella wondered how many other promises Lydia had made to ensure that Andrew would choose to stay with her. But perhaps he didn't need to be bribed. She longed to get him on his own so she could be sure that this was what he really wanted.

Soon, Lydia was thanking Tibby for the tea and saying that they should be leaving.

Stella addressed Andrew. 'Before you go, I've got something I want to give you. It's upstairs but it won't take a minute.'

Andrew looked at his mother and Stella was surprised when she gave him a reluctant nod. 'Just a minute then,' she said sternly.

Outside the library, Stella took his hand and pulled him up the stairs. She took him into her bedroom and said, 'Sit down, close your eyes and hold out your hands.'

While he perched on her bed, she fetched a pair of book ends and placed them in his open palms.

'Now open your eyes,' she ordered. 'Walter made them and I painted them. Not very well – it's supposed to be Dal Lake on this one and The Raj-in-the-Hills on the other.' She watched him turn them over. 'Anyway, I wanted you to have something from me – you can put your school books between them.'

He sat staring at them, his face flushed. 'Thank you.' His voice was husky. 'They're . . . really nice.'

She sat down beside him and put an arm around his shoulders. He bowed his head and she could see him swallowing hard. 'Don't be upset.'

'I'll miss you, Stella,' he croaked.

She kissed his head. 'I'll miss you too – very much. Andy,' she said gently. 'Is this what you really want – to stay with your mother and go to school in Durham?'

After a pause, he nodded. 'I like it in Ebbsmouth. I feel proud of being a Lomax here – of knowing where I come from. I didn't expect that. And I like Durham and being with Noel and the other boys – I think I'll be happy at Dunelm School. I know it's not India, but . . .'

'And you're happy about living with your mother and grand-mother?' Stella asked.

He glanced away. 'I'll be living in Durham most of the time.'

'I'm sorry, Andy. I feel so guilty about leaving you here with your mother.'

'I know you don't like Mamma but she's been a lot nicer to me since we've been away in Durham. She really wants me to stay – I think she needs me . . .'

'You shouldn't be staying just because she's making you feel somehow obliged to – that's not fair on you, and it's wrong of her.'

He shifted away. 'At least she tells me the truth and doesn't pretend to be someone she's not.'

Stella retorted. 'Like pretending to still be in love with your father?'

Andrew was defensive. 'Maybe she is still in love, but Esmie did her best to come between her and father.'

'You can't really believe that?' Stella cried. 'It was your mother who chose to desert your father and come back to Scotland – none of that was Esmie's doing.'

'How do you know?' Andrew asked in agitation.

'Because Tibby told me,' said Stella, 'and I remember what it was like when your parents ran the Raj in Pindi. I don't think your mother ever loved your father.'

'That's not true! Mamma said she was devastated when Dad left her and went back to India to be with Esmie.'

'That's your mother twisting the facts again. Your dad wasn't unfaithful to her – she was to him! Your mother was having an affair with an army officer.'

Andrew sprang up. 'I don't want to hear any more. I thought you'd understand why I want to stay here – but I don't care if you don't. It's my choice and that's that.'

'Sorry,' Stella said, quickly getting to her feet. 'I do understand. I just think you're being unfair to your father and Esmie. I don't know what I'm going to say to your father – I feel responsible that you're not coming home with me and I know he's going to be so sad—'

'You're not responsible for me,' Andrew said. 'And you don't need to worry about Dad – I've written a letter explaining that it's my decision and I want to stay in Britain. No one is forcing me.'

'And Meemee?' Stella questioned. 'Have you written to her too?'

He glared. 'She's not my Meemee any more. She came between my parents.'

'Don't say that,' Stella rebuked him. 'She couldn't have been a more loving mother to you. She's loved you your whole life. You've only known your mamma for a few weeks.'

'Only because I was stolen away from her,' Andrew replied.

'Those are your mother's words,' Stella said in exasperation. 'If you want the truth, she could have kept you here in Ebbsmouth years ago but she chose not to. She sent you back to India with your ayah when you were a baby. Esmie has always loved you ten times more than she has!'

He gave her a fierce look, his blue eyes accusing. In that moment he reminded her of Lydia. He thrust the book ends back at her. 'Take them. I don't want them. I'm glad I'm not coming back with you, Stella!'

He spun round and fled from the room. She threw the book ends on the bed and went after him.

Andrew was already standing at the main door with his mother as she said goodbye to Tibby. Willie was hovering in the rain with an umbrella, ready to escort Lydia to her car.

'Goodbye, Stella.' Lydia turned and gave her a brief nod.

'Mrs Lomax,' Stella said, forcing a smile. 'I believe you have a letter of mine that I left behind by mistake. Lily said she gave it to you. I wondered if you'd brought it. If not, I don't mind cycling over to get it before I leave.'

She saw Lydia colour. 'A letter? No, I don't recall . . . Lily must've been mistaken.'

Stella persisted. 'She found it the day I left and offered to deliver it here but you said you'd do it.'

Lydia gave one of her dismissive waves. 'I don't remember any such thing.'

'The letter from Dublin,' Stella reminded her.

She saw a flicker of realisation in Lydia's eyes and knew she remembered the incident.

'Oh, the letter from a fellow passenger,' said Lydia. 'Some widow, wasn't it? Aren't you making rather a fuss over it?'

Stella flushed. Lydia was enjoying her discomfort.

'Well, if it turns up,' Lydia said, 'I'll send it on.'

'Thank you,' Stella said, trying to remain calm.

'Come on, darling.' Lydia chivvied Andrew out in front of her and dashed under the umbrella.

'Goodbye, Andrew,' Stella called.

He half-turned as he hitched his jacket over his head. 'Bye, Stella,' he mumbled. Then he was running down the steps and leaping into the car.

She watched and waved until the car disappeared beyond the trees, even though he probably wasn't looking.

Tibby sensed her unhappiness. 'I'll keep an eye on Andrew,' she promised. 'I'll be his link to his father and Esmie. I won't let Lydia deny me that.'

Stella nodded, too full of emotion to answer.

After that, Stella couldn't wait to be gone. The next day, Tibby took her shopping for small presents to take back to India, then early on the final morning, Tibby and Dawan drove her down to the railway station to catch the train to London. From there she would join a boat at Tilbury Docks. There was no chaperone organised this time; she would be turning twenty-one in a few days' time and travelling on her own for the three-week voyage.

At the station, Stella turned to Tibby and raised her voice above the noise of the steam engine.

'I can't thank you enough, Miss Lomax, for taking me in when . . . well you know . . . and for making me feel so at home. I'll never forget your kindness or my time at The Anchorage.'

Instead of shaking hands, Tibby enveloped her in a huge hug. 'It's been an absolute pleasure, dear girl. Hasn't it, Dawan? We'll miss your pretty smile about the place – not to mention your baking.'

Stella's eyes smarted with tears. 'I'll miss you all too.'

Dawan nodded. He put his palms together in a farewell gesture. 'Give my love to Lahore when you pass through,' he said, with a wistful smile.

Stella turned and hurried up the platform to where the porter was putting her case into a carriage. Her heart was heavy; the final goodbyes had been harder than she'd imagined.

How she wished she had parted on better terms with Andrew. It might be many years before she saw him again; she was not convinced that Lydia would allow him to go on holiday to India as he hoped.

Climbing on board, Stella pulled down the window in the carriage door and leaned out to wave. Doors slammed shut, a whistle blew and the train shunted forward. It picked up speed. As she came alongside the barrier, she saw Tibby and Dawan waving through the engine smoke. Then she was past. She gazed out for her final view of Ebbsmouth, its pretty curving bay glinting in the early sun.

For an instant, she thought she saw someone waving from beyond the fence – a dark-haired youth? – and then the train pulled away from the town. Stella's chest tightened. The figure made her think of Andrew, though it was very unlikely to have been him. With a heavy sigh, she leaned in and closed the window against the smoke.

Stella sat down and closed her eyes, conjuring up India and home in her mind.

Andrew leaned on the fence, staring at the retreating train, breathless from his cycle. He'd left it too late. All night he'd tossed and turned, wondering whether he should go and see Stella off at the station. It would be a chance to say sorry for arguing with her and for petulantly rejecting her gift. He felt terrible about that now. Was he right to have chosen to stay? How would he cope here without her? Stella was his last link to India and home. Andrew felt overwhelmingly alone.

Was that Stella leaning out of the carriage window? He was sure it had been. Had she seen him waving at her? He hoped so. Sadness pressed on his chest. When would he see her again? If only he'd been able to say goodbye properly – tell her how much she meant to him . . . She was the one person in the world he could tell anything to and not feel foolish.

Andrew climbed back on his bicycle and turned towards Templeton Hall. Then, on a whim, he changed direction and began cycling towards The Anchorage. He would go and see his Auntie Tibby – she would be sad at Stella's going too – and he'd retrieve the book ends that Stella had made for him. The thought gave him a small amount of comfort.

Chapter 18

Stella fought her way through the chaos of the customs hall, already drenched in sweat from the sticky heat. But she was fortified by the note that had been delivered on board when they'd docked the night before. Esmie would be coming to meet her!

She searched the crowds of topee-wearing British as she queued to have her luggage processed and sent on to the mail train that they would be catching that evening. They found each other at the entrance. The sight of Esmie looking slim and composed in a yellow summer frock made Stella dissolve into tears of relief.

They hugged tightly. Stella tried to speak. 'I'm s-so s-sorry . . . for not b-bringing Andrew h-home . . .'

Esmie rubbed her back. 'None of this is your fault, Stella. Come on, let's go and have coffee somewhere quieter.'

Esmie steered her into a taxi and instructed the driver to take them to a mission house in the city.

'I stayed there last night. It's a bit staid but they do passable coffee and cake – and they'll let us freshen up before we get the train.'

Stella sat back and took in the sight of the magnificent stone archway, the Gateway of India, as they left the teeming dockside and threaded their way through the busy tree-lined streets of the city. Joy surged inside her at the familiar sights of India: women in colourful saris, cows holding up traffic, coolies pushing cart-loads piled high with goods and dazzling white buildings offering glimpses of cool interiors. How she had missed it all!

Soon they were turning into a narrower street and drawing up outside a modest three-storey building next to a church. Esmie led her into a tiny deserted courtyard and ordered refreshments. They sat in the shade of a jacaranda that made Stella think tearfully of home and her parents.

Esmie kept the conversation light. 'Your family are well and looking forward to seeing you,' she said. 'The baroness will be returning soon from Srinagar – I saw her on my way down from Gulmarg – and she's in good health too. Ada has been a great help over the summer and I think Felix is rather taken with her. Your cousin Lucy has managed fairly well with Mrs Shankley, though she's not as patient with her as you are.' Esmie smiled. 'But Lucy is now devoted to Frisky so you might have a hard job winning your dog back.'

When the coffee and Madeira cake had been served and the waiters had withdrawn, Esmie said quietly, 'Tell me what happened in Ebbsmouth, Stella. We don't blame you for anything – we just want reassuring that it's really Andrew's choice to live there.'

Stella poured out her story about the rift with Lydia and the drunken revelations that Lydia had made in front of Andrew that had caused him to take refuge in Durham with his friend Noel and opt to go to school there. She told her about Lydia banishing her to The Anchorage and her failure to get Andrew to see things from his father's point of view.

Esmie sat very still, listening to her unburdening herself about the final argument with Andrew.

'I was trying to defend you from the wicked lies that his mother has been telling him – blaming you for coming between her and

Mr Lomax,' Stella said. 'I'm ashamed to say I told him what Tibby had said to me in confidence: that it was his mother who'd had an affair – and also that she'd rejected Andrew as a baby. I was so cross with him for believing her every word. I should never have said such things – and I've felt wretched ever since for hurting him.' Stella's eyes flooded with tears.

Esmie put a hand over hers. 'I feel so bad that we put you in this situation in the first place. I should have known that Lydia would try and blacken my name and turn Andrew against me. Even after all these years she still can't bear the thought of me being with Tom.'

Stella felt she needed to be totally frank. 'There's more to it than that. I'm afraid it just confirmed the taunts Andrew was subjected to at Nicholson's about you – gossip that you and Mr Lomax weren't really married. Even before Andy left India, he had doubts about that . . .'

Esmie glanced away, turning pink-faced. 'Oh, I see. That explains why he was distant with me before he went. Poor, dear Andy. Why didn't he say anything?'

'He didn't want to believe it,' said Stella. 'He told me but made me swear I wouldn't tell you. If I had, maybe everything would have been different.'

'No.' Esmie was adamant. 'It was always going to come out eventually – we were foolish to think it wouldn't. I'm just so sorry Andy had to hear it from his mother. No wonder he doesn't want to come home – he must feel very let down by his father and me.'

Stella tried to comfort her. 'I can't pretend he isn't upset by it all, but I think his decision to stay is also because he really loves Ebbsmouth and he's excited about going to Dunelm School. He's already made good friends in Durham – and it's a cricketing school so I think that probably swung his decision.'

Esmie gave a wistful smile. 'That's good.'

For a moment they both fell silent. Stella knew Esmie was as heartsore as she was, so kept to herself the fear that Andrew was also staying out of an obligation to keep his mother happy.

Stella plucked up the courage to ask, 'How is Mr Lomax?'

Pain flickered across Esmie's face. 'He's not taking it well. He can't sleep or settle to things.'

Stella felt renewed anger at Lydia. 'I will never forgive Andrew's mother for destroying his belief in his father – calling him a coward and saying he brought shame to the Peshawar Rifles. I tried to remind Andrew that Mr Lomax had been a brave soldier long before the war as well as during it. I was right, wasn't I?'

Esmie nodded vigorously. 'Oh, of course you were! As you know, Tom endured more than most men, losing his first wife, Mary, and their baby girl while he was away on active service. He bottled up his grief and carried on, but the strain of warfare finally brought him to breaking point.'

Stella was distressed at the reminder of this early tragedy in Tom's life. 'Did Lydia know?'

'Eventually she did.' Esmie looked burdened. 'I wrote and told her what Tom had been through – in the hopes it would help her understand him better and save their marriage. But Lydia resented that I knew about it before she did and it just made matters worse.'

'Poor Mr Lomax,' Stella said, leaden at the thought of his suffering. 'If he was court-martialled then he must have been at the end of his tether.'

Esmie nodded. 'It's true he was court-martialled, but I bet Lydia didn't tell you the real reason why? It wasn't for cowardice – it was for disobeying orders. He refused to carry out the execution of one of his sepoys who had thrown away his weapon. To me that was a mark of extreme bravery and humanity.'

Stella was indignant on Tom's behalf. She had always admired him and now she did even more. She let out a long breath. 'How wicked that people called him cowardly.'

'Only those who didn't know the real story,' said Esmie. 'Some were very unforgiving of Tom for turning his back on the army – but they weren't the men he'd served with; they were the jealous types who thrived on gossip in a garrison town.'

'If only he'd told Andy this,' Stella exclaimed.

'I encouraged him to.' Esmie sighed. 'But Tom finds it very difficult to talk about the past – and he still feels a sense of shame about succumbing to shell shock and being put in the dock.'

'What can we do to help Mr Lomax now?' Stella asked.

Esmie met her look. 'Reassure him that Andrew is not unhappy with his mother and that Lydia has not forced him into this. Tom's instinct is to want to rush off to Scotland and rescue his son – despite Andy's letter telling him he wants to stay in Ebbsmouth. Tom's finding it very hard to accept.'

Stella nodded. 'Perhaps his mother will tire of the responsibility – once the novelty of having him around has worn off and she has to deal with a boisterous youth in her household. She's not the most patient of women.'

Esmie shook her head. 'Even if Lydia does get fed up with Andrew, she'll never admit to it. She sees this as a great victory over us – over me in particular – and she'll make sure he stays in Scotland.' Her look was dispirited. 'I can't blame Lydia for wanting to mother Andy – not once she'd got to know him. I'd have fought to keep him with me if I'd been her.' Her grey eyes glinted with tears. 'And there's one thing that makes me think that Lydia might be genuine in wanting to make a success of being Andy's mother.'

'What's that?'

'Her most recent airmail letter to Tom says she's prepared to give him a divorce as long as he allows Andrew to stay with her.'

Stella gaped in surprise. 'That's good news, surely? For you, I mean.'

Esmie fidgeted with her necklace. 'If she's really serious about it. Tom thinks it's to stop him appearing in Ebbsmouth or taking her to court to assert his rights over Andrew.'

'But at least something good might come out of this horrible situation,' said Stella. 'Then you can marry properly and not be the victims of unkind gossip.'

Esmie smiled at last. 'Yes, I long for that, but . . .'

Stella waited for her to elaborate.

After a pause, Esmie shrugged. 'It just makes Tom feel more guilty towards Andrew – that he has to give him up in order to marry me. Lydia still manages to manipulate Tom even after all these years.' She let out an agonised sigh. 'I fear he may grow to resent me for it later.'

'He won't,' Stella cried. 'Mr Lomax adores you!'

'Oh, Stella, you are such a tonic.' Esmie gave her a tearful smile. 'I'm so glad you are back.'

Stella smiled. 'And so am I.'

Chapter 19

> *Dear Andy,*
>
> *Happy New Year! My New Year's resolution is to write to you again. I'm not sure if you ever got any of the letters I wrote to you after I returned to India at the end of the monsoon season. Perhaps they weren't sent on to you at school? At least I know from your father that you are well and enjoying school in Durham. I haven't seen him since the start of the cold season but Esmie tells me he's started painting again, which is good.*

Stella paused, wondering if she should mention Esmie. Things had been far from well when she'd returned to The Raj-in-the-Hills for the final month before it closed for the season. Tom had abruptly disappeared with a hunting rifle. Esmie had been frantic, but Felix had assured her that Tom had taken a tent and had gone on shikar. Tom had turned up four days later, contrite that he'd made them worry so much.

'I'm sorry, Esmie. I should have told you I was going hunting. I thought you'd guess . . . It's what I used to do as a young man, remember?'

'Not since I've known you, Tom.'

Later, Esmie had confided in Stella. 'Does Tom seem confused to you? It's as if he thought I was his first wife, Mary. He's never gone on shikar since he's been with me.'

'Perhaps he's worried about Andrew,' Stella had said. 'Things will get better once the hotel closes and you have time together. Perhaps you should take him away for a change of scene?'

But the Lomaxes hadn't gone away. Tom didn't want to leave Gulmarg, telling Esmie he felt safe in the mountains. Instead, he had begun to spend time in his studio, painting.

'Your talk of Dawan and his colourful art has inspired Tom again,' a delighted Esmie had said to Stella.

Stella had returned to Rawalpindi encouraged that all would be well between the Lomaxes.

She returned to the letter.

Do you visit The Anchorage? I wonder which artists are there at the moment? I'm sure Dawan will be. Did he ever finish that one of your aunt as the goddess Manjusri? How is your Auntie Tibby? Please pass on my best wishes to her when you next see her.

The residents here are just the same as ever – Ansom and Fritters are twittering like a couple of parrots over the imminent arrival of a new guest because he's an Indian. Pa is trying to reassure them that he's a retired Gurkha soldier and so one of the British army's elite – and also Nepalese, not Indian. But Fritters keeps muttering about being attacked in the night by a kukri-wielding native. Jimmy thinks Fritters is a bit jealous because the Gurkha was probably a much better soldier than he was.

Talking of Jimmy, my brother has been court-ing the same girl now for eight months, which is a record for him. She's called Yvonne Harvey and works in Lovell's haberdashery. She's pretty with short wavy dark hair like Clara Bow and seems quite sweet – she's definitely smitten on Jimmy and even goes to watch him play cricket on her rare Saturday afternoons off. Must be love.

Stella put down her pen and sighed. She wasn't going to tell Andrew how disappointed she was never to have heard again from Hugh. Even if she couldn't be sure that her letter to his sister in Dublin had been delivered, she had also written to him care of the Agricultural Department in Quetta in Baluchistan. Perhaps he had extended his leave? Or maybe he had been moved to another posting?

But even if he had, his mail would have been sent on and he could have replied. She had to face the likelihood that Hugh was no longer interested in pursuing a friendship with her; he had written on a whim and hadn't really meant what he'd said about wanting her to be his girl.

Lydia had never sent on the precious letter from Hugh, and over the intervening months Stella had begun to forget exactly what he'd written. Perhaps she had read too much into it and had mis-taken his friendly banter for something more serious. For Stella, it had been the most thrilling experience of her life. But perhaps for Hugh it hadn't been anything more than a friendship over card games and a few pleasurable kisses that had helped him while away the long hours of inactivity.

Picking up her pen again, she began to write about her day-to-day life at the hotel.

Ma and Pa are fine – although Pa always finds the cold season difficult as his chesty cough comes back. The weather has been wet and windy, but that didn't stop the British from enjoying the usual festive cheer of Christmas parties and New Year dances.

I hope you had a happy time in Ebbsmouth. Give my regards to your mother and grandmother. Write to me when you get the chance and tell me how you are getting on at Dunelm School. Give my best to Noel and his grandparents too.

Love from Stella x

May 1934

Dear Andrew,

This card is just to wish you a very happy fourteenth birthday! I hope you have a great day. Are you going to come out to India for the summer holidays? I'm looking forward to going up to Gulmarg next week.

Love from
Stella

June 1934

Dear Stella,

I'm writing this at the end of prep. It's still light outside and I can't wait for the bell to go so that I

can go and play cricket with Noel. I'm on the Second
Eleven already and I'm the youngest on the team.
   How is everyone at The Raj?
   The Langleys are well

Andrew hesitated, tapping his pen against his teeth. Should he tell Stella that he wouldn't be coming out to India this summer? His mother had got upset when he'd raised the idea during the Easter holidays.

'Oh, darling, this is our first full summer together! Do you really want to leave me and Mummy for the whole of your holiday?'

'Well, no . . .' Andrew had been alarmed at the sight of her eyes welling with tears.

'It would break my heart!'

'Perhaps just for half the holidays then?' he'd suggested.

'You couldn't go all that way for a couple of weeks! No, it would have to be all or nothing. And I've been making plans – happy plans. I thought we could take your grandmamma to see your Aunt Grace in Switzerland – Mummy loves it there – and you've never met your Swiss cousins. It'll be a big family holiday – your *Templeton* family for once. But if you've made up your mind, I won't stand in your way—' She'd fumbled for a handkerchief and dabbed her eyes.

'Please don't cry, Mamma.' He'd patted her shoulder. 'I can go to India next year. I'd like to meet Aunt Grace and the cousins. It's just . . .'

'Just what?'

'Well, I've half-promised Noel that he could come with me to India. He's mad keen to visit and has been reading about the Mutiny and the Indian Army and—' Just in time, he'd stopped himself from adding that Noel wished to meet Andrew's dad so he could ask him all about the Peshawar Rifles.

His mother had looked aghast. 'Honestly, Andrew! You shouldn't have made such promises!'

'Sorry.'

She'd relented a little. 'Noel can come with us to Switzerland. I'm sure Grace won't mind.'

Andrew had brightened. 'Are you sure?'

'Of course! The more the merrier.' She'd smoothed back his uncombed hair. 'Oh, darling! We'll have such fun.'

Andrew had managed to mask his deep disappointment at not being able to return to Pindi and Kashmir. But Noel had leapt at the chance to visit Switzerland, and Andrew began to look forward to the summer break.

He looked at the half-written letter to Stella and sighed. He kept a photograph of her in his tuckbox which had been taken on the beach at Ebbsmouth by Noel's grandfather on his Box Brownie. It showed Stella in her swimming costume, her arms draped over his and Noel's shoulders, grinning at the camera. The photo – as well as receiving letters from an older girl – gave him kudos with the other boys in his house and on the cricket team. He'd told Stella to write directly to him at school – partly so he could show off her letters, but also because he suspected his mother had opened some of his home post and not sent it on.

He had never admitted to anyone his feelings for the Dubois girl. Her photograph was like a talisman. Whenever he was feeling homesick for India, he'd slip Stella's image into his pocket and carry it with him, kissing her goodnight after the dormitory lights were turned out.

Refilling his pen with fresh ink, Andrew decided not to tell Stella that he wouldn't be seeing her – or Gulmarg – this summer. That was something he was going to have to put in a letter to his father; a letter he kept putting off writing.

The Langleys are well. Noel sends his regards. Mamma and Grandmamma are going to come and watch me play cricket on Saturday. Please give my best wishes to your parents and Jimmy – and to all the friends at the Raj.

Love from Andy

September 1934

Dear Andy,

I was really happy to get a birthday card from you.

We were all sad that you didn't come out to India this summer but I hope you enjoyed your holiday in Switzerland. Were the Alps as beautiful as the mountains in Kashmir? Did you and Noel spend the time walking and climbing? Fishing perhaps? Your dad still goes off fishing – though I know he misses taking you with him.

Stella broke off. Maybe she would ink over that last line. She didn't want Andrew to feel guilty about not coming home for the holidays.

It was nearing the end of the season at The Raj-in-the-Hills and she would soon be travelling back to Pindi. She wouldn't tell Andrew that things were strained between Tom and Esmie. Stella was worried about them. So far, Lydia had not kept her promise to instigate divorce proceedings against Tom.

'Why did I ever believe she'd stick to her side of the bargain?' Tom had fulminated. 'Under Scottish law she can divorce me for desertion. We don't even have to resort to adultery as a reason.'

'I don't see why you won't divorce her!' Esmie said, her patience snapping.

'Because it wouldn't be the gentlemanly thing,' Tom had said in agitation. 'And I'd have to go to Edinburgh to do so. We can't afford it.'

'We could scrape the fare together, surely? Then we could see Andy – and visit my Aunt Isobel.'

'But it could take months – maybe a year. We can't leave the business for that long.'

'The Duboises could cope with both hotels—'

'They shouldn't have to! I'm not leaving Gulmarg. I'll write again to Lydia and make her see sense.'

Stella resumed her letter-writing.

> *The baroness came up here for a fortnight, which was lovely. She went riding nearly every day – she looked so elegant in her old-fashioned riding habit and still rides side-saddle! She must be about eighty but she still won't tell anyone her real age. As she always says, 'Young at heart, darling, that's what counts.'*

May 1935

Dear Andy,

This is to wish you a very happy fifteenth birthday!

Jimmy is still playing a lot of cricket, which is annoying his girlfriend Yvonne – she thinks he should be spending his free time taking her to dances at the Chota Club. My brother just laughs it off. I can't see him ever settling down. She'd be better off transferring her affections to another man – someone like my cousin Rick or one of the Gibson twins, as they all love to go dancing.

The residents at the Raj are getting a bit creaky but they're all still with us. Ansom and Fritters have become quite friendly with Mr Tamang, the retired Gurkha soldier, and he now joins them for chota pegs before dinner. What are you doing this summer? Your dad would love it if you could come out here. You are probably the most hopeless letter writer I've ever known but at least we hear occasionally from Tibby how you're getting on. She tells me that Dawan has been giving you drawing lessons.

Write soon!
Stella x

August 1935

Happy Birthday, Stella!

I hope you like the sketch of the boathouse below The Anchorage. Dawan calls me a Persian miniaturist! I thought he would be quite a critical teacher but he's very encouraging and says I should think of doing Art at Glasgow or London. He's jealous that I'm on holiday on the French Riviera because lots of artists come here. I find it too hot and can't wait to go to the Highlands with the Langleys at the end of the holidays.

Andrew glanced out of the villa window at the view of shimmering sea beyond a fringe of pine trees and craggy rocks. He wouldn't risk posting the card till he got back to Scotland in case his mother asked questions. He'd had his biggest row ever with Mamma at Easter. This year, he'd been determined to go to India for the summer holidays and had begun mentioning it in letters to his mother during the Lent term.

On Easter Sunday, he'd gone with his grandmother and mother to lay flowers on his Grandfather Jumbo's grave in St Ebba's churchyard. Lydia had wept openly and later taken Andrew aside.

'I can't bear the thought of Mummy dying too. She's growing frailer by the day. You must have noticed a difference since Christmas? I hate the idea of something happening to Mummy while you're away all summer in India. You'd feel dreadful, wouldn't you?'

'Nothing's going to happen—'

'It could easily. And I'd have to deal with it on my own – and with you thousands of miles away.'

'But Dad's expecting me . . .'

'You've had thirteen summers with your father and that woman! And you'd deny your grandmother a few weeks of your company? It might be her last summer on earth! Don't you think you're being a little selfish?'

'You're the one being selfish,' Andrew had retaliated. 'You're just making up an excuse so I can't go to India.'

She'd flinched as if he'd hit her. 'How can you say such a hurtful thing to your own mother? I'm not doing this for me – I'm doing it for your poor dear grandmamma! But if being with your father means more to you, then I'll be the last person to stand in your way!'

Andrew had stormed out of the house and marched around the clifftops in a fury. However much he strove to please her it never seemed to be quite enough. She was impossible! He loved his grandmother and was sure that she would encourage him to go to India, but what if something did happen to her while he was away? He would feel terrible. Perhaps she was a bit doddery compared to a few months ago. Mamma was with her daily and would have noticed any changes. Perhaps he was being unfair to his mother. He shouldn't have called her selfish – she was the most generous person he knew. Yet he longed to visit Gulmarg again and to see Stella.

Andrew had taken refuge at his Auntie Tibby's for a couple of hours and it was then that he'd asked Dawan if he would teach him to paint. If he wasn't going to be allowed to go to India that summer, he would spend time with the Lahori artist and indulge his passion for drawing. It would be his small rebellion against his emotional mother.

Looking at the shimmer of heat haze over the Mediterranean, Andrew felt the urge for a swim. He quickly signed off the card to Stella.

> *I hope you have a great day!*
> *Love from Andy*

May 1936

Dear Andy,
> *Happy sixteenth birthday! Have a lovely day.*
> *Best wishes*
> *Stella*

P.S. Your father is really hoping to see you this summer.

October 1936

Dear Andrew,

We were so disappointed when you decided not to come this summer. Perhaps you are still angry towards your dad and Esmie? That's a shame as they are two of the most special people in the world and would do anything for anyone.

I wanted you to know that they are very happy to be married properly at last. They went to Lahore for a very quiet ceremony as soon as The Raj-in-the-Hills closed for the season. I'm glad that your mother finally agreed to a divorce – she has put them through hell for far too long. I think their hotel business has suffered as a result – only their most loyal customers have returned each summer to the hotel in Gulmarg and they've been wondering whether to sell on the lease. The Raj in Pindi continues to do well because Pa and Ma put so much effort into keeping it going. I hope they won't think of selling that as Jimmy hopes to manage it one day.

I wonder if the hotel business interests you at all?

I hope you continue to be happy. I shan't be writing again, as I think I must be embarrassing you with my letters – you hardly ever reply. I just want you to know that I think of you often.

Regards
Stella

October 1936

Stella,

> *You are quite wrong about so much. I've wanted to come back to India for the past three summers but Mamma has always put up a reason not to every year. This time I had to prove my loyalty because she needs so much reassurance. Having agreed to give my father a divorce she was frightened that I would go to India and not come back – and then she would have lost everything again, all because of Esmie. I couldn't put her through that, even though I had no intention of staying longer than the summer holidays. I'm happy at school in Durham and my friends are here. I'm also very happy in Ebbsmouth. But I do miss Kashmir and The Raj Hotel. I don't think I'd make a very good hotelier – I prefer being outdoors too much – but it doesn't mean I don't care about it or the people there.*
>
> *I'm glad that Dad is happy. I feel bad about not coming this summer but I don't think it's fair blaming me for everything. He's got what he wants now – Esmie – and Mamma has me. So why don't we just leave it at that?*

Andrew shoved the half-finished letter in his jacket pocket and climbed out of the study window. He crept behind the gardener's shed and lit up a cigarette.

Earlier that year, he'd braced himself for the usual battle with his mother over going to India but had been utterly unprepared for her semi-hysterical story about a long-ago kidnapping.

'I hate India and I don't want you to go!'

'But why—?'

'I'll tell you why! It's where I was abducted by savages and taken into the mountains and held in a stinking fortress where I thought I was going to die and your father and the police had to come and rescue me.'

'Abducted?' Andrew had been dumbfounded. 'Where? How . . . ?'

'I was snatched in Taha – that horrible primitive little place where the Guthries lived. It was all Esmie's fault – she'd insulted some Pathans and they seized me thinking I was her. It was dreadful. I still have nightmares about it.'

'How terrible, Mamma! Why have you never told me this before?'

'I didn't want to upset you. It was the most traumatic thing – I just wanted to bury the memory. And I can't bear the thought of you going out there and being with Esmie when she's caused me such pain. I know you won't come back!'

His mother had grown so distraught that Andrew, shocked by her tale, had quickly acquiesced and abandoned his plans for a holiday in Kashmir.

Andrew was reluctant to raise this in a letter to Stella – his mother could be prone to exaggeration – but perhaps he should tell Stella that he did care a lot about his father. When his parents' divorce came through, he'd got maudlin drunk on brandy and been sick among his grandmamma's rose bushes. Deep down, he was hurt that he hadn't been told about or invited to his father's wedding – even though he wouldn't have been able to go as it was in term-time.

Why on earth did Stella's opinion of him still matter? He hadn't seen her for over three years and he sometimes found it difficult to conjure up her face in his mind. The tiny photo he had of her was so creased and faded that it was no longer possible to make out her dimpled cheeks or the laughter in her eyes.

It was probably for the best that she stopped writing to him.

Besides, he'd had a good time in Italy this summer with his Swiss cousins, and Noel had come too. They'd teamed up with an Italian family in the next villa and Andrew had half-fallen in love with one of the daughters, Mirella. He'd had his first proper kiss – several – and they had agreed to write to each other. Perhaps he'd write to her now. Andrew finished his cigarette and then took the letter to Stella from his pocket.

Striking up a match, Andrew set the letter alight and dropped it on the cold earth. With a heavy heart, he watched it burn and then ground down the ashes.

June 1937

Dear Andrew,

I know I wasn't going to write again but I thought you'd want to know that Frisky passed away two weeks ago.

He hasn't been that energetic for a long time but he remained the most wonderful companion right up until his final days. I'm crying as I write this. He'd gone into your old bedroom (your parents have never let it be used by anyone else) and managed to climb onto the bed. Frisky went to sleep there. It was Esmie who found him.

We've buried him up on the marg above the hotel – on the way to the shepherds' huts. I wish you were here – you are the one person who would understand how I'm really feeling.

Kind regards
Stella

P.S. A belated happy seventeenth birthday.

July 1937

Dear Stella,

I'm very, very sorry to hear about Frisky passing away. I loved that dog – maybe almost as much as you did – and I can't imagine The Raj Hotel without him. Gulmarg won't be the same either but I'm glad his resting place is there. I know nothing I say will make you feel better, so instead I've done this drawing of Frisky and hope it makes you smile rather than cry. It's instead of a hug.

    Warm regards,

    Andy

Chapter 20

'Congratulations, Yvonne!' Stella kissed her new sister-in-law on her flushed cheeks. 'Welcome to the family.'

'Thank you, Stella.' Yvonne smiled, her thin lips made to look plumper with ruby-red lipstick. 'Though I hope you already think of me as one of the family after all this time.'

'Of course,' Stella agreed. 'I've always wanted a sister.'

'Me too,' Yvonne said, laughing.

Stella moved aside for other guests to greet the newly-weds. Jimmy winked at her. He was beaming. She'd never seen her brother looking quite so smart, in a new suit with his round face freshly shaven and brown hair gleaming with brilliantine. She gave him a quick peck on the cheek.

'Settling down at last,' she teased. 'You've made Ma and Pa very happy.'

'It'll be you next, Stella,' he said with a grin and a nod towards Monty Gibson. 'Can't keep him hanging on forever.'

'You're one to talk.' Stella nudged him and laughed.

She glanced at Monty and sighed inwardly. It would be so much easier to marry Monty than put up with her family's constant questions about her courtship with the Gibson boy. The pressure for Stella to marry had increased since her cousin Ada had married Monty's twin brother Clive the previous year. Monty was passably handsome, despite a crooked nose from a cricket injury that marked him out from his twin. He was sociable and had a steady job as an engineer in the Public Works Department. He didn't seem as ambitious as Clive, who was gaining promotions in the Posts and Telegraphs Department, but that didn't bother Stella. He was thirty years old and she was twenty-six. Recently her mother was beginning to despair of her.

'It's high time you were married and making a home of your own. If you're not to have a vocation like nursing, then marriage is the next best thing. Surely you don't want to end up an old maid?'

Only her father defended her reluctance to get engaged. 'Sweet Pea will decide in her own good time. If we nag and nag, she will run off to sea with a captain and never come back.'

'Charlie, you do talk nonsense!' Her mother couldn't help laughing. Her father was good at defusing people's bad tempers.

But today was Jimmy and Yvonne's special day and Stella was happy to be in their shadow. An hour ago, the young couple had married in St Joseph's Roman Catholic Church, with Yvonne's uncle from Lahore leading her down the aisle. Now the guests – Jimmy's family outnumbering Yvonne's tenfold – were being greeted in the hotel foyer, handed a drink and shown into the dining room.

Stella's parents had gone to great lengths to decorate the hotel dining room with bunting and flowers, and the tables were groaning with food. All the residents had been invited to the wedding feast. Ansom was dressed in old-fashioned tailcoat and spats, while Fritwell was squeezed into army uniform. Baroness Hester was wearing a green velvet gown – rather frayed at the collar – and an eye-catching headdress of green and orange feathers. Mr Tamang had taken it upon himself to be in charge of pushing Mrs Shankley in her wheelchair so that Stella didn't have to worry about looking after the elderly missionary.

'Welcome one and all!' Charlie greeted the wedding guests, his round face creasing in a wide smile. 'It is a great honour and a privilege to be your host.'

Stella was glad to see her father was wearing the red bow tie with the black polka dots that she had brought him back from Scotland over five years ago and that he only wore on very special occasions.

The Lomaxes had been invited, but Esmie had sent a message to say that Tom had come down with influenza and couldn't travel. They had sent a canteen of silver cutlery in a beautiful walnut box as a wedding present. She knew how her parents – her father in particular – had been disappointed by the news. Privately, Stella had wondered if it was just Tom's reluctance to travel that kept them away. His nerves had been playing up this past summer, ever since they had got word from Tibby that Andrew had decided not to go to university but to join the army instead.

Both Andrew and his friend Noel had been accepted for officer training and would now have already been at the Royal Military Academy Sandhurst for nearly three months.

Tom had been deeply upset by the news. 'The bloody fool! I bet Lydia's been filling his head full of nonsense about honour and sacrifice.'

'Maybe he just wants to prove that he can be a soldier too,' Esmie had dared to suggest.

'Well, it doesn't impress me,' Tom had railed. 'I'd have told him that soldiering just perpetuates war – and warfare is a terrible thing.'

Against Esmie's advice, Tom had written a hasty letter to Andrew telling him not to throw away his chance of doing a degree. A university education would be a far better attainment than blindly following his Lomax ancestors into the army as cannon fodder. The indignant reply he had received a month later was a further blow. Tom had been very upset by it. Esmie had later shown it to Stella.

> . . . I'm sorry if you think so little of me that you believe I haven't thought long and hard about my future.
>
> You have been out of Scotland for too long, Dad, otherwise you would know that there is a real fear of Hitler. There is talk of war.
>
> How could I possibly put my studies first? I have talked to many people about this – not just Mamma and Grandmamma – and have had nothing but encouragement. Even Auntie Tibby says it is entirely my decision.
>
> I have also been talking at length with an old army friend of yours and Mamma's. He's recently been invalided out of the cavalry but spent six years out in India – the North West Frontier – just like you. He sends his regards. His name is Captain Dickie Mason and he's now living just down the coast from here in Berwick.
>
> I'd hoped that you might have been proud of me, but I intend to join up anyway.
>
> Your (not so) obedient son,
> Andrew

'He seems very determined,' Stella had said. She couldn't help being impressed by Andrew's passionate conviction that he was doing the right thing.

Esmie had confided, 'It's not so much Andy's determination to join the army as the mention of Dickie Mason.'

'Why, who is he?'

Esmie had given her a harrowed look. 'He's the young officer that Lydia had an affair with – he's the main reason Tom's marriage to her fell apart. He's furious that she's introduced him to Andrew as an old friend of his.'

'Oh my goodness!' Stella had been shocked. 'No wonder Mr Lomax is upset.'

'He can't think of anything else,' Esmie had said in distress. 'He wants to know how long Lydia has been seeing Dickie – whether he's married or unmarried. Tom thinks he might be the reason why Lydia finally agreed to a divorce. And it may be true. For myself, I don't care – we got what we finally wanted – but for Tom it's different. He's torturing himself that his son is taking advice from that cheating man rather than him.'

Neither Esmie nor Stella had been able to prevent Tom from succumbing to another bout of depression. In October, when the hotel was closing up, Stella had offered to stay on with Esmie and keep her company. Tom was fighting his 'black monsoons' by trying to paint, but more often than not was to be found restlessly walking the high margs and bivouacking in the woods. He seemed to lose all track of time and sometimes called Esmie 'Mary' when she came to coax him back home.

Esmie, knowing how Jimmy's wedding was imminent, had insisted that she go home. 'That's very kind of you, lassie, but your family will be needing you and looking forward to having you back. We'll see you at Jimmy's wedding.'

Stella had left Gulmarg deeply worried about the Lomaxes and Tom's fragile mental state. How long would they be able to run The Raj-in-the-Hills if his health continued to deteriorate? She was desperately sorry for Esmie, who had finally been able to marry

Tom after all these years only to find she was increasingly becoming his nurse.

As she watched the guests enjoying her parents' hospitality, Stella couldn't help wondering what made the best kind of marriage. Was she foolish to continue to put Monty off because of some unattainable ideal of a love match that she still hoped for?

The truth was that Stella still hankered after someone who she knew now almost certainly didn't even give her a passing thought. Hugh Keating was her measure of the ideal man; handsome, fun, interesting and with the most charming accent she'd ever heard. Whenever Monty tried to kiss her, all she could think of was how much better Hugh's passionate embraces had been. Five years later she was still filled with longing for him. But the letter she'd sent to Baluchistan at the end of 1933 had eventually been returned nearly a year later with 'gone away' written across it.

Had he been moved to another posting in India or left the service and returned to Ireland? Stella had tried to find out by contacting the local agricultural office in Rawalpindi, the 'Grass Department' as it was nicknamed by the other governmental services. But the officer in charge had been a little suspicious and not very helpful.

The Indian clerk had seen her disappointment and offered to send a note of enquiry on her behalf. It was three months before she heard back.

> . . . *Mr Keating is no longer with the Agricultural Department. He resigned his post in November 1933. I am sorry to say they will not give out a forwarding address to non-family members . . .*

Assuming Hugh had never returned to India from Ireland, she wrote again to the sister in Dublin in the vain hope that a letter might reach him, even though she didn't have the correct address.

That had been back in 1935. Over three years later, Stella had not heard back. She knew it was hopeless to hanker after him. If he'd really wanted her to be his girl, he would have tried harder to stay in touch.

Stella tried to quell thoughts of Hugh. She should be looking forward to the future and not back at what might have been.

The servants were clearing tables and pushing back chairs to make more room for dancing. Her father announced the Grand March and they all fell into a procession around the room while Jimmy's friends made a human arch for them to duck under. Then the bride and groom cut the magnificent three-tiered cake that Stella's parents had commissioned and shortly afterwards the hired band struck up for the first dance.

'May I, Miss Dubois?' Monty stood there grinning.

'Of course,' Stella said, allowing him to take her hand and lead her onto the dance floor.

He was a good dancer and she knew that her mother was keeping a keen eye on them as they moved effortlessly around the floor. He chatted and she half-listened.

Later she did the two-step with her father.

'This is all going swimmingly, don't you think, Sweet Pea?'

'It's been a lovely day,' Stella agreed. 'I think Jimmy and Yvonne really appreciate what you've done for them.'

'We'll do the same for you,' he said with a smile of affection. 'In fact, we will push the boat out further to sea for our beloved daughter!'

'Pa!'

'But only when you are ready,' he added quickly.

She swiftly changed the subject. 'It's very kind of the Lomaxes to let Jimmy and Yvonne use their flat in the hotel. It'll be so much better than squeezing into the bungalow with us.'

Charlie nodded. 'It saddens me, though, to think that our dear Lomaxes are not intending to visit much any more.'

'Well, they can still use one of the hotel rooms,' said Stella. 'It doesn't mean they'll never come.'

'I so hoped they would be here today . . .'

Stella had kept to herself just how difficult things were for Tom and Esmie, not wanting the Lomaxes' business being discussed around Rawalpindi.

Soon the newly-weds were getting ready to leave. Although the first snow had already come to the foothills, they were honeymooning in Murree, where Jimmy had secured an off-season rate at The Birchwood Hotel. He was borrowing his Uncle Toby's car and was keen to get his bride up the mountainside before dark descended.

The guests crowded together under the blue-roofed portico and waved them away with much noise and shouts of encouragement. Clive and Monty had tied tin cans to the car bumper which made a din as Jimmy drove up the street. Rick led the Dixon cousins in running behind letting off firecrackers. On the hotel lawn, the resident peacock gave a cry of alarm and displayed its feathers.

Stella slipped an arm through her father's and squinted in the low sun at the far hills with their dusting of snow. She had a familiar tug of longing for Kashmir. It would be months before she was there again. If she ever did get married, she would like it to be at The Raj-in-the-Hills – a quiet affair with the Lomaxes, her close family and the baroness – with Felix laying on a lunch of fish curry and custard tarts.

But, no matter how hard she tried, she couldn't imagine Monty as the groom.

Chapter 21

Ebbsmouth, December 31st 1938

'You'll have to go without me, darling,' Lydia said, emerging from under a towel and releasing a waft of scented steam from the bowl she was bending over.

'Oh, Mamma!' Andrew said in concern. 'Are you really feeling that bad?'

'Terrible,' Lydia said, pressing a hand dramatically to her forehead.

'Keep under the towel,' Minnie fretted. 'You're letting out all the infusion.'

Lydia pulled off the towel. 'It's making me feel worse,' she said in irritation. 'My head is pounding.'

'Better go to bed, dear,' Minnie said. 'I'll send Lily up with a cup of tea.'

'Lily's got the night off,' Lydia reminded her.

'Has she?' Minnie asked in confusion.

'Yes, Grandmamma,' Andrew said. 'It's Hogmanay, remember?'

His grandmother looked bemused, so he said quickly, 'I'll stay in and look after Mamma – and then we can play cards like old times.'

'Certainly not,' Lydia said. 'You must go to the Murrays' party – you've been invited – it would be rude not to— Atchoo!' She broke off with a loud sneeze.

'I hardly know them,' Andrew protested, 'and I don't want to leave you when you're ill. I might pop over to see Auntie Tibby for a dram at midnight if you're both in bed by then.'

Lydia gave him a glassy-eyed look. 'That sounds very dull – and you've already been to The Anchorage twice this holiday. The Murrays' house will be full of young things – far more suitable company than Tibby and her unwashed bohemians.'

Andrew wasn't going to tell her that it was Tibby's newest resident that he hoped to see tonight. Red-haired Ruth was a furniture-maker and sometimes modelled for Dawan. She wasn't conventionally pretty but there was something very alluring about her wild unbound hair and plump lips. Besides, Andrew knew it was pointless to argue with his mother.

Since he'd been away at Sandhurst on military training, he suspected Lydia had been turning to the sherry bottle even more than usual. Minnie was becoming more forgetful and so a worry to his mother, and Dickie Mason had gone to stay with relations in the south of England over Christmas and hadn't yet returned. Andrew wondered if his mother's sudden 'fever' was an excuse to avoid going to a party without Dickie on her arm.

His mother and Dickie had been close companions for over two years now, and Andrew liked the amiable captain but was fairly sure that Dickie had no intention of marrying Lydia. He was obviously quite happy with his casual frequent visits to Templeton Hall, the occasional winter foray to the south of France and periods of absence when he needed a break from Lydia's smothering attention. His mother had forbidden him to mention Dickie to his father and Andrew still felt a little guilty for doing so in his letter. But he'd been hurt by his father's scathing rejection of his decision to join the army and thought that mentioning Dickie's support might help his cause.

Andrew stood up. 'I'll go and get changed.'

Lydia smiled. 'You'll have a marvellous time. Wear your tartan trews, you look so handsome in your mess kit.'

By ten o'clock, Andrew was feeling bilious at the amount of sickly ginger cordial he'd consumed along with the wedges of fruit cake and slightly stale shortbread that had been handed around. The Murrays, a cheery couple who had recently bought a Victorian mansion on the outskirts of Ebbsmouth, were gaining a reputation for throwing lively parties.

The downstairs drawing room and adjacent dining room were packed with guests drinking cocktails and champagne, their glasses being constantly topped up by the ever-present servants. The chatter was loud and the laughter raucous. The Murrays, it would seem, thought a good party was measured by the amount of alcohol served rather than the food. Andrew thought wryly that his mother would have loved it.

He glanced at the clock and wondered if it would be impolite to slip away. His face ached from smiling and his voice was hoarse from having to talk loudly to make himself heard to a series of people he hardly knew. He didn't much care for parties. Even mess dinners could be boring – it was the side of the army he least enjoyed. Noel thought it amusing that he, a Scot and a Lomax, had no taste for whisky.

Andrew decided to go. He searched around for his hostess but could see no sign of her. He wouldn't be missed and would write a note of thanks tomorrow. He made for the entrance. As he stepped into the cold air, a hand on his sleeve stopped him. He turned to see a tall young woman in a tartan silk dress smiling at him.

'Hello, Andrew.'

There was something familiar about her. She had a slim face framed by wavy fair hair and regarded him with hazel eyes – pretty eyes.

'You don't remember me, do you?'

Andrew flushed. 'Sorry, I don't,' he admitted.

She laughed. 'At least that's honest. You came to play at my house years ago, when you first came back from India. You were so exotic – I'd never known anyone from that far away before.'

He still had no idea who she was. His mother had dragged him all over the county that summer when he'd rather have been spending it with Stella.

'Oh, yes.' He tried to sound convincing. 'I'm sorry, you'll have to remind me of your name.'

'Felicity.'

This was becoming embarrassing. The name meant nothing to him.

Her smile turned into a pout. 'You still don't remember, do you? I made you play with my dolls and you spent half the time in the loo – I thought you had tummy trouble 'cause you'd been in India, but afterwards I realised you were probably hiding from me.'

Finally, Andrew remembered. 'Flis-Tish!' he exclaimed.

She gave him a quizzical look.

He laughed bashfully. 'It's the name I called you because I couldn't remember Felicity.'

She raised an eyebrow. 'Well, I'm glad I made some sort of impression on you.' She held out her hand. 'I'm Felicity Douglas. Pleased to meet you, Andrew Lomax.'

Andrew shook hands. 'Delighted to meet you, Miss Douglas.'

'So, why are you leaving?'

'I – er – my mother's not well and I don't want to leave her too long on her own.'

'So, it's not because you're bored?'

He found her directness disconcerting.

'I am,' she continued. 'Or I was until I spotted you – which wasn't hard considering you're one of the tallest people here – and you look very handsome in your outfit, by the way. Are you in the army now?'

'Yes. Officer training.' He reached inside his doublet for his cigarette case, his interest piqued. 'And what about you?'

'Still at boarding school. Can I have one of those, please?'

Andrew hesitated and looked back at the throng of people beyond the entrance. 'Are you allowed?'

'Mummy won't mind and anyway, no one can see us in the dark out here.'

Andrew gave a grunt of amusement and offered her a cigarette, lighting hers and then his own. He blew out smoke, feeling relief ripple through him. He expected her to cough or gasp at the strong tobacco but she smoked like someone who was used to it.

'Do you enjoy school?' he asked.

She made a derisive sound. 'You sound like an aged uncle. You're not really interested, are you? And no, not much is the answer.' She eyed him through a gauze of smoke. 'I noticed that you don't drink. Not alcohol, anyway. Why is that?'

Andrew shrugged. 'I don't like the taste.'

He wasn't going to tell her that having a father and mother who drank too much had put him off for life. He never wanted to be that out of control.

'I'm not supposed to drink but I quite like the taste of sweet sherry,' Felicity admitted.

Andrew tried to remember how much younger she was than him. She must be about sixteen but she seemed older. Precocious, his grandmother would say.

'What do you want to do when you leave school?' he asked. 'If that's not too much of an aged-uncle question.'

She smiled. 'The truth is I'm not sure. My parents want me to go to finishing school – learn how to arrange flowers and boring things. I'd rather go to India and hunt tigers.'

Andrew laughed. 'Something tells me that you'll get your way, Miss Douglas.' He ground out his cigarette and put the butt into his pocket.

Felicity stubbed out hers on the stone wall and threw it into the dark.

'You're not really going home to your mother at ten o'clock on Hogmanay, are you? I bet you're going to sneak off to a more interesting party now you've done your duty here.'

Andrew tried to hide his surprise. He decided to be honest. 'I might go and first-foot my aged aunt later.'

'Now that does sound boring!'

'It won't be. Auntie Tibby lives with a houseful of artists.'

'Gosh, really?' Her eyes opened wide with interest. 'Is she the woman who dresses like a man and lives at The Anchorage?'

Andrew nodded.

'I wish I had an aunt as exciting as her.' Felicity gave a pleading look. 'Will you take me with you? Please do!'

Andrew shook his head. 'Maybe another time, Miss Douglas.'

'I'll hold you to that, Lomax.' She grinned.

'Goodnight.' He turned and hurried down the steps, shivering in the frosty air. Looking back, Andrew saw the girl still standing in the entrance, watching him. He waved and she waved back before retreating inside. All the way home he couldn't stop thinking about how the annoying eleven-year-old Flis-Tish had turned into a startling vivacious young woman.

Back at Templeton Hall, Andrew found his mother and grandmother had already gone to bed. He grabbed his bicycle from the garage and set off for The Anchorage. Moonlight bathed everything in ghostly silver and cast shadows as he cycled the empty lanes.

He thought about how he'd not heard from his father since he'd started at Sandhurst and he now regretted having sent such a hostile letter in reply to his father's plea for him to go to university.

He'd received a Christmas card from Esmie telling him that his father had been unwell but sent his love. It had mentioned that Jimmy Dubois was now married and was living at the Raj with his new wife. There was only a passing reference to Stella being back in Rawalpindi and helping her parents once more.

Long ago he had stopped blaming Stella for the hurtful things she had said about his mother and for keeping the truth from him about Esmie not being married to his father. She had been in a difficult position, tasked with looking after him while he was in Scotland and yet resented for doing so by his mother. It wasn't surprising that her loyalties had lain with his father and Esmie.

What would have happened if he had gone back? He would never have been as happy at school as he had been in Durham or had such a close friend as Noel. Neither would he have got to know his mother or grandmother – or his wonderful Auntie Tibby – in the way he had. His father and Esmie would have kept up the lie of being married and he would have grown up thinking that his own mother didn't love him. But for all her faults, she did love him.

She had been prepared to go through the shame and indignity of divorce so that he, Andrew, could remain with her. She had sacrificed her reputation for him.

His father, on the other hand, had chosen Esmie over his own son. He had agreed to let Andrew stay in Scotland in order to secure a divorce so he could marry Esmie. Andrew sighed. Was he being unfair to them both? After all, it had been his choice to stay in Britain. And deep down, Andrew knew how strong the love was between his dad and Esmie – it had been a part of his childhood. No matter what – or who – had caused the breakdown of his parents' marriage, didn't Tom and Esmie deserve to be happy together?

Andrew pounded along on the bicycle trying to rid his head of thoughts of India, but glittering stars always made him think of Stella. He'd expected to hear of her engagement before now – dreaded it because she had captured his heart years ago. Every girl he met, he measured against Stella. Tonight, meeting Felicity again, he'd been drawn by her fair looks and pretty eyes because they reminded him a little of his former friend.

Probably if he saw Stella now, he wouldn't find her nearly as attractive as in his memory. It had been a boyhood infatuation that he should have let go of years ago. His New Year's resolution would be to find a woman who didn't remind him of her in the slightest.

Andrew found Tibby and her friends playing charades in the library in front of a roaring fire. He was pleased to see Ruth among the long-time lodgers: Dawan, Mac and Walter. Willie the gardener and his wife Elsie stood up as he came in.

'Come and join us!' Tibby cried in delight. 'We're having a hard time trying to guess what film Mac is acting.'

'How smart you look,' said Ruth admiringly, making room for him on the sofa. He'd never seen her in an evening dress before and it showed off her cleavage. 'I love a man in uniform.'

'Leave him alone,' said Dawan. 'He's too young for you.'

Ruth gave a deep-throated laugh. 'As you are for Tibby?' she teased.

Andrew sat next to her and she kissed him on the cheek. He smelt a waft of her perfume and her unruly hair tickled his face. He tried not to stare but couldn't help wondering what she looked like with her clothes off modelling for Dawan.

Mac continued his energetic mime, throwing his hands in the air and pulling faces.

It suddenly struck Andrew that the Duboises and the residents at the Raj would probably be playing charades this very night too. As a small boy, he had relished being allowed to stay up late and take part. He pushed the thought from his mind as the game rolled on, and all at once it was his go.

'Okay, I'm ready.'

'Shush, everybody.' Tibby silenced her chattering guests.

Andrew signalled that he was doing the whole title, then stood legs apart and pulled on an imaginary bow and arrow.

'*The Adventures of Robin Hood*?' Elsie suggested.

Andrew grinned. 'Yes. Well done, Elsie.'

'Oh, you made that far too easy,' said Ruth.

Andrew flopped back on the sofa and Ruth leaned towards him.

'Masterful on the bow and arrow,' she teased.

Mac came round topping up drinks and Tibby began a new game of 'guess where I am', which quickly petered out when Dawan chose a 'hiding place' in Lahore that no one, apart from Andrew, had heard of.

After that, Tibby declared they should dance and that Willie should play his bagpipes. They pushed back the furniture and danced a chaotic 'strip the willow'; Ruth made sure she partnered Andrew, who swung all the women around with gusto.

They collapsed into chairs while Elsie came round with cups of tea and thick wedges of her homemade black bun, a rich fruit cake encased in pastry.

Then, abruptly, Tibby was clapping her hands. 'It's nearly midnight! Andrew, you be our tall dark stranger.' She thrust a piece of coal from the scuttle at him and pushed him towards the door. 'Stand outside till Willie pipes you in!'

For a couple of minutes Andrew stood shivering in the hall, clutching his piece of coal and wondering if he had time for a quick cigarette. The New Year was nearly upon them. What would it bring?

Willie came out of the library clutching his pipes. 'It's midnight,' he said. He clasped Andrew's shoulder like he used to when he was younger. 'I wish you the very best o' luck for the year ahead, Master Andrew.'

'Thank you, Willie.'

Then the gardener was striking up his pipes and leading him back into the library to a chorus of cheers and clapping led by his irrepressible Auntie Tibby. 'Happy New Year, everybody!'

The party went on into the small hours. At three o'clock, Tibby retired to bed and insisted Andrew must stay the night and not attempt to ride back on treacherous black ice. He needed little persuasion. He liked to bed down in his father's old turret room – and he had an excited feeling that he might get a visitor tapping at his door later.

He'd fallen asleep in the chilly bedroom, buried under several blankets, when he became aware of someone there. He started awake. A figure stood over him; he could just make out the outline of a woman in the dark.

'Ruth?' he whispered, catching a whiff of her powerful perfume. His heart was thudding.

He heard her laugh softly. 'Well, I hope you weren't expecting Elsie.'

Before he could say anything else, she was lifting the bed covers and climbing in beside him. Cold air wafted in. She shivered and snuggled up, touching him with cold hands.

Andrew flinched. 'You're freezing!'

'Warm me up, then,' she answered, pulling his arms around her.

She was wearing a cotton nightgown. He rubbed her back vigorously, trying not to shake with nerves.

'I didn't mean like that.' She sounded amused. 'Am I your first?'

Andrew said hoarsely, 'No, second. That's if we . . .'

'Do you want to?' she asked.

'Yes.' He hated the way his voice croaked, betraying his nervousness.

'Good. I've been longing to go to bed with you all holidays.'

It was light when Andrew woke again. Ruth was lying with her back to him, snoring gently. They'd made love twice before falling asleep. He couldn't resist kissing her pale shoulder, marvelling at the sight of this woman in his narrow bed. He craved a morning cigarette but didn't want to wake her, wanting to prolong their time together. Perhaps they could have sex again before breakfast.

He lay back smiling, his breath like a cloud in the chilly room. This had been so much better than his first fumbling attempt with the older sister of a school friend in the dunes of some Northumberland beach the previous summer.

He had no idea how old Ruth was – thirty, perhaps?

Stella was twenty-six. Andrew tried to stop himself imagining it was Stella and not Ruth lying beside him. He cursed under his breath. Even now, he couldn't get her out of his mind.

Ruth stirred, yawning and stretching.

'Good morning,' Andrew said, leaning over and kissing her.

'Goodness, what time is it?' She sat up.

'No idea. Does it matter?'

She gave a brief laugh, fumbling for her nightgown and slipping out of bed. He watched in dismay as she pulled it on.

'You don't have to go, do you?'

'Yes, I'm sitting for Dawan this morning.'

'On New Year's Day?' Andrew protested.

'Start the year as we intend to go on.' She smiled. 'Nineteen thirty-nine will be the year Dawan receives true recognition – and I will be famous as his muse. Can I borrow this dressing gown?' she asked, picking the one that hung on the door.

It was his father's. He never used it, but liked it hanging there as if it still held an essence of Tom.

'Of course.' He sat up. 'Will I see you later?'

'Won't you be going back to Mamma?' Ruth's mouth twitched.

Andrew reddened. She came back and kissed him on the forehead. 'You look really handsome with your hair in a mess. Call in and say goodbye before you leave for Sandhurst, won't you?'

Then she was gone. He felt deflated. It certainly didn't seem to be the momentous night for Ruth that it had been for him. What a fool he was to think it would.

Andrew reached for his cigarettes. The beginning of 1939 had already been eventful. As he smoked, he wondered where the year would take him. Andrew had a surge of restlessness. He was impatient to get back to officer training and his new comrades.

Chapter 22

Stella was picking flowers for the hotel dining room when she became aware of Tom and Esmie crossing the lawn towards her. It was a gloriously sunny morning and most of the guests were out for the day, riding, golfing or walking. Shading her eyes, she could tell at once from Tom's face that something terrible had happened.

'Stella.' His handsome, lined face was creased in pity.

'What's happened?' Stella stood up.

'We've had a letter from Pindi. Your mother . . .'

Stella's heart lurched. 'Something's happened to Ma?'

He shook his head. 'No, no, she's fine. Well, not fine, but . . .'

Esmie said quickly, 'It's your father – he's had a heart attack. I'm so sorry, lassie. He's . . . He passed away two days ago.'

Stella stood stunned. She couldn't take in what they were saying. Tom was mumbling something about his good friend Charlie and then tears were spilling down his cheeks. Esmie reached out and took Stella in her arms, pressing her head into her shoulder and stroking her hair as if she were the one crying. But she wasn't – couldn't. She was too shocked. A life without her pa was inconceivable.

Stella pulled away. 'But he's not even ill. He never gets ill in the hot season, only in the cold. He can't be dead. It's a mistake.'

Esmie spoke calmly. 'It's not a mistake. Your mother wrote to us so we could tell you in person rather than you read it in a letter. The doctor thinks Charlie's heart was weakened by the pneumonia he had last winter.' Gently, she took Stella by the arm. 'Come inside, lassie, and sit down. You're in shock.'

Stella allowed Esmie to shepherd her onto the veranda. A servant was sweeping the floor but with a nod from Esmie, he left them alone. Esmie sat Stella down on the wicker sofa next to her. Tom stood looking out at the view, trying to bring his emotions under control.

Esmie spoke in a low, soft voice. 'We'll make arrangements for you to return to Pindi as soon as you can. One of us can take you, if you like? Or you can wait a day or two. Your mother says that Jimmy is arranging the funeral and Yvonne is helping with the hotel, so you're not to worry about rushing back before then. But I imagine you'll want to be with your mother . . .'

'Funeral?' Stella repeated.

'It's likely to be next week,' said Esmie. 'They want to give time for Charlie's brother to come from Ceylon if he wants.'

Stella recalled the last thing her father had said to her before she'd set off for Kashmir in May. He'd kissed her on the top of her head and pinched her cheek as he'd done since she was a child.

'Take care, Sweet Pea! Transport my many felicitations to the dear Lomaxes. And tell the baroness, if she can't be good, be careful!'

Stella buried her face in her hands and tried to breathe. It was as if a lead weight were pressing on her chest. She let a sob escape and then the tears came. As she wept uncontrollably, Esmie held her tight and rocked her in her arms.

'Cry all you want,' she soothed.

Stella didn't know it was possible to feel such pain. Her father was her rock.

She tried to stem her tears. The Lomaxes too must be deeply saddened by the news. It may have been her mother who had the business head and had kept the hotel from going bankrupt in the early days, but it was her father's cheerful gregarious presence that had given the Raj a reputation for hospitality and homeliness.

Stella took a deep breath and sat back. Tom was standing in front of her holding out a large handkerchief.

'Thanks.' She blew into it.

Tom laid a hand on her head. She felt the warmth of it flow into her.

'Charlie was one of the greatest friends I ever had,' he said quietly. 'I'll miss him more than I can say, Stella. You were lucky to have such a loving father.' Tom gave a wistful smile. 'I never knew a man more besotted with his daughter than Charlie.'

Stella smiled through her tears. 'I know I was lucky.'

Tom's chin trembled. 'Esmie and I will come with you to Pindi to say farewell to our dear friend.'

Stella knew what an effort that would be for Tom, as he didn't like to venture beyond Gulmarg and hadn't been to the city now for over two years.

'Thank you, Mr Lomax,' she said, full of gratitude.

Charlie's funeral was held on the 23rd of August at St Joseph's Church on a sweltering, thundery day. The pews were packed with family, friends, colleagues and hotel staff who had all come to pay their respects. Stella had been in a state of numbness for days, trying to be strong for her mother, but on the funeral day it was Myrtle who remained dry-eyed and dignified while Stella sobbed throughout the mass.

Yvonne, who was noticeably pregnant, cried too. She clutched onto Jimmy and wailed that their baby would never see either of its grandfathers.

Jimmy seemed to have taken on the role of his father, thanking people for coming and inviting them back to the hotel for the wake. Tom had said that he would pay for everything and laid on plenty of whisky alongside the sandwiches and tea.

The baroness, who had travelled down from Srinagar for the funeral, seemed to know what to do in such circumstances. She slipped brandy into Stella's tea and said, 'Darling, knock it back and go and talk to your young man. Charlie would have hated all these long faces, so put a smile on for your pa.'

Stella glanced over to see Monty, hands in pockets, looking morose. She didn't really want to talk to him but he looked so sad that she did as Hester ordered.

'Thanks for coming,' she said, touching his arm briefly.

'I thought the world of your pa,' he said, his brown eyes shining with emotion.

'And he was fond of you, Monty.' Stella gave a wan smile. 'He used to say, *"That boy is full of promise – one day he'll box for India!"*'

Monty gave a soft laugh. 'I'm not even the best in C Company.'

'Have you been away on camp with the Auxiliary Force?' she asked, realising that she hardly knew what he'd been doing while she'd been in Gulmarg.

Monty nodded. 'Some of the men think . . .' He broke off. 'Sorry, now's not the time to talk of such things.'

'What things?' Stella scrutinised him. 'What do the men think?'

'There's been a lot of talk of us going to war,' he said quietly. 'Britain being dragged into war in Europe.'

Stella's insides clenched. 'The Lomaxes are worried about that too – especially with Andrew being in the army.'

Monty nodded. 'This pact between the Nazis and the Soviets makes it more inevitable.'

'But it won't affect us in India, will it?'

Monty shrugged. 'We'll have to be prepared – support the mother country in any way we can.'

'You're right, of course,' Stella agreed. 'But let's hope it can all be avoided.'

'Stella,' he said, his look unsure. 'When you feel up to it, I'd like to take you out for a drive.'

'I don't know when I'll feel like doing that—'

'There's something I need to speak to you about.'

Stella tensed. She couldn't face a proposal from Monty so soon after her father's death. She could only manage the grief by taking each day at a time. He would have to wait.

'Not yet,' she said. 'I need time.'

'Of course.' He stepped away. 'Let me know when you want to see me.'

The days that followed had a strange unreality about them. Stella coped with her loss by keeping as busy as possible around the hotel, but it seemed that in her absence over the hot season, Yvonne had largely taken over her role. Her sister-in-law helped Myrtle with drawing up menus, instructing the cook and ordering foodstuffs. Stella's mother was also teaching Yvonne bookkeeping.

'She's so quick to learn things,' Myrtle told Stella one evening as they sat alone in the bungalow. 'And it's more important than ever that she knows the business. Charlie always wanted Jimmy to take over one day – we just never thought it would be this soon . . .' Her mother broke off, overcome with sadness.

Stella was quick to give her a hug. 'Oh, Ma, it's so hard to believe Pa's gone! I miss him so much.'

Myrtle kissed the top of her head. 'You were always such a daddy's girl. I think it's harder for you than Jimmy. He's got Yvonne – and the baby to look forward to.' She touched Stella's cheek. 'I wish I could see you settled too.'

'I am settled,' said Stella. 'I'm happy at the hotel and I want to be with you, Ma. It's the only life I've ever wanted.'

Myrtle sighed. 'What about Monty? He's been very patient waiting for you to make up your mind.'

Stella's insides twisted. 'I like Monty – I suppose I'm fond of him. But I'm not in love with him.'

Her mother looked disappointed. 'Stella, I should tell you something. Monty came to see your father the week before he died – to ask his permission to marry you.'

Stella was winded by the news. 'What did Pa say?'

'He said he'd be very happy to give his permission – joyous was the word he used – but that the decision had to be yours.'

Stella's eyes stung with tears. She could hear her father giving his blessing in his enthusiastic way. She felt wretched. Not only was her avoidance of marriage frustrating for Monty but it must have been worrying her father too, otherwise he would not have been so keen on giving his permission. He had never pressed her on the issue but secretly must have been hoping she would accept marriage to Monty.

Myrtle put a hand over Stella's. 'If you don't want to marry Monty then you must put him out of his misery and tell him. It's not fair to give him hope where there is none.'

Stella nodded in agreement.

193

Two days after this conversation, on the first day of September, news came through that forced domestic issues from Stella's mind. Jimmy dashed into the bungalow as Stella and her mother were getting ready for bed.

'I've just been listening to the wireless,' he said, his face aghast. 'The news from home is that the Germans have begun to invade Poland. Our government is sticking to their promise to help Poland – and so are the French.'

Stella asked anxiously, 'What does that mean? What will happen?'

Jimmy said, 'I don't know, but they're calling up our army and naval reserves.'

On the Sunday, they learnt the worst, when Chamberlain announced that an ultimatum given to Hitler that morning had been ignored and that Britain was at war with Germany. Late that night, the Duboises and the residents sat around the radio in the lobby under the cooling whir of the electric fans and tuned in to a broadcast by King George to his Commonwealth subjects.

The king spoke in his precise, sombre voice. *'For the second time in the lives of most of us, we are at war.'*

For the first time it began to dawn on Stella that this might not be some distant conflict between a handful of nations in Europe; all their lives were under threat. The king was exhorting his people – both at home and across the seas – to face the dark days ahead together and be ready for whatever service or sacrifice was demanded of them.

'With God's help we shall prevail.'

The speech ended. They sat in silence as Jimmy switched off the wireless. Then Fritwell stood up and began to clap. Others followed.

Jimmy ordered Sunil to pour out whiskies for all those who wanted one. Fritwell raised his glass and made a toast: 'To the King and our Empire!'

The others chorused, 'To King and Empire!'

Stella gazed around the dimly lit lobby and wondered what her father would have thought. Everything looked exactly as normal; the guests gathered for a final nightcap. Outside insects hummed and a night bird screeched. Someone rode past ringing their bicycle bell. Soon, everyone was dispersing and bidding each other goodnight.

By day, the routine of the hotel resumed as before, with Jimmy taking up his father's role; by night, the residents gathered for the evening ritual of tuning into the news from London on All India Radio. The very next day after Britain and France had declared war on Germany, Viceroy Linlithgow had announced that India was at war with the Nazis too.

The news was sobering; Poland was being quickly overrun by fast-moving German Panzer divisions, and by the middle of September, the Soviets were invading from the east. The French had lost no time in attacking Germany in the west by marching over the border into the Saar.

Britain was on a war footing, but there was no talk of going to the rescue of the Poles. Merchant ships were being sunk at an alarming rate.

Fritwell complained, 'All we seem to hear from the broadcaster-wallahs is depressing news of German successes.'

'Will ships be able to get through to India from Britain?' Hester asked anxiously.

'Well, we appear to still be getting sea mail,' said Ansom. 'And airmail letters, for that matter.'

Prompted by her mother's words, Stella sent a note to Monty asking to see him. It was time she put an end to their lukewarm romance. She suspected that he had only come to ask her father's permission to marry her as a face-saving act after pressure from his own family to follow Clive's lead and get married.

Not wanting to have her mother and Yvonne interfering, Stella arranged to meet him under the clock tower in the Saradan gardens. He was waiting for her, his expression wary.

He kissed her lightly on the cheek. 'How are you?'

'I'm okay, thank you. Keeping busy.' To put him at his ease, Stella suggested, 'Let's walk through the park.'

For several minutes they strolled a little aimlessly, Stella talking about the family and the hotel. 'You were right about war breaking out,' she said. 'That's all the residents can talk about.'

'I'm not happy to be proved right about it,' Monty said glumly.

'It all seems so far away, though,' said Stella, 'that I find it hard to believe it's actually happening.'

'But it is,' said Monty, becoming animated. 'And it's already causing division in India, with Congress holding a gun to the government's head, saying they'll only support the war effort if they get independence at the end of it.'

Stella wasn't greatly interested in politics, but she held the same opinion as her father had had: that one day – perhaps in her life-time – India would become self-governing like other former colonies, such as Canada and Australia.

'Some day, that might happen anyway,' she pointed out.

'Don't say that!' Monty exclaimed. 'Imagine what would happen to the likes of us. We'd be left high and dry if the British handed over rule to Indians. It's unthinkable.'

Stella was more optimistic about such a future but decided to say no more on the subject. They walked on in silence.

Abruptly, Monty stopped. 'Stella, can we sit down? I've something to tell you.'

Stella nodded, her insides knotting. Now was the moment she was going to have to let him down as gently as possible. They chose a bench in the shade of a peepal tree.

Monty turned to her, his look resolute. 'I'm leaving my job. I've enlisted with the army.'

Stella gaped at him. 'Enlisted? When?'

'Last week,' he said. 'I've been accepted for military training with the King's Own Bengal Sappers. I'll be leaving in a couple of weeks. Their headquarters are at Roorkee in United Province. A couple of days' train ride away.' He gave her an earnest look. 'I'll try and get back to Pindi as often as I can.'

She was trying to absorb his surprising news when Monty took hold of her hand. 'Stella, I know this is a shock but it's made me think more than ever about what I want for the future. I hate to leave Pindi and everyone here – but especially you. Do you think before I go – that we – that we could become engaged?' His hand felt hot and sticky as he clasped hers. 'Stella, will you marry me?'

Stella squirmed. 'Monty, I do care for you but I don't want to get married.'

He looked crestfallen. 'Is there someone else? Someone in Kashmir? Is that why you go there every hot season?'

'No,' Stella said. 'There's no one in Kashmir. I go there because I love Gulmarg and working for the Lomaxes.'

He carried on clutching her hand, his words turning desperate. 'Do you mean you don't want to get married yet – or you never want to marry me? Because it would mean such a lot to know that you might one day – if I could go away knowing that you hadn't dismissed it altogether.'

Stella's resolve began to weaken. 'I don't know if my feelings will change – or if yours will either. Everything seems so uncertain at the moment – I don't want to make promises . . .'

'Even if you agreed to keep an open mind,' said Monty quickly, 'I'd be happy with that. You're right; we're at war and nothing is certain. But couldn't we just say there's a bit of an understanding between us – see how things are after I've completed my training? I won't hold you to it if you still feel the same then.'

It seemed a fair request. She had told him how she felt; if he wanted to believe she might change her mind in the future then that was up to him. Stella was sure that Monty didn't really love her either; he wanted to join the army on this new adventure and be able to say he had a girl waiting for him at home. When he asked to pay for a studio photograph of her, she was even more certain of his motives.

But there didn't seem any harm in it and Stella kept remembering that her father had been prepared to welcome Monty into the family. It would be unkind to send him away with a brusque rejection and rob him of his pipe dream.

The cold season arrived with dusty winds bringing hail and rain. The town filled up again with regiments and families who had spent the hot months in the hills. The rumoured Nazi attack on their western neighbours didn't materialise, and to Stella it seemed as if life in the cantonment was continuing as normal. She saw the usual games of tennis being played at the Gymkhana Club and officers exercising their horses along the Mall. Jimmy advertised that the hotel would do special rates for children's birthday parties and bridge club teas.

Her brother threw a farewell drinks party for Monty, and Stella was persuaded to go on to the dance at the Chota Club with Monty and their friends. It was the first time she had been to one since her father had died, and although she still had little appetite for dancing, she put on a cheerful face. Monty left, giving her a kiss on her lips and asking her to write to him when she could. She felt a guilty relief at his going and hoped that his desire to get engaged would diminish with time and distance.

Yvonne, now a month away from giving birth, was being made to rest by a fussing Myrtle. Stella was more than happy to take over her duties and was growing as excited as the others about the imminent arrival of a baby in the family. She could see how it gave her mother something to look forward to. Myrtle was stoical and put on a brave face to the outside world, but only Stella knew how much her mother was grieving. Often, she woke in the night to hear her ma weeping. It made her heartsore to remember how throughout her life she had been comforted by the muffled sound of her parents' chatter and laughter beyond the bedroom wall.

Once, on hearing her mother crying, Stella had knocked on her door.

'Can I come in, Ma?'

Her mother had stifled her sobbing. 'N-no, don't. I'm all right.'

'Can I fetch you anything? A hot drink?'

'G-go back to bed, Stella. I'm sorry if I woke you.'

As Christmas approached, Stella knew her mother would be dreading it as much as she was. All the festive rituals at the hotel were so bound up with Charlie's exuberant personality that it was impossible to think of them without him.

They debated whether to hold the traditional Christmas Eve party and Jimmy decided that they should.

'Our friends at the hotel will be feeling Pa's absence too,' he said. 'We owe it to them to put on a show that Pa would have been proud of. What better way to honour him?'

Stella helped her brother prepare their father's signature whisky punch and decorate the foyer and dining room with colourful streamers and lanterns. As the sun set and the guests gathered, Stella spun around at the sound of familiar voices in the hotel entrance.

'Mr and Mrs Lomax!' she gasped, rushing forward.

Esmie enveloped her in a hug and explained, 'We wanted to be with you all this Christmas.'

Tears sprung to Stella's eyes. 'Thank you! Ma and Jimmy will be so pleased.'

Tom put an affectionate hand on her head. 'What better way to cheer ourselves up than to see your smiling face, dear girl?'

'We've made Pa's special punch,' Stella said.

'I was hoping you would,' Tom said. He looked thin and drawn, but his handsome blue eyes shone with warmth.

Soon spotted by Hester and her friends, he was beckoned into their midst.

Later, as Stella sat with the Lomaxes in the chilly courtyard outside the bungalow, she was able to ask about Andrew.

Tom pulled hard on a cigarette and said, 'As far as we can make out, he's been doing further training in the Highlands. Kicking his heels, as he calls it. He'd rather be on active service.'

'But that news is a couple of months out of date,' said Esmie. 'Tom hasn't heard from him since October. It might mean he's already in France.'

Stella squeezed her hand. 'I'm sure you would have heard if that was the case. Tibby would have let you know.'

'You're right; she would.' Esmie looked reassured.

'Besides,' said Stella, 'Andrew has always known how to take care of himself. I'm sure the Borderers are training him well.'

Chapter 23

It was Felicity's idea to go and see a matinee film in Edinburgh.

'You've been prowling around here like a caged tiger for the past fortnight,' she accused Andrew, 'and I'm dying to see Cary Grant in *Gunga Din*, aren't you?'

'Not really,' said Andrew, stopping to stare out of the drawing room window at the icy landscape that was finally beginning to thaw. His embarkation leave had been extended because of the snowstorms and freezing weather of the previous month, which had brought the country to a standstill. In the Highlands he'd seen post delivered by skiers and milk by sledge.

'But it's about the army in India,' said Felicity, 'fighting wild tribesmen – just like your ancestors.' She slipped her arms around his waist and lowered her voice. 'Besides, it'll give me a chance to have you to myself – your mamma monopolises you and there's so little time left . . .'

Andrew looked down at her and smiled. 'You're very pretty when you pout at me like that.' He kissed her on the nose.

'Good. So does that mean we can go to the pictures in Edinburgh?'

Andrew nodded. 'I'll go and tell Mamma not to expect us for lunch.'

Andrew was exhilarated as they drove up the coast towards Edinburgh, the North Sea sparkling and benign under a cobalt-blue sky. It was hard to imagine that danger lurked out there: a deadly game of cat and mouse between shipping and U-boats. Soon, he too would be crossing the sea to join the British Expeditionary Force in France. He was impatient for it – Noel had been there since October with his battalion – and he itched to join him and start doing his bit.

'Penny for your thoughts?' Felicity asked.

He glanced round guiltily. 'Just thinking what a lucky man I am to be taking you out.'

'Liar.' She gave a huff of amusement. 'You were miles away. Probably already in France.'

Andrew flushed. 'You know me far too well.'

She slipped a hand onto his thigh. 'Not as well as I'd like.'

He experienced a jolt of excitement. It had surprised him how quickly their friendship had blossomed since the previous New Year. They'd met up every time he'd been on leave. As soon as Felicity had turned seventeen last spring, she'd insisted on leaving school and had been one of the first recruits locally for the Women's Voluntary Services, helping to look after evacuated children. When she wasn't doing that, she was working in her father's stables because his stable hand had been called up by the navy.

She was emotionally mature beyond her years and was outspoken and lively – and was keen to take their relationship further. Andrew, though, was hesitant. He was about to be sent abroad into conflict and there was a chance he might not come back.

Andrew picked up her hand, kissed it and then gently placed it back on her lap. 'We don't want this car going off the road,' he joked.

By the time they got to Edinburgh three-quarters of an hour later, the sky had clouded and a chill wind was blowing down the rows of elegant terraced streets. Andrew parked down a cobbled lane near the main thoroughfare of Princes Street and then walked hand in hand with Felicity.

'First, lunch at Jenner's,' he decreed, 'to fortify us for *Gunga Din*.'

Despite the recent introduction at home of rationing of bacon, butter and sugar, restaurants so far were under no such restrictions. Andrew and Felicity tucked into a meal of fish pie and carrots with cheese sauce, followed by sponge pudding and custard, and a large pot of tea.

Afterwards, they made their way towards the New Victoria Cinema. Felicity slipped her arm through Andrew's in excitement as they stepped into the brightly lit foyer and across its marble floor to the ticket kiosk.

Buying tickets for the stalls, they entered a long curving lounge dotted with pot plants and cane chairs. People were milling about, chattering and laughing. Andrew had a sudden sensation of having been there before, and then it hit him: it reminded him of The Raj Hotel. He stopped and took a deep breath.

Felicity looked at him in concern, pausing in unbuttoning her coat. 'Are you all right, Andrew?'

He recovered quickly. 'Yes, of course. I'm just taking it all in.'

'Fabulous, isn't it?' She grinned, pulling him forward.

The auditorium was even grander; it resembled a Greek amphi-theatre with figurines in niches and Corinthian columns arrayed either side of the massive screen. An usherette showed them to their seats near the back of the stalls. Above them jutted the sweep of balcony and behind was a row of private boxes.

Andrew pulled out a couple of boiled sweets that he'd been keeping for the cinema and handed her one.

'Goodness, you do know how to spoil a girl, don't you, Lomax?' she teased. 'That couple in the box behind are gorging on chocolates.'

Andrew glanced round. A man in civvies was saying something to make his blonde-haired companion laugh.

Andrew said dryly, 'We'll still be sucking on these when they've finished their chocolates.'

Something about the man seemed familiar. Andrew looked over his shoulder again but Felicity nudged him.

'Don't stare,' she hissed. 'They'll think we envy them.'

Andrew grunted. 'We do envy them.'

Then the lights went down and they both settled to watch the film.

Andrew thought the film a rather ridiculous parody of both the army and India, but still it unsettled him. The scenes of barren mountains, dusty plains and soldiers being drilled in the heat trans-ported him back to his boyhood home.

At the intermission, he lit up a cigarette. Surreptitiously, he glanced around to look at the man in the box again. He was defi-nitely familiar. Had he seen him in Ebbsmouth before?

Felicity leaned closer and whispered, 'Why do you keep look-ing at that couple behind? Do you know them?'

Andrew shrugged. 'I'm sure I've seen the man before.'

'He's rather a dish.' Felicity smirked. 'But I still prefer you.'

Soon the second half of the film was beginning and Andrew put the man from his mind. He surrendered to the slapstick and melodrama as the film reached its climax, and found himself unexpectedly moved by the quasi-tragic ending. He recognised the comradeship of the British soldiers and felt a pang for the places of his childhood.

'It was filmed in America, you know,' Felicity said, as the lights went up. 'Did it look anything like the Khyber Pass?'

'It looked a bit like the North West Frontier from what I remember,' admitted Andrew. 'Although I've only been once and I can't have been older than five or six.'

They began to shuffle out of their row behind other cinemagoers. Andrew watched the couple in the box as they stood up. The man reached for a walking stick and moved stiffly towards the door. That's when it struck him. Hugh Keating! It was the Irishman on the boat from '33 whom Stella had been in love with. He was sure of it.

'I *do* know that man,' he told Felicity. 'Come on, I'd like to catch him.'

He took her hand and they weaved their way through the slow-moving crowd. Back out in the stalls' lounge, Andrew craned over heads to try and spot Hugh, but there was no sign. They filed out into the foyer.

'Let's just wait here for a few minutes,' he said. 'He might not have left yet.'

'Can I have one of your ciggies, then?' Felicity asked, already rummaging in the breast pocket of his uniform. She lit up.

A minute later, Andrew saw Hugh stepping into the foyer on his own, limping slightly and aided by his silver-topped cane. Andrew pushed across the crowded space and hailed him.

'Mr Keating? Hello, Mr Keating!'

The man stopped and turned around.

Andrew reached him. 'It is you, isn't it? Hugh Keating.'

He smiled in bemusement. 'It is. And you are?'

Andrew held out his hand. 'Andrew Lomax. I was your cabin-mate on the SS *Rajputana* in 1933.'

'Good heavens!' Hugh stared in surprise, and then shook his hand vigorously. 'Look at you, young Lomax! Tall as a tree and a soldier now, I see. How the devil are you?'

'Very well, thanks.' Andrew grinned. 'I'm on leave in Ebbsmouth. I joined the Borderers. And what about you? Are you still with the Department of Agriculture in Baluchistan?'

Hugh whistled. 'That seems a lifetime ago. No, I resigned from the service.' He tapped his lame leg. 'Never recovered from being shot at and didn't think it fair to stay on when I couldn't get about easily on horseback and do the job properly.'

'Very honourable,' Andrew said. 'So what do you do now?'

'I work for agents in Calcutta – McSween and Watson – selling agricultural supplies and the like. Not very glamorous, but they won't take me in the forces.' He gripped Andrew's shoulder. 'I envy you lads in uniform.'

'You're on furlough, then?' Andrew asked.

'No, it's a work trip to our headquarters in Dundee,' he explained. 'But I'm not a priority for getting back to India, so will have to wait my turn for a passage out.'

'What brings you to Edinburgh?'

'Well, introduce me to your friend,' interrupted Felicity, appearing at his side. Andrew did so and she held out her hand to Hugh. 'Felicity Douglas.'

Hugh smiled and pressed her hand lightly to his lips. 'Charmed, Miss Douglas. Young Lomax is a lucky man.'

Felicity laughed. 'Andrew spent half the film craning round to stare at you. I should be jealous. Where is your wife?'

Hugh looked nonplussed and then said, 'Oh no, there's no wife. I'm – er – visiting my cousin – Cousin Caroline. She's just gone to powder her nose, as you ladies say.'

Hugh chatted easily to Felicity for a minute or so; it reminded Andrew what good company Hugh had been on the ship and how guilty he had felt afterwards for discouraging a romance with Stella. Poor Stella! Andrew was pretty sure that his mother had deliberately got rid of Hugh's letter to her out of petty jealousy.

It prompted Andrew to ask, 'Did you ever hear from Stella – our family friend on the boat?'

'Your companion?' Hugh queried. 'No, never. I was very taken with her, but plainly she didn't feel the same way. I wrote to her but she didn't reply. Left me a broken-hearted Irishman.' He clutched his chest in self-mockery.

'She wanted to,' Andrew told him. 'She was very pleased to hear from you and wanted to write back but I think your letter got thrown out by mistake.'

Hugh seemed taken aback to hear this. His fair face coloured and he looked momentarily sad. 'Well, that's a great pity,' he said. 'A great pity indeed. If only I'd known . . .'

'I'm sure she would still like to hear from you,' said Andrew, trying to make amends.

Hugh gave a huff of disbelief. 'Surely the beautiful Stella will have married long ago.'

'No, she hasn't,' said Andrew. 'At least not that I've heard of. She still writes to my aunt in Ebbsmouth. Stella's father died recently so she's been comforting her mother.'

'Is she still at The Raj Hotel in Pindi?' Hugh asked with interest.

'Yes, she is.'

Felicity said in amusement, 'Well, I've never heard such blatant matchmaking. Men are far worse gossips than we women.'

Andrew laughed and, to cover his embarrassment, asked, 'Mr Keating, would you and your cousin like to come for a cup of tea with us before we drive back to Ebbsmouth?'

Hugh gave a regretful smile. 'I would like nothing better, but I have to get my cousin home before dark or I'll be in trouble with my aunt and uncle. In fact, I'd better go and hurry Caroline up.' He shook Andrew's hand again. 'It's been wonderful bumping into you again, Andrew. Take care and all the best of luck. Maybe one day we'll meet in Pindi.' He smiled and bowed at Felicity. 'Pleasure to meet you too, Miss Douglas.'

He turned and disappeared back through the foyer doors.

Felicity linked arms with Andrew. 'I think we've been dismissed,' she said with a wry look. 'If that woman's his cousin, I'll eat my hat.'

'What do you mean?' Andrew asked in surprise.

'I'd say she's someone else's wife,' Felicity remarked. 'Come on, let's not embarrass them.'

Andrew marvelled at Felicity's perspicacity and allowed her to lead him outside.

On the road home, Andrew could only half-listen to Felicity's chatter about the film as his mind was too full of the strange day. Why had he encouraged Hugh to write to Stella and then immediately regretted doing so? Was it because Felicity's suspicion about Hugh being with a married woman made him worry that the Irishman might not be a reliable suitor – or was it because deep down he still harboured feelings for Stella?

He tried to push such thoughts from his mind. He was in love with Felicity and didn't need to hang onto his ridiculous boyhood crush on the Dubois girl.

They reached Ebbsmouth as the sun was setting and Andrew turned down the lane towards the Douglases' large Victorian villa, built as the seaside home of a Glasgow industrialist.

'Park up out of view of the house,' Felicity ordered.

Andrew was reluctant. 'I must get back before it's dark or the ARP warden will be after me.'

'Just a few minutes,' she cajoled.

He did so and then she reached across and started kissing him. Andrew felt desire stirring at the taste of her moist lips. They embraced and fondled each other's hair.

'Let's climb into the back seat,' Felicity suggested, a little breathless. 'Then we can kiss more easily.'

Andrew knew where this was leading. He pulled away and caught her hands in his.

'This isn't the way,' he said gently. 'One day, we'll make love but it won't be in the back of my mother's freezing car. We'll do it properly. I'm not going to risk leaving you in the family way while I'm on the battlefront – or wherever they're sending me.'

She gave him one of her direct looks. 'I'm disappointed but I think also flattered. Are you saying we have to get engaged first?'

Andrew felt a flicker of alarm. He wasn't thinking that far ahead.

'Possibly,' he said, unsure. 'Let's see what happens.'

She gave a smile of satisfaction and kissed him one more time. Then she was swinging her long legs out of the car.

'Call round before you leave, won't you? I'm going to miss you like stink.'

He promised he would. He drove quickly home, his emotions see-sawing between exultation and relief. Felicity loved him like no girlfriend had before – and he desired her too – but part of him was thankful he was about to leave Ebbsmouth and go into action. Soon he would be fighting for his country; it was as simple as that.

Chapter 24

The night pulsed with the sound of insects and the intermittent screech and howl from the forests above the hotel. Stella and the Lomaxes were gathered in the small back sitting room of the annex, listening in disbelief at the latest grim war news on the wireless.

'Belgium has surrendered too?' Stella said in shock. 'What does that mean for our British troops?'

'They will carry on fighting beside the French,' said Esmie stoutly. 'Like we did in the last war.'

'We're already in retreat,' Tom pointed out, looking utterly haggard. 'Our army will be wiped out or taken prisoner. It's happening all over again. Except this time the Nazis are much more organised and ruthless than the Kaiser. They've gone through Holland and Belgium like a knife through butter! As well as Denmark and Norway – countries that have declared themselves neutral. Hitler has shown time and time again that he can't be trusted.'

'You're right.' Esmie tried to calm him. 'But don't upset yourself.'

'How can I not be upset?' Tom cried. 'Andy is in the middle of this hell!'

'We must pray for Andy's safety,' said Esmie. 'For everyone's safety. It's all we can do.'

Stella couldn't speak. She felt overwhelmed with anxiety for Andrew. Earlier that month they had raised their glasses at supper to his health on his twentieth birthday, knowing only that he was somewhere on the Western Front. He was the age she had been when they'd embarked together on their adventure to Scotland. Andrew had had to grow up quickly, and judging by the photograph Tibby had sent of her nephew in uniform, he was physically a man now too.

In the picture, taken outside The Anchorage, he towered over Dawan and Willie the piper. Stella had been struck by how alike he was to Tom with his dark hair and lean features. Yet his eyes resembled his mother's and his shoulders were broader than his father's.

Tibby had told Stella that Andrew was courting a very pretty and spirited girl, Felicity Douglas – or Flis-Tish as Andrew called her – and that they seemed very smitten with each other. She was happy for him. It distressed her now to think of Andrew being in danger.

Lying in bed sleepless that night, Stella chided herself for thinking so much about Andrew and not about Monty. She had seen him once, briefly, in March when he'd had a few days' leave. They had gone dancing and to a party at Clive and Ada's, but she had avoided being alone with him and couldn't wait to get back to the hotel.

Stella was completely besotted with her new nephew, Charles Franklin (named after his two grandfathers) who had been born in January. At her suggestion, Jimmy and his young family had moved back into the bungalow, while her mother and she had taken over the smaller hotel flat.

Baby Charles was plump and contented, and although he had an ayah who lived in the servants' compound, Stella often took charge of him. She'd found it a wrench to leave him in early May to come up to the hills.

Stella even had pity for Lydia. How she must be waiting anxiously for news of her son too! Stella had long ago come to the conclusion that Lydia did love Andrew, in her own way.

Over the next few days, Stella tried to keep up the Lomaxes' morale by playing the piano each evening and organising sing-songs with the guests. Esmie joined in, but Tom retreated to his studio. He'd begun to drink heavily again. The women watched helplessly while he became more withdrawn as the news from Europe worsened. Once Belgium had capitulated, the Nazis were racing for the French coast, intent on cutting off the retreating British Expeditionary Force and its allies. The cream of the British Army – tens of thousands of men – were fighting a fierce rear-guard action.

Then in early June, news began to filter through of a miraculous escape by thousands of the beleaguered combatants; a modern-day armada of naval ships and merchant vessels had come to their rescue across the Channel and plucked many of them to safety. Tom chain-smoked as they listened to the hissing broadcast on the wireless as it came and went, one moment clear as a bell and the next an indistinct crackling.

'Do you think Andrew could be among those who got away?' Stella asked in hope.

'We have no way of knowing,' said Esmie, trying to hold back tears.

Tom gave them a ghost of a smile. 'My boy won't give up; wherever he is, he'll never give up.'

The waiting and not knowing were purgatory. Guests, aware that the distracted hotelier was in daily dread of bad news, spoke in platitudes.

'It's not over till it's over.'

'I'm sure you'll hear he's safe soon.'

'Chin up, Mr Lomax.'

To the delight of them all, the unexpected arrival of Baroness Cussack from her houseboat raised their spirits. Where others had failed, she managed to tempt Tom out of his den with chota pegs and games of whist. But as June advanced, the daily bulletins grew worse. Fascist Italy entered the war on the side of Germany and immediately invaded France across the Alps and began bombing British dependency Malta. The RAF was already retaliating with raids on Italian air bases in Libya, but it meant that the airmail service to India was suspended. The Nazis were marching on Paris and by the middle of the month had taken the French capital. They heard a little-known French general called De Gaulle exhorting his fellow officers and soldiers who had escaped to Britain to join him and fight on. *'The flame of the French Resistance must not go out and it will not go out.'*

At the same time as France was being overrun, they learnt that the Soviets had invaded the Baltic state of Lithuania. It seemed as if the totalitarian forces were gaining a stranglehold on Europe. Stella knew they were all thinking the same thing, even if they dare not say it; it would only be a matter of time before Britain was Hitler's next target.

Stella was the one to spot the chaprassy bounding effortlessly up the hill. She was on the veranda playing ludo with Hester, along with a forester's wife and her small daughter.

'Girls,' Hester was saying. 'Do you know that ludo is based on an ancient Indian game called pachisi? The Mughal emperors used to play it and Akbar had a giant board—'

'Baroness,' Stella interrupted, getting to her feet. 'I think the chaprassy is holding a telegram.'

Hester put a hand to her chest. 'Oh, my goodness! Go and get Esmie.'

Stella ran into the dark interior of the hotel, calling, 'Mrs Lomax! Come quickly!'

Esmie came dashing out of the small office. 'What is it?'

'The chaprassy's outside,' she gabbled. 'He's brought a telegram.'

Esmie said calmly, 'Get Bijal to fetch him a drink while I go and get Tom.' Then she was hurrying round to the studio.

Stella instructed the bearer to take the messenger round to the kitchen while she and the other women waited on the veranda. The telegram lay unopened on the table. It seemed an eternity before Esmie reappeared, though it could not have been more than a couple of minutes.

'Tom's not there,' she said. 'He must have gone for a walk.' She picked up the telegram with a trembling hand and then put it back down again.

'Open it,' Hester said. 'Better to know.'

Esmie looked torn. 'I can't – it's addressed to Tom.'

Stella felt nauseous. 'Do you want me to go and look for him?'

Esmie replied, 'No, I'll go.'

'I'll come with you,' Stella insisted. 'It'll be quicker with two.'

Esmie gave a brief smile and nodded. 'Thank you.'

They swiftly changed into walking shoes and set off up the hill and across the high marg. Stella couldn't have borne remaining at the hotel playing games. She sent up a fervent prayer that Andrew

216

was alive – and that Tom had not set off on one of his long melancholic wanderings.

They found him up near the Gujjars' huts chopping wood. He looked up and gave a bashful smile, and then his expression changed. 'Esmie, what is it?'

'A telegram,' she said simply. 'We haven't opened it.'

At once, Tom dropped his axe and went to her. She took his hand and they set off down the hill almost at running pace, with Stella trying to keep up.

When they got back to the veranda, only Hester was waiting. The other guests had made themselves scarce. Tom went straight to the table and seized the envelope. For a moment he stared at it. Stella could see him swallowing hard and then he tore it open. She held onto Hester, heart pounding.

With shaking hands, he read the message. He let out a groan.

Esmie gripped his arm. 'Tom?' she gasped.

Stella started to shake.

Tom's eyes filled with tears. He cleared his throat. 'Andy . . . Andy's alive. Tibby says he was rescued from Dunkirk.' He let out a sob.

Esmie took the telegram from him and read it herself. 'Oh, thank God!' she cried.

Stella and Hester hugged.

'Is he at home?' asked the baroness.

'Tibby doesn't say,' said Esmie, 'so I suppose not yet. It was wired four days ago. But he's definitely back in Britain.'

Stella couldn't hold back her tears. 'Oh, what a relief! I'm so glad!'

Tom reached for Esmie and clung to her. Gently she guided him onto a sofa and sat beside him. Tom broke down weeping. Esmie held him and stroked his hair.

'It's all right, my darling,' she crooned. 'He's safe. Our boy is safe.'

Stella's chest constricted at the sight. With a nod from Hester, they both retreated inside the hotel and left the Lomaxes alone.

Chapter 25

Ebbsmouth, June 1940

The overcrowded train shunted into Ebbsmouth late at night. They had travelled without lights on but the midsummer night shed an eerie glow through the windows. Andrew could see the outline of figures around him, hunched on benches or hunkered down on the floor, asleep or smoking in silence. Some, like him, were still in grubby combat clothing, stinking and utterly exhausted. Most were heading on to Edinburgh or Glasgow.

Stiffly, Andrew stood up and stepped over sleeping bodies to get to the carriage door. He felt a mix of relief to be in sight of home and dread at leaving the other soldiers who had been through what he had. Every time he closed his eyes, he saw the horror of the retreat through Belgium and France; the roads clogged with fleeing civilians being bombed from above. He couldn't rid his senses of the stench of rotting flesh and cordite, the screams of the dying and the sight of lifeless children strewn in ditches like rag dolls.

'Good luck, sir.' One of the soldiers – Jocks as they were affectionately known in the Scottish regiments – saluted him.

Andrew shook him by the hand. 'And good luck to you too, Private.'

In the half-dark, Andrew saw indistinct figures at the station barrier. He could see that one wore a large hat with a feather: Auntie Tibby. His eyes smarted and he felt a flood of affection. It took him back to his very first arrival as a callow youth on this very same platform – with Stella at his side – meeting his Ebbsmouth relations for the first time. Fleetingly, he wondered if word had got through to his father that he was safely returned from France. Did Stella know and, if so, how much would it mean to her?

Andrew shook off the thought. He was about to be reunited with some of the people he cared for most.

His mother rushed at him first. 'My darling!' Lydia clasped him, swallowing down a sob.

He patted her back. 'I'm fine. A bit smelly, but all in one piece.'

She pulled away and fumbled for a handkerchief. 'Yes, you do rather whiff.' She half-laughed, half-cried. 'Surely they could have given you a good bath and fresh clothes?'

'It was all a bit chaotic,' Andrew said, suppressing the memory of being crammed onto an overloaded merchant ship with men dying of their wounds and medics frantically trying to staunch blood and save lives. 'They just wanted to get people onto trains and north as quickly as possible.'

Tibby hugged him, not caring what state he was in. 'I'm so glad to see you home, dear boy. I've wired your father to let him know you're safe.'

'Thank you, Auntie.' Andrew kissed her cheek.

'Where's your kit bag?' Lydia asked.

'In France, Mamma,' Andrew said with a grim smile.

'Oh goodness. Oh, yes. I really can't bear to think what you've been through,' said Lydia. 'We'll not talk about it. Come on, let's get you home.' She steered him out of the station, chattering in relief. 'Felicity wanted to come and greet you too, but I said she would have to wait till tomorrow. I want you to myself for a few hours – I know how she monopolises you once you're home. Will they let you stay long?'

'Not long,' said Andrew, feeling weak with fatigue. He could hardly put one foot in front of the other. He was relieved Felicity wasn't going to see him like this.

'You look dead on your feet,' said Tibby. 'Go straight home. No need to drop me off at The Anchorage, Lydia, I'll walk back.'

Lydia didn't insist. As she drove Andrew up to Templeton Hall in the gloaming, she said, 'Tibby's been a bit of a brick while you've been gone. She comes over with eggs and cheese, and she sits with Mother and talks to her about flowers. Every Tuesday she has your grandmother for the day and gives me a break.' She glanced at Andrew. 'I never thought I'd say this, but your aunt is really rather a nice person. Still mad as a March hare – but a kind soul.'

'Yes, she is,' Andrew agreed, not adding that he'd always known Tibby was special but had never said so for fear of upsetting his mother. Lydia needed constant reassuring that she was loved above all others.

'There's hot water for a bath,' said Lydia as they entered the house. 'And a cold supper of cheese, oatcakes and potato scones. We'll crack open a nice Vouvray I've had chilling.'

Andrew hardly had the energy to speak, let alone bathe and eat.

'I just want to crawl into bed, Mamma,' he said. 'I hope you don't mind?'

She didn't mask her disappointment. 'Oh, well, I suppose not.'

'We'll have plenty of time together tomorrow,' said Andrew. 'I promise.'

Lydia put a hand to his cheek, her eyes filling with tears. 'I can't tell you how glad I am to see you home . . . Whatever happens in this beastly war, I feel so much safer with you around, my darling.'

He kissed her forehead. Better to say nothing rather than promise he would be around to protect her – he had no idea where he might be sent next. The country would be bracing itself for invasion. These next few days at Ebbsmouth would be precious because none of them knew what lay ahead.

While his mother wanted no talk about the horrors of the retreat, Felicity demanded details. Andrew was rather taken aback by her curiosity at the carnage and heroics on the beaches of northern France.

They were walking along the cliff close to The Anchorage – the cove was fenced off and out of bounds to civilians – when she pressed him for more stories.

'I feel so useless here,' said Felicity. 'The most exciting thing I do is try to catch people out for not closing their blinds properly. But you've seen real life-and-death action. Tell me more about the rescue from Dunkirk.'

Andrew felt a wave of anxiety overcome him as his mind recalled what had taken place. The fighting had been hard and attritional.

'We were trying to protect those getting onto the ships first,' he said. 'Allow the medics time to patch up and evacuate the wounded.'

'Were you being bombed the whole time too?' she asked.

'Yes.'

'Did it go on for days?'

'Days, yes.'

'You must have been one of the last off?'

'No.' Andrew stopped and gazed out over the blue-grey sea. 'There were Indian troops still there firing on the Germans as we waded out to a boat.'

'Indian?' Felicity echoed in surprise. 'Whatever were Indians doing in France?'

'They were part of the Expeditionary Force,' Andrew explained. 'Mule companies – providing transport.'

'Carrying the baggage, you mean?'

'Not just that – pulling guns – and fighting too,' said Andrew.

He thought of the muleteers he'd seen having to shoot their animals to stop them falling into enemy hands and then spiking abandoned guns. Just hearing them shouting above the din in Urdu, the language of the Indian Army, and seeing them stoically turning to fight off the advancing Nazis with bayonets, had raised his morale.

Thinking about them now and wondering if any of them had survived stirred something deep in the core of him. He had had snatched conversations with a couple of them – men from the Punjab – whose weary faces had lit with smiles of delight at his greeting them in a language they understood.

'So it wasn't just the British troops at Dunkirk?' she asked.

Andrew looked at her. 'Of course not. There were French and Belgian – and soldiers from our empires – Africans and Algerians. Men from all over.'

'How interesting.' Her eyes were wide in amazement.

Suddenly, Andrew didn't want to talk about it any more. For a few short, blessed days, he wanted to bury the memories and think only of the present. He filled his lungs with sea air and put his arm about Felicity's shoulders.

'This is far more interesting being here with you.' He smiled.

She turned into his hold and slipped her arms around his neck.

'Kiss me then.' She grinned up at him.

Andrew did so gladly.

Chapter 26

The Raj-in-the-Hills, Gulmarg, late June 1940

The Lomaxes' relief at hearing of Andrew's safe return to Britain was followed swiftly by worry over his safety in Scotland – and that of Tibby and others. News came through of serious bombing raids on Scotland. The radio bulletins were vague, citing only that there were attacks from over the North Sea. Tom scoured the newspapers for further details but it was only when a wire came through from Tibby that all was well in Ebbsmouth that Esmie could persuade him to stop worrying.

Tom, however, continued to be obsessive in listening to radio broadcasts and reading the papers to know what was going on at home.

'Now that the Nazis have taken over Norway,' he fretted, 'they can launch attacks easily on east-coast Scotland.'

Yet up at Gulmarg, in the tranquillity of the mountains, Stella found it hard to believe they were at war. The Gujjars appeared with their herds and flocks as they did every hot season and the 'grass widows' of public servants brought their children on holiday. The baroness returned to spend a leisurely summer on her rented houseboat on Dal Lake just as usual. The hot temperatures broke as the monsoon rains came in thunderous downpours and laced the mountains in mist.

One day, a consignment of sea mail arrived from Scotland. Mostly it was magazines sent to Esmie by Tibby, but there was also a letter for Stella.

'Looks like Andrew's handwriting,' Esmie said, handing it over with an enquiring look.

Stella took it. Andrew hadn't written to her for three years. She pretended that she didn't mind, but it had hurt her a little that he hadn't written to give his condolences when her father had died. Charlie had always made a fuss of Andrew at the hotel. She had blamed herself for writing a reproachful letter criticising him for never returning to his parents in India. She'd vented her frustration on Andy instead of the real culprit, Lydia, and had regretted it ever since.

'It's months out of date,' she said, tearing it open with a finger. The postmark was from February.

> *Dear Stella,*
>
> *I feel very bad for not having written this earlier but I'm arranging my affairs before getting my marching orders with the battalion. I wanted to say how very sorry I was to hear of your father's sudden passing. I can't quite believe he isn't still standing in the lobby of the Raj greeting everyone with a cheery good morning and a comment about how lovely the weather is – even when it was as hot as hell and everyone was sweating like the proverbial pig!*
>
> *Mr Dubois was one of the kindest and most considerate men I've ever met. He was only ever interested in others – no matter how young or*

unimportant they were. He always made me feel
special as a cherished boy whom he treated like one
of his own.
I know how much you cared for your dad . . .

Stella's vision blurred with tears. She sat down abruptly on a cane chair in the office and pressed her hand to her chest.

'Stella, are you all right?' Esmie asked in concern.

Stella nodded, unable to stop tears rolling down her cheeks. 'It's such a lovely letter about Dad,' she said, croakily.

'Can I get you anything?' Esmie asked gently.

'No, thanks.' She wiped at her tears and read on.

I know how much you cared for your dad so can
only imagine how bereft you must be feeling – your
mother and brother too. Charlie Dubois touched
many, many lives and we'll all miss him greatly.
I'm sorry, Stella, that I've been tardy in writing
to you. It's a lame excuse, but I felt that as long as
I didn't write about it then it didn't seem real – a
selfish reason, I know.
Take care of yourself and please pass on my deep-
est sympathies to Mrs Dubois and Jimmy.
Fond regards,
Andrew

Stella let out a sob and passed the letter to Esmie. 'Read it. It's beautiful.'

As Esmie was about to take it, she said, 'There's a P.S. on the back of the sheet. I didn't see you read it.'

Stella turned it over.

P.S. I hesitate to put this in the same letter but time is short and I thought you should know. Last week, I was in Edinburgh seeing a film with my girlfriend when I bumped into an old acquaintance of yours – Hugh Keating . . .

Stella gasped. Her hands shook.

He was there with his cousin Caroline. We had a brief chat and it turns out he's still working in India (though not in the agricultural service). He's with McSween and Watson Agricultural Agents in Calcutta.

He asked after you and said he was heartbroken that you'd never replied to his letter, so I took the liberty of telling him that you had very much wanted to but his letter had been lost. I also told him you were still at the Raj and (as far as I knew) fancy-free. I've since rather regretted doing so – in case it causes you embarrassment if he contacts you. My girlfriend seemed convinced his so-called cousin was actually some other man's wife – based on nothing but instinct, so perhaps unfair on poor Mr Keating. Anyway, it's done and you're forewarned. If I know anything about you, Stella, it's that you are perfectly capable of handling amorous Irishmen and the like, if needs be.

Stella's heart pounded. What a shock to hear about Hugh after all this time. He'd asked after her. He was still in India! Had he enquired about her just to be polite or did he still have feelings for her? She could just imagine him claiming to be 'heartbroken' in his joking, self-deprecating way.

She passed the letter to Esmie who read it quickly.

'What a very loving letter,' said Esmie, her eyes shining with emotion. 'Andy puts it so well – how much everyone loved Charlie.'

'Yes, he does.' Stella could feel her cheeks burning.

Esmie eyed her. 'And this Hugh Keating?'

Stella knew she could say anything to Esmie in confidence and she longed to unburden herself about Hugh. 'I met him on the ship to Britain,' she said. 'We started a romance but I think Andrew put him off – he was being overprotective, I suppose – even though I was meant to be the one looking after him.' Stella gave a rueful look. 'Hugh wrote to Ebbsmouth and asked me to be his girl. But I'm pretty sure Lydia destroyed the letter and I couldn't remember the address in Dublin he gave me. I wrote to him in Baluchistan too – but it was sent back, as he'd left government service and there was no forwarding address.'

'So, is this welcome news that you know where Mr Keating is?' Esmie asked.

'Yes,' Stella admitted. 'Very welcome. I've never felt such an instant attraction to any man before or since.'

Esmie gave her a smile of understanding. 'Will you write to him in Calcutta?'

Stella hesitated. Andrew had bumped into Hugh over four months ago and yet Hugh hadn't attempted to get in touch so far. Of course it was possible he was still in Scotland and hadn't been able to get back out to India – even so, he could still have written. Tom had been full of an anxious story the other day about a ship full of evacuees from Britain being torpedoed in the Arabian Sea just a couple of days away from Bombay. Lives had been lost. Suddenly she was worried that Hugh might have been on it.

'No, I'll wait and see if he writes to me.' Stella met Esmie's look. 'I know that I still feel strongly for Hugh but I don't want him feeling sorry for me or that he has to reply out of a sense of duty. If he does contact me then I'll know it's because he really wants to see me again.'

Esmie covered her hand with hers and squeezed it. 'That sounds very sensible.' She smiled and gave back the letter.

Stella knew she would be racing to check the post every day from now on.

The summer passed swiftly, but no letter came from Hugh. Stella wavered in her resolve not to contact him first. What harm would there be in sending him a note via his company to say that Andrew had told her about their chance meeting in Edinburgh? But she resisted. Some instinct told her to be patient.

The Lomaxes were cheered by a letter to Tom from Andrew saying that he was in good fettle and back with his regiment on defensive duties. He was sad to report, though, that his good friend Noel Langley had been taken prisoner in France.

August came and Tom kept Stella informed of the increasingly grim daily bulletins about the war at home with air raids, mass casualties and destruction.

The talk on the hotel veranda was more about the situation in East and North Africa where the Italians had captured British Somaliland and were now bombing Egypt and the Suez Canal. Airmail had once again been stopped and troops were being mobilised in India.

'This is where the Indian Army will come in,' said a police officer on leave from Lahore. 'We've run down our fighting force since the Great War but now we'll be needed.'

Stella turned twenty-eight. She dwelled on the thought that life was passing her by. What had she done with her life since returning from Scotland? She had been content to carry on helping run the two hotels with no real ambition to do anything else. She was nearly the same age as Yvonne, yet her sister-in-law had shown far more initiative. Not only was she making herself indispensable at the Raj, she was a wife and mother.

It made Stella realise how much she wanted to be a mother herself. But there was no point hankering after something she couldn't have; that joy would only come once she was married. She wondered if Monty wanted to be a father. They had written very spasmodically to each other while he was away training at Roorkee. She suspected that he wasn't any more enthusiastic about marrying her than she was at being his wife.

Stella decided that, now she knew that Hugh was still in India, she would break off her courtship with Monty once and for all. Even if nothing came of it with Hugh, she wouldn't hold Monty back from finding someone he really loved and could love him back in the way he deserved. She knew that her feelings for Hugh were still strong and she wouldn't settle for a husband whom she didn't love wholeheartedly.

In this new determined frame of mind, she also decided she would take her future in hand and do something for the war effort. She would volunteer in Rawalpindi for the Women's Auxiliary Corps of India.

Stella told the Lomaxes of her reasons why she wished to return to Rawalpindi more promptly than in previous years. 'Apart from wanting to sign up for the WAC, I'm missing baby Charles,' she admitted. 'He'll have changed so much in the past four months. I hope you don't mind?'

'Of course not,' said Esmie. 'The numbers are dropping off now and we'll soon be shutting up the hotel.'

'And it's a fine thing you're doing,' said Tom, 'offering to help out as a volunteer.'

Stella was touched by his encouragement.

'You'll let me know if you hear anything more from Andrew, won't you?' Stella asked. 'Or from Tibby about how things are in Scotland.'

'I promise we will,' Tom replied.

'And,' Esmie added, 'we'll be down to see you all at Christmas time.'

Stella met up with the baroness in Srinagar and they travelled back to Rawalpindi together. She told Hester the latest news about Andrew and also confided about her hope that Hugh Keating would get in touch.

'It seems ridiculous that I should still have such strong feelings for a man I haven't seen for over seven years, but I do.'

Hester said, 'True love takes no account of time or distance. You just have to listen to your heart. If I were you, I'd write to him.'

'Really?' Stella was doubtful.

'Darling, life is so uncertain. None of us knows what will happen in this war with Germany and Italy. If I was young like you, I'd seize whatever happiness I could get. If he doesn't reply, then he's not worth it and you won't be any worse off.'

As soon as Stella was back at the Raj, spurred on by Hester's words, she wrote a brief but friendly letter to Hugh and sent it off to McSween and Watson's in Calcutta.

Chapter 27

Ebbsmouth, October 1940

The country had been braced for invasion since the summer. Andrew's machine-gun company was on constant alert along the Berwickshire coastline. The beaches were bristling with rows of barbed wire defences and hastily positioned concrete tank traps. Crouched in dank pillboxes, their guns pointing through narrow loopholes, they watched out for enemy ships. Now that Norway had fallen to the Nazis, it seemed a matter of time before an invasion across the North Sea began.

There had been damaging air raids on Edinburgh and its port of Leith in late September. One clear night, Andrew had seen the sky glowing to the north and knew that the docks were aflame from incendiary bombs. The sky had filled with the scream and flash of anti-aircraft fire as the Scottish units retaliated. The toll of merchantmen sunk was rising weekly. Yet the invasion did not come.

Andrew snatched a welcome two days' leave and went back home. Lydia was ecstatic to see him.

After he'd helped her get his grandmother to bed, Lydia settled him by the fire with a glass of port. His mother was obviously managing to find something in her father's cellar to drink.

'At least I have one of my boys home,' she said with a contended sigh.

'Where is Uncle Dickie?' Andrew asked.

'London. Something in intelligence, I think. Not that he's allowed to say what he's doing. I've been terribly worried about him with all this awful blitz on London.'

Andrew grew drowsy by the fire and found it comforting just to listen to his mother gossiping without interruption.

Having rung Felicity and made plans to see her at teatime, Andrew cycled over to his aunt's while his mother had her hair done. Tibby shrieked in delight and kissed him on both cheeks.

'I'm just on my way out to deliver these vegetables to the old folks,' she told him.

'Let me help you,' said Andrew.

'No, you go and see Dawan. He's missing male company. Walter's been called up and Mac's gone home to Greentoun to look after his mother as both his brothers are now in the forces. I'll be back as soon as I can.'

Andrew found Dawan in the library sewing by hand. He quickly abandoned the work to greet Andrew.

'Your aunt is teaching me to mend clothes,' he said bashfully.

'Gandhi would be proud of you,' Andrew said in amusement. 'We army boys know how to sew on buttons too, you know.'

They sat by the fire and had a few minutes catching up about Walter and Mac leaving and the general war situation. But without Tibby there to complain about them talking politics, it wasn't long before they were having a robust conversation about the political situation in India.

'I think Congress is missing a trick in not supporting the war effort,' said Andrew. 'It won't do them any favours in the future when it comes to wanting more self-rule.'

Dawan waved his hands. 'They offered to do just that but the Britisher government turned them down. Wouldn't even consider independence.'

'Maybe not independence,' said Andrew, 'but they could have asked for something lesser, like home rule. It just seems petty to resign all their positions on the provincial governments.'

'You are looking at it through the eyes of a Scotsman,' Dawan said dismissively. 'You have forgotten how to look with Indian eyes.'

Andrew was wounded by the remark but could hardly deny it. His time in India seemed like a remote dream – vivid but no longer part of his life.

'Who's got Indian eyes?' Unexpectedly, Felicity bounded into the room, pulling off her hat and patting at her neat fair hair.

'Not me, apparently,' said Andrew, leaping to his feet. 'This is a nice surprise.' He kissed her cold pink cheek.

'I think you have gorgeous eyes,' said Felicity, kissing him on the lips.

'And have I ever told you how alluring you look in uniform?'

Felicity laughed. 'Yes, often.' She turned to Dawan. 'Hello, Mr Lal. I hope you don't mind me barging in on your cosy chat. But I haven't seen Andrew for weeks.'

'Of course not, Miss Douglas.' Dawan gave a gracious nod.

'So did Mamma tell you I was here?' Andrew asked.

'No, I bumped into Tibby distributing cauliflowers to the old folk up the lane. She told me where to find you. I'm not sure your mother would have.' Felicity laughed.

Dawan made for the door. 'Let me leave you lovebirds alone. Tell Tibby I'll be in the studio.'

As soon as he was gone, Felicity pushed Andrew back onto the sofa, sat on his lap and began kissing him.

'I've missed you so much,' she said, as they caught their breath.

'Me too,' said Andrew. 'Do you want to go for a walk while it's not raining?'

'No, I hate walking.' She traced a finger across his jaw. 'I can think of other exercise I'd rather be doing with you.'

Andrew laughed. 'Miss Douglas, I'm shocked.'

'That's the trouble with you, Andrew,' she said. 'You're far too honourable. I get propositioned weekly by chaps in the Home Guard. Trust me to fall for Scotland's most morally upright second lieutenant.'

'What chaps in the Home Guard?' he asked.

'Oh, do I detect a twinge of jealousy?' She smirked.

'I hope they're over sixty and missing most of their teeth,' he teased.

'How rude!' She gave him a playful pat on the cheek. 'Don't you think I can attract other young men?'

'I don't doubt it,' said Andrew. 'But I hope you resist their advances. Otherwise I'll have to start challenging my rivals to a dual.'

'Then give me a good reason to remain constant to you, Andrew Lomax.'

'Meaning?'

'Show that you love me – and only me,' she said. 'Enough that you want to marry me.'

Andrew tensed. 'I thought we'd agreed to take things steadily? It's all too uncertain – we could be fighting off an invasion any day.'

She gripped his chin. 'Exactly! That's why we should just do what we're both dying to do and say to hell with the consequences. This time tomorrow, we might both be blown to kingdom come by a Nazi bomb. I don't want to die a virgin!'

Andrew began to laugh.

Abruptly, she smacked his cheek and climbed off his knee. 'Don't laugh at me! I'm not some silly girl who you can trifle with. I'm nearly nineteen and I know my own mind.'

Andrew felt chastened. 'Of course you do. I'm sorry.'

'You obviously don't feel the same way as I do,' said Felicity, her eyes glistening with angry tears. 'So let's just forget about it. I'll find some other man who appreciates what I have to give – a real man.'

She picked up her discarded hat and marched to the door.

Andrew got up. 'You don't mean that? Don't go, Flis-Tish—'

'I'm not your Flis-Tish!' she cried. 'And I do mean it.'

She slammed the door behind her and left him staring at it in disbelief.

Tibby found Andrew out in the garden smoking a cigarette.

'Felicity gone already?' she asked.

He nodded.

'Want to talk about it over a pot of weak tea? We still have one precious caddy of Darjeeling left that Esmie sent.'

Andrew gave a grateful smile. Some of his happiest moments had been at Tibby's kitchen table drinking potfuls of tea. He liked the way she never foisted liquor on him as his mother and fellow officers did.

Later, as they sat sipping tea in the gloom of a kitchen only lit by weak autumnal sun, Tibby listened to his outpouring about Felicity.

'So, basically,' Tibby summed up, 'she wants to rush headlong into marriage and you don't?'

Andrew looked sheepish. 'I'm not sure she does want to marry me   I think she just wants to have intercourse.'

Tibby gave a snort of laughter. 'Most men I know would be happy with that.' Seeing his embarrassment, she added quickly, 'Dear boy, you're far more special than most men. I know you're shying away from taking advantage of Felicity but it seems to me she knows her own mind. The question is, do you love her?'

'Yes,' said Andrew.

He can't have sounded convincing, because Tibby pressed him. 'Enough to marry her?'

'I think so.' Andrew wrestled with his thoughts. 'I just want us to take our time over things. We're both young . . .'

'A lasting relationship needs more than just sex,' said Tibby. 'You need common interests too. Can you see yourself with Felicity in five – ten – fifty years' time?'

Andrew gave a self-conscious laugh. 'Is that how you and Dawan feel about each other?'

'Don't change the subject.'

Andrew shrugged. 'We're at war and I'm in the army. I can't see beyond next week let alone next year or the year after.'

'You're still avoiding the question,' Tibby pointed out. 'If you can't answer it then you probably shouldn't be marrying Felicity.'

Andrew tried to make light of it. 'That's the trouble with having frank conversations with my unconventional aunt – you tell me the brutal truth.'

Tibby gave a compassionate smile. 'Dear Andy, you don't need to take any heed of my advice. I will support whatever you decide.'

His heart squeezed at her calling him Andy. It was the childhood name his father and Esmie had always used – and Stella. He didn't want to think of them. To do so was too unsettling. His life was here, and the choice he had to make was whether he wanted to share his future in Scotland with Felicity or not.

Chapter 28

Stella carried around Hugh's letter and pulled it out to read whenever she had a moment alone. The paper was tearing at the creases with the constant folding and unfolding. Her insides somersaulted every time she reread it, even though she knew the words by heart.

> *My dear Stella,*
>
> *What a surprise and a delight it was to receive your letter! I was on the point of writing to you myself, having discovered from Andrew that you were still in Pindi. It was fate brought me and young Lomax together that night. If we hadn't met, I would never have known that you had tried to write back to me. All these years I have lived with the thought that you didn't care for me and hadn't thought of me since. But now I'm daring to hope that you still have some affection for me. Do I hope in vain?*
>
> *I'm travelling a lot at the moment and only picked up your letter this week. I'm helping the government with sourcing supplies for the forces. I hope very much to get up to the Punjab soon and will*

endeavour to visit you in Pindi if I can. First, I must
know if the lovely Dubois girl with the pretty green
eyes would want to see me again? Please write to me
soon, Stella, and let me know.
    Affectionately yours,
    Hugh

Stella had written straight back but had heard nothing since. That was three weeks ago. She assured herself that he was away travelling again and would reply as soon as he was back in Calcutta. She was thrilled at the turn of events. How clever of Andrew to have spotted Hugh in Edinburgh. She would write and thank him when she wasn't so busy.

Her life was filled with purpose these days. She got up early to help in the hotel and then went to do clerical duties for the WAC at one of the metal workshops that were making hinges and handles for army supplies. She returned home in time to play with Charles before he was bathed and put to bed by his ayah.

By the time Stella had returned from Gulmarg in September, Charles had developed a lot since she'd last seen him in May. He was sitting up, pointing and laughing, and four more teeth had come through. She loved his soft dark hair, round brown eyes and chubby chin. Recently he had been attempting to crawl.

One November day, on the bungalow veranda in the mellow afternoon sunshine, Stella was encouraging her sturdy nephew by putting him on his tummy, getting down beside him and crawling herself. Her mother watched from a cane chair where she was putting up her feet for five minutes.

Stella then sat him on her knee and began singing nursery rhymes, helping him clap his hands and count his fingers.

Her mother rolled her eyes but couldn't help an indulgent smile. 'I don't know why you turned down that Gibson boy – it's obvious you're longing to have your own child.'

Stella was startled at the truth of it. 'Monty wasn't the right man for me,' she replied.

Her mother was frank. 'You can't be too choosy at your age.'

Stella tried not to show the remark hurt. 'So you keep telling me, Ma.'

'Well, I just want to see you settled. Your father did too . . .'

Stella cuddled Charles closer.

Just then, Jimmy appeared in the courtyard. 'Stella, there's someone to see you. I've just checked him into the Lytton Room and he said he'd wait for you in the sitting room.'

Her heart skipped a beat. 'Oh?'

'Says he knows you from your trip to Scotland. A Mr Keating.'

Stella could feel the heat flood her cheeks. She handed Charles to her mother and quickly stood up, brushing the dust from her skirt. She tried to calm her thumping pulse by tidying her hair and taking deep breaths. He hadn't replied, but he'd come in person instead!

'Is this the mystery man whose letter you keep on you the whole time?' her mother asked suspiciously.

'Yes,' Stella admitted. She didn't want to deny it and her mother was about to find out how she felt about Hugh anyway.

'Jimmy, go and keep an eye on your sister,' Myrtle fussed.

Jimmy chuckled. 'Stella's quite old enough to deal with this herself. Give me my little treasure for a minute. The baroness is complaining she hasn't seen him all day.'

Stella didn't wait. She hurried across the courtyard and down the hotel corridor to the far sitting room. As she entered, she heard his still-familiar laugh.

Hugh was sitting and chatting with Mr Tamang and Mrs Shankley. He rose on sight of her and smiled. He looked older, his wavy hair receding at the temples and his fair face more lined. But his dark-blue eyes shone with merriment and his broad smile made her stomach flip again. He reached for a walking stick and came towards her, limping slightly. Andrew hadn't told her he was still lame in the leg. Her heart went out to him. Perhaps that was the reason why he'd left Baluchistan.

She crossed the room to meet him.

'Mr Keating.' She put out her hand.

'Hugh, please.' He took her hand and kissed it. 'You're even more beautiful than I remembered. It's so wonderful to see you, Stella.'

Stella felt ridiculously happy and yet tearful at the same time. 'You too.'

They gazed at each other for a long moment, grinning.

Breathlessly she asked, 'Have you been practising your backgammon?'

He gave her a quizzical look. She prompted, 'When we parted on the boat, you said you would practise so that when we met again you might beat me.'

Hugh laughed. 'So I did. I can't say I'm much better, but I'm happy to try.'

Stella was aware of the other guests watching them with interest. She recovered her poise. 'Please, Hugh, sit down. I'll join you for a few minutes.'

They sat in armchairs next to each other. Hugh raised his voice so that Mrs Shankley could hear. 'Stella, I've been chatting to two of your fans here. Mrs Shankley couldn't speak more highly of you.'

'She's the dearest girl,' agreed Winifred.

'I'm so sorry to hear that your father passed away. You talked about him a lot on the boat.'

242

Stella nodded, clutching at his hand. Her throat constricted. 'I wish you'd met him. I think you both would have got on so well together.'

Mr Tamang and Mrs Shankley began reminiscing about Charlie. Stella was touched by the way Hugh encouraged them with questions and patiently repeated himself to the deaf missionary. Yet she longed to speak to him alone.

'How long are you in Pindi?' she asked.

'Four days. I'll be busy with meetings during the day but I intend keeping my evenings free for backgammon with the Raj champion.'

Stella smiled. 'Good. I was hoping you'd say that.'

'After dinner tonight then?' Hugh suggested.

'Agreed.' She stood up. 'I must go and help with Charles.'

He looked at her enquiringly.

'My nephew,' she explained. 'Jimmy's son. He's the most adorable ten-month-old baby in the whole world.'

'Ah, a baby! I'm glad I'm not competing with a grown man,' Hugh teased.

Stella laughed. 'I'll see you later.'

'I'll look forward to it,' he said, standing politely as she left.

Stella felt joyful. Hugh hadn't changed; he was still the warm, amusing, attentive man that she had fallen for so easily on the ship. It was as if the years in between had never been. The baroness had been right; time and distance didn't matter when you loved someone enough. She knew instinctively that Hugh was the man for her.

'You caused quite a stir at dinner tonight,' Stella said in amusement, sitting under the portico with Hugh much later that evening. It was chilly and she had a rug tucked around her knees. The residents and her family had gone to bed and only the chowkidar was within hearing distance as he patrolled the front lawn. 'I'm sorry if the baroness bombarded you with questions, but I'd told her about you before. She's finding it very romantic that you've come looking for me after all this time.'

'Hester is delightful,' said Hugh. 'They all are. I can see why you're so fond of the regulars. Though I'm not sure I can keep up with Fritters and his chota pegs. Just as well I'm only here a few days.'

The comment made Stella sad. 'Don't say that. You've only just arrived.'

He took her hand quickly and kissed it. 'I didn't mean it like that. I'm the happiest man in India to be sitting here in the dark with the prettiest girl in the world.'

Stella chuckled. 'Oh, Hugh, I've missed you. Tell me what you've been doing since we met. I've told you my story – not that there was much to tell.'

He threaded her fingers in his. 'I've not much to tell either.'

'Why did you leave your job in Baluchistan?'

He sighed and tapped his leg. 'I'll always be lame in this leg. I couldn't ride well and didn't feel I could do my job properly. Horseback was the main way to get around the deserts and mountains – it's the way I gained respect among the tribesmen. Perhaps it was stubborn of me, but I decided to leave the service rather than do a job badly.'

'Stubborn maybe,' said Stella, 'but honourable. Is that when you decided to join McSween and Watson?'

'Not immediately.' He paused. 'I stayed in Ireland for a while. My father needed help on the family farm – I'm the only son – and I felt duty bound. But then . . .'

He paused again and Stella had the impression he was finding it difficult to talk about.

'You don't have to tell me if you don't want to.'

'No, I do want to.' He cleared his throat. 'My father died after a long illness and the farm was sold. I wanted my mother and sister to have a secure income so the money went on an annuity and a smaller place to live in.'

'I'm so sorry,' said Stella. 'Were you close to your father?'

Hugh nodded.

'I know how that feels.' Stella squeezed his hand. They fell silent, then she asked, 'I thought your sister was married and lived in Dublin? Mrs Henry French.'

He looked momentarily startled. 'Fancy you remembering that. Yes, that's my other sister – the older one.'

'I wrote to you care of her,' Stella said, 'but I couldn't remember the address. Andrew's mother pretended she'd mislaid your letter but I'm sure she destroyed it.'

'What an unpleasant woman,' Hugh said. 'You haven't really told me about the Scotland trip in any detail. Is now the time?'

Stella sighed. 'No, let's leave it. It's a long sorry saga and I don't want to dwell on it when I've got you here to myself.'

'Fine,' said Hugh, moving closer. 'Then maybe we can do what I've been longing to do all evening?'

Stella's pulse quickened. 'Which is?'

He leaned over and kissed her on the lips.

Heart thudding, Stella said, 'Again, please.'

She parted her lips and this time Hugh kissed her for longer. Stella thrilled at his embrace and the way he touched her face. She could have sat there all night kissing, but the chowkidar called out at something or someone beyond the gate. They broke apart.

'I must let you get to bed,' she said huskily. 'And Ma will be waiting up to make sure I do too.'

Hugh smiled and kissed her on the nose. 'I'll have to be content with dreaming about you then, Miss Dubois.'

They went inside together. As she climbed the stairs, she heard Hugh walking off down the lower corridor to his room. She couldn't stop grinning. It was like being on the ship again with them going off to separate cabins. Except she was no longer a naive twenty-year-old and she wanted more from Hugh than stolen kisses and games of backgammon. She wished him to be a part of her life.

The four precious days that Hugh spent at the Raj flew by far too quickly for Stella. In the early mornings, she met him at dawn for a stroll along the Mall. Dew sparkled like jewels on the grass and wreaths of mist hung in the trees as the sun broke through. The air was filled with the pungent scent of dung fires and out of the mist trotted horses being exercised by their officers. Hugh, despite his limp, was an energetic walker. With Stella on his good side, he linked her arm in his and encouraged her to chat about the day ahead.

In the evenings, after dinner, she would join him in the sitting room by the fire and they'd play whist with Ansom and Hester, and then backgammon together. Stella would wait with impatience for the others to retire to bed so she could be alone with Hugh and sit out on the porch kissing in the dark.

'They all adore you,' Stella said on his final evening. 'The baroness said if she was half her age, she'd be vying with me for your attention.'

Hugh chuckled. 'Don't tell Hester, but you'd win the contest by a mile. You're the girl for me.'

'And you're the man for me, Hugh.'

He stroked her cheek, looking reflective. 'I'm not sure your mother thinks I am.'

Stella felt uncomfortable. Her mother had not taken to Hugh with the enthusiasm she had hoped for – despite Jimmy and Yvonne's approval. In fact, Stella had argued with her about Hugh the previous night.

'You hardly know the man and yet you're throwing yourself at him,' Myrtle had fretted. 'We know nothing about his family or what he gets up to in Calcutta. Can you even be sure he's not married?'

'Ma, don't say such a thing! Hugh is a man of honour and I love him.'

Her mother had relented. 'Stella, I know you do. I'm sorry, but I just don't want you rushing into anything with someone you met on a ship when you were twenty.'

'I won't do anything rash, I promise.'

Now sitting beside Hugh, she realised that he had been well aware of her mother's wariness towards him.

'Ma is just being protective of me,' said Stella. 'With Pa not being here to take care of things, she worries more.'

'Then she's a good mother,' said Hugh. 'What is it she's worried about?'

Stella steeled herself to be frank. 'Not knowing enough about you. The other boys who've courted me – she's known them and their families for years. She's afraid you might already be married.'

Hugh looked at her dumbfounded. 'Is that what you think too?'

'No, of course not. I know you better than that. But maybe you could reassure her?'

He seized her hand. 'I feel I've been waiting all my life for you, Stella. How can your mother not see how much I'm in love with you?'

Stella hesitated. He hadn't actually said he wasn't married. She pressed him. 'So, there's no Mrs Keating waiting for you back in Calcutta?'

He looked at her gravely with his mesmerising blue eyes and she held her breath.

'I swear to you there isn't.' He said it with such vehemence that Stella felt ashamed for asking.

'Kiss me,' she whispered.

'Do you believe me?' Hugh persisted, hurt in his eyes.

'Yes, of course. I'm sorry for doubting . . .'

He silenced her with a passionate kiss.

Afterwards, he said, 'I just want to make you happy, Stella.'

'You do make me happy,' she insisted. 'I can't bear the thought of you going away tomorrow. When will I see you again?'

'I'll come back when I can. Will you write to me, Stella, so I know you're thinking of me?'

She gave him a tearful smile and nodded. Then they kissed one last time.

Chapter 29

The Raj Hotel, spring 1941

Stella's romance with Hugh blossomed over the next few months. He managed to be sent on regular trips to the Punjab for work. Even if it was in the south of the state, he would snatch a night or two in Rawalpindi to see her. She was especially pleased that he went out of his way to charm her mother and reassure her.

'I cherish your daughter, Mrs Dubois. I'd do nothing to hurt her, I promise.'

Stella had never been so happy. Her life was fulfilled; she had work, family life and frequent visits from Hugh. She was deeply in love and it made her optimistic about the future, even with the war.

Unexpectedly, Monty got leave in April. Stella wasn't surprised that he didn't come to see her, though she was concerned to hear from Jimmy that he was likely to be shipped out soon.

Jimmy told her, 'Most likely Iraq, he thinks. He's—' He hesitated as if changing his mind about saying something.

'Go on,' Stella said.

'He's heard about you and Hugh.'

Stella blushed. 'We broke up before Hugh came back into my life.'

Jimmy nodded. 'Then you won't mind that he's already courting someone else too?'

'No, I'd be pleased if he was,' she assured him. 'Do you know who?'

'Yes, our cousin Lucy.'

'Lucy? That's a surprise. But I'm glad for him, and for her,' said Stella. 'I think they'll make a lovely couple.'

Before Monty's leave was up, Stella heard that he had proposed to Lucy.

By May, Stella was making plans to travel with Hester to Srinagar and go on to Gulmarg as usual. She was more reluctant to leave Pindi than in previous years, knowing that it would be much more difficult for Hugh to visit her in Kashmir, but she had promised the Lomaxes that she would join them.

She had seen them only briefly at Christmas, and messages from Esmie were frank about how concerned she was over Tom's health. He worried obsessively about the war at home, and the news of heavy bombing over Scottish cities and ports since March was causing his depression to deepen. He was drinking too much still and sleeping badly.

Stella took a leave of absence from her voluntary work with the WAC and said a tearful goodbye to baby Charles, who was now toddling about and shrieking her name on sight: 'Ste-wa! Ste-wa!'

She had hoped that Hugh would get to Rawalpindi in early May before she left for Kashmir, but he wired her to say that he was being sent to Bangalore. Pining for him, she wrote expressing her wish that he might take some leave and try and get to Gulmarg to see her.

250

To Stella's dismay, she watched Tom's nerves continue to deteriorate with the worsening news from Europe. Yugoslavia had fallen to the Nazis, who had pushed on into Greece and the swastika was now flying in Athens. In early June they heard that the last troops on Crete had been evacuated by the Navy to Egypt, with heavy losses.

Esmie confided in Stella. 'However much I reassure him that Andrew is relatively safe in Scotland – that he hasn't been deployed to North Africa – Tom won't be consoled. He just goes on and on about the destruction from the bombings and the loss of civilians. I really think the only thing that would ease his mind was if Andrew came back to India and he saw for himself that his son was safe and well.'

'But that's not likely till after the war is over,' Stella pointed out. She kept to herself the concern that even then, Andrew might choose not to rush back. He appeared very settled in Scotland and had a girlfriend there.

Esmie said, 'I can't bear to think that Andy might never come back home – I think that's what's at the core of Tom's anxiety too. He feels terrible guilt about it – that somehow we pushed him away.'

'That's not true,' Stella said. 'You gave him a loving home here. It's Lydia who's to blame for turning him against you both. She was never going to let him go once he was back with her.'

'That's not how Tom sees it.' Esmie's voice was full of sadness. 'He feels that he was forced to give Andrew up as the only way of being able to marry me. I can't deny it's put a strain on our marriage – we both feel guilty for choosing to be with each other.'

Stella was aghast. Long ago, she had thought that Tom and Esmie were the epitome of a love match that nothing could break. But she saw how the strain of long years of not being able to marry properly and then their pretence at being married must have taken its toll. Even when Lydia had finally given Tom a divorce, it had been a hollow victory. By gaining marriage they had lost what they loved most: Andrew.

'I feel selfish for marrying Tom, knowing how important Andrew is to him,' Esmie agonised. 'I, of all people, knew what he'd gone through losing his first wife and baby daughter – how fragile his mental health was because of it. If we'd never married . . .'

'Don't say that,' Stella remonstrated. 'Mr Lomax wouldn't have survived without you. You've done more than anyone to help him battle his demons – and to bring up Andrew till he was thirteen years old. Andrew is the loving man he is because of the home you gave him and the example of what it is to love unconditionally.'

Esmie's grey eyes filled with tears. 'Stella, you are a kind lassie.'

'It's not kindness, it's the truth,' Stella insisted. 'And I can't believe you and Mr Lomax won't get through this bad patch. Everyone is worried about this war. But when it's over – God willing all our loved ones come through it – you could go to Scotland to visit Andy.'

Esmie nodded. 'You're right; we must stay optimistic.'

'Yes,' Stella urged, 'give Mr Lomax something to hope for.'

Esmie smiled, encouraged. 'You would make a wonderful nurse.'

In June, unexpectedly, a wire came from Hugh saying he had a week's leave and was coming to Gulmarg. Stella was overjoyed at the news.

'I haven't seen him for over two months,' she said eagerly to Esmie and Tom.

'Then you must take some time off from the hotel and spend it with him,' Esmie declared. 'Don't you think so, Tom?'

Fleetingly, a smile lit his gaunt and lined face. 'Of course she must,' he agreed. 'It's time we met this man who causes our Stella such excitement. He must be special.'

Stella grinned, gladdened to see a spark of the old teasing Tom. 'He is,' she said.

Hugh arrived on a warm afternoon, looking fit and suntanned. Stella felt the familiar butterfly sensation in her stomach at the sight of his handsome, smiling face. She ran down the path to meet him and flung her arms around him, not caring what the hotel guests on the veranda thought. She was euphoric at seeing him.

He took her hand and they mounted the hotel steps together while his luggage was brought up behind on a mule. Hugh raised his walking stick in greeting to the Lomaxes, who came onto the veranda to meet him.

Stella proudly introduced him. 'This is my friend Hugh Keating.'

Tom shook him vigorously by the hand. 'Pleased to meet you at last, Mr Keating. Stella has talked about you non-stop.'

'As I do about her to my friends,' Hugh said cheerfully. 'I know from Stella that you and Mrs Lomax are like family to her. I'm so honoured to meet you, sir.'

'Less of the sir,' Tom answered.

Esmie welcomed him warmly too. 'You must treat this like home while you're here, Mr Keating. You lead a busy life, by all accounts, so you deserve some relaxation.'

'I've got lots planned for us to do,' Stella said happily. 'I know you like golf and swimming. And we can take short walks – I'm longing to show you the high marg.'

Hugh laughed. 'Not so much relaxation then.'

'Whatever you want, of course,' said Stella quickly.

He smiled at her. 'Just being with you is all I need.'

'You Irish and your charm,' Esmie said in amusement. 'Come in, Mr Keating, and have some refreshment.'

Chapter 30

As long as Stella was around in the evening to play the piano for the guests, Esmie told her she was free to spend her time with Hugh.

'Better take Karo to chaperone you,' said Tom protectively.

The days of Hugh's leave went by too quickly for Stella. He shied away from activities with other people, so they didn't go to watch tennis or swim as she'd planned.

'I just want to be with you,' said Hugh. 'This time together is precious.'

At the end of the first day, he also persuaded Esmie that it wasn't necessary for her Pathan sewing woman to follow them about.

'We'd like to go out riding and poor Karo can't keep up,' he said. 'Stella is a mature young woman and hardly needs chaperoning – and I hope you can trust me, Mrs Lomax?'

Esmie quickly acquiesced. For the next few days, Felix packed them a picnic and they went for rides up through the woods and across the marg. Despite Hugh's knee injury he was still a skilled horseman and Stella thought it a pity he'd given up his civil service job in Baluchistan because of it.

After a morning's gentle riding, they would spread out a blanket in the shade of the trees and eat the picnic. Replete, they would lie and doze to the sound of bees buzzing among the wild flowers.

Before they left, they would kiss and cuddle, Hugh becoming more amorous as the week progressed.

Stella resisted his attempts to make love, though each day she was finding it harder to do so. She wondered at the wisdom of spending so much time alone with him away from the hotel, but she craved his company and was falling more deeply in love than ever. He made her laugh and she could talk to him about anything and everything. Above all he made her feel special and cherished.

She let him pet her but she wouldn't allow anything further. 'I won't do it until I'm married. It's the way I've been brought up.'

'I respect you for that,' said Hugh. 'But I can't deny how much I desire you.'

She hoped it might prompt him to propose, but he didn't broach the subject.

On the second to last day, Hugh seemed preoccupied and ate little of the picnic.

'What's wrong?' Stella asked. 'Aren't you feeling well?'

He took her hand in his, his expression hard to read. 'I've been putting off telling you this – I haven't wanted to spoil our week together.'

Her heart lurched. 'Tell me what?'

He looked full of regret. 'The reason I was able to snatch a week's leave is that I'm being sent to Singapore.'

Her insides plummeted. 'Singapore? But why?'

'They're reinforcing the garrison there,' said Hugh, 'and I'm to help with supplies.'

Stella clutched his hand. 'Oh, Hugh, it's so far away – and it sounds dangerous.'

He gave a brave smile. 'I'm sure it won't be. But I don't know when I'll be able to get back to India. It could be months.'

Stella's eyes stung with tears. 'I can't bear the thought of not knowing when I'll next see you.'

'I feel the same way too.' He raised her hand and kissed it. 'Stella . . .' He gazed at her with intense blue eyes. 'Will you marry me?'

She didn't know if she was more shocked by the unwelcome news or his sudden proposal. She was in turmoil; her unhappiness turning to euphoria. She threw her arms about his neck and hugged him.

'Oh yes, yes!' she cried.

He smiled in relief. 'Good! It's the only thing that will keep me going when we're apart – to know that I'll have you to come back to – that you'll wait for me.'

'Of course I will. There's never been anyone else for me.'

Hugh kissed her passionately. Stella was light-headed at such a bittersweet moment. Hugh was committed to marrying her and yet was about to go far away to the east for months on end.

Hugh whispered in her ear, 'I'm mad about you, girl. I want to show you how much I love you.'

Stella's pulse was racing. She knew what he meant.

He twirled a strand of her hair. 'But I won't do anything you don't wish me to. Do you want me as much as I want you, my green-eyed girl?'

'Yes,' she admitted. 'More than anything.'

'I'll be very careful,' Hugh said, kissing her again.

In the sweet-scented meadow, Stella finally gave herself up to his caresses and love-making.

As they made their way back down to the hotel, Stella's heart was still beating wildly at the intimacies they had shared under the sighing trees. She couldn't stop exchanging grins with Hugh at what they had done. She wished they hadn't wasted most of the week just kissing; if Hugh had proposed sooner, they could have been making love every day.

'Can we tell the Lomaxes our good news?' Stella asked.

Hugh hesitated. 'I'd rather we did it properly and I bought you a ring first.'

'But there isn't time,' Stella said in frustration.

'On the day I leave,' said Hugh, 'come down with me to Srinagar and we'll buy a ring.'

Stella's spirits lifted. It would mean precious extra hours with the man she loved.

When they returned to the hotel, Stella couldn't hide her joy or resist confiding in Esmie. 'I'm not supposed to say anything yet, but Hugh has proposed.'

Esmie stifled an exclamation and hugged her. 'I was hoping you'd say that! I'm very happy for you, lassie. I can see how much in love you are.'

'We're going to buy a ring in Srinagar when he leaves. I hope that's all right for me to take one more day off from my duties?'

'Of course it is,' said Esmie.

Then Stella told her about Hugh being sent to Singapore. 'I don't know when we can get married,' she said, feeling a wave of unhappiness again.

Esmie tried to reassure her. 'Maybe he won't be gone that long. You can still plan for a wedding. You know that you can use either of the Raj Hotels for your wedding party whenever you want.'

'Thank you!' Stella smiled in gratitude. 'Do you think Mr Lomax would agree to give me away?'

Esmie looked overcome by the suggestion. Her voice trembled as she replied. 'Dear lassie, I think he would be honoured. You're like a daughter to him.'

They clasped each other in a tight hug.

That night, after sitting up late on the veranda holding hands, Hugh said, 'Leave your door unlocked and I'll come to you tonight.'

Later, Stella lay on top of her bed in a loose nightgown waiting impatiently for the dead of night. When all sounded quiet, Hugh let himself in to the small back bedroom and groped for her in the dark.

He lay down beside her and they began urgent kissing, trying to keep as silent as possible. Removing their clothes, Hugh whispered, 'You're so beautiful – let me see you properly.'

He pulled back the curtain, letting in a faint silvery light from the setting moon. Stella caught the look of desire on his face as he lay over her and began a leisurely love-making. Rapture flooded through her – even more than the first time in the woods – and she struggled not to cry out.

Afterwards, they lay wrapped in each other's arms on the narrow bed, her cheek pressed to his chest, which rose and fell rapidly.

'You make me so happy,' she murmured.

He kissed her head. 'And you me, my beauty.'

They fell asleep. Stella was woken by Hugh climbing stiffly off the bed, rubbing his bad leg. Grey pre-dawn light filtered in. She watched him pull on his clothes and ached with renewed longing. She felt reckless and would rather risk being discovered with Hugh if it meant another half an hour in his arms.

'Don't go,' she urged, sitting up.

She saw the indecision on his face as he stared at her nakedness. She could see the lust in his eyes. He limped back to the bed.

'You've got me under your spell, girl,' he said with a soft groan.

They made love quickly and vigorously, with none of the slow preamble of the night. It was over in a few minutes. Hugh left her panting and yearning for more.

'See you at breakfast.' He blew her a kiss and was gone.

They went for their final ride together up to the marg. The sky was cloudy and thunder rumbled around the mountains, forewarning of a pre-monsoon storm. They went further into the shelter of the trees, startling a troop of monkeys that scampered away into the interior.

Hugh hurriedly laid out the rug. 'We might not have much time before it rains.'

They shed their clothes quickly and made love with a passionate desperation. In the subdued light, Stella explored his body with kisses, wanting to remember every detail about him. She could hardly bear to think beyond the day and having to say goodbye.

She found the scar on his knee and caressed it with her fingers. 'Did they ever catch the tribesman who did this to you?'

'No,' he said, catching her hand and kissing it.

She stared at the livid scar. 'Tell me how it happened.'

'A Baluchi, out to get me.'

'How terrible,' said Stella, bending to kiss it.

Before she could question him further, Hugh was pushing her gently on to her back and pleasuring her again.

Soon the sky grew darker and the wind picked up. They abandoned their picnic, packing up swiftly and heading down the slope. They arrived just as the first fat drops began. Within minutes, the rain was bouncing off the tin roofs and flooding the flowerbeds.

The servants shut the veranda windows so that the guests could settle down to read or play cards. But while they'd been out, word had spread that Stella was engaged to the genial Mr Keating and people came up to shake Hugh by the hand.

'Congratulations,' said Mr Davidson of the Public Works Department. 'You're a lucky man. We thought no one was ever going to win Miss Dubois's heart.'

'We hear you're off to buy a ring tomorrow,' said his wife eagerly.

259

Hugh seemed a little taken aback, but nodded and smiled. 'Yes, we are. I'm the luckiest man in India.'

Esmie gave Hugh an apologetic look. 'I'm sorry – I mentioned it to Tom and he seems to have told the world. He's so pleased for you both.'

Stella was touched. 'I don't mind at all. I want people to know.'

That evening, the Lomaxes asked Stella and Hugh to dine with them in their annex. Felix had cooked Stella's favourite spicy fish cutlets served with coconut rice and his sweet and sour home-made chutney. She was with three of the people she loved most in the world and yet she was already experiencing dread at Hugh's going.

Tom was more animated than she'd seen him in a long time. Hugh had a way of putting people at their ease and drawing out anecdotes. To her and Esmie's surprise, Tom even spoke about his time in the army.

'I was stationed in Baluchistan briefly before the war,' he reminisced. 'Quetta was a pretty cantonment, though I hear it was nearly all destroyed by the earthquake six years ago. Terrible business.'

'Yes,' said Hugh. 'Appalling. If I'd gone back to my old job I'd probably not be sitting here to tell the tale.'

Stella shuddered. 'I can't bear to think of it. It makes me thankful you gave up your post.'

Tom nodded. 'You must have known colleagues that perished.'

'Yes, some very good friends.' Hugh looked sombre.

Stella wanted to steer the conversation away from the Quetta tragedy but didn't want to stop Tom's reminiscing. He carried on chatting about people and places he'd known before the Great War and asked Hugh questions about the area and its tribal people in more recent times.

Abruptly, Hugh rose from the table. 'I'd like to make a toast. To my beautiful Stella!'

Stella blushed as the Lomaxes raised their glasses and joined in: 'To Stella!'

Tom added, 'And to you both. May you find great happiness together.'

Esmie smiled. 'To the happy couple!'

After that, the conversation took a lighter turn as they discussed the imminent monsoon and the flowers Stella had picked on the marg to press into her diary.

Soon Hugh was excusing himself.

'This has been a delightful final dinner,' he said. 'I couldn't have asked for better company. Thank you very much. I hope you don't mind me taking Stella for a final walk around the garden – we have so little time left together.'

'Of course we don't mind,' said Esmie.

Outside, the air was cooler after the rain. Stella linked arms with Hugh and they strolled down the garden path and across the springy turf. The lower slopes were dotted with lights from private cabins, Nedous Hotel and the club. Overhead, the sky was littered with a myriad of stars.

'I feel selfish keeping you all to myself this week,' said Stella. 'You haven't been once to the club or mixed with the other bachelors on holiday.'

Hugh answered, 'Why would I want to spend my time with boring officials when I've got you here? You're the only reason I came, Stella.' He stopped and regarded her. 'You have no idea just how attractive you are, do you?'

She gave a laugh of embarrassment. 'You make me feel attractive.'

He kissed her gently on the lips. 'Let's make the most of our last night together, eh? I'll come to your room when all is quiet.'

Their love-making in the dead of night was passionate. For Stella there was a new urgency about it; in a few hours they would be parted. Afterwards, as she lay encircled in his arms, she began to weep.

'Shush now, don't cry,' he whispered.

'I c-can't bear the thought of you going,' she answered, trying to smother her sobbing.

'I'll come back as soon as I can,' he promised.

'I wish I could go with you,' Stella said with yearning. 'What if I came with you to Calcutta? We could get married there before you have to leave. Then at least we would be husband and wife – it would give me such comfort.'

Hugh kissed her tenderly on the forehead. 'You know how much I wish for that too. But there isn't time. I'll be sailing next week or the week after, at the latest. And I won't risk taking you to Calcutta and leaving you to make your own way back. I would worry too much.'

'Perhaps Esmie could come with me?' Stella suggested in desperation.

'Stella!' Hugh chided. 'You shouldn't ask that of Mrs Lomax. She has enough on her plate running the hotel and looking after Mr Lomax – you've told me that yourself.'

'I know, I'm sorry.' Stella was ashamed of herself. Her needs were frivolous in the face of what Esmie had to cope with. 'I'll just miss you so much.'

'And I, you.' Hugh sighed. 'But it will give me comfort to think of you here – to remember this magical week we've had together. I'll always be grateful for that.'

Stella didn't like the way his words sounded final, as if he feared for the future and had been making light of the danger he might be soon facing. Then he began kissing her again and soon she was losing herself in the moment and banishing dread thoughts.

Before dawn, Hugh slipped out of her room. Stella couldn't sleep, so got up early. She was exhausted, but she was determined not to miss a minute of being with Hugh on their final day. After an early breakfast, Hugh said farewell to the Lomaxes.

'Good luck, Mr Keating,' said Tom, exchanging firm handshakes.

Esmie said, 'We'll take good care of Stella for you until you come back.'

'Thank you,' said Hugh, looking grateful. 'You've both been very kind.'

Bijal, Tom's long-time bearer, was to drive the travellers to Srinagar and return with Stella that evening. They set off while the sky was still pink from the dawn. They rode on mules downhill, birdsong filling the still air while the pockets of snow on the surrounding peaks turned golden in the rising sun.

At the foot of the settlement, Bijal transferred Hugh's luggage from the baggage mule to the Lomaxes' van.

'I'll drive us there,' Hugh told Bijal, 'and Miss Dubois will sit up front with me.'

The sturdy Pathan glanced at Stella and when she nodded in agreement, he helped her up into the front seat and then went round the back and climbed in with the luggage.

As the van rattled along the rough road descending towards Srinagar, Stella sat close to Hugh, holding his left hand while he drove with his right. He sang popular songs to her that made her laugh and cry in equal measure. All too soon, the two hours it took to drive to the ancient town by Dal Lake were over. Hugh had arranged for a car and driver to be at the Srinagar Nedous Hotel to take him back to Rawalpindi, from where he would get the train south and east back to Calcutta.

'We've just over an hour to buy your ring, my sweet girl,' said Hugh.

Leaving Bijal to meet them at the hotel they continued on foot, crossing one of the many bridges that arched the Jhelum River, and scoured the narrow streets for jewellers. Hugh rejected the first two dark shops as being 'too native'.

'It doesn't have to be grand or expensive,' she said. 'Please don't spend too much on a ring. Anything you give me will be special.'

But Hugh ignored her pleas. 'I'm not buying you a trinket to hang from your nose,' he said with a laugh.

Finding a shop he was happy with, he ushered her inside. The owner was welcoming, inviting them to sit down on wooden chairs with gaily embroidered cushions. His offer of tea was waved aside by Hugh.

'We haven't time for the niceties,' he said. 'Show us what you have in precious stones – diamonds or maybe a ruby. And be quick about it.'

The Kashmiri made a great show of laying out a dark-green velvet cloth on a low table in front of them and then placing rings on it like delicate flowers. Stella was entranced, gasping at the jewels in their gold settings.

The jeweller gave her an encouraging nod. 'Please, memsahib, you can try them on.'

'Come on, let me help you find the right size,' Hugh said.

He picked up one with a large diamond and slipped it onto her finger.

'It feels too big,' said Stella. She also thought it would be impractical and would catch on things when she was working, but didn't think Hugh would want to be told that.

'What about this emerald?' Hugh picked up another one. 'To match your beautiful eyes.'

It fitted, but Stella thought it too showy in its circle of diamonds. She took it off and picked up a more modest ring: a simple sapphire set in a crown of tiny gold claws. It fitted well. The Kashmiri nodded with approval.

'I love this one, Hugh,' she said with enthusiasm. 'What do you think?'

Hugh looked a little disappointed. 'If that's the one you want.'

'Oh, yes, please.' She gave a bashful smile. 'The dark blue will be a constant reminder of your handsome eyes.'

Hugh laughed. 'Then it shall be yours.'

He began a robust haggling with the shopkeeper. Stella sat with stomach knotted in case Hugh would refuse to pay a sum that the dignified but stubborn Kashmiri would accept. To her relief, they both settled on a price. Hugh drew a wad of cash from his wallet and counted it out.

When the seller offered to wrap the ring, Stella said, 'I'd like to wear it.'

He handed her a box to keep it in.

They walked out of the shop arm in arm into the sunshine. It was already hot and motes of dust rose from the dry unpaved streets. The rank smell of effluent and rotting vegetation from the river was growing stronger and people were calling to each other from wooden balconies that jutted precariously over the water.

'Smells worse than a pigsty in Ireland,' Hugh joked. He hailed a tonga to drive them to Nedous.

Stella snuggled close to Hugh. The moment of parting was almost upon them.

Bijal was waiting with the van outside the hotel. 'Keating Sahib, I've taken your luggage inside for safekeeping.'

'Thank you,' Hugh said distractedly and turned to Stella. He took her hands in his and said, 'Let's not make this worse for ourselves. A swift goodbye is best.'

Stella's throat watered; she swallowed hard and nodded in agreement.

'I'm going to miss you every minute of every day,' she said huskily, smiling through her tears.

He kissed her hard on the mouth. 'Take care of yourself, my green-eyed girl.' He gave her one of his heart-melting smiles.

'And you too,' she croaked. 'Write to me from Singapore and let me know you're safe, won't you?'

'Of course.' He kissed her one more time and then let go of her hands. 'Off you go back to Gulmarg,' he ordered. 'I want to see you leave so I know you're not here on your own.'

He led her round to the passenger side of the van, helped her in and closed the door. Stella felt a sob rising in her chest but she kept smiling for him. Bijal climbed into the driver's seat and started the engine. Hugh tapped the side of the van for them to go.

As they began to move, Stella wound down the window and shouted out, 'I love you!'

He blew her a kiss and waved. She gazed at him as long as she could, straining round for one last glimpse and waving back. When she could no longer see him, Stella sat back and, putting her face in her hands, began to cry.

Bijal looked at her in concern. 'Stella-Mem'?' he asked. 'Shall I get you chai?'

'N-no, thank you, Bijal.' She fought to stop her weeping. She felt as if her insides had been torn out and sat hugging her stomach. How could the world be looking so beautiful in the sunshine when she was feeling so bereft? The Dal Lake sparkled beside them as they drove north.

Suddenly a thought came to her. 'Bijal,' she said, 'can you take me to see Baroness Cussack on her houseboat? Do we have time?'

He glanced at her and nodded. Turning off the road he made towards the lake. Stella's spirits lifted a fraction to see the spread of waterlilies and the vivid green of the floating vegetable gardens beyond the wharves.

Soon she was in a shikara being paddled across the still water towards the *Queen of the Lake*. As it glided in beside the houseboat, Stella could see Hester sitting on deck having a late breakfast. It was astonishing to think it was only eleven o'clock. The elderly woman stood up to see who was approaching, and on seeing Stella gave a cry of delight.

'My darling, this is a lovely surprise!'

Stella almost fell up the houseboat steps in her haste to be with her. She threw her arms around Hester's bony shoulders and hugged her.

'Whatever is the matter?' Hester asked in concern. 'Has something terrible happened? Is Captain Lomax all right?'

'Yes, everyone is fine,' Stella gabbled, ashamed of making her worry. She made a supreme effort to bring her emotions under control and speak calmly.

'It's good news really,' she said. 'Hugh and I got engaged two days ago – we've just bought the ring.' Stella held out her hand to show off the sapphire.

'How marvellous!' Hester clasped her hand. 'And what a pretty ring. Congratulations, darling. But where is your young man?'

'I've just said goodbye to him in Srinagar,' Stella said, her voice wobbling. 'He's going to Singapore and I don't know when I'll see him again . . .'

Hester put her knobbly hands either side of Stella's face. 'Ah, my poor Stella,' she sympathised. 'Come and sit down and tell me everything.'

Stella let her elderly friend steer her into a comfortable seat. Looking across at the romantic gardens and the glimmering Himalayan peaks beyond, Stella poured out her heart to the baroness.

Chapter 31

Ebbsmouth, late September 1941

Andrew hadn't told his mother that he was coming home for a few days. He made straight for The Anchorage to see his aunt. Somehow it seemed easier to talk to Tibby first. She would understand better – or at least not get too emotional at his news. He found his aunt picking blackberries in an old pair of jodhpurs, a woolly jumper and her favourite purple hat, which was looking more battered than ever.

'Dear boy!' she cried. 'How lovely.'

He swung his kit bag from his shoulder, kissed her cheek and popped a blackberry into his mouth.

'As sweet as my favourite aunt,' he said with a grin.

'You look like you're on manoeuvres?' she said with a questioning look.

Andrew savoured another berry before deciding to tell her outright. 'I'm being transferred to a different battalion,' he said.

Tibby eyed him. 'And where do they think they need you most?'

Andrew glanced up at the fluttering canopy of beech trees and the pearly grey sky beyond and felt a tug of sadness. He had grown to love this place.

'East,' he replied, meeting her look. 'India.'

Her eyes widened. 'India? But there's no war there, surely?'

'The Nazis have been stirring up the tribes in the North West Frontier to rebel again.'

Tibby gave a little gasp. 'That's where Tommy was. Will they send you there?'

Andrew shrugged. 'I don't know – but that is where the Second Battalion of the Borderers is stationed at the moment.'

'How strange,' said Tibby, 'if you end up where your father served.' She touched his arm and smiled wistfully. 'You'll be able to see him again after all this time – and Esmie.'

Andrew felt a familiar tension in the pit of his stomach at their mention. 'Perhaps – although it's quite a way from Kashmir. And I might not be sent to the frontier. All I know is that in a few weeks I'll be embarking for India.'

She scrutinised him with a shrewd look in her hazel eyes. 'Come inside and tell me more.'

As they shared a pot of weak tea in the library, Dawan received Andrew's news with excitement.

'I can't deny I'm a little bit envious that you'll be going back to India. Plentiful curries and hot sun on your back,' he said with a wry smile.

'Does your mother know yet?' asked Tibby.

Andrew shook his head. 'I'm summoning up the courage to tell her.'

'Poor Lydia.' Tibby sighed. 'Talking of India then, have you heard from your father recently?'

'No,' Andrew said. 'Not for a couple of months.'

'Well, it's the busy time of year for him at the hotel,' Tibby said in his defence.

Andrew didn't like to say that he hadn't written to his father for longer. He found himself agitated by his father's constant harping on the dangers of the war and his demands for reassurance that he, Andrew, was safe. He would write and let him know about being deployed to India. Or would that just make his father fret about the dangerous sea voyage? Perhaps it might be best to say nothing until he was on Indian soil.

'Have you heard the news about Miss Dubois?' Dawan asked.

Andrew's heart jumped. 'Stella? What about her?'

'Oh, yes,' said Tibby, 'with all this excitement over your news, it went out of my head. Stella's engaged at last. Did Tommy not tell you?'

Andrew's mouth dried. 'No, he didn't. Who is the lucky man?' Even as he asked, he knew.

'Hugh Keating, of course,' said Tibby. 'Isn't that super? Stella is such a lovely lassie; she deserves to be happy.'

'Yes, she does.' Andrew felt a sudden constriction in his chest. He always knew that one day he would hear of Stella's betrothal but he hadn't expected to feel so upset at the news. He should be happy for her – and for Hugh, whom he liked – and yet he was overwhelmed with disappointment and envy.

Tibby carried on. 'It was all very romantic apparently. He proposed to her in Gulmarg and bought her a sapphire ring in Srinagar. She's as happy as a skylark. Except poor Hugh's been sent to Singapore with government work so there's no date been set for the wedding. Perhaps you'll be in India when it happens. Wouldn't that be wonderful if you were there to celebrate with them? You were their cupid, after all.'

Finally, Tibby stopped talking and gave him one of her beady-eyed looks. 'You're very quiet, dear boy. Are you all right?'

He forced a smile. 'Yes, fine. I'm just a bit anxious about facing Mamma.'

Chapter 32

The Raj-in-the-Hills, early October 1941

Stella was trying to put on a brave face. She hadn't heard from Hugh in over a month. A wire had come in July to say that he was safely in Singapore, which had been followed by a brief letter in August telling her very little. He was travelling in Malaya requisitioning materials for the army; it was hot and humid.

> *I'd give half my salary to be in the cool of the mountains with my darling girl. I miss you. Keep writing and thinking of me. Your loving Hugh xx*

She had written to him; at first almost daily and then weekly, but she'd heard nothing from him in six weeks. She wondered if she had the wrong address – or if his firm had moved – or whether he had been sent somewhere else. But surely, he would have written to tell her if this were so?

She needed to know he was safe and she needed to be reassured that he still wanted to marry her. Each day, she grew more certain of her condition. It had started with tiredness and a metallic taste in her mouth, then frequent biliousness and an aversion to certain food.

Esmie had noticed too. 'You seem to have gone off Felix's curry puffs. Are you unwell?'

Just the mention of the spicy, oily puffs was enough to make Stella retch. She brushed off Esmie's concern. 'I'm fine. Just a bit anxious about Hugh.'

That was in August. Now she was absolutely certain that she was pregnant; she hadn't had a bleed in four months. The thought of carrying Hugh's baby thrilled her and yet filled her with trepidation. What on earth would her mother say? Myrtle had written to express how pleased she was at the engagement, which had been a relief given that she had been so cautious about Hugh in the early days of their courtship.

How she longed to see Hugh and tell him the news! Perhaps he would then be able to get leave and return to marry her before her pregnancy was too obvious – or at least before the baby was born. She went cold thinking of the disgrace it would bring on her mother and family to bear a child out of wedlock.

As the number of guests began to dwindle and the Lomaxes prepared to close up the hotel, Stella went to Esmie for help. Finding her in the office, Stella closed the door and gabbled out her problem.

'I'm carrying Hugh's baby. I think I'm four months gone. What am I going to do?' She felt her chin tremble. 'I haven't heard from him in weeks and don't even know if he's still in Singapore. Why haven't I heard from him? Oh, Mrs Lomax!' She pressed her hand over her mouth to stop a sob.

Esmie went straight to her and hugged her. 'Oh, lassie. I was beginning to fear you might be. You've not been yourself recently.' She steered her into a chair and poured out a glass of lime juice from a covered jug she kept on the desk. 'Sip this.'

As Stella did so, Esmie asked, 'Are you absolutely sure?'

Stella nodded. 'I haven't had a "monthly" since the beginning of June.'

'Oh, lassie!' Esmie let out a long sigh. 'Have you written to Hugh to let him know?'

'Not yet,' Stella admitted. 'I've hinted that I have something important to tell him but none of my letters are being answered. I don't like to put it in writing in case someone else is opening his post . . .'

'Then you must.' Esmie was adamant. 'He needs to be told. Perhaps he could get a few days' leave and you could meet him in Calcutta – arrange a swift marriage licence.'

Stella latched onto the idea. 'Do you think that's possible?'

'Once he knows the situation, I'm sure he'll do his best.' Esmie gave her a look of sympathy. 'It's a shame you couldn't have waited . . . but I understand why you didn't – what with Hugh going away and not knowing when you'd next see him.'

Stella covered her burning cheeks.

'What about telling your mother?' Esmie asked.

Stella's insides curdled. 'Oh, I can't tell her! Not yet. She'll be so ashamed of me. I can only face her with Hugh by my side.'

'She'll be expecting you home sometime this month,' Esmie pointed out.

'Can I stay on here for a bit longer? Please, Mrs Lomax!'

'Of course you can,' Esmie reassured her. 'Perhaps Tom could contact McSween and Watson and find out exactly where Hugh is.'

Stella gasped. 'Does Mr Lomax have to be told?'

Esmie gave her a pitying look. 'He's going to find out sooner or later, isn't he? And I can't keep this from him – Tom and I don't have secrets from each other.'

Stella felt chastened. 'No, of course not.'

'But we'll keep it from anyone else at the moment,' said Esmie.

'Thank you,' said Stella gratefully. She twisted her engagement ring – a solid reminder that she and Hugh were betrothed – and was comforted by her friend's support. It was a relief that someone else now knew. 'I long to be with him.'

'Let's hope you will be soon, lassie.'

The women sought out Tom in his studio. His reaction was more forthright.

'How dare he take advantage of you?' he fulminated. 'And to think he was doing so under our noses! I thought he was more honourable than that. And I didn't think you would be that foolish, Stella. You've always been so sensible.'

Stella cringed at his rebuke. 'I'm sorry you've had to be brought into this situation and I know I've behaved badly, but we were engaged . . .'

'I'm not blaming you,' said Tom. 'It's Keating's fault for not showing restraint—'

'Tom!' Esmie interrupted. 'Getting angry isn't going to change anything. Stella needs our help.'

Tom stopped pacing around the hut and looked at his wife in amazement. Then he ran a hand over his haggard face. 'I'm sorry. It's just the shock. Of course we'll stand by you, dear girl. You're one of the family.'

'Thank you,' said Stella, her eyes brimming with tears at his defence of her.

'We need to find out quickly where Mr Keating is,' said Esmie, 'and make him aware of the situation.'

'I haven't heard from him in six weeks,' Stella said, 'so I'm not even sure he's still in Singapore. He may be somewhere else in Malaya.'

'I'll send a wire to McSween and Watson in Calcutta,' Tom said at once.

'That's what I thought we should do,' agreed Esmie.

'I should have done that before,' Stella admitted, 'but I didn't want to make a fuss until I was sure . . .'

'Well, I'm not afraid of making a fuss on your behalf,' said Tom stoutly. 'We must track Keating down and make him face up to his responsibilities.'

Chapter 33

'Are you in the army now?' Minnie asked, smiling at Andrew in bemusement. She was dead-heading geraniums in the conservatory while Andrew held a basket for her.

'Andrew's been with the Borderers for three years now, Mother!' Lydia said in exasperation. 'How many times do I have to tell you?'

'Have you?' Minnie exclaimed. 'You do look very smart in your uniform, Tom.'

His mother retorted, 'For goodness' sake, it's Andrew, not Tom. It's your grandson!'

'It's all right, Grandmamma, you can call me what you want,' Andrew said quickly. His grandmother often mistook him for his father or muddled up their names.

'I don't know what I'm going to tell her once you've gone,' Lydia said reproachfully. 'She'll be asking where you are every five minutes.'

'I am here, Lydia dear,' said Minnie. 'You don't have to talk about me as if I'm not.'

His grandmother's memory might be failing but she was still attuned to people's moods.

'So where are you going?' Minnie asked him.

'I'm being posted out east,' Andrew explained again. 'India.'

'Ah, India!' Minnie seized on the name. 'Jumbo and I had a lovely holiday there when your mother was first married. What was the name of the place, dear?'

'Pindi,' said Lydia.

'That's it. Pindi. We stayed at a rather quaint hotel. What was it called?'

Lydia rolled her eyes.

Andrew answered, 'The Raj, Grandmamma.'

'That's it! Such a friendly family running it – Anglo-Indian – charming man, Charlie-something. Made us so welcome.'

'He was useless at business,' Lydia said dismissively. 'It was Tom and I who ran the place. The Duboises were little more than hangers-on. No wonder Tom couldn't make any money out of it.'

'The Duboises are fine people.' Andrew leapt to their defence. 'Poor old Charlie died two years ago, Grandmamma.'

'Did he?' said Minnie. 'How sad.'

'I told her that,' Lydia muttered under her breath.

'And their daughter,' Minnie continued. 'She was a delightful girl – Sylvia . . . ?'

'Stella,' Andrew answered.

Minnie's expression brightened. 'Yes, I remember her well. Didn't she come and stay here once?'

Lydia huffed. 'Yes, she did. We put her up all summer but she did her best to turn Andrew against us – always taking Esmie's side and painting me out to be the wicked witch.'

Andrew didn't like to hear his mother malign Stella, so he cut in. 'Stella's engaged to be married.'

Lydia gaped at him. 'Are you still in touch with her?'

'Tibby told me.' He tried to sound unconcerned, but could feel the warmth creep into his jaw.

'Who to? Some half-half railwayman, no doubt?'

'Mamma!' Andrew protested. 'Don't be unkind. And no, he's not an Anglo-Indian.'

'Well, who then?' Lydia's interest was piqued.

'Hugh Keating – the Irishman she met on the ship in '33.' Andrew had a twinge of satisfaction telling her. 'She ended up with Hugh despite your attempts to keep them apart.'

'What do you mean?' Lydia was indignant.

'That letter from Hugh that you never gave her back,' he reminded her.

Lydia gave a dismissive wave of the hand. 'I don't remember any letter. And anyway, why should I care? I'm happy for Stella that she's found a husband at last. At her age she must have thought she was on the shelf. But she's not my concern. You are, darling. I'm trying to be brave about you going away. Dickie will simply have to come up from London and console me. And I'm worried that once you get back to India, you'll forget us and not want to return.'

'That's not true,' said Andrew, putting down the flower basket and going to sit beside her. He put an arm about her shoulders. 'Of course I'm going to come back.'

'How can I be sure?' Lydia demanded. 'I know the sway your father can have over people.'

'Not over me,' Andrew said.

'I wish you had something pressing to come back for – like being in love with a girl,' Lydia persisted. 'What about Felicity? Why did you stop seeing her?'

'You used to complain that I spent too much of my leave with Flis-Tish,' Andrew teased.

'No, I didn't. I liked her. She had spirit and her family are very well-to-do.'

'She ditched me for an older man,' Andrew said ruefully. 'A farmer in the Home Guard.'

'The Home Guard?' Lydia cried. 'She's far too young for one of them. I bet he's toothless.'

Andrew chuckled. 'I don't think so. I thought you would have heard from Mrs Douglas. Aren't you still friends?'

'I don't go anywhere these days – my life is spent looking after your grandmother. But I'll make some enquiries – see how serious Felicity is about this toothless farmer. You liked her, didn't you?'

'Yes,' Andrew admitted. 'A lot actually.'

'Then we must invite the Douglas girl over before your leave ends. I'm sure, at the very least, Felicity will want to say goodbye.'

Andrew should have known that once his mother got an idea into her head, nothing would stand in her way. Within two days, she had Felicity round for lunch to fit in with her ARP warden duties.

Before the soup course, Lydia had ascertained that Felicity was no longer being courted by the farmer in the Home Guard.

'Goodness, I haven't seen him in months,' said Felicity, giving Andrew a bold look. 'I'm not seeing anyone at the moment.'

As soon as the simple lunch was over, Lydia said, 'Andrew, why don't you take Felicity for a walk? It's a glorious afternoon. I want to get some letters written while your grandmamma has her rest.'

Outside, Felicity said, 'Your mother is shameless. That was a blatant attempt to push us together.'

Andrew laughed. 'Yes, subtlety is not her middle name. I apologise.'

'Why should you? Only say sorry if you didn't go along with the idea.' She scrutinised him with attractive hazel eyes. Her shorter bobbed hair suited her and her lips were looking particularly red and kissable.

'I wanted you to come,' Andrew replied. 'I've missed you, Flis-Tish.'

She smiled and linked her arm through his. 'Good, because I've missed you too.' They walked down the terraced steps and round the side of the hot houses. Felicity stopped and faced him. 'I'm really very upset to hear you're being sent abroad. Why didn't you get in touch sooner?'

'I thought you were with another man.'

'That was never serious – just a fling.'

'How was I supposed to know that?' he asked.

'You should have got in touch when you were on leave before.'

Andrew held her look. 'The last time I saw you, you stormed out of The Anchorage and said you never wanted to see me again.'

She arched her eyebrows. 'You weren't supposed to take that seriously. In fact, you were supposed to run after me and beg me to come back.'

Andrew gave an amused huff. 'Was I now?'

'Yes.' She reached for his hand and pulled him closer. 'I was annoyed that you didn't want to make love to me – so I went and found someone who did. But he was terribly boring. It's you I've always wanted, Andrew.'

He reddened. He'd forgotten just how forthright she could be, yet it excited him.

'The thing is,' said Felicity, 'do you still want me? You don't have to worry about being responsible for my virginity any more.' She ran a finger across his jaw. 'I love it when you blush like a schoolboy.'

He caught her hand and kissed it.

'Is that an acceptance that we should try again to be friends?' she asked.

'Yes,' Andrew said. 'I'd like that.'

'Then let's start by you kissing me properly,' she ordered.

Andrew bent and kissed her long and hard on the mouth. She responded with enthusiasm. Breaking off, he said, 'You taste of something sweet.'

She giggled. 'It's beetroot. I've run out of lipstick. It stains them rather a gorgeous red, wouldn't you say?'

Andrew licked her lips. 'Umm, tastes surprisingly delicious too.'

Felicity held his face captive and started kissing him again.

Chapter 34

The Raj-in-the-Hills, mid-October 1941

Stella had an anxious week awaiting a reply from Hugh's head office in Calcutta. She had a letter written and waiting to send, depending on where they said Hugh was. Still no communication had come from her fiancé. She was plagued with fear that something terrible had happened to him; some accident in the jungles of Malaya, or that he had fallen ill with malaria or worse. There must be a reason why he hadn't written to her.

The day the last of the guests left at the start of the cold season, Tom walked into the office where Esmie and Stella were doing bookkeeping. He was holding a telegram in his hand.

'It's from Calcutta,' he said, handing it over to Stella unopened. 'You should be the one to read it.'

Stella took it with trembling hands, her pulse racing.

'Would you like to be left alone?' Esmie asked. 'Tom and I can wait outside.'

'No, please stay,' Stella said at once. She took the letter opener, cut the envelope and pulled out the message.

Keating in Burma – STOP – returning to Malaya
– STOP – advise she writes here and I shall forward

– STOP – was unaware he has fiancée – STOP –
Arthur Lamont

Stella swallowed hard. She felt dizzy with relief that Hugh was all right.

'He's been in Burma,' she said. 'That's why he hasn't written – and he won't have got any of my letters for ages either. I thought something dreadful must have happened . . .'

She handed the telegram to Esmie, who read it and gave it to Tom.

Esmie said, 'I'm thankful to hear he's just been busy and travelling, but you mustn't waste any time in writing to him about your situation.'

Tom was frowning. 'What's all this about Lamont not knowing Keating has a fiancée?'

Stella blushed. 'There was so little time before he went to Singapore that he mustn't have mentioned it.'

Esmie added, 'Men don't talk about these things like women do.'

Tom looked incredulous. 'Well, I think it's odd that Keating wouldn't have told his colleagues of something so important.'

'Just because this man hasn't heard,' said Esmie, 'doesn't mean Mr Keating hasn't told others.'

'But why does Stella have to write to Calcutta?' Tom continued to fret. 'Why couldn't he give a forwarding address?'

'Because Hugh's moving about so much,' Esmie pointed out.

'How do we know Lamont is going to pass on any letters?' said Tom.

'Oh, Tom!' Esmie grew exasperated. 'Because he says he will. I'm sure he's perfectly reliable.'

Stella hated to see them arguing over her; it was her problem and she must sort it out. The last thing she wanted was to make Tom ill again.

'I'll send my letter at once,' said Stella, 'and I'm sure it'll be sent on swiftly by head office. They must be sending post daily to their agents abroad. Please don't worry, Mr Lomax. I know my Hugh and he'll do what's right when he hears from me.'

That day, she sent off the letter to Hugh telling him that she was expecting his baby and urging him to return quickly to marry her.

Chapter 35

Ebbsmouth, November 1941

Andrew's departure was delayed until mid-November. Recent torpedoing of ships in the Mediterranean had meant it was deemed unsafe to risk a large convoy of troops to be taken east using the Suez Canal, so they were to travel the longer route around the Cape. The welcome reprieve gave him another snatched leave with his mother and grandmother – and also with Felicity.

Two days after Lydia had invited her round for lunch the previous month, Felicity had engineered for Andrew to stay over at her house one night. In the blacked-out rambling villa, she had come to his bedroom, armed with 'French letters', and seduced him. It had been very pleasurable.

'Better than doing it in the back of your mother's car, then?' she had teased him, her tone triumphant.

'Much better,' he had agreed.

'I suppose it was worth the wait.' Felicity had given a throaty laugh and instigated another bout of love-making.

Andrew saw Felicity each day of his final week at home. They went for cold autumnal walks and talked about inconsequential things, both knowing that the end purpose was to find somewhere sheltered to make love. Their final time alone, he took her to Tibby's summerhouse overlooking his favourite cove with the boathouse.

'I'd like to have taken you there.' Andrew pointed down at the fenced-off beach. 'It's a favourite spot. When this war is over, we'll make passionate love in the boathouse.'

Felicity wrinkled her nose. 'Doesn't look very inviting or comfortable to me.'

'I'll make it comfortable,' Andrew promised, staring down at the sandy bay and the wheeling sea birds glinting white in the low wintry sun. He had first fallen for this place as a youth – that summer with Stella when she had supervised his games with Noel. Poor Noel, who was incarcerated in a fortress somewhere in Germany. And Stella, who might already be married to Hugh.

'So you're planning on returning after the war?' asked Felicity. 'If we win it.'

'*When* we win it,' Andrew answered. 'And yes, of course I'm coming back.'

'Your mother doubts you will,' she said.

'Has she been talking about me to you?'

'Of course we talk about you. That's practically all your mother can talk about. She's convinced you'll be seduced back into life in India by your dad and his scheming wife who usurped her.'

'She shouldn't have bothered you with all that. And it's not true. I didn't choose to go to India – I'm being sent because I can speak Urdu. I'd much rather be fighting the fascists in Europe than chasing around after rebellious tribesmen in the North West Frontier, which is what I'm likely to end up doing.'

Felicity slipped her arms around his waist. 'I'm glad to hear that I win over India. Come on, I'm getting cold. Let's try out this summerhouse.'

Afterwards, Andrew felt a wave of contentment lying with Felicity in his arms. He found her desire for him flattering and enjoyed her outspoken chatter. Felicity was pretty, his mother approved of her and he could imagine a future in Ebbsmouth in which they were together.

She was lying with her hand on his chest. He took hold of it and kissed it.

'Flis-Tish,' he said. 'Will you marry me?'

She leaned up and looked at him enquiringly. 'Marry you? Are you getting the jitters about going away? You don't have to ask me just because we're lovers.'

He reddened. 'I'm not getting the jitters, as you call them. I've come to really care about you and think we'd be happy together. Don't you?'

She eyed him. 'I'm pretty potty about you, that's true. But I'm not sure you feel the same way. Don't just ask out of politeness because you're about to go away.'

Andrew smothered his discomfort that what she said might be true. Yet, he could see a happy life with her beckoning to him beyond the uncertainty and horrors of this war. He clung to it.

'It's nothing to do with politeness,' he insisted. 'I want to marry you and be with you.'

She smiled and reached up to kiss his cheek. 'Then I accept.'

'You do?'

'Yes!'

'That's wonderful!' He kissed her on the lips.

She drew back a fraction. 'On the understanding that we both feel the same way when you come home.'

Not for the first time it struck Andrew that Felicity was far more insightful than he was.

'Not very romantic of you,' Andrew said wryly. 'But I'd never hold you to an engagement if you change your mind.'

'It wasn't me I was thinking of,' she said. 'Now we've got the formalities over, how about a final consummation of our agreement?' Grinning, she began kissing him again.

Early the next morning, on the day of his departure, Andrew went to say goodbye to his grandmother. In a moment of lucidity, she sat up in bed and said, 'I know it will be difficult for you going back to India but don't be too hard on your father. He did all he could to try and make your mother happy – but you and I know what a challenge that can be at times.'

'I don't really blame Dad for what happened,' Andrew admitted. 'I know it was more Esmie's fault.'

'Esmie?' Minnie sounded surprised. 'Esmie was a lovely girl. She married that missionary doctor – what was his name? Harold something.'

'Guthrie,' Andrew prompted. 'Dr Guthrie.'

'So very sad when he died.' Minnie shook her head. 'His mother never really recovered. Poor Agnes.'

'But then Esmie muscled Mamma out of the way and went after Dad.' Andrew felt familiar indignation on his mother's behalf.

Minnie looked confused. 'No, no, that's not right . . .'

'What do you mean, Grandmamma?'

She looked at him as if he could provide the answer. She gave up with a shrug. 'I can't remember what it was I wanted to say. I'm sorry.'

He leaned over and kissed her cheek. 'Don't be. It doesn't matter. Just remember that I love you and want you to be here when I get back from India.'

'Sweet boy,' Minnie said, with a fond smile. As he stood up to go, she added, 'You will try and make her happy, won't you?'

'Who, Grandmamma? Do you mean Felicity?'

'No, Lydia, of course.'

Andrew stepped back. His grandmother was mistaking him for his father again. He was about to tell her that he wasn't Tom, when he stopped. It only confused and upset her to be told she was mistaken. He felt a pang of sadness that her mental faculties were diminishing and yet she bore it with good humour. Perhaps she liked dwelling in a past that was inhabited by his grandfather Jumbo and filled with memories of happier times.

'I will look after her, I promise,' said Andrew with a smile of reassurance.

At the door he turned and saluted. The last sight he had of his grandmother was of her raising a frail hand in farewell and blowing him a kiss.

Tibby arrived to take him and Lydia to the station, as his mother didn't like to drive in the dark. He was reassured to know that Tibby would be there to keep his mother company after he went. He'd told Felicity not to come and see him off, and she'd agreed.

'I hate goodbyes,' she'd said. 'Everyone just gets upset. It doesn't mean I won't be thinking of you every minute. I'll let your mother hog the last moments with you or she might resent me forever.'

'Well, you're in Mamma's good books for agreeing to marry me,' Andrew had said. 'You know you'll be welcome at Templeton Hall anytime.'

'I'll keep an eye on your mother, don't worry,' Felicity had said, guessing as usual what he'd meant.

At the station, a raw wind was picking up dead leaves and hurling them onto the railway tracks. The train was late. Shadowed groups lined the platform, waiting; they stamped their feet to keep warm.

Tibby fished something from her pocket. 'I nearly forgot. This is from Dawan. It's a talisman to keep you safe – Ganesh the elephant god.' She pressed it into his hand.

Andrew stared at the small intricately carved ivory head strung on a thin strip of leather. 'The one he wears around his neck?'

'Yes,' said Tibby.

'But it belonged to his father, didn't it? He shouldn't be giving it to me,' Andrew protested.

'He said you're the nearest to a son he'll ever have,' Tibby said with a loving smile. 'So he wanted you to have it.'

Andrew's throat constricted. 'Please thank him,' he said huskily, greatly touched by the gesture.

Lydia peered at the necklace. 'How gruesome – and not at all Christian. I don't think your grandmother would approve.'

Andrew exchanged wry looks with Tibby and stowed it in his coat pocket. 'Don't wait in the cold,' he said. 'The train might be ages.'

'Don't be silly. I want to see you safely on board.' Lydia was adamant.

Just then, he heard the distant sound of a steam engine approaching. This was it.

Tibby stepped forward quickly and hugged him tightly, just as she had when he'd first arrived in Scotland over eight years ago. She still smelt of mothballs and cigarette smoke; she never changed. He gripped her, his eyes smarting.

'Take care of yourself, dear boy,' she said tenderly. 'And when you see Tommy, give him my love – and Esmie and Stella too.'

Andrew knew that as soon as he was gone, his mother would take Tibby to task for mentioning Esmie. But it was typical of his aunt not to care; she was incapable of being mean-spirited about anyone, and he loved her for it.

'I will,' he murmured and then let her go. 'Mamma.' He turned to his mother and held out his arms. She wasn't one for hugs but he wasn't going to allow her to dismiss him with a kiss on the cheek and a pat on the shoulder. Throughout his childhood he had wanted to feel a mother's arms around him and it had fallen to Esmie to try and assuage his deep need. But even as a grown man, he still sought Lydia's love and approval.

For a moment, Lydia allowed herself to be held. 'I pray for your safe return, my darling,' she whispered.

'Thank you,' he said.

They gazed at each other with tear-filled eyes. There was so much he wanted to say. He had left a letter for her to find that would save them both the embarrassment of tender words being said aloud, and she would have something to remind her of his love for her while he was gone.

From the train, as it shunted out of the station, he could just make out the figures of the two women standing close together, waving. The dawn was being heralded by a streak of gold light lying over a dark sea. Ebbsmouth passed – a dark mass of houses huddled on the cliffs – and then was gone from sight.

Chapter 36

The first of the snow had arrived in Gulmarg. The other hotels and chalets had already closed for the winter. Most of the staff at the Raj-in-the-Hills had been paid off until the spring. Only Tom's bearer Bijal, Esmie's sewing woman Karo and a couple of part-time house servants – a sweeper and a cook – remained.

Stella's five-month pregnancy hardly showed yet, especially under baggy woollen clothing, but she was very aware of the baby growing inside. She felt it moving daily now, a gentle fluttering like a moth tapping at a lightshade. She would cup her hands over her stomach, wanting to capture the sensation, but it was too elusive.

She was thrilled at the thought of carrying a baby and realised that this was what she had craved for so long.

Why hadn't Hugh written back? She clung to the belief that her letter of the previous month had taken a long time to catch up with him – wherever he was. Surely, he would not ignore such momentous news? He wouldn't deliberately let her suffer such anxiety; he was a kind and loving man. She couldn't wait for the day when they were together – husband and wife – and bringing up their precious child.

Yet in the dead of night, when she lay huddled under extra blankets and felt the baby stir inside, she allowed doubts to flood in. Perhaps he didn't love her as much as she loved him and was having second thoughts about marrying her. After all, it was she, not Hugh, who had first got back in touch, following Andrew's chance meeting with him in Edinburgh. And he had been with another woman then.

What if this woman was more to Hugh than a 'cousin', as Andrew's girlfriend had suspected? Perhaps she was living with him in Calcutta and he had lied to her. The worst thought of all – that she hardly dared entertain – was that Hugh had only proposed to her so that she would agree to lie with him.

By dawn, Stella would feel ashamed of such disloyal and suspicious thoughts. Hugh loved her. She had a beautiful sapphire ring to prove it. The delay in his reply was simply because of the disruption to post during these chaotic times.

She was so caught up in her own problems that she hardly listened to Tom's litany of woes about the war. HMS *Ark Royal*, Britain's invincible aircraft carrier, had been sunk off Gibraltar; Rommel's Afrika Korps appeared to be gaining the upper hand in fierce counter-attacks against the Allies in North Africa and the Nazis were reported to be on the verge of taking Moscow from the Russians.

One day, Esmie took her aside. 'In another month we'll be cut off here,' she warned. 'Don't you think you should go back home and talk to Myrtle – face this situation together?'

Stella was appalled at the thought. 'Ma would never understand. Unless I'm married in the next couple of months, she'd make me give the baby away, I'm sure of it. They'd all put pressure on me to do that – the aunties and uncles; I'd never be allowed to keep it.'

Esmie sat with her hands in her lap, contemplating what she'd said. Stella always found her troubled state of mind eased by Esmie's calm manner. It was so different from the scolding and recriminations she knew she would get if she went home.

'Is that what you really want?' Esmie asked. 'To keep your baby, no matter what happens – even if Hugh doesn't come to the rescue?'

'Hugh will stick by me, I'm sure of it.'

'But if he doesn't?' Esmie pressed her.

Stella swallowed hard. How many times had she asked herself that question in the lonely sleepless nights?

'Yes,' she said with conviction. 'I want this baby more than anything.'

Esmie took her hand and squeezed it. There was no need for further words; Stella knew that the Lomaxes would support her.

The following month Esmie wrote to Myrtle explaining that she was suffering from bouts of tiredness and Stella was kindly staying on through the winter to help her. She hoped Myrtle wouldn't mind. Stella's mother wrote back full of concern and suggested that the Lomaxes come to stay at the Raj in Pindi where she could visit a doctor.

Esmie wrote a second time, reassuring Myrtle that there were good doctors in Srinagar and she would get more rest in the hills than during the busy social season in Rawalpindi. To Stella's relief, her mother accepted this state of affairs and gave her approval of Stella staying on to help.

The snowline was down to Gulmarg now and it was turning bitterly cold. Tom helped Bijal fix the shutters to the hotel windows and shut up the main building. Stella moved into the small annex with the Lomaxes. Since she had asked to stay on, Tom's mood had improved. He started painting again and on days when he wasn't, he suggested that he and Esmie went for walks with Stella riding beside them on a pony. They never went far, but Stella relished the sharp air and the sight of glistening white mountains under a deep blue sky. On such days, she was optimistic. Hugh was her fiancé and one day soon they would be together – it's what they had planned.

Shortly afterwards, on a day of snow flurries, when Stella was sewing a patchwork blanket with Karo, she heard Esmie call out, 'We've got post!'

Stella leapt to her feet and pulled on a thick coat that Esmie had lent her. She felt the baby punch with a tiny fist or foot. The women went out together to meet the chaprassy. He handed over an airmail letter and then went to claim a hot drink from the kitchen.

'It's from Tibby,' said Esmie with a pitying look. 'Sorry, Stella.'

Stella could not hide her disappointment. She'd been so certain that Hugh had finally written to her. Feeling overwhelmed with sadness and disappointment, she returned inside. Perhaps Hugh would just turn up without warning like he had in Rawalpindi. Had she made a mistake hiding out in the hills instead of going back to the city? He was more likely to be able to snatch a visit to The Raj Hotel than up here. But as far as she knew he wasn't even in India, so the chances of him coming to the Punjab, let alone Kashmir, were slim.

Minutes later, Tom was bursting through the door waving the airmail letter, Esmie at his heels.

'He's coming home!' Tom cried, pumping the air with his fist.

'Who is?' Stella looked up in confusion.

'Andy!' Tom's lined face was creased in a broad grin. 'Tibby says he's been sent east to join the Second Battalion, the Borderers. They're stationed at Taha in the North West Frontier.'

Stella gasped. 'That's wonderful news!'

'Isn't it?' said Esmie, clutching onto Tom in delight.

'No doubt they're beefing up the numbers against the rebelling Waziris before another spring offensive,' said Tom. 'According to Tibby, Andy didn't want to tell us until he got to India in case we worried about the dangers at sea. But she thought we'd be cheered by the news and should know.'

'When will he get here?' Stella asked.

'Tibby doesn't say,' said Esmie. 'And he might well be sent to the Borderers' headquarters in New Delhi first, so we mustn't be too impatient.'

'And that's not his only news,' said Tom, waving the letter. 'My boy has got himself engaged!'

Stella's hand instinctively went up to her mouth in surprise. 'Andrew's getting married?'

'Well, in time,' said Esmie. 'Tibby said it was a spur-of-the-moment thing before he left.'

'Who to?' asked Stella, still not quite able to believe it.

'To that Felicity Douglas that Tibby wrote about,' said Esmie. 'Rich local family.'

'That'll please his mother,' Tom said with a note of derision.

Stella recognised the name; she was the girl who had been with Andrew when he'd met Hugh in Edinburgh – the girl who'd suspected Hugh had been with someone else's wife. She tried to stifle her disquiet. How ironic it was that both she and Andrew should undertake hasty engagements within months of each other. She was certain that he wouldn't have left his fiancée alone and pregnant. The Andrew she knew was kind and honourable. Felicity Douglas was a lucky young woman.

Suddenly Tom let out a strange sound; part groan, part sob. Esmie quickly put her arms around him.

'I know, I know, it's a shock,' she said softly. 'But a happy one.'

Tom nodded, his eyes brimming with tears. 'Our boy is coming home,' he repeated in a voice raw with emotion.

The electrifying news of Andrew's imminent return was swiftly followed by alarm at the shocking turn of events in the war. A belligerent Japan had made a surprise attack on the American naval base of Pearl Harbour in Hawaii, badly damaging the US fleet and killing thousands. Within days, Japan declared war on America – and Britain declared war on Japan – as Japanese forces landed in the Philippines and Malaya.

'Malaya?' Stella's head reeled. 'But Hugh . . . ?'

'We don't know if that's where he is,' Tom said bluntly. 'He could still be in Burma – or back in Singapore.'

'I need to know he's safe,' Stella cried. 'I can't bear this not knowing!'

But daily the news grew more alarming.

Tom stopped Stella listening to the broadcasts, but she overheard him talking in grave whispers to Esmie about the naval losses. 'Losing such ships will seriously damage the defence of Malaya and Singapore. We mustn't talk about it in front of Stella – she's making herself ill with worry over wretched Keating as it is.'

Stella was distressed to hear Tom talk about her fiancé so disparagingly but she could hardly blame him. So far, Hugh had failed her, and it was the Lomaxes who were bearing the burden.

So she went to them and said, 'I want to go to Srinagar and send a telegram to Calcutta – before the snow cuts us off here – and demand that Arthur Lamont puts me in touch with Hugh directly. If Malaya is under attack, then surely McSween and Watson will be pulling out their men? He might already be back in Calcutta.'

'You're not going anywhere in your condition.' Tom was firm. 'I'll make the journey to Srinagar – I can pick up extra supplies while I'm there. And I'll put in a call to the Raj and assure your mother that all is well.'

'Thank you,' Stella said, curbing her frustration at not going too. Despite her swelling womb and growing tiredness, she hated the enforced idleness but knew that at six months pregnant she would only be a liability to Tom if she went.

For four days Esmie and Stella looked out anxiously for Tom's return as the snow around the house deepened and the tracks down the mountainside disappeared. Then on a clear crisp December day, they spotted a distant blanket-wrapped man zigzagging between the chalets with a mule laden with supplies. Even though clothed like a native, they recognised Tom's tall lean figure.

Esmie pulled on her boots, coat and hat and went to meet him. When Stella tried to follow, Esmie was firm. 'We're not going to risk you slipping on the icy paths. Stay with Karo and I'll be back soon.'

It seemed an eternity before they appeared outside the small chalet. While Bijal led the mule away to be unloaded, Tom and Esmie came inside, wafting in cold air and stamping the snow off their boots.

Stella could see immediately from Esmie's expression that she had momentous news.

'Tell me!' she urged. 'Have you heard back from Calcutta?'

'No,' Tom answered, shedding his thick woollen blanket. 'But this was at the post office waiting to be delivered.' From his jacket he pulled out an airmail letter. 'It's for you – from Singapore.'

Stella stood up so fast she went dizzy. Tom reached out to steady her.

'Sit down, lassie,' Esmie urged. 'Karo, will you bring us tea, please?'

The servant nodded and left the room.

Tom guided her into a comfortable chair and handed her the letter. Stella gulped for breath. The writing on the envelope was Hugh's. At last! Not waiting for Esmie to fetch a letter opener, she tore it open.

The Lomaxes went to sit by the fire. She pulled out two flimsy pieces of paper with shaking hands. She saw that it was dated before the invasion of Malaya in Hugh's large expansive writing.

> *My darling girl,*
> *Your letter was awaiting me on my return to Singapore. I'm furious with Lamont for failing to pass on that you had been trying to contact me by telegram. Useless man! But what a letter!*
> *I can't pretend I wasn't shocked by the news – dumbfounded even. I thought I had been careful, but then passion for you must have clouded my senses.*

How long ago that seemed now! She read on eagerly.

> *But what's happened has happened and we will face the future together.*

Stella put a hand to her chest to still her hammering heart; rereading the words with exultation: '. . . *face the future together.*'

She turned over to the next page. The writing was smaller and more closely written.

Now, my darling Stella, I have a confession to make. I feel terrible that you have to hear this in a letter and not in person. If I'd had more time with you in Gulmarg I would have spoken of this sooner – there's a little fly in the ointment to our being married. You see, although I have long been estranged from her, I have a wife in Ireland. I haven't lived with her as her husband for years – she refused to live in India and sometimes I even forget she exists. Rest assured I will divorce her as soon as I can – and it does not alter for one moment my desire to spend the rest of my life with you. I cannot wait for us to be reunited – and plan to leave Singapore as soon as possible but it may not be for several weeks, maybe months.

Stella was winded by shock. She thought she would vomit. Pressing a hand over her mouth she read on in utter disbelief.

I know this might come as a blow to you, dear Stella, and it does not help your 'delicate' position at this point in time. I must thank the Lomaxes for taking care of you for me – perhaps they can advise you on what to do. I can't help feeling that it might be for the best if you place your baby in the care of others. I'm sorry that this complicated situation has arisen. Please write back and assure me that you don't hate me for this.

Someday soon, we will be together. I am still committed to marrying you, Stella, I promise. Perhaps in the meantime we could pretend we are married? After all, you told me that's what the Lomaxes did for years. If you are as set on keeping

the baby as you say you are, then I encourage you to
wear a wedding band. I will put my name to it when
it is born, no matter what happens.
   Take care of yourself, my green-eyed girl.
   With all my love,
   Hugh xxx

Stella sat with the letter on her lap, stunned, her head spinning with what she had just read. She didn't know what to think. The letter was a mass of contradictions. In one sentence Hugh was dropping the bombshell that he was married to a woman in Ireland and in another promising that he still loved her and wished to marry her. He advised her to give away the baby – *her* baby, he called it – and then backtracked and said if she wanted to keep it then to pretend they were married and he'd give it his name.

A part of Stella desperately latched onto this idea. Why not? As he said, the Lomaxes had lived with the pretence of being married. But just as quickly she dismissed it. The lies had eaten away at Tom and Esmie's relationship and had shattered the trust of their beloved Andrew. She felt ashamed that she had ever told Hugh their secret. Besides, her mother and family would see through the ruse at once; a feeble attempt to cover up that she was having a child out of wedlock.

Panic overwhelmed her.

Esmie glanced over anxiously. She rose. 'Stella?'

Stella stood, her legs nearly buckling underneath her. The airmail pages scattered to the floor as she hurried from the room, reaching the thunderbox just in time to vomit into it. She retched and retched. Gradually she became aware of Esmie standing over her, gently rubbing her back.

Without asking any questions, Esmie led her into the small bedroom that Stella was using and helped her under the covers.

'I'll get a hot water bottle and some tea with honey.'

Before she went, she stoked up the fire.

Stella lay – her throat and stomach sore from being sick – numbed to the core. Through the wall she could hear Tom's raised voice asking anxiously after her. When she felt the baby kicking, her tears came. She buried her head under the covers and wept. Esmie returned and tried to comfort her, coaxing her to sip the hot sweet tea. Bit by bit, Stella told her what was in the letter.

'What a cowardly man!' Esmie said in contempt. 'Even if he is estranged from his wife, he should have told you about her. You would never have got engaged if you'd known – and none of this would have happened.'

'I don't know what to believe,' Stella said in distress. 'How can I trust that he'll come back and support me when he's kept such a big secret from me?'

Esmie stroked the hair from Stella's brow. 'You can't trust him. What do you really know about him?'

Stella was no longer sure. Long ago, on the ship from India, Hugh had told tales of daring deeds in Baluchistan that had captivated Andrew. Yet when Tom had questioned Hugh about Quetta, he had been vague about the tribal outpost and seemed to know little about the army cantonment.

Hugh had told her that he was a farmer's son from somewhere outside Dublin and had stayed on in Ireland to help his mother and sister after his father died. But all the time he must have been married to this other woman. All his talk about supporting the family farm might have been fabricated to make him appear in a good light. What she did know now was that he had a wife in Ireland for whom he had such contempt that he sometimes forgot she was there. And who was it in Edinburgh that Hugh had been with when Andrew and Felicity had met him?

She was gripped with a sick fury. How had she allowed herself to be taken in by his charm and promise of marriage, which he was in no position to fulfil? He had seduced her knowing that. For years, she had chased a ridiculously romantic dream – that there was only one man for her – a handsome, sensual Irishman. She had been so certain of this that she hadn't stopped to question why he had suddenly turned up in her life after years apart and single-mindedly wooed her. Had it been nothing more to him than an opportunistic affair while he was thousands of miles away from his wife?

And yet, his letter insisted that it was she, Stella, whom he really loved.

'He says he still wants to be with me,' Stella said, 'and that he'll divorce his wife as soon as possible.'

Esmie shook her head sadly. 'So why hasn't he done so before now? What if she turns out to be like Lydia and refuses a divorce? Are you prepared to put up with that? It's not just you, Stella – you have your unborn child to consider. Do you trust that he will take on the baby?'

Esmie had never been so forthright with her; it was a measure of how upset she was. Stella could only imagine what Tom would have to say about Hugh's deception.

Her eyes stung with fresh tears. 'I don't know if I do,' she whispered.

Esmie let out a long sigh. She leaned over and kissed Stella tenderly on her forehead, like a mother would her child. 'Try and rest for now,' she said kindly. 'All this upset is not what your baby needs. You and your child are what matter to us, Stella, not Mr Keating.'

She stood and lifted a small brass bell from the tea tray. 'Ring this if you want anything. I'll look in on you later. Sleep, dear lassie.'

After she'd gone, Stella lay staring at the fire, trying to empty her mind of everything except the dancing pattern of the flames. Her baby stirred. It felt like it was somersaulting in her womb. It brought her sudden comfort. Whatever happened after today, she would love this child of hers with her whole heart and do whatever was best for him or her.

Chapter 37

The converted troop ship dropped anchor in the night. Standing at the rail, there was little to see, but Andrew could smell India on the night breeze: warm, pungent and oily. There was general euphoria on board that the long sea voyage was over and they had safely dodged the underwater terror of the U-boats.

Yet Andrew's pulse raced not from relief but from nerves. He had left India as a boy of thirteen, and now – eight and a half years later – he was returning as an adult. He gripped Dawan's talisman tightly in his pocket. The last time he had been here, he had clung to his father at their emotional parting, thinking that he would only be gone for the summer holidays. How he had worshipped his father in those days.

Over the past years he'd discovered from his mother how difficult a husband Tom had been: short-tempered, neglectful and ultimately unfaithful. Lydia had been even more vitriolic about Esmie. *'She usurped my place as your mother for years – I can never forgive her for that.'* Yet his Auntie Tibby – who always thought the best of everyone – had painted a different picture of his father and Esmie. *'Don't you think that the main reason they pretended to be married might have been to give you a stable, loving home?'*

As a youth, smarting from discovering the deceptions, Andrew had taken his mother's side. But adulthood had moderated his opinion. Relationships could be complicated, with no one side being completely guilty or innocent.

He let out a long breath. All those years ago, standing on the Bombay dockside, he had been embarking on an adventure with Stella by his side. If she had never gone with him, she would never have met Hugh Keating. How strange were the twists of fate where spur-of-the-moment decisions could lead to momentous consequences. Over the years, it was Stella's chatty, loving letters that had kept alive his connection to India. Now here he was, finally about to step back onto Indian soil – and somewhere on this vast subcontinent she was still here.

Then he chided himself for thinking more of her than of Felicity. He would write to his fiancée once he got to their headquarters in New Delhi.

As dawn broke, business on the dockside stirred. Andrew watched as coolies did their ablutions and heated up pans of chai. Acrid cooking smells filled the air and porters weaved among the squatting tea-drinkers with large bundles balanced on their heads. He'd forgotten the mark of the porter in India: a red cloth wound around his crown to give some modest protection from his burden.

Andrew caught a whiff of aromatic smoke: bidis. He remembered being in the compound at The Raj Hotel trying one of Sunil's small brown cheroots; it had ended in him having a coughing fit. Charlie Dubois had roared with laughter and promised not to tell Andrew's parents. His eyes smarted to think he would never see Charlie again.

Below, someone went by singing a high-pitched melodious song in Urdu. The sky over the city was rose pink and the outline of palm trees and ethereal pillared buildings began to emerge. Over the cries of stevedores, he could hear the chatter of exotic birds. He felt a sudden unexpected surge of excitement – India was welcoming him back.

Chapter 38

For the past few weeks, Stella and the Lomaxes had been marooned in the mountains. The snow in January had been so thick that for several days they had not even attempted to dig their way out. When Tom and Bijal eventually set out, the drifts of snow were chest-high in places.

Only Bijal and Karo had stayed on after December, both hardy Pathans used to the hardships of mountain winters and both discreet, neither passing comment on Stella's pregnant state.

The news that they had gleaned from the temperamental radio was deeply worrying. Hong Kong had fallen to the Japanese in late December and by January they had overrun Borneo and most of Malaya. Now Singapore was under siege, with bombing raids being carried out in broad daylight. A few weeks ago, the idea of this British-held territory being surrendered to Japan had been unthinkable; now it seemed only a matter of time.

Stella had no idea if Hugh was still there or whether he had managed to escape. She had never replied to his explosive letter and didn't know if he'd written again – no mail had been delivered since the end of December.

She had been cocooned in this icy, white world, content to hibernate from the dangers beyond it. She knew that her time was running out and she would have to face the world soon. Her thoughts about Hugh still see-sawed from day to day. One moment she clung to the hope that he would make good his promise to marry her and give their baby a name; the next she was filled with anger that he was a married man who had deceived her and left her pregnant.

Esmie was right when she'd said that Hugh might never divorce his wife – and even if he eventually did, it didn't help her in the here and now. Did she have the courage to brazen out her situation as an unmarried mother in the hopes that he might one day stand by her and their child?

Yet it distressed her to think Hugh might still be in Singapore and in danger. No matter what he had done, he was the father of the child she was carrying and she still cared for his safety. The thought of him being taken prisoner – or worse – seized her with panic.

Only a month away from giving birth, her belly and breasts were large, though the rest of her body was trim. Esmie had made sure that she kept healthy with indoor exercises, simple food and plenty of rest.

The Lomaxes had been like doting parents, cossetting her and keeping her occupied. With Tom she had learnt to draw flowers and found that she could be absorbed for hours – time in which she stopped dwelling on her situation. With Esmie and Karo, she sat on the floor propped up by cushions and stitched patterns of birds and flowers onto a blanket for the baby.

By the middle of February, when a slight thaw began, Tom made plans to go into Srinagar.

'I can't bear this waiting,' he said. 'I need to find out what's happening and where Andrew is.'

Tom was the epitome of a loving father. No matter that Andrew was now grown up, Tom still worried about him and loved him with the same fierce intensity that he had when he was a boy.

The night before Tom set off to trek into town, Stella lay sleepless and uncomfortable, her hands resting on her large belly. She'd had sharp twinges on a couple of occasions that Esmie had reassured her were normal in the late stages of pregnancy.

With Esmie – an experienced nurse – and Karo there to help her through the birth, Stella didn't fear it. But thinking of her life once the baby was born kept her troubled and awake. Slowly in her mind a plan began to form.

She hardly slept more than an hour or two. When she heard the Lomaxes stirring, she got up, wrapped a blanket round her and went to join them.

'You didn't have to get up to see Tom off,' Esmie said with a fond smile.

'No,' Tom agreed. 'Go back to bed and keep warm.'

Stella stood facing them, her heart pounding. She screwed up courage to say what she'd decided in the night.

'I want to ask you something,' she began. 'A very great favour.'

'Of course,' said Tom. 'What is it?'

'I've finally come to accept that Hugh is not the man for me or my baby. I don't think he will stick by me – but even if he intends to, I can't be sure he won't reject our child or come to resent us both.'

'I'm glad you're not going to be taken in by that man's empty promises,' Tom said. 'I've been worried that—'

'Tom,' Esmie interrupted, 'let Stella speak.'

Stella swallowed. 'Mr Lomax, you and Esmie are the kindest and most compassionate couple I know. I'm asking, for the sake of my baby, whether you could . . . whether you would agree to be parents . . . to him or her?'

They looked at her open-mouthed in astonishment and confusion.

'What do you mean?' asked Tom.

'Stella, are you saying you want to give up your child?' Esmie gasped.

Stella began to shake with emotion. 'I don't want to,' she said unhappily, 'but to keep it would be selfish. I can't give the baby a home – not one where it'll be treated normally. We'll both be outcasts. I don't want my child to be taken from me and given to strangers or end up in an orphanage where it might not be loved in the way it deserves.' Her eyes flooded with tears. 'But if you take my baby, I know that you will be the best parents he or she could have. I've seen the way you've loved Andrew and the way you've taken care of me these past months, not bothered about the shame I've brought you.'

Esmie was pressing her hand to her mouth to stop a sob.

'I can't make you do this,' Stella said, 'but the only way I can face giving him or her up is if I know you will be looking after it.'

Esmie rushed over to Stella. 'Sit down, lassie. You're shaking like a leaf. This is all such a shock. Are you sure you've thought it through?'

Stella nodded.

Esmie looked at her husband. 'Tom? Say something.'

Tom cleared his throat, struggling to speak. A single tear ran down his lean cheek. 'Yes,' he said hoarsely. 'I'd be a father to the baby – if you agree as well.'

Esmie smiled through her tears and nodded. 'Yes, Stella, we will. But would it not be better to wait and decide after the birth?'

'No,' said Stella, not wanting to weaken her resolve. 'I want my mother to be told that it's you who's expecting – and that I've stayed to help. I've thought about it so much and I think that this way is best for all of us. If Karo and Bijal don't say anything, then who is to know that it's not yours?'

Esmie encircled her with her arms and kissed her head tenderly. 'My poor, sweet Stella. What a brave lassie you are.'

Stella felt her tears come. She looked over to see Tom openly weeping.

A few days later, Tom returned full of joy about Andrew.

'I wired the Borderers' HQ in New Delhi. Andrew's there. He arrived last month.'

'Oh, darling!' cried Esmie. 'That is good news. When will we see him?'

'He thinks they'll be sent up to Taha by next month. I've asked him to let us know when he's likely to be passing through Pindi.'

'I can't wait to see him!' Esmie hugged him.

Stella's spirits lifted to think that Andrew was back in India. She was eager to see him too and catch up on the years apart. They probably would never recapture the close bond they'd once shared – their lives had diverged so much since she'd left him behind in Ebbsmouth. But if he was still the affectionate Andrew of his boyhood then she was sure they could rekindle their friendship. She was anxious, though, on Esmie's behalf. She had seen at first hand how intent Lydia had been on turning Andrew against his stepmother and wondered how awkward the reunion would be between them.

At the mention of Pindi, Stella asked nervously, 'Did you speak to Ma?'

'Yes.' Tom looked awkward. 'I told her that Esmie is expecting – that we hadn't said anything in case the pregnancy went wrong. I felt a fraud saying it, but that is what you want, isn't it?'

Stella nodded. 'What did she say?'

'She was delighted for us. And she said you were to stay on as long as we needed you.'

Stella's chest tightened. The deed was done and there was no going back. For the past few days she had forced herself to begin thinking of the baby as belonging to the Lomaxes and not her. She gave Tom a small smile of assent.

Esmie, sensing her unwillingness to dwell on the subject, asked, 'So what else did you bring from Srinagar?'

Tom had newspapers and post. The papers confirmed the frightening news that they had heard on the wireless: Singapore had fallen to the Japanese forces with the surrender of tens of thousands of troops. Hundreds of civilians had also been taken prisoner. Stella felt leaden at the thought that Hugh might be among them. But there were no further letters from him.

'I've wired Calcutta on your behalf, Stella,' Tom said, 'as I knew you'd be worrying about Keating.'

'Thank you,' Stella said, trying not to be tearful.

His look turned grim. 'The Indian Army must be fighting to hold onto Burma too – they're evacuating Rangoon.'

Stella's stomach churned. 'Evacuating them to where? India?'

'I imagine so,' said Tom.

'So India could be next?' she asked fearfully.

Esmie squeezed her arm. 'Not necessarily. You mustn't worry. The war's still a long way from here.'

Tom said quickly, 'I didn't mean to cause alarm. The jungles and mountains between Burma and India are almost impenetrable. And the British will never allow India to be taken.'

Three weeks later, as the March thaw came to the mountains and valleys of Kashmir and the frozen rivers turned to thundering rapids, Stella went into labour. It was late afternoon and she'd been having occasional sharp pains on and off since the morning. Suddenly, she broke off from doing paperwork with Esmie and let out a gasp. She clutched her belly.

Esmie looked at her in alarm. 'Are you feeling pains?'

Stella nodded.

'Come on,' said Esmie, 'let's get you to bed.'

Four hours later, as she lay half-prone on her narrow bed in the annex, the labour contractions were coming in relentless waves. Karo wiped her face with a damp scented cloth while Esmie held her hand and encouraged her.

'Squeeze my hand when the contractions come,' she said, timing them on her old nurse's watch.

Stella gritted her teeth as each fresh bout of pain assaulted her.

'That's good,' said Esmie. 'You don't have to be so brave – shout if you want – but keep some breath for the pushing.'

Esmie examined her. She exchanged rapid words in Pashto with Karo, who took over holding Stella's hand.

'Is everything all right?' Stella panted.

'You're doing very well,' Esmie assured her with a smile. 'The baby's in position. I can see the head – it won't be long now. Karo says you're lucky – you've been blessed with a short labour.'

Stella had never experienced such pain. It gripped her like a vice. Each time it subsided she dreaded its return. But Esmie talked to her calmly and Karo murmured words that she couldn't understand, yet were soothing.

'Don't fight it,' Esmie said. 'Save your energy. Breathe . . . in and out . . . That's it – keep it steady. And again.'

Beyond the stuffy room, she knew that Tom was waiting anxiously. Half an hour ago, Esmie had gone out and reassured him that all was going well. Now, Stella just wished it to be over. She never wanted to go through such an ordeal again. She panted and cried out.

Abruptly, Esmie ordered, 'When the next contraction comes, start to push. Ready? Push!'

Stella pushed and howled. She clung onto Karo.

'Again!' Esmie urged.

As sweat ran down her face and soaked her body with the exertion, Stella cursed aloud. 'Hugh-bloody-Keating! I hate you! I wish I'd never met—!' Her cries were swallowed up by another roar of pain.

'That's it,' Esmie coaxed. 'Nearly there! One last big push this time. Go on, Stella, push!'

This time, Stella felt the difference. The excruciating red-hot pain was followed by the strangest sensation – as if she were expelling half of her insides – and then sudden relief. Moments later, Esmie let out a triumphant cry.

'Well done, lassie!'

Stella lay back, heaving for breath, her eyes stinging with sweat. She heard the tiniest bleat of protest. Through blurred vision she watched Esmie and Karo deal with the bloodied newborn; clearing its airways, cutting the cord, wiping off the mucus, wrapping it and cooing over it.

'Girl or a boy?' Stella whimpered, euphoric with relief that it was over, and yet anxious.

Esmie gently held up the mewling bundle. 'It's a wee lassie. A beautiful girl – just like her mother.'

'Let me see.' Stella struggled to sit up. One thing still plagued her thoughts – unspoken to the Lomaxes, although they must have been worrying too: what did the baby look like?

As Esmie brought her daughter close, Stella could see dark sticky hair and a petite crinkled pink face screwed up against the light of the kerosene lamp. Stella's fears subsided. Apart from the hair colour, the baby didn't look Anglo-Indian. The dark hair could be passed off as being like Tom's. But the true mother's heritage would not betray her. Stella sank back with relief.

'Would you like to hold her?' Esmie asked with a tentative smile.

Stella fought the desire to do so. 'No, you keep her. Show her to Mr Lomax.'

Chapter 39

Stella fell asleep. She woke to a strange sound. The lamp had been turned down low but she could make out the shape of the cradle beside her bed. It was gently rocking. Leaning up, Stella saw Karo sitting cross-legged on the floor, pushing it.

She smiled at Stella and then called out for Esmie.

At once, Esmie appeared in the doorway. 'How are you, lassie? Could you manage a bowl of soup and some chapatti?'

Stella realised that she was hungry. 'Yes, I'd like that, thank you.'

Without being asked, Karo rose and went to fetch some food.

Esmie sat down on the edge of the bed. 'I know you'll want a bath,' she said. 'But do you think you could try and feed the baby after you've had a bite to eat yourself? Karo can help show you how.'

They had agreed this was what they would do for the first days; Stella would nurse the baby herself. Then when the hotel opened up again, Karo's daughter Gabina would return from Srinagar to be the baby's ayah – and Stella would go back to Rawalpindi.

Stella was sore and still exhausted – and not sure any more that she wanted to nurse the infant. But it didn't seem a lot to ask; Esmie had done so much for her these past months. Nothing she did could repay the Lomaxes for standing by her when she had needed them so badly.

'Of course,' Stella said, wincing as she tried to sit up.

Esmie helped prop her up with pillows and then lifted the baby out of the cradle. The snuffling sound that had woken Stella was growing into a querulous cry.

Esmie held the tiny girl in her arms and stroked her cheek. 'There, there, wee lamb,' she crooned. 'Milk is coming.'

She walked around the small room, patting and soothing. Tears sprang to Stella's eyes at seeing Esmie – childless for so long – treating the baby with such tenderness. If she'd had doubts about her decision to give her to the Lomaxes, this moment of intimacy dispelled them. Esmie would love her daughter with a devotion that she might not be able to match herself.

Karo returned with an aromatic bean soup, and Stella devoured it. The queasiness she'd experienced for months at the smell of spicy food was miraculously gone. Afterwards, Karo helped Stella put the baby to her breast. Stella gasped at the sharp tug from such a tiny mouth. It was the strangest sensation – neither painful nor comfortable – and she stared at the creature feeding from her, amazed at the newborn's instinctive ability to know what to do. She had dark eyes that fixed unfocused on the creamy curve of Stella's breast.

Soon the baby stopped sucking, her eyes closing. Karo showed her how to unlatch the small mouth without it hurting. Stella felt a flicker of disappointment when the warm, snuffling infant was removed and placed back in the cradle.

'What do you want to call her?' Esmie asked.

Stella had fleetingly thought of naming her daughter Myrtle, after her mother, but dismissed the idea at once. There must be no connection with her family at all.

'You and Mr Lomax must decide,' she said, forcing a smile.

Esmie seemed about to say something and then changed her mind. She nodded. 'Karo will prepare a bath for you. Then you can sleep.'

Stella sank back in the bed and tried to stop the tears that were leaking between her closed eyelids. She was glad of the subdued light in the room, which hid her emotional state.

The Lomaxes decided to call the baby Isobel.

'It's after my Aunt Isobel in Scotland,' Esmie explained. 'I know she wasn't my real aunt but she was a wonderful guardian after my parents died – and a great friend.'

Stella remembered Esmie being upset about the woman's death five years ago.

'My only regret in staying out east was that I never saw her again,' Esmie said with emotion.

'She was a wonderful woman,' said Tom, 'and a great doctor too.' He gazed down at the baby in his arms. 'If you have half of Isobel Carruthers's spirit, my wee girl, you'll take on the world.'

Esmie smiled. 'Tom, we don't want her to take on the world – just to thrive in it.'

Stella felt a pang at their happy talk, glad that the baby was already bringing them joy as well as a renewed tenderness towards each other. Where the upset over Andrew had put a strain on them for years, the two weeks that Isobel had been in their lives had lifted their jaded spirits.

Tom chuckled. 'But Isobel sounds a bit serious for such a delicate creature, so we'll probably call her Belle for short. What do you think?'

Stella's eyes glistened. 'I think that's a lovely name.'

'Belle it is, then,' Tom declared, his lean face creasing in delight.

During the time that Stella was feeding the baby, she carried on living in the annex. Esmie stayed close to home too, making sure that both mother and baby were feeding and resting. Meanwhile Tom and Bijal began opening up the hotel for the new season, fixing up the gutters and repainting the verandas. They had a telephone installed – something Stella had been suggesting they do for years but Tom had resisted – as now they wanted Andrew to be able to contact them more easily.

As the spring came and wild flowers pushed up from the warming soil, Esmie and Tom would take Belle out in a makeshift pram – a box on wheels that Tom had made – and push her down the garden path and across the deserted golf course. It was too early for any visitors to the chalets or hotels, but Stella knew it was only a matter of time before word spread that there was a baby in the Lomax household up at the remote hotel.

Stella existed in a strange state of limbo – of living purely in the present. She focused on the job in hand: feeding Belle. She was glad they had chosen a name that would never have occurred to Stella; it made the baby seem less like hers. Her milk had come in strongly now, and the baby was thriving on it. Already Belle was changing shape, her crinkled face filling out into soft plump cheeks and her budlike mouth latching on eagerly to Stella's breasts.

Most startling of all were her eyes: round dark-blue eyes that fixed on her trustingly. Eyes like sapphires: the one trait that betrayed that Hugh was the father.

Stella would stroke the baby's soft brown hair as she fed and for a moment indulge in a fantasy of being Belle's mother in a home that Hugh had created for them. It was the way it should have been – but now never would. Even if Hugh reappeared, Belle's future had been determined. She would grow up as a Lomax.

One afternoon, while the Lomaxes were out with Belle, Stella was sewing on the veranda and heard the telephone ringing in the hotel. Bijal came onto the front steps and waved across.

'Telephone call, Stella-Mem'! Sahib on the line!'

Stella jumped. Could it be Hugh? Had he made it back safely to India? Perhaps he had been trying to get in touch with her all this time . . . Dropping her sewing, she raced inside.

She grabbed at the receiver on the office desk.

'Hello! Hugh, is that you?'

There was a pause at the other end and then a man's deep voice answered. 'No, sorry. It's Andrew. Is that you, Stella?'

Stella's first reaction was huge disappointment. Even after all that had happened, for a few dizzying moments she had dared to hope that it was Hugh trying to reach her.

She swallowed hard. 'Yes, it's me. Andrew . . . goodness! How are you?'

'I'm well, thanks. How are you?'

'Fine,' she lied. 'You sound so different. It's like hearing your father. I mean, you have a man's voice.'

She heard him give a huff of amusement. 'Well, I suppose that's what I am.'

She cringed. 'Of course you are. What a stupid thing to say! I'm just caught by surprise at your call. But it's lovely . . .'

'I didn't think you'd be up at Gulmarg this early in the year – or at all – now you're engaged. Sorry if you were expecting it to be Hugh. How is he?'

Stella gripped the receiver. 'I . . . I'm not sure. He's been in Singapore – I don't know if he's safe – I've had no news . . .'

'Oh, Stella! How awful for you! I'm so sorry.'

'Don't worry,' she said hastily. 'Knowing Hugh, he'll have escaped any trouble. Might even be back in Calcutta by now. It's just we've been cut off up here. But tell me about yourself. Where are you?'

'Still in Delhi – we've been training here since January, but—' The line crackled and Stella missed some of his words. '. . . up to Taha so I'm hoping to get a night or so in Pindi.'

'Oh, Andy, that would be wonderful. Your dad and Esmie are longing to see you.'

'Is Dad there?' he asked.

'No, sorry, he's out with Esmie.' Just in time, Stella stopped herself mentioning the baby. 'He'll be so disappointed that he's missed your call. Can you ring back later?'

The line crackled again and she missed his reply. She strained to hear. 'What did you say?'

'. . . give my love—'

Abruptly, the line went dead.

Shaking, Stella sat down. She felt suddenly winded. It had been so long since she'd heard Andrew's voice and yet, although older, he sounded just as friendly and affectionate as ever. She blushed to think of her flustered greeting about him having a man's voice. What must he think of her? And to mistake him for Hugh . . .

Unable to settle to her sewing again, Stella went in search of the Lomaxes. Spotting them meandering back across the golf course, she ran to meet them, gabbling breathlessly about Andrew's telephone call.

They started talking at the same time.

'How is he?'

'What did he say?'

'Is he coming here?'

'When will we see him?'

Stella berated herself for not having asked more questions; she'd hardly learnt anything about how he was or what it was like being back in India.

'It was difficult to hear,' she admitted, 'but he said something about Taha and hoping to pass through Pindi. I'm sorry, I can't really tell you any more than that. We got cut off.' Seeing the disappointment on their faces, she quickly added, 'But he sent his love.'

'I wish I'd been there to speak to him,' Tom said in frustration.

'Oh, Tom,' Esmie said, kissing his cheek. 'It sounds like he's on his way north. I'm sure we'll see him very soon.' She looked at Stella and her expression clouded. 'Did you tell him about Belle?'

Stella stammered. 'No. Perhaps I should have?'

Tom shook his head. 'It's not something he should be told about over a crackling line to Delhi.'

They returned to the hotel, the Lomaxes talking excitedly about the thought of seeing Andrew soon. Stella's spirits lifted too. The conversation had warmed her heart, and yet it had been too frustratingly brief. How good it would be to talk to Andrew properly and to see him again.

At the end of March, a telegram arrived from Calcutta. Stella felt faint with anxiety as she opened it.

> *Report good news – STOP – Keating safe in South Africa – STOP – will remain there while India uncertain – STOP – Arthur Lamont*

Tom was scathing. 'Typical of the man to have got out of Singapore when thousands didn't – like a rat deserting the sinking ship.'

'Tom, don't,' Esmie reproved. 'At least he's not a prisoner, as Stella feared.'

Stella gripped the telegram, her stomach churning. Her initial relief at hearing he was safe quickly turned to anger.

'No, Mr Lomax is right,' she cried. 'Hugh is a rat! He's not even tried to contact me and tell me he's all right or ask how I am. I've heard nothing for months – not even a telegram.'

She tore the telegram in pieces and jammed them into a brass ashtray.

'I'm sorry,' she said, turning and rushing from the sitting room.

Stella escaped to her bedroom and shut the door firmly behind her. The noise woke Belle. She began to grizzle. Stella tensed, balling her fists. Belle was living proof of her naive stupidity; a constant reminder of her weakness in falling so heavily in love with a silver-tongued adulterer.

Belle's protests grew. Stella knew it would be seconds before the baby was yelling lustily to be fed. She leaned over the cradle and picked her up. For a moment, Belle fell silent and fixed her with curious blue eyes, as if she sensed her misery. She looked so solemn and trusting. Then her rosebud mouth flickered in the ghost of a smile. Even though Stella knew that babies didn't smile as young as three weeks old, it pierced her heart.

She kissed her daughter tenderly on the forehead and then sat down with her in the nursing chair that Karo had furnished with colourful cushions and a warm wool blanket. Cradling Belle to her breast, Stella felt the familiar tug and her milk beginning to flow. It released the tears that had been welling in her eyes. Stella sat cuddling her baby and quietly weeping. She already knew how hard it would be to leave her and return to Rawalpindi. But she refused to think of the life she must lead beyond this moment. All that mattered was this time with her daughter, giving her what she needed that no one else could.

Through the gauze muslin curtain that blew gently in the breeze at the open window, Stella could make out the fir trees beyond the hotel, stretching up to the marg. She breathed in the sweet scent of pine as her heartbeat slowed and the baby sucked rhythmically at her breast. Calmness settled on her like soft falling petals.

April came, and with it a message from Rawalpindi. When Tom came rushing round from the hotel, the women were on the small veranda of the annex enjoying the secluded view of the sloping forest behind. Stella was experimenting with painting flowers onto fabric while Esmie helped Karo sew cushion covers for the hotel. Belle lay gurgling in the cradle.

'It's from Jimmy,' said Tom, excitement in his voice. 'He says Andrew has booked into the Raj next week for a couple of nights on his way to Taha.'

'Next week?' Esmie exclaimed. 'That doesn't give us long to get organised and down to Pindi.'

Stella saw Tom's look alter. He glanced at Belle, who was waving her hands in the air. 'I think, given the circumstances, that I should go down to Pindi on my own.'

Esmie looked crestfallen. 'But I so want to see him.'

'I know you do, my darling – but you should be here with Belle – and Stella.' Tom looked awkward. 'I think I should meet him alone on the first occasion – there has been so much misunderstanding – I can set the record straight. And he doesn't know about Belle yet . . .'

Stella reddened. Would Andrew be glad to hear he had a baby sister? She hoped so. The last thing she wanted was for her actions to cause further tension in the Lomax family.

'Yes, I suppose you're right,' Esmie said, putting on a brave face. 'You must have as much time with Andy as you can get. You'll press him to come and visit us here, won't you?'

'Of course,' said Tom, brightening. 'This is the place he loved the best in India – I'm sure he'll jump at the chance as soon as he can.'

Stella felt overcome with excitement. How she would love to see Andrew too! The recent tantalising phone call had made her all the more curious to see what sort of man he had grown into.

Chapter 40

Andrew peered through the slats of the train window and caught his first sight of Rawalpindi emerging out of the plain in the dawn light. In the distance, across the rocky scrubland, he could just make out the fringe of foothills that led east into the Himalayas. That way lay Murree and beyond it, Kashmir and his father. He quickly dismissed an unsettling thought. He'd been given two days' leave on his way to Taha, which didn't give him time to get to Gulmarg. He should have told his father he would be in Rawalpindi but he didn't want to drag him down from the mountains for such a short time – and the roads might still be hazardous for another month – although deep down he longed to see him.

Andrew craned for a view of the city – a dark bulky mass of buildings under wreaths of smoke from early fires, the glint of a temple roof, a flock of birds rising into golden light – and then the train was slowing and pulling into the station. As it juddered to a halt, Andrew eagerly alighted from the carriage, breathing in the smell of dung fires and ghee. The air was already warm. Across the platform, he was greeted by the familiar sight of the imposing brick-built station building with its mix of eastern arches and gothic turrets and battlements.

Manek, the wiry bearer whom Andrew had hired in Delhi, was already commandeering a porter to carry Andrew's luggage. Manek was pockmarked and small in stature but had a breezy manner that seemed to make others want to do his bidding.

For the first time in years, Andrew heard Punjabi being spoken around him and delighted in seeing local men dressed in baggy salwar kameez and extravagantly large turbans. These Punjabis paused at wicker tables to eat a quick breakfast of chapatti and dahl, while beside them chai-wallahs brewed pans of sweetened milky tea.

For a moment, Andrew drank in the first sights of his old home town. Traders weaved around him pushing trolleys laden with sacks and bundles. Across on the far platform, camels snorted in protest at being loaded onto open bogies. It struck Andrew that they were probably being transported to the frontier to help with army convoys. Soon he would be following them, but for now he had a reprieve. He hurried through the station after a beckoning Manek.

The hired horse-drawn tonga took them through the Saddar Bazaar. As Andrew revelled in the sights of low-lying balconied buildings and the open-fronted stalls that were already doing brisk business with their piles of ochre and yellow spices and sacks of green chillies, it struck him that little had changed.

As the tonga went under an arch of the Massey Gate, Andrew pointed out the sign above to Manek. 'That's the Dhunjibhoy Public Library. Parsi family. They run the tongas going up to Murree and Kashmir. At least they used to. Maybe most people do it by car these days.'

Manek nodded in agreement. 'Parsis are good at business, sahib.'

They emerged into the regimented tree-lined streets of the cantonment with its pencil-straight roads and grander buildings running down to the Mall. Officers were out exercising their horses before the temperature climbed higher and, through the trees,

Andrew glimpsed soldiers doing physical fitness on a dusty patch of ground.

'Pindi's always been an army town,' he said. 'I used to love going to watch the parades and the polo games – never imagining that one day I'd be a soldier too.'

Turning down Edwardes Road towards Dalhousie Road, Andrew began to feel nervous once more. He held his breath as they turned into Nichol Road. There, across the neatly cut lawn set back from the street, was his former home: The Raj Hotel. Andrew peered past the two palm trees that guarded the path and a riot of bougainvillea that half-hid the entrance; the building looked newly whitewashed. The window frames and iron-roofed portico were still painted pale blue, but Charlie's garish red and gold signage had been replaced by a more tasteful and subdued green, declaring Mr T. Lomax as the proprietor.

Andrew felt a pang of sadness. He braced himself for meeting the Duboises for the first time since Charlie had died. His palms began to sweat. Would Stella be here too? During their tantalisingly brief phone call, he'd not had time to ask when she was returning to Pindi. He knew that it was highly unlikely she'd be here but, even so, he had to admit that this was the real reason he was feeling so nervous at returning. Speaking to her had churned up his emotions. One minute he'd been ecstatic at hearing her voice; the next he'd felt punched in the guts at her mistaking him for Hugh. He didn't know which would be worse; seeing her or not seeing her.

As Andrew climbed down from the tonga he heard a mournful cry and turned to see a peacock strutting towards him across the lawn, which was strewn with a carpet of deep-pink bougainvillea petals.

'Percy, my old friend!' Andrew grinned. 'Glad to see you're still alive. Or maybe you're son of Percy?'

The bird gave another shrill call and then bent to peck at the ground. At that moment, a familiar grey-haired figure came hurrying down the path and gave him a toothless grin.

'Welcome, sahib.'

'Sunil!' Andrew cried. 'How are you? You haven't changed a bit.'

Sunil nodded and his smile widened further. 'Very well, sahib.'

'Manek,' Andrew said to his bearer, 'this is the man who taught me the art of smoking. Sunil will help you bring in the bags.'

Andrew walked ahead of them, his confident strides belying the anxiety he felt inside. Petals fell on him as his head brushed against the creeper over the entrance; he'd definitely grown taller since he'd last been here. He entered the gloom of the lobby, which still smelt of beeswax polish and the slight mustiness of overwatered plant pots. To his delight, the décor had remained pale green and the tiled floor was cluttered with cane chairs, drinks tables and drooping ferns as it had been when he was a boy.

A thick-set man with a round face, pencil moustache and dressed in a dark suit came forward, hand outstretched. For a stunned moment, while his eyes adjusted from the glare outside, Andrew thought it was Charlie.

'Master Andrew!' The man beamed. 'You are the image of your father.'

'Jimmy!' Andrew shook his hand warmly. 'And you are the image of yours. I was so very sorry—'

'Yes, yes.' Jimmy cut him short. 'We all miss the old boy like the devil. The residents will be delighted to see you – they have been growing quite giddy at the thought of you coming.'

'I can't wait to see them too,' said Andrew. He asked quickly, 'But first, how is the rest of the Dubois family? I must congratulate you on becoming a father. From the wedding photograph that Stella sent to my Auntie Tibby, you have a beautiful wife too.'

Jimmy smiled and nodded.

'And how is your sister? I had the briefest of conversations last month and was surprised to find she'd gone to Gulmarg early this season.' He hoped his voice sounded neutral despite his drumming heart.

'Ha, my sister! It's so long since she's been here that we've forgotten what she looks like!'

Andrew noticed that he immediately felt a slight easing of the tension he'd been feeling. 'Oh?' he said, keeping an even tone.

'Yes,' said Jimmy, 'she's been in Gulmarg since last summer.'

'Right through the cold season?' Andrew asked. 'Why?'

Jimmy's round face turned pink. 'Well, helping your parents of course . . .'

Andrew was baffled. 'But there's nothing to do there once the snow comes.' He grew alarmed at the sight of Jimmy's wary look.

'Surely you've heard?'

'Heard what? Dad's all right, isn't he?'

Jimmy nodded vigorously. 'Never better. And I'm glad to say that Mr Lomax is on his way here to greet you. I took the liberty of alerting him to your impending arrival.'

'My father's coming here?' Andrew gasped.

'Yes, sir. You will soon be reunited. Mr Lomax will be here by this evening.' Jimmy was beaming again. 'He can explain everything.'

'Explain what? You're being very mysterious, Jimmy. Is he coming on his own?' For a brief moment he hoped Stella would be returning too.

'Yes, yes, alone.'

Just then, there was a shout from along the corridor. 'Subaltern Lomax! Is that you? By golly, you've grown.'

Andrew turned in amusement to see who was greeting him with the old-fashioned army title for second lieutenant and saw two familiar figures coming towards him.

'Mr Ansom! Mr Fritwell!' Andrew greeted them. He wanted to throw his arms around them in delight that they were both still living there, but shook them eagerly by the hand instead.

Jimmy waved them towards the dining room. 'Master Andrew is going to join you for breakfast.'

'Best scrambled eggs outside of Britain,' said Ansom. 'Even though Chef's never mastered the art of crisping the bacon.'

'We want to hear all about your exploits,' said Fritwell. 'Heard you were at Dunkirk. Terrible business.'

Andrew gave distracted answers to their volley of questions. He was still reeling from the news that his father was on his way. To be truthful, a part of him yearned to be reunited with his dad, yet he was nervous too. Even after all this time, it was hard to clear his mind of his mother's bitter words about her former husband.

The dining room appeared to have changed little: the walls darkly panelled and the tables laid with crisp white linen and glinting cutlery. Each had a centrepiece of a spray of fresh flowers. He thought fondly of how Stella had always delighted in doing that job; perhaps Yvonne had taken it on.

Andrew worked his way through a large plateful of bacon, eggs and tomatoes, followed by fried puffs with syrup, toast and apricot jam, washed down with several cups of strong tea. Baroness Cusack joined them, with squeals of surprise at seeing Andrew, and as he ate he attempted to satisfy Hester's curiosity about his life in Ebbsmouth, his mother, his aunt, his school days in Durham and his love life.

'Do you have a photograph of your beloved?' she asked in her forthright way.

When Andrew produced a photo of Felicity from his pocket, Hester peered at it through the pince-nez that hung from a thin chain around her neck. She handed it back with an assessing look.

'Well?' Andrew asked. 'Does she pass muster?'

'Very pretty,' said Hester. 'She looks quite determined.'

Andrew said in amusement, 'She is.'

'I hope she's kind to you, darling.'

Andrew wasn't sure if that was a word he would use about Felicity. 'I'm fairly sure she loves me,' he said with a self-deprecating smile.

'And you're in love with her?' she pressed him.

'Of course.'

'Well, that's good,' said the baroness. 'It's wonderful to see you young ones falling in love. First Stella and her Irishman and now you and your Scottish girl.'

'I hear Stella isn't sure of Mr Keating's whereabouts. Has there been any more news of him?' Andrew asked.

'Good question,' said Hester. 'It's been a bit of a drama for the poor girl. He was working in Malaya and Singapore but got safely away. Myrtle had a letter from Stella just the other day to say that her fiancé is in South Africa. Must be a relief to know he's safe but it doesn't sound like they will be marrying in the near future.'

Andrew was just turning this news over in his mind when in walked Myrtle Dubois. He got up at once to greet her, repeating his condolences about Charlie's death while she expressed the common view that he, Andrew, was just like his father. She had aged; her pretty brown eyes were sunk in patches of bluish skin and her hair had gone grey. When she wasn't smiling, her mouth drooped in sadness.

But she seemed pleased to see him. Myrtle had always made a fuss of him as a boy and indulged him more than her own children.

'I hope Jimmy has been looking after you. With Stella away, I've moved back into the bungalow to help with my grandson. You must settle in and then come and see our Charles – he's such a dear little thing. It's such a tonic having a little one in the family after my Charlie . . .' Tears sprang into her eyes.

'I'm sure he's a great comfort,' Andrew said kindly.

Myrtle smiled. 'He is. And you'll soon find out the joy of having a baby in the family too, won't you? We're so delighted for you all.'

Hester commented, 'Surprised but delighted. After all this time, who would have thought it?'

Andrew looked bemused. 'A baby? Whose baby?'

Myrtle's look faltered. 'Mr and Mrs Lomaxes'. Surely you've been told?'

Andrew gaped at her in disbelief. 'They've had a baby?'

'Oh dear,' said Hester. 'We've let the cat out of the bag. Obviously, your father wanted to tell you in person.'

Andrew was speechless.

'I'm sorry,' said Myrtle, 'I thought you'd know by now. Of course, we've only recently been told. With Mrs Lomax coming to motherhood late, they were being very cautious. Stella's been helping out.'

'When did this happen?' he managed to ask, still in shock.

'She was born last month,' said Myrtle.

'She?'

'Yes,' said Hester. 'You have a sister called Isobel. Isn't that lovely news?'

Andrew didn't know what to think. Was he pleased? 'Yes, happy news,' he forced himself to say. He suddenly felt terribly constricted, though; trapped. 'Well, after that wonderful breakfast, I think I'll go and freshen up.'

'Of course,' said Myrtle. 'Is there anything else we can get you?'

'No, nothing,' said Andrew. 'Nothing at all.' He made for the door, waving at the men at the far table who had been unaware of the awkward conversation.

'Catch up with you at tiffin!' Ansom called over.

Andrew walked smartly past Jimmy at reception and took the stairs two at a time. He raced along the corridor to the family flat at the far end. Inside, he slammed the door shut and breathed in deeply.

He had a month-old baby sister. Why hadn't they told him sooner?

The baby must just have been born when he'd spoken to Stella. She should have said something.

Try as he might, Andrew couldn't put his mother's bitter words out of his mind. *'Andrew, the plain truth is that your father would rather be married to that woman than have you live with him. I thought he'd fight harder for you.'*

Now they had a child of their own. Had they been trying for years for another son or daughter? He could hardly blame them if they had. It wasn't so much them being parents to someone else that bothered him; it was the not telling him that hurt.

Andrew pulled out his cigarette case and stepped onto the veranda. As he smoked, he stared into the courtyard below. Someone was peeling vegetables in the shade of the jacaranda. He'd fallen out of that tree as a boy and twisted his ankle. Charlie had carried him into the bungalow and strapped up his ankle while Stella had given him a sherbet sweet and told him a story about giants to take his mind off the pain.

Andrew inhaled smoke furiously. It was futile getting upset over domestic wrangles that no longer mattered. His father and Esmie were entitled to do what they wanted – live how they chose – and enjoy late parenthood. Esmie would make a devoted mother.

And he shouldn't blame Stella for not saying anything on the telephone. It wasn't her news to tell.

As a boy, all he'd wanted was to be part of a conventional family like his school friends. But life wasn't like that for everyone. From what he could gather, his parents' love for each other had been as transient as the bougainvillea petals blowing across the rooftop of the hotel. By the time he was born, they already seemed to be out of love. Life was messy and didn't always work out as planned.

Andrew would not make the same mistake as his parents. If he survived the war, he would be going back to Scotland and marrying for love. Grinding out his cigarette stub, he retreated to the smaller bedroom, stripped off and lay down on the green counterpane. In minutes he was asleep.

Chapter 41

Andrew woke feeling groggy and thick-headed as if he'd been drinking spirits. For a moment he thought it must be night-time already and then realised the shutters were keeping out the light. Emerging from the bedroom he saw that a tray of food had been left for him in the sitting room; he must have missed tiffin. He lifted the metal lids to be met by wafts of curry and rice. It made him feel a little sick. Instead he glugged down a glass of mango juice – his favourite as a boy – and pressed the semi-cool glass to his forehead.

The startling news he'd heard this morning came back to him: his father and Esmie had a baby daughter called Isobel. He dreaded to think how Lydia would take the news of the Lomax baby. Would she be jealous that Esmie had now completely eclipsed her in Tom's life, giving him a longed-for daughter?

He would write to his mother and assure her that it made no difference to their relationship – he would always be her son first and foremost – not Esmie's.

Padding to the bathroom, Andrew saw that Manek had run a cold bath for him. Stripping off, he immersed himself in the tepid water, plunging his head under to banish his feverish thoughts. While he shaved, Andrew tried to steady his nerves at the thought of seeing his father in a matter of hours. Walking through the flat towelling his hair, he found Manek laying out fresh clothes on the bed. His young bearer must have been listening at the door for sounds that he was up and about.

'Are they treating you well in the compound?' Andrew asked.

'Yes, sahib.' Manek smiled.

'Have you noticed if they still keep bicycles there? I'm going to go out this afternoon and would like to borrow one.'

'Yes, sahib, they do. Would you like me to bring one round to the hotel entrance?'

'Please,' Andrew said.

Downstairs in the foyer, Ansom was snoozing under a copy of the *Military and Civil Gazette*. Andrew saw a headline about Gandhi telling Indians not to resist the Japanese if they invaded India and to continue their campaign of civil disobedience; they wanted immediate independence.

Andrew felt a flicker of alarm. The last thing he wanted was for his regiment to be dragged into a policing role of rounding up and imprisoning Indians when they had a war to fight. He felt a renewed frustration that he had been deployed to the Frontier rather than to help in the battle over North Africa or in the Middle East. Yet if these rumours were true of their army being pushed back through the jungles of Burma by rapidly advancing Japanese forces, perhaps the spectre of India being invaded was no longer so fantastical.

To take his mind off grim war news and his growing nervousness at seeing his father again, Andrew spent the afternoon cycling aimlessly around the town and the military cantonment. Finding himself in the Anglo-Indian quarter of Lalkutri, he called into Dixon's garage, run by Stella's relations, and was greeted warmly by her cousin Sigmund, with whom he had often played cricket as a boy.

339

'I didn't know you were back in Pindi,' said Sigmund.

'I'm just passing through,' said Andrew. 'I've been posted to Taha. I'm with the Borderers.'

Sigmund gave him a cheerful salute. 'Come upstairs and have some refreshment,' he insisted. 'My sister Ada is visiting. This will make her day to see Andrew Lomax dressed in khaki.'

Andrew felt a pang of nostalgia as he climbed the outside staircase to the flat, remembering how Stella used to take him there. It conjured up happy memories of visits to the lively and noisy household – Auntie Rose pressing him to eat mounds of cake and playing raucous games of cards with Stella and her cousins.

As soon as he saw Ada it was obvious she was heavily pregnant. He'd heard she'd married one of the Gibson twins a few years ago.

Ada kissed him on the cheek and laughed. 'Yes, you are allowed to mention it. I'm expecting in June.'

'Congratulations.' Andrew smiled. 'So, you've beaten your cousin Stella to marriage and motherhood.'

Ada rolled her eyes. 'Stella has always been too fussy. She could have had her pick of the Lalkutri boys but she's always had her sights set on marrying a pukka Brit.'

'Now, now, sister,' Sigmund chided, 'don't be unkind about Cousin Stella or Andrew here will have something to say.'

'Sorry, Andrew,' said Ada. 'I'd forgotten how you were always coming to Stella's defence.' She laughed. 'Oh, how sweet; you still blush at the mention of her name.'

Stella's aunt welcomed him and plied him with afternoon tea while talking proudly of her eldest son Rick being in the Indian Air Force and training down at Walton, outside Lahore. The visit provided a welcome distraction as well as a chance to talk about Stella.

Andrew lingered until the shadows lengthened and he knew he couldn't put off returning to the hotel any longer; it would be dark in half an hour. He said his goodbyes to the Dixons and pedalled home as he'd done countless times as a boy, the sky turning pink and flocks of birds settling noisily into the trees.

Drawing near to the Raj, his heart skipped a beat as he turned into Nichol Road. There, in front of the hotel, was parked the Lomaxes' battered green van. His father had arrived.

Andrew took deep breaths as he wheeled the bicycle up the pathway to the portico. He could hear laughter coming from the lobby – Jimmy's infectious giggle – and a deeper voice, one he also knew. Handing over the bicycle to the waiting Manek, he braced himself, as if going into battle, and strode into the hotel.

A middle-aged man with his back to the door was sitting in a cane chair next to Ansom and Fritwell. A bald patch on the crown of his head gleamed in the dim electric light and long bony hands clutched a tumbler of whisky and a half-smoked cigarette.

'Ah, our young subaltern returns!' Fritwell cried, catching sight of Andrew.

Their companion turned and for a moment he locked eyes with Andrew. Andrew felt a strange sensation; it was like looking at himself in thirty years' time. The familiar face was deeply scored with wrinkles and the hair at his temples was grey. Then his father plonked his glass on the table, abandoned his cigarette and sprang to his feet.

'Andy!' he called out, pushing past another chair to get to him.

Andrew felt his chest swell with emotion at the use of his child-hood name and the delight on his father's face. Then he saw the look falter as his father hesitated about how to greet him.

Quickly Andrew stuck out his hand.

'Hello, Dad.' His voice sounded croaky.

Tom clutched his hand in both of his and held on.

'My boy,' he said, his eyes glinting with tears. 'So good to see you again.'

'You too,' Andrew responded, a lump in his throat.

They stood like that for a moment, then Ansom was calling them over. 'Here's a chota peg for you, young Lomax!'

'A celebration indeed!' Fritters said, red-faced and jolly.

Andrew wondered how many drinks they'd already had with Tom.

Jimmy hurried over and directed Sanjeev to pull out a chair for Andrew next to his father and place a whisky and soda on the table in front of him. They sat down. Andrew pulled out his cigarette case and offered it to his father. Tom looked taken aback and then smiled and took one. They both lit up.

For a few minutes it was the residents who kept up the conversation, first asking Andrew about his trip out and then switching to the day's news and the likelihood of Sir Stafford Cripps's mission failing.

'What do you think, Andy?' his father asked.

Andrew was startled by the sudden question. He toyed with his untouched whisky. 'I don't really know much about Indian politics. Not for me to say . . .'

'Of course it is,' said Tom. 'You young are the future of this country.'

'I'm British,' said Andrew, meeting his look, 'and my country is thousands of miles away.'

'As it is for all of us,' agreed Fritwell. 'But we have responsibilities here – to govern India well. When the future of the Empire and our nation is at stake, then we have to crack down hard on the enemies within.'

'Or you give them self-rule,' suggested Tom, 'and all fight on the same side.'

Ansom chuckled. 'Captain Lomax! Living in the hills has turned you into a radical jungli,' he teased.

Tom gulped his whisky and gave Andrew an encouraging nod. 'So, what are they saying about India at home?'

Andrew shrugged. 'To be frank, not much. But when I left, the Japanese hadn't begun to invade our territories. India was seen as safe – apart from the North West Frontier – which is why the Borderers are being sent to bolster our presence in the tribal areas. The big fear is if the Axis powers defeat Russia and attack India via Afghanistan and the Frontier.'

'Same old story,' said Tom. 'We've always been vulnerable along the Frontier. It used to be fear of Russia and now it's the Nazis.'

'We should fear them,' said Andrew, stubbing out his cigarette and growing animated. 'The fascists are the biggest threat to world peace there's ever been. Europe is under the jackboot and it looks like the fascist Japanese forces are trying to do the same all over Asia. That's why I joined the army because I saw what was happening – from Czechoslovakia to Spain the fascists were destroying democracy.'

There was silence. Tom broke it. 'Well, you joined for far more honourable reasons than me. I took a commission in the Rifles because my father told me to.' His eyes shone. 'You are a young man of principle.'

'Chip off the old block,' said Ansom.

'I'll drink to that,' said Fritwell, waving at Sanjeev to refill their glasses.

A voice from the stairs called out, 'What are you all celebrating down there?'

'Baroness!' cried Ansom. 'Come and join us. It's the reunion of Lomaxes.'

'Darlings! How delightful.'

Hester stood on the halfway landing dressed in a dark-blue velvet gown and a feathered headband that Andrew was sure he remembered her wearing when he was a boy. It delighted him that she still dressed up as if she were going to dine with the Viceroy. He leapt up and went to guide her down the steps. The men stood up as Andrew steered her into a seat. Tom kissed her hand in greeting.

'Ah,' said Hester with a gracious smile, 'all my favourite men gathered in one place. How lucky I am.'

'We're the lucky ones, Baroness Cussack,' said Andrew.

'Darling, you're as charming as your father. I'm so happy to see you both together again after such a long separation. It's a big sacrifice for parent and child,' persisted Hester, 'having to endure years apart. Isn't that right, Andrew? You must have missed home terribly.'

Andrew tensed. He glanced at his father, who was looking at him warily. He might as well be honest with them.

'I had my mother,' he replied, 'and she gave me a happy home. And there was Auntie Tibby too. Scotland is where I belong. I didn't choose to come back to India – the army sent me. But I'm delighted that it's given me the chance to meet all of you again.'

Hester looked momentarily lost for words. 'And we're delighted too,' she said hastily.

There was an awkward pause; the men swigged their drinks. Andrew hadn't wanted to embarrass them but neither was he going to let them talk as if his mother didn't exist or he'd been living an enforced exile.

He decided to get the other contentious topic out of the way too. 'So, Father, I hear congratulations are in order. You have a baby daughter. I hope mother and baby are doing well.'

Tom gaped at him, reddening. 'Y-yes, very well. Thank you. I was going to tell—'

'Mrs Dubois gave me the happy news.'

Tom looked stricken. 'I'm sorry you didn't hear it from me first. We didn't tell anyone until near the birth . . .'

'No need to apologise,' said Andrew. 'I'm very happy for you both.' He watched his father, who seemed ill at ease.

344

'Does she have Esmie's lovely grey eyes or your blue ones?' asked Hester.

'Blue eyes,' Tom answered. His expression suddenly softened. 'She's a contented wee thing and Stella's convinced Belle has started smiling already. Esmie says it's wind. She seems to like my singing. Though Belle doesn't sleep well at night so we're all a bit tired.'

'Esmie will have an ayah for her, surely?' asked Hester.

Tom knocked back his whisky. 'Stella is helping at the moment but Gabina – Karo's daughter – is going to come and be ayah soon.'

'So, what will Stella do then?' Andrew asked.

Tom looked confused. 'What do you mean?'

'Will she stay on and help in Gulmarg for the summer or come back here?'

'Oh, I see.' His father ran a hand over his face. It was a gesture Andrew had forgotten until now, a sign that his dad was agitated. 'I think Stella wants to come back here – she hasn't seen her family for nearly a year and misses them.'

'Let's have a toast to the return of our darling boy, Andrew – and the arrival of his sister, Belle,' Hester suddenly exclaimed.

'To Andrew and Belle!' the men chorused.

Heart drumming, Andrew stood up. 'Thank you.' He smiled. 'If you'll excuse me, I'll go and get changed for dinner.'

He left them ordering further refills and hurried away. It was the use of the endearment Belle that had made him emotional. Suddenly he had seen the happiness on his father's face and realised that this half-sister really did exist. Belle was a contented baby with blue eyes. He couldn't pretend that she was nothing to do with him. One day he would have to meet her and he didn't know how he felt about that.

Andrew was pleased to get through dinner without any further talk about the war or family. He made sure he sat with Mrs Shankley and spent most of the meal getting her to reminisce about her time as a missionary.

He noticed how his father drank steadily throughout the meal. After dinner, the residents dispersed, some drifting along to the sitting room to play cards while others sat in the foyer under the cooling fans.

Tom fell in step with Andrew. 'Want to go for a walk round the block?' he suggested.

Andrew nodded.

Father and son set off down the hotel path. Andrew noticed how their strides were the same length and their shoulders at the same height – though he was broader in the chest. His father looked diminished, his dinner jacket hanging loose on his thin body. They marched in silence down the street, turning into Dalhousie and then down to the Mall. At the entrance to the Gymkhana Club grounds, Tom stopped and leaned against the wall.

'Want a smoke?' he offered, holding out his silver cigarette case.

Andrew took one from under the elasticated string, a frisson of memory stirring. As a boy he'd once stolen a cigarette from this very case. Esmie had caught him but let him off with a cautionary word not to take without asking. As far as he knew, she had never told Tom.

They smoked in silence, Andrew nervous at what his father might say. Would he start apologising again for not telling him about Belle or would he chide him for not returning to India sooner? He had no idea how to begin speaking to this man he hadn't seen for almost nine years.

'How is your mother?' Tom asked.

Andrew flinched at the unexpected question. He dragged on his cigarette before answering. 'The last time I saw her she was trying to be brave about me going away but not very good at hiding how upset she was.'

Tom gave a ghost of a smile. 'I can imagine that.'

'She spends most of her time looking after Grandmamma – she's very forgetful these days.'

'Ah, Minnie.' Tom nodded. 'I always liked her.'

Andrew hesitated and then said, 'I think Mamma is lonely at Ebbsmouth. She liked it when I was home from school and had friends to stay.'

'I thought she had Dickie with her these days?' Tom said, his tone tightening.

'Uncle Dickie's working in London for the government so doesn't get north much.'

Tom ground out his cigarette. 'And Tibby?'

Andrew was relieved that his father wasn't going to harp on about Dickie. His mother had told him how ridiculously jealous Tom had been.

He smiled. 'Auntie Tibby is wonderful. I miss her a lot. She somehow manages to keep that old pile of stones from falling down, as well as giving a home to a bunch of eccentric artists. She's developed a passion for gardening and avant-garde art – and for years she's had an Indian lover, Dawan Lal.'

'Goodness! She's having an affair with Dawan?' Tom laughed. 'I bet that has the county matrons gossiping.'

'They're very discreet,' said Andrew. 'And Auntie Tibby couldn't care less what anyone says about her.'

'That's true,' Tom agreed. 'I'm glad to hear she hasn't changed. Dear Tibby.'

Andrew immediately lit a fresh cigarette from his old one and offered one to his father. They continued to smoke.

Tom said quietly, 'I can't tell you how much Esmie and I have missed you, Andy. She sends her love and hopes you will come

347

up to Gulmarg when you next get leave to see us. She was very disappointed not to come this time but it wasn't possible . . .'

Andrew murmured, 'No, not with a baby to look after.'

Tom put a hand on his shoulder. 'I'm so sorry you had to hear about Belle from Myrtle and not me.'

'I'm pleased for you both that you have a daughter,' Andrew answered tensely. 'Honestly I am. But it makes little difference to me.'

Tom looked saddened. 'You might change your mind when you meet the wee lassie.'

Abruptly, Andrew felt a deep resentment rising up inside. 'I hope you don't expect me to start playing happy families after all these years?' he said. 'Because my family is Mamma and Grandmamma and Auntie Tibby in Ebbsmouth. And my fiancée is there too. That home is more real to me than here or up in Gulmarg. I want you to understand that.'

'I'm sorry to hear that,' Tom said, looking pained. 'We never wanted you to leave India in the first place. It's been very hard for me and Esmie to endure this long separation—'

Andrew threw away his cigarette. 'You were hardly rushing to Scotland to get me back, were you? I know the bargain you made with Mamma – that she could keep me as long as you were free to marry Esmie.'

'It wasn't as simple as that,' said Tom, grinding out his own cigarette.

Andrew felt a sudden rage. 'Why did you lie to me about being married to Esmie? I had to find out the truth from a bully at school. I punched another boy in the face defending Esmie's honour – and yours. Do you know how guilty I felt when I found out Gotley hadn't been lying? But at least leaving India meant I got to meet my mother properly. And do you know what? She wasn't the unlovable ice-queen you'd made her out to be.'

His father looked stunned, but Andrew couldn't stop now he'd started. Years of resentment that he thought he'd overcome came pouring out.

'She still loves you, you know? Though heaven knows why after the way you neglected her and caused her such pain.'

'I caused her pain?' Tom asked, seemingly bewildered.

'Yes, going off with Esmie and taking me too. You both robbed me of my real mother.'

Suddenly his father looked furious. He lurched at Andrew, his breath sour with whisky. 'Don't you dare accuse Esmie! She's completely innocent. She's never had a bad word to say about your mother, though God knows, she's had reason to. She's been loyal to Lydia for years – even when my selfish ex-wife took you away from us for good.'

'Loyal?' Andrew said in contempt. 'After Harold Guthrie died, Esmie took advantage of Mamma's sympathy to get close to you. She went off with her best friend's husband. How is that loyal?'

Andrew saw the punch coming too late. His father's fist landed on his jaw and sent him staggering backwards. He bit his lip at the impact. As he clutched his chin, blood started trickling out of his mouth. His head pounded.

'Andy!' Almost immediately Tom looked aghast at what he'd done. 'I'm sorry. I shouldn't have.' He tried to put his arm about him. 'God forgive me; did I hurt you?'

Andrew pushed him off and groped for a handkerchief.

'Let me,' Tom pleaded, trying to dab at his swelling lip.

'I'm all right,' Andrew said, turning away. He didn't want his father to see how shocked he was.

'I want to explain about Esmie,' Tom said in distress. 'She had nothing to do with your mother and me separating. It was your mother who—'

'Please don't say any more,' Andrew pleaded. 'Let's just agree to disagree.'

His father's shoulders sagged as he steadied himself against the wall. Perhaps he was drunker than Andrew had thought. It had been a mistake to embark on such a painful subject when his father was intoxicated and he was so riled up. He felt instant remorse for his outburst.

'I'm sorry for arguing,' said Andrew, relenting. 'Let's just go back to the hotel before we're arrested for disturbing the peace. That would be hard to explain to my CO.'

Tom hung his head.

'Come on, Dad,' he said, taking him by the arm and steering him along the path. It pained him to see how diminished his father had become – both physically and in spirit.

By the time they got back to the Raj, Andrew's lip had stopped bleeding and Tom had regained something of his old composure. They were both subdued. Andrew was glad to see there were no residents in the lobby to ask how he'd split his lip or to entice his father into drinking more. Andrew told a waiting Manek to bring them up a pot of tea and they headed upstairs.

Father and son got ready for bed in silence. When the tea came and Andrew dismissed Manek for the night, they sat tensely, Andrew slurping his tea while his father smoked.

'Dad,' Andrew said, keeping calm. 'I don't want us to talk about Mother again. Let's keep off sensitive subjects. We've got so little time together – I hate that we're spending it arguing.'

His father gave him a desolate look and nodded in agreement.

'Tell me about Stella,' Andrew encouraged. 'It must be hard for her being separated from Hugh Keating. I hear he's safely in South Africa.'

Tom gave a snort of derision. 'Keating! He's given poor Stella the runaround. If he comes back and marries her, I'll eat my hat.'

Andrew was astonished. 'Why do you say that? I thought they were madly in love?'

'She was,' said Tom. 'Still is, I'm afraid. But he's not to be trusted. Did you know he's got a wife in Ireland?'

Andrew gasped. 'He's what? A wife? I don't believe it!'

Tom was full of indignation. 'I'm afraid it's true.'

'That's terrible. How did she find out?'

'He wrote and told her himself,' Tom said. 'Full of promises about how he's going to divorce his wife and marry her. I think hell will freeze over first.'

'Poor Stella!' Andrew was shaken by the revelation. 'Why on earth then did Hugh ask her to marry him in the first place?'

Tom gave him an impatient look. 'Why do you think?'

Andrew felt the heat rise into his face. 'I feel awful,' he admitted. 'I was the one who put them in touch again.'

'You weren't to know what he was like,' said Tom.

'Felicity had a hunch he was a womaniser,' Andrew admitted. 'We bumped into him at a cinema in Edinburgh and she thought he was with someone else's wife.'

'I think he's probably fabricated a lot about himself,' Tom said in disdain. 'I questioned him about his service in Quetta but he seemed to know little about the place.'

'Oh Lord!' Andrew grimaced. 'I remember him telling me great tales of his heroics in Baluchistan. That's how he got his leg injury – shot by a tribesman. Perhaps he was making it all up?'

Tom grunted. 'If a Baluch had wanted him dead, they wouldn't have wasted a bullet on his knee. I doubt Keating's ever been to Baluchistan.'

Andrew was distressed on Stella's behalf. She must have felt both betrayed and humiliated. She was such an open-hearted, trusting person.

'Is that why she stayed with you all winter?' Andrew guessed. 'I suppose she didn't want to face everyone here and admit to Hugh being married.'

Tom didn't answer immediately. He looked torn. 'Andrew . . .'

'Yes?'

'Stella's had a difficult time . . .'

'I understand that,' Andrew said.

'What I mean is . . . well, what I've told you is in confidence. No one here knows about Keating being married. So, we must leave it up to Stella to decide what she's prepared to tell anyone.'

'Of course,' Andrew agreed. 'I'd never break her confidence.'

Tom nodded in relief.

'But I don't promise not to give Hugh a bloody nose,' said Andrew, 'if I ever see him again.'

'You and me, both.' Tom looked suddenly contrite. 'I'm so sorry I hit you. I'm an awful father. All I've really wanted to do for all these years is give you a bloody big hug – and within hours of seeing you again I end up attacking you. Can you ever forgive me?'

Andrew felt a wave of pity. 'Of course I forgive you,' he said quickly. 'I was just as much to blame for losing my temper. And I'm sorry for being unkind about Esmie. It's been difficult over the years, but I suppose I understand now about your marriage, and why you had to pretend.'

Tom clenched his jaw and swallowed, wiping at his glistening eyes. 'Thank you.' He cleared his throat and reached for another cigarette. Once he'd lit up again, he squinted at Andrew through a puff of smoke.

'Now, tell me all about this fiancée of yours. I remember her father, Archie Douglas – he used to have a soft spot for your Auntie Tibby.'

'Really?' said Andrew. He felt a jolt of guilt that Felicity had hardly crossed his mind all evening. Quickly he pulled out the photograph that he carried of her and handed it over to his father.

He felt on safer ground chatting about the Douglases and Felicity. He told his father about her work as an ARP warden. For a short while he could conjure up Ebbsmouth and home again – and not have to dwell on disturbing thoughts about Stella and her doomed romance with Hugh.

Chapter 42

Andrew slept badly in his old bedroom, his mind disturbed by the argument with his father over his mother and Esmie, as well as the revelation about Hugh's betrayal of Stella's love. The recent telephone call and hearing her voice again had reignited deep feelings. It was unsettling to be staying in the room that had last been used by Stella. He still felt her presence about the place. He was touched to find that the sketch he had sent her years ago of Frisky was displayed in a silver-plated frame by the bedside.

In the middle of the night, as he tossed restlessly, he realised for the first time that he was really disappointed that she hadn't been there, and acknowledged that he had held out an absurd hope that she might have travelled down specially to see him – as he would have done for her – even after nine years apart. He still kept the dog-eared photograph of her, taken with him and Noel on the beach that fateful summer in Ebbsmouth. It was tucked into his wallet and kept like a guilty secret.

But she wasn't there, and it was ridiculous of him to hold such childish feelings for Stella after all these years. So he made up his mind, there and then, that he would cut short his stay at the hotel and travel on to Taha in the morning. With the decision made, he fell into fitful sleep.

Woken at seven by Manek bringing him a pot of tea, Andrew found that his father had risen earlier and wasn't in the flat. He winced at the stiffness in his jaw and probed at his bottom lip. The swelling had gone down, though he could still feel tenderness. Glancing out of the open veranda window, he glimpsed his father smoking under the jacaranda and talking intently to Jimmy.

Andrew felt renewed regret that they'd wasted the previous evening in fruitless argument. It struck him that they would need far more time than this snatched moment at the Raj to get to know each other again. Time that they didn't have.

At breakfast there was consternation. His father was sitting with Ansom and Fritwell. He met his father's sheepish look and gave an encouraging smile.

'Young Lomax!' Ansom called him over. 'Have you seen the morning papers?'

'Terrible business,' Fritwell said, puce-faced. 'Ceylon. Out of the blue.'

'What's happened?' Andrew asked.

'Japs have bombed the naval base at Colombo,' Tom explained.

'Sounds like our air force boys chased them off,' said Fritwell. 'Shot down thirty enemy planes.'

'Where on earth were they attacking from?' Andrew asked, dumbfounded. He knew that the island of Ceylon, which lay off the southern tip of India, was crucial for protecting shipping through the Bay of Bengal and up to Calcutta.

Tom answered, grim-faced. 'It means they must have at least one aircraft carrier operating in the Indian Ocean.'

Andrew was horrified. If Ceylon was vulnerable to attack, then so was mainland India. He sat down with the men; there was no sign yet of the baroness or Winifred Shankley. He had no appetite and after forcing down some tea and toast, he got up.

'I've decided to travel on to Taha today and meet up with my fellow officers. I'll come and say goodbye in half an hour or so,' he promised.

No one protested.

Andrew went swiftly to the lobby and asked Jimmy to make arrangements.

Back in the flat, Andrew waited for his father to follow him up, but he didn't come. Perhaps he was wary of saying the wrong thing, just as Andrew was.

A short while later, Andrew was back down in the lobby saying goodbye to the residents while Manek went to supervise the loading of luggage. Myrtle and Yvonne were there to wish him well, and Charles was hopping from one leg to the other, not wanting to be constrained by his grandmother.

'Soldier!' he cried, pointing at Andrew in his uniform.

Andrew crouched down and produced one of his grandfather's toy soldiers that he carried as a keepsake.

'This is for you, Charles.' He put it into the boy's small hand and saw him look up at his grandmother in questioning excitement.

'I hope it's all right to give him this? It belonged to Grandpapa Archibald.'

Myrtle smiled. 'That's very kind of you. We'll make sure he's careful with it.'

'Say thank you,' Yvonne instructed her son.

'T'ank you, soldier,' Charles said, his round face creased in a huge smile.

Andrew ruffled the boy's hair and then stood up. He glanced around, wondering where his father was. Just then, Tom appeared with Jimmy.

Jimmy shook his hand in goodbye. 'Your father wishes to take you to the station.'

'I hope that's all right?' Tom gave him a wary look.

Andrew nodded in relief. 'Thank you.'

Outside, he saw that Manek was loading the luggage into the Lomaxes' green van and was waiting for him too. Andrew climbed in the front beside his father.

They drove in silence through the cantonment and into the busy streets of Saddar Bazaar. They bumped along in the van, his father tooting the horn at wandering cows and pedestrians.

He glanced at his father, whose face was tight with suppressed emotion. Andrew felt suddenly protective towards him. Over all these years, how hard had it been for his dad to be the subject of gossip about his cowardice and court-martial? As a boy, Andrew had been ashamed of his father being talked of as a mental case, but that was before he had experienced war for himself. In France, he had seen brave men – veterans of the Great War – paralysed with fear, and at times he had felt sheer terror himself. He should have stuck up for his father more in the face of his mother's criticism.

He recalled something Stella had said long ago about his father being a hero despite being court-martialled. *Think of all the years of war he went through – all he had to endure – and he was a brave Rifleman on the North West Frontier for years before that. It's not true that he was a coward.'*

'Penny for your thoughts?' Tom asked him with a sideways glance.

'Nothing,' said Andrew, with a stab of guilt.

'I believe an old friend of mine is still in Taha,' said Tom. 'The Reverend Alec Bannerman. They call him the Padre – was an army chaplain in his day. He's as old as the hills – in his nineties, I believe – but judging by his Christmas letters, he's still sharp as a pin. I'm sure he'd give you hospitality if you looked him up.'

'Was he in the Peshawar Rifles?'

'No, but I came across him in Peshawar,' said Tom. 'And again in Taha when . . .' He hesitated. 'When my friend Guthrie lived there.'

Perhaps he was the old white-haired man that Andrew vaguely remembered from his visit to Taha as a small boy. He had little wish to go looking up people from the Guthries' past or to stay longer in the frontier town than he needed. Taha had bad associations for his mother.

But to keep his father happy, he said, 'If I get the chance I will.'

His father looked anxiously over at him. 'You won't do anything foolhardy, will you? I know what it's like to be a young subaltern and wanting to prove oneself to fellow officers.'

'Dad, I'm a professional soldier,' Andrew said. 'I'm not here to play games.'

'Sorry,' Tom said quickly. 'I just worry . . .'

'You don't have to.'

His father gripped the steering wheel. 'I've never asked you about your time in France – what it was like and how you got away—'

'You were in the Great War,' Andrew said gently, 'and know more than most what fighting is like. I don't need to tell you.'

'But we've had so little time together and I've wasted it.'

'We needn't have argued,' Andrew admitted. 'But I shouldn't have flown off the handle with you either.'

Soon they were at the railway station and Andrew jumped out. He busied himself supervising Manek, glad of the bustle around them which prevented further heart-searching by his father.

'You don't have to wait around,' Andrew said to him. 'Best to say goodbye here.'

Tears welled in his father's eyes. 'Please believe me when I say that Esmie longs to see you too. You're dearer to her than anyone.'

'She has a daughter now,' Andrew pointed out. Swiftly, he put out his hand and said, 'Send her my regards and congratulations about the baby. Thanks for the lift, Dad.'

Tom took his hand and held onto it; he was struggling to speak. Clearing his throat, he said, 'Promise me you'll come and visit us in Gulmarg when you get leave?'

Andrew nodded. 'I'd like that.'

He thought his father was going to burst into tears, so hurriedly withdrew his hand. Abruptly, his father grabbed his shoulders and with surprising force, pulled him into a hug.

'Look after yourself,' he said croakily. 'God go with you, my dearest boy.'

Andrew suddenly felt deeply overwhelmed with sadness and regret for his father. He nodded and stepped back. Unable to express how he felt, he turned away, leaving his father standing on the dusty pavement.

Even after he'd boarded the train and it was pulling out of Rawalpindi, Andrew felt downcast. He shouldn't have let old resentments get in the way. He had squandered the opportunity to allow him and his father to make amends and find true reconciliation. It might be months – even years – before he had another such chance.

Sitting watching Rawalpindi being swallowed up by the dun-coloured landscape, Andrew felt leaden at the thought. His father was no longer a robust man – not the giant presence of his childhood – but someone bedevilled by mental breakdown and too much drink. His overriding emotion was one of pity. Yet he had broken away and left his father standing alone and miserable, perhaps thinking that he was no longer loved by his son.

Then Andrew reminded himself that he was more alone in this country than his father was. Tom would soon be returning to Gulmarg – to Esmie and Belle – his new family. And to Stella.

If she had been around in Pindi, he would probably never have argued with his dad. She would have smoothed the way with her intelligence, warmth and humour.

But as he had realised in the night, for his own sanity he must rid his mind of her, once and for all. She belonged to a time and place that no longer existed – his Indian boyhood.

Chapter 43

The evening Tom returned, Stella was settling Belle in her cradle after a long feed. She heard Esmie's cry of delight and voices on the veranda. They were all still living in the annex but the hotel would be reopening in May and staff hired for the summer season would soon be arriving. She knew that she would only have another week or so of feeding the baby before she would have to hand over nursing duties.

Stella stroked Belle's pink cheek and soft brown hair and wondered how she was going to be able to leave her. Belle watched her with drowsy eyes as Stella set the cradle rocking. She remembered Esmie soothing Andrew in this very same crib. She longed to hear Tom's news about his son and how her family was, so kissed Belle and hurried along to the veranda.

There was still a chill in the air once the sun slipped behind the mountain behind them. Tom was already sprawled in a cane chair clutching a tumbler of whisky. Even in the soft lamplight he looked exhausted. He half-rose.

'Please don't get up,' Stella said. 'How was your journey?'

'Two punctures and a landslide near Baramullah,' said Tom. 'But otherwise uneventful. How is Belle?'

'Almost asleep,' said Stella.

'She's been good as gold,' said Esmie.

'I can't wait to see her,' Tom said with feeling.

'So now that Stella's here,' said Esmie excitedly, 'tell us how everyone is at the Raj. Was Andrew in good heart? Tell us everything.'

Tom took a swig of his drink and addressed Stella. 'Your family are very well – missing you of course – but all is running smoothly at the hotel.'

'And how is Myrtle?' asked Esmie.

'Putting on a brave face,' Tom answered. 'She's obviously missing Charlie a lot but keeps busy with Charles, whom she adores.'

'What is Charles like now?' Stella asked eagerly. 'Is he saying much?'

'The wee lad is full of chatter,' Tom said. 'Some of it incomprehensible but he's going to be another sociable Dubois.'

'And Andy?' Esmie pressed him. 'It must have been wonderful seeing him again.'

'It was.' Tom's face twisted in a half-smile. 'He's a fine young man – tall and good-looking. The residents were cooing over him.'

'Is he still the loving Andy we remember?' Esmie questioned.

Tom put down his glass with a sigh. 'He's kind and loving about his mother. But she's obviously spent the past nine years blackening our names. To be frank, he's angry at us.'

'What has Lydia been saying?' Esmie asked in dismay.

Tom hesitated and glanced at Stella.

'Do you want me to leave you to discuss this alone?' she asked.

Esmie shook her head.

Tom said grimly, 'Lydia claims that I left her for you – that I was the adulterer – and that you stole me away.'

'How dare she!'

'Not just that,' said Tom, 'but she's convinced Andy that we also took him from his mother against her wishes.'

Esmie put a hand over her mouth to smother a cry. Tom quickly leaned across and gripped her other hand. 'I tried to tell him it wasn't true – that you are a complete innocent in all this – but he won't hear a bad word said against Lydia.'

'Does he hate me?' Esmie gasped. 'He must do if he believes me capable of such a thing.'

Stella spoke up. 'He can't hate you. I know how much he adores you deep down. That sort of love doesn't just go away. You need to see him again so you can tell him the truth yourself.'

Esmie gave her a grateful look. 'Tom, do you think he'll agree to see me?'

Tom said, 'He did promise that he would try to come to Gulmarg, if he got leave. He sent you his regards, which is encouraging—' He paused, looking uncomfortable, before adding, 'And congratulations about the baby.'

Stella's heartbeat grew erratic. 'D-did he believe you about Belle?'

Tom nodded. 'Unfortunately, he got to hear about her from your mother before I could tell him. I don't in the least blame Myrtle – I curse myself for not letting him know sooner.'

Stella shifted in her chair uncomfortably. 'That must have been embarrassing for him. I'm so sorry if I've made things more difficult for you and Andy.'

Tom let out a long sigh. 'I'm afraid it's me who's made things ten times worse.' Abruptly, he buried his head in his hands. 'I can't forgive myself for what I did . . .'

Esmie asked in alarm, 'Tom, what do you mean?'

Tom looked at her, his face suddenly grey and lined. 'I – I punched him. I hit my boy.'

Esmie gasped.

Tom swallowed hard. 'We were arguing and I couldn't bear the things he was saying about you . . .'

'Did you hurt him?' Esmie asked in agitation.

'I made his lip bleed. Oh, Esmie, how could I have done such a thing? I don't deserve to be his father. He took it like a man and didn't retaliate. In fact, he apologised for losing his temper too. That made me feel worse. I wish he'd knocked me senseless.'

'Don't say that!' Esmie reached out and put her arms around him. They clung to each other.

Tom's voice was desolate as he said, 'He cut his stay short – he couldn't get away from me quickly enough. It was like talking to someone I hardly knew.'

'Andy will grow to love you again, I'll make sure of that,' Esmie insisted. 'It's like Stella said: a love that deep doesn't just vanish.'

Tom pulled away and gave Stella a guilty look. 'Andrew asked about you in particular. I'm afraid I told him about Keating betraying you – being married already.'

'What did he say?'

'Blamed himself for putting you in touch with Keating again. He was angry on your behalf – it's the only thing we agreed on.'

Stella put her hands to her burning cheeks. She was mortified that Andrew should know how foolish she had been over Hugh – how ridiculously naive she had been. Yet she was touched that he had been indignant. Like Esmie, she longed for the opportunity to see him again and let him know that, despite the long years apart, she wanted them to be friends once more.

Stella got up. 'If you don't mind, I think I'll eat in my room tonight and give you both a chance to talk things over on your own.'

Long into the night, Stella pondered her situation. Had she been right to give up Belle to the Lomaxes or had it brought them an extra burden? She could see now how Andrew must have resented not being told about this new addition to his family. She perhaps should have told him on the telephone. Poor Andrew! None of them had thought hard enough about how this would affect him.

She must do the best she could for her daughter. Listening to Belle's gentle breathing, Stella was still convinced that being brought up by the Lomaxes was the best thing for her, and that Andrew would, must, eventually come to love his new sister.

In the early hours of the morning, at the first glimmer of light, Stella wrote a letter to Hugh.

> *Dear Hugh,*
>
> *Many times, I have sat down to write to you and given up, not knowing how to reply to your letter sent at the end of last year. You must have known how devastated I would be to hear that you were already married and had a wife in Ireland. You claimed that you are estranged but how can I believe you? If it were so, you would have told me about her from the beginning of our courtship. I fear you only proposed to me so that you could seduce me – knowing how utterly in love I was with you.*
>
> *I'm ashamed now of my naivety. So, this is to tell you that I am breaking off our engagement and releasing you from the pretence of wishing to divorce your wife and marry me. The child I bore you has been given up for adoption so you have no further obligation to me.*
>
> *I can't say I don't still have feelings for you, Hugh. Although you have not attempted to let me*

know that you are safe, I'm glad that my fears that you were captured by the Japanese didn't turn out to be true. Mr Lamont wired me to say you had escaped from Singapore and are now in South Africa. I imagine he will send on this letter to you there or that you will eventually get it if you return to Calcutta.

You have broken my heart, Hugh, and I do not want you to contact me again. Perhaps the most honourable thing you can do is to return to Ireland and be reconciled with your wife.

This is farewell,
Stella

For a long time after she'd finished writing the letter, Stella sat at the window watching the dawn break over the eastern peaks. She had shed tears and felt such turmoil – longing, anger and desolation – as she wrote the words. But now that it was done, a calmness settled over her. Never again would she allow herself to be so infatuated by a man. She had wasted years fantasising about a life with Hugh and pining for him. But it had been based on nothing more than an on-ship dalliance. She had been too eager to believe Hester Cussack's ideas of romantic love – that there was only one person in the whole world who was the right one for her. Nobody could live up to such an ideal – least of all a womaniser like Hugh.

At breakfast, Stella handed over the letter to be put in the post.

Tom, who had Belle in the crook of his arm and was making a fuss over her, gave Stella a wary look. 'You're writing to Keating?'

'Yes. I've not replied to him until now. I'm telling him that I'm breaking off our engagement.' Even as she said it, she felt a twist of regret. 'And I've told him not to contact me again.'

'Brave lassie,' said Esmie in approval. 'You're doing the right thing.'

'And I want you to sell this.' She held out the sapphire engagement ring. 'Use the money to buy clothes and things for Belle. It's the least he can do for his daughter.'

Stella felt a lump in her throat at the sight of Tom clutching Belle protectively, his careworn face softened in love. It was both touching and devastating. It struck her how Belle's real father would never have held her like that or talked to her as if she were precious to him. Stella wondered if Tom gazed at Belle and thought about the baby from his first marriage – Amelia – who had died soon after birth. Perhaps, after all these years, Belle could bring comfort to Tom's grieving heart, as well as happiness and peace of mind.

'I think Gabina should come as soon as she can,' Stella said, digging her nails into her palms to stop herself crying. 'And that we should begin bottle-feeding the baby.'

Esmie said in concern. 'Stella, are you all right?'

'Then I can move into the hotel and help when the first guests arrive. That's if you're happy for me to stay on for the season. I don't feel ready to go back to Pindi yet.'

'Of course we are,' said Tom at once.

'Dear lassie,' said Esmie. 'Only if you think you can manage it – if it won't be too hard for you with Belle around . . .'

Stella swallowed. 'I can manage. But I think it will be better if I'm kept busy at the hotel and no longer live in the annex.'

Esmie nodded. 'I understand.'

For all her brave words, Stella found being separated from Belle excruciating. Within a week, Gabina arrived from Srinagar and took over her duties as Belle's ayah.

Gabina was twenty-three, cheerful and efficient, and took to Belle at once. Stella remembered a young Gabina following her adoringly around The Raj Hotel.

'I was like your shadow,' Gabina laughed as they reminisced. 'I wanted to do everything you did – and you were so patient with me. Do you remember the dolls we both had and you insisted on giving me yours to keep? I've brought them for baby Lomax.'

To Stella's astonishment, Gabina produced two rather worn rag dolls with dark plaits, one in a crimson sari and the other in a faded green salwar kameez. They'd been presents from Esmie one Christmas.

'Fancy you still having them! I'd long forgotten about those dolls.'

For the first few days, Stella stayed on in the annex while her milk dried up. Although it was Esmie who gave Gabina her instructions, the young woman was quick to see Stella's bond with the baby and the pain she was going through. Stella hadn't expected such soreness in her breasts as they continued to fill up with milk. It was Gabina who suggested that Stella bind them up in rolls of bandages.

'I understand the situation,' Gabina said with a compassionate look. 'I will help swaddle you and then you will feel relief.'

Stella was alarmed that she had guessed so easily. 'You mustn't tell anyone. The baby belongs to the Lomaxes now.'

'On my word, Stella-Mem', I will tell no one.'

The binding brought temporary relief, but at night Stella lay unable to get comfortable, yearning to suckle her baby. It was torture to hear Belle crying in the next room and know that it was not her place to comfort her, listening out for Gabina's crooning and soothing words.

Once the swelling had gone down, Stella moved into the hotel and immersed herself in making the place ready for guests, taking bookings, putting up newly washed curtains, helping the Lomaxes with supervising new staff, ordering supplies and planning menus.

Steeling herself, Stella put in a call to her mother. She assured her that although her engagement to Hugh was over, she was fine. Stella was grateful that her mother accepted her words without a stream of questions.

'Keep busy, my dearest,' Myrtle advised. 'It's the best way to get through difficult times.'

Chapter 44

North West Frontier, July 1942

Andrew, drenched in sweat, crouched as still as possible behind a piquet wall of boulders and rubble. Perspiration ran under his pith helmet into his eyes. The sun beat down relentlessly in a cloudless sky, and the glare from the barren mountain slopes blinded him. After three months on the frontier he still couldn't get used to such searing heat. Even though his company had trained on the hot plains around Delhi for this type of warfare, it was hotter, dustier and more nerve-wracking than he'd imagined.

The enemy were swift and elusive. While the Indian Army and supporting British regiments moved in long convoys of armoured vehicles along the valley roads, the Waziris and Mahsuds travelled light on horseback or foot, ready to swoop on infantry or pick them off with sniper fire.

Andrew's commander and frontier veteran, the craggy-faced Major McBain, had warned him on first arrival, 'They're the past-masters at guerrilla warfare, Lomax. Like our Scottish Highlanders of old. They can cover miles with just a crust of bread in their bellies, carrying only rifles and ammunition, and sleep out in bitter cold with a single blanket. Hard as bloody nails.'

The full-scale tribal war of the previous year had abated and the fears of a fresh rising once the winter snows had melted had not materialised. Yet his commander was cautious.

'Don't be fooled.' McBain had laughed grimly. 'It's like summer sport for them to take on the ferenghi devils, as they call us. And as long as the Afghans are still prepared to arm them, they'll cause us as much trouble as they can.'

'So, is it the Nazis who are bankrolling the rebellion?' Andrew had asked him.

'Yes, it seems to be the case. We just have to pray to God that the Russians can hold out against the new German offensive.'

Andrew's head pounded and he licked his cracked lips, trying to concentrate on the job in hand. Half an hour ago, he had led a dozen men up the precipitous slope to secure the piquet, something that they had done with textbook efficiency. Now they were keeping watch on the valley below as the convoy passed on its way to Razmak to resupply the army outpost. The Borderers were responsible for piquets on a ten-mile stretch to the next camp. *Keep eyes in the back of your head as well as on the convoy.* McBain's words were drummed into him.

This was the most challenging stretch of the route, carved out of the steep flank of hillside above a gorge. Andrew was in awe of the sappers and miners who must have blasted this road through the rock with its sheer drop to the green-grey waters below.

It made Andrew think of ex-cavalry officer Dickie Mason, his mother's friend, who had been stationed at Razmak in the early twenties. One day, Andrew hoped, he'd return safely to Britain and be able to swap stories with the amiable Dickie. Andrew wondered if his father too had ever patrolled this rock-strewn valley or defended these same treeless slopes.

Andrew craved a cigarette. He wiped the sweat from his eyes. He'd like to chat to his dad about the Frontier – compare experiences – and once again chided himself for wasting the opportunity to talk to his father in Pindi.

The convoy of armoured cars, trucks and mules snaked into view around the bend below. The dust raised by the rumbling vehicles could be seen from afar and the noise filled the silence like distant thunder.

Every Waziri for miles around would be able to see it and would know of its coming; the convoys were weekly. But part of the exercise was to try and draw out the enemy and engage them in open warfare, so that the British-Indian forces could use their Vickers machine guns and superior fire power to rout the tribesmen.

'Wily Pathans won't be drawn,' McBain had told him. 'They know there's little point attacking motorised transport. It's the piquets where they understand we're vulnerable – and we're at our weakest when we withdraw from one piquet and move to the next.'

Two weeks ago, Andrew had lost one of his men to a Waziri sniper. Private Henderson was from a village outside Ebbsmouth and Andrew had had to write and tell his parents. It was the hardest letter he'd ever written.

Andrew's jaw clenched as he surveyed the road below and the mountain terrain around them. He must concentrate. The train of vehicles shimmered in the heat, writhing in his vision. His temples thumped.

Corporal Mackenzie passed him a canteen of water and whispered, 'Sir, a wee sip?'

Andrew took it with a grateful nod. It was he who should be looking after the men, not the other way around. He gulped at the water, which tasted oddly metallic. After a moment of relief, he was as thirsty as ever.

Eventually, the convoy was almost past. Andrew gave the signal for his men to withdraw from the piquet. With weapons drawn, they descended as quietly and swiftly as possible. Halfway down, bullets suddenly began spraying the scree around them, sending loose stones bouncing into the air.

'Take cover!' Andrew shouted out across the men.

They scrambled behind clumps of thorny scrub – the only protection on the stark mountainside – and returned gunfire. Andrew saw a flash of white turban from behind the wall they had been guarding just minutes earlier. He took aim and fired. The head bobbed out of view. The sniper fire continued. They were pinned down and partially exposed.

Andrew motioned to Mackenzie to put into action the drill they had practised. While the corporal and the others kept up a constant barrage of bullets against the snipers, Andrew wriggled on his belly to the slight overhang below the piquet. Finding a foothold, he hauled himself up, his lungs labouring for breath in the thin air, and dived behind a large boulder. Swiftly, he pulled a grenade from his belt and released the pin.

Standing up, Andrew hurled the grenade with all his force at the tumbledown piquet and then threw himself flat behind the rock, praying it would withstand the blast. Seconds later, the grenade went off. Stones and dust rained down beside him. Andrew burrowed into the ground, his mouth filling with grit and his ears ringing.

Looking up, he could see nothing through the billowing clouds of smoke and dust. He heard no answering gunfire. Quickly, he hurtled back down the overhang, skinning the palms of his hands, and landed back beside his men.

'Think that's cleared the nest, sir,' said Mackenzie.

Andrew, heaving for breath, gave the order for them to head down to the convoy.

They executed three more piquet duties that day without incident and arrived in camp before sundown, in time for the men to erect bivouacs and set up the various mess tents for the evening meal. Andrew sat on a camping stool eating chicken and rice next to a fellow Scots officer, Lieutenant John Grant, who had heard of his grenade attack.

'All that cricket practice, eh, Lomax?' he joked. 'Best overarm in the platoon, I hear.'

Andrew shared his cigarettes with Grant while the amiable lieutenant chatted about fishing on the Tweed. It amazed Andrew how Grant always managed to have immaculately groomed auburn hair and moustache even in the desert.

'Fishing in Kashmir is supposed to be good,' said Grant.

'It is,' said Andrew. 'I used to fish there with my father as a boy.'

Andrew stared at the ball of fire that was sinking behind the mountains of Waziristan. He could still see the sun imprinted on his eyelids when he closed them. He felt heady. What on earth were they doing chasing tribesmen on this remote western frontier when a vast fascist army was pressing at the eastern borders of India?

'Did you say something about fascists?' Grant asked him in bemusement.

Andrew wasn't sure if he'd spoken aloud. 'Sorry, just rambling.'

'Are you okay, Lomax?' he asked in concern. 'Touch of sun, maybe? Here, have a swig from this.' He handed over a whisky flask.

Andrew hesitated and then took a sip. It stung his lips and throat.

'Thanks.' He handed it back.

'Get some rest,' Grant said. 'We have to do it all over again in the morning.'

That night Andrew crawled thankfully onto his bedroll and fell into exhausted sleep.

He dreamt of rain. It was lashing at the window of his tower bedroom at The Anchorage. He got up to close the window but couldn't; he stood shivering and naked until the rain stopped. Then abruptly he was under the horse chestnut trees along the drive to Templeton Hall. He was walking hand in hand with Felicity under the russet autumnal canopy and they were laughing as the ripe chestnuts split from their casings and bounced around them.

But, horrifyingly, the nuts turned to bullets and Felicity started screaming. Andrew was trying to drag her to safety but she wouldn't move. Then suddenly they were running and he was gripping her hand so he wouldn't lose her, but when he turned it was Stella's face he saw . . .

Andrew woke with a jerk, panting with fear. He stared around him and gradually remembered he was sleeping under the desert stars far from Ebbsmouth. He sank back, heart still beating hard. His dreams had been so vivid; he'd smelt the rain and felt Felicity's warm hand in his. Or had it been Stella's? The thought was disturbing. He had felt a flare of desire as he'd turned to face the woman whose hand he'd grasped.

Andrew was unsatisfied and ached with regret. Rolling onto his front, he tried to regain sleep. He wanted to get back to the part of the dream where he was with Felicity under the trees before the bullets began to fly. It was useless. He lay shivering, his mind filling with anxious thoughts about Felicity and his loved ones at home.

The Stella in his dream had looked like the twenty-year-old he'd last seen, but she would no longer be like that. He was now twenty-two, so he worked out that Stella would be twenty-nine. She'd sent him a card on his birthday with a puzzling message that he knew by heart.

I hope you can come to Gulmarg soon. We all long to see you and I have things to explain about your

375

*half-sister – things that might make you think more
kindly of your father and Esmie. Take care of yourself, love from Stella.*

Andrew sighed. What did she want to tell him? Yet it raised his
spirits that she wanted to see him again. Was that just Stella being
typically generous-hearted or did he mean something more to her
than just the boss's son?

Andrew dozed, his thoughts flitting incoherently between the
past and dread of the days ahead.

The following night they reached the barracks at Razmak: a huddle
of low-lying fortified stone dwellings. Within the expanded perimeter of the fort were rows of white army tents to accommodate the
increased number of troops.

Razmak had a commanding view of the valley – a tributary
of the Tank Zam River. McBain had told him it was bitterly cold
with snow in winter but pleasantly green in spring where the lower
slopes were cultivated by peasant farmers. But this was the peak of
the hot season and the vegetation had shrivelled in the harsh sun
and the river dried up.

They arrived to find an outbreak of enteric fever.

'We thought it was a few cases of heatstroke,' McBain told
Andrew and John Grant, 'but then the men got sicker with stomach problems and fever. The colonel wants them transferred to the
hospital at Taha before it spreads any further. Sorry, lads, you'll have
to turn right around and escort the convoy back again.'

Andrew felt exhausted at the thought. He couldn't shake off
the malaise he was feeling; his muscles ached and his head still

pounded. All he wanted to do was crawl into his bedroll again and sleep.

'I'm not sure Lomax is up to it, Sir,' said Grant. 'He's fatigued – maybe a touch of sunstroke himself. I suggest we leave him here for a few days.'

'Lomax?' McBain asked in concern.

Andrew drew himself up. He wasn't going to shirk his duties just because of the heat. He'd lived in India for years and should be able to cope better than most of the Scottish soldiers toiling in the fierce sun for the first time.

'I'm perfectly fine, sir,' said Andrew. 'I'll go.'

'I'd rather you did,' said McBain. 'The medical orderlies speak Urdu so we'll need you to translate.'

The next day at dawn, when the convoy of patients set off back down the road to Taha, Andrew was with them.

The journey was a blur. Andrew felt as if his body was on fire, but even the setting sun brought little relief. At the end of the day he was glad that the Scotsman Grant was there to take charge. Andrew began to hallucinate; he saw giant birds with human faces. He remembered vomiting, and then he passed out.

Chapter 45

Andrew knew he was under attack – a turbaned Pathan leaned over him and muttered threats in Pashto – but he was too weak to defend himself. They had bound him up and although he struggled, he couldn't get free. This was how he would die, in a remote corner of the frontier, far from family and friends. He would never get to tell her how much he loved her. Andrew couldn't quite remember who it was he had been thinking of. The woman's face kept swimming before his closed eyes, smiling but elusive.

Voices drifted over him. '. . . fighting for his life . . . Should we let his family know? . . . Temperature's sky-high . . . Send for the padre . . .'

Andrew tried to open his eyes. Someone was touching him and it made his skin burn. For a brief moment he saw a woman's face – a slim face with dark intelligent eyes – not the woman in his dreams. She was trying to tell him something. But he couldn't keep his eyes open. He surrendered once more to the heat and the darkness.

The next time Andrew awoke, an ancient man with a sweep of white hair, a weathered, crinkled face and huge beaky nose stared at him. He wondered if he might be dead.

'You look like God,' Andrew said in a cracked voice.

The man, dressed in a faded linen suit and clerical collar, bellowed with laughter. 'I've been called many things, but never that.'

'You're Scottish.' Andrew recognised the accent.

'Aye.' He smiled. 'Name's Alec Bannerman – but just call me Padre.'

Something about the name was familiar, but Andrew's head felt too fuzzy to concentrate.

'And we're very pleased to see you've pulled through,' said the old man. 'I've been praying for God to spare you.'

'Where am I?'

'In the mission hospital at Taha. Your friend Grant brought you in. We thought we'd lost you but I told Mrs Desai that you Lomaxes are made of sterner stuff.'

Andrew realised he was lying in a single iron-framed bed with a curtain drawn around it. A woman appeared at the sound of their voices – the one he'd seen during his delirium.

'This is Mrs Desai,' said Bannerman. 'She's the ministering angel who saved your life.'

'Along with my orderly, Malik,' said the woman, scrutinising him with solemn brown eyes. 'You've had a severe case of heat-stroke. Luckily Malik spotted it when you brought in the typhoid cases.'

Following behind her, Andrew saw the moustachioed Pathan that he'd thought, in his delirium, had captured him.

'Malik is helping me arrange for you to be brought to my house,' said the padre. 'You can recuperate there and free up a bed for another soldier.' He rose to his feet and Andrew realised he must be as tall as he was.

Andrew was bemused and light-headed. It might be possible he was still hallucinating. But shortly afterwards he was helped onto his feet by Malik and another orderly and half-carried to a car outside. It was evening, and a welcome lick of breeze prickled his skin. To his delight, he saw his bearer Manek waiting for him with a kitbag of clothes and a cheerful 'namaste'.

'Your bearer has been lighting candles for you at the temple,' said Bannerman.

To Andrew's surprise, the old padre clambered into the driving seat. With Manek in the back, they set off at speed, driving out of the hospital compound and through the army cantonment towards the civilian lines. Andrew winced as the car bumped over the rutted road and only half-listened to Bannerman's chatter about the army town.

As they drew up outside a whitewashed bungalow set back in a neat garden with a large mulberry tree, Andrew asked, 'Why are you being so kind to me, sir?'

'You're a Lomax,' said Bannerman, 'and I consider myself a good friend of your family.'

Then Andrew remembered: this must be the friend his father had encouraged him to contact if he was stationed in Taha. Unwillingly, he recalled his mother's harrowing tale of being kidnapped by tribesmen who'd mistaken her for Esmie. He'd been shocked the first time he'd been told the story fully. His father and Esmie had never done so, probably unwilling to admit the mistaken identity.

He closed his eyes in exhaustion. He didn't want to be here – didn't relish staying in Taha any longer than he had to. It was a place of terrible memories for his mother – one of great fear – and he was keen to go back to Razmak as soon as he could.

'I can see you're not up to having a chinwag this evening,' said Bannerman. 'You must go straight to bed and I'll have my bearer send in a little supper. We can talk tomorrow.'

Andrew woke, wondering at first where he was. Through the mosquito net around his comfortable bed he could see a starkly furnished room bathed in soft dawn light from the unshuttered window, and he realised that he was at Bannerman's home.

He lay for a moment, and then, realising that his pounding headache was finally gone and that he was hungry, he sat up and attempted to climb out of bed. On wobbly legs, he made it to the door and put on the silk dressing-gown that was hanging there on a hook. Someone had laid out fresh clothes, but Andrew didn't have the strength to get dressed.

Reaching the veranda, he collapsed into a chair, dizzy with the effort.

'Morning, Lomax!'

Andrew gasped at the sight of Bannerman emerging out of the shadows, dressed only in a pair of flannel shorts. His limbs were thin and strangely hairless but his body still moved with a sinewy strength.

'Always start the morning with prayers and exercise,' he said cheerfully.

'I didn't mean to disturb you,' said Andrew.

'Not at all. I'm glad to see you up and about. Though you mustn't overdo it. Lieutenant Grant said you're to stay here until you're fully recovered – and that he's greatly relieved he's not having to write a letter of condolence to your parents.'

'Was I really that ill?' Andrew asked.

'Death's door, laddie. But with your Lomax willpower and a wee bit of help from the Almighty, you've pulled through. We'll have chota hazri together on the veranda. That's if you're up to eating something?'

'Thank you. Do you mind if I just stay in pyjamas?' He still felt weak as a newborn.

'Don't mind in the least. I'll get the bearer to rustle up some tea.'

He disappeared and Andrew sat watching the sun come up over the rocky hills, spilling golden light over the low rooftops of the cantonment and spreading across the garden. Raucous birdsong came from the mulberry tree. The air smelt of dewy earth and the freshness of a new day before the temperature climbed towards suffocating heat. He caught a whiff of dung fires from the compound behind the bungalow and his eyes prickled.

There was something familiar about this place and he felt calmness settle on him for the first time since coming to the frontier. He liked Bannerman and was touched by his enthusiasm to help him.

The retired padre joined him for breakfast but didn't linger.

'Got hospital visits to do,' he explained, 'and must call on the brigadier about baptising one of his bairns. We'll have a proper chat this evening. Just tell the bearer if there's anything you want. Help yourself to any of the books in my study.'

Then with a wave he was striding off down the pathway. Andrew found it hard to believe Bannerman was in his nineties – he had the energy of a much younger man.

After washing in cool water and dressing in the loose shirt and trousers he'd bought in a bazaar in Delhi, Andrew wandered into the padre's study and then spent the day reading and dozing in the subdued light of the half-shuttered veranda, under the soporific whirring of an electric fan.

That evening, after dinner, Andrew sat with the padre on the veranda. Insects buzzed and hummed beyond the screens. Bannerman nursed a whisky. The talk at dinner had been of the padre's visits and the general war situation. Andrew felt they had both been skirting around more personal subjects, but he had been put at ease by the old man's genial manner.

'I feel as if I've been here before,' Andrew mused.

'You have,' said Bannerman. 'You came here as a small boy with your father and stepmother.'

Andrew's grip on his chair arm tightened. 'I do have flashes of memory . . . I think I might remember meeting you, Padre.'

'I certainly remember you. You can't have been more than five or so,' Bannerman recalled. 'They came to pay their respects to Dr Guthrie – Esmie's first husband; he's buried in the cantonment cemetery here. He was a very well-liked and respected doctor in Taha.'

'Yes, I know who Harold Guthrie is,' Andrew said. 'He was a family friend of my mother's.'

'That's true,' said the padre, 'but he was also your father's oldest boyhood friend. They had gone to the same school and served together in Mesopotamia. He was distraught when Harold died.'

'More so than my stepmother?' Andrew asked, unable to mask his bitterness.

Bannerman looked surprised. 'No, not at all. Esmie grieved deeply. She blamed herself for not being here when he died of blood poisoning – thought she might have been able to prevent his death.'

'So why wasn't she here?' Andrew asked. 'Was she visiting my father, by any chance?'

Bannerman leaned forward, frowning. 'Why ever would you say that?'

Andrew decided to be frank. 'I'm sorry, I know you're a friend of my stepmother's. But according to my mother, Esmie was always in love with my father and did her best to come between them.'

The old man sat back, his expression difficult to read. He took a sip of whisky and said nothing. Andrew cursed himself for offending his kind host. He shouldn't have spoken his thoughts aloud, but he had been disarmed by this ancient father-confessor on his tranquil darkened veranda.

When Bannerman spoke, it was without the reproach that Andrew expected. 'You've been here twice before. The first time was as a baby with your mother.'

Andrew was startled. 'Really? So, you've met my mother too?'

'Indeed. I was utterly charmed by her. She spent quite a bit of her stay keeping an old man company. She was delightful, though a little distracted, as it turned out.'

'Were my parents visiting the Guthries?'

'Your father wasn't with you – he stayed in Pindi. Your parents weren't getting on well by then. But nobody realised how unhappy Lydia was.'

Andrew tensed as the truth dawned on him. 'Was this when my mother was kidnapped?'

Bannerman gave him a sharp look. 'Ah, you know about that?'

'Yes. My mother told me she was mistaken for Esmie and snatched by Pathans in revenge for some slight that Esmie had done to them. Mother still has nightmares about it all.'

The padre put down his glass and leaned forward, clasping his knees. 'I'm not surprised she has nightmares. What else did Lydia tell you?'

'That she was taken into tribal territory and kept in a filthy fortress – terrorised by her kidnappers – and then finally rescued by the British police after my father led an expedition to find her.'

'So, she never mentioned that it was Esmie who rescued her?' he asked.

'Esmie?' Andrew was confused. 'No, of course not. No woman would have been allowed on such a rescue attempt.'

Bannerman sighed. 'I can see that you've never been told the whole story – no doubt your father and Esmie kept quiet to save

Lydia from embarrassment. But I can't let you carry on believing a half-truth.'

'What do you mean?' said Andrew, feeling a mixture of excitement but also dread at what the padre was saying.

'Your mother may have been snatched because the kidnappers thought she was Esmie,' he answered, 'but she put her life in danger in the first place by deliberately driving off on her own into the hills.'

'She wouldn't do such a thing!'

'I'm afraid she did. She took my car – and one of my maps.' He nodded towards the table. 'Strangely enough it was the one you've been looking at today.'

'The one of Razmak and the frontier? Why on earth would she try and go there?'

'Esmie believed your mother was attempting to reach a friend – a man she knew who was stationed there – a Major Mason. But she never got further than a few miles outside of Taha.'

'Uncle Dickie?' Andrew cried in disbelief.

'Then you know Dickie Mason?'

Andrew flushed. 'Yes, he's a friend of Mamma's at home.'

Bannerman nodded. 'I knew him too when he was first posted to the frontier – a very charming young man. The Guthries were very kind to him and his fellow officers. That's how your parents met him in the first place, through Esmie.'

Andrew was indignant. 'If you're saying my mother was having an affair, I don't believe it. It's just Esmie trying to justify going off with my father.'

Bannerman's voice hardened. 'Esmie was the best friend your mother ever had. She was the one most concerned about Lydia's mental state. And what's more, your mother went off without you. It was Esmie who looked after you – your mother was in no fit state to do so. She was prepared to leave you behind to go after Dickie Mason and that's the sad truth of it.'

Andrew was winded by his words; his mother wouldn't have abandoned him.

'I don't believe you,' he said quietly, but his heart no longer felt in it.

'Andrew, I wouldn't lie to you. When your mother was kidnapped for ransom, she unknowingly put a lot of people's lives at risk. There had been uprisings the year before and the army didn't want to go in heavy-handed to Otmanzai country looking for her. That would have led to your mother's abduction further beyond British jurisdiction – or worse.' Bannerman's faded blue eyes held his look. 'The brigadier here asked Esmie to lead a small band of men to go beyond the border and bargain for Lydia's release. Not only was she a trained nurse, but she was a woman – and the brigadier and the chief of police were banking on her being given more leniency than military men by the Otmanzai. A brave young mullah also agreed to go as her protector.'

Andrew shook his head, sad and confused. 'This all sounds too fantastical – and nothing like Mother described.'

'Ask Malik,' Bannerman challenged. 'He went with Esmie and was there at your mother's rescue. Esmie put her life in danger for Lydia – went knowing that there was a strong possibility that she would never return – and for a time she was held captive too. I'm sorry to hear your mother no longer acknowledges the great debt she owed Esmie for saving her life. If Esmie hadn't gone, she would have been able to nurse Harold when he fell ill. He died while she was away.'

Andrew said in agitation, 'Where was my father in all this?'

'We summoned him from Pindi as soon as my car was found abandoned on the Razmak road. He insisted on going on the rescue mission too.'

'So, what happened when they all returned safely?'

'Your mother offered to look after Esmie but she wanted to be left to grieve on her own,' he replied. 'Your parents took you back to Pindi and then to Scotland. Lydia was keen for Esmie to go with them but she chose to stay on in Taha at the mission for a while. I think she felt closer to Harold here.'

Andrew was at a loss as to what to think. 'Are you saying that my mother and Esmie were still friends at that point?'

Bannerman nodded. 'If there's one thing I know about Esmie, it's that she would never have deliberately come between your parents. She was too fond of both of them. And she loved Harold. If he hadn't died, I have no doubt that she would still have been here with him working at the mission hospital. It's what she came to India to do.'

Andrew felt a sudden surge of conflicting emotions: confusion at his mother's behaviour, guilt at believing the worst of Esmie and anger at being kept in the dark about the full story. But could he really trust this old man's memory? Perhaps, over the years, the padre had embellished Esmie's part in the rescue attempt and grown more critical of his mother's actions.

Andrew swallowed. 'Do you know what happened between my parents after that – when they went to Scotland?'

Bannerman sighed. 'No. Only that your mother never returned to India. That's something you'll have to ask them about.'

Then Andrew recalled the wounding words that Stella had once hurled at him just before she was sent away from Ebbsmouth, about his mother packing him off back to India as a baby with his ayah. He hadn't believed it for a moment and had deliberately tried to forget her words, but now they seemed to have a sudden power.

Bannerman got stiffly to his feet and put a gnarled hand on Andrew's head.

'Dear boy, I can see this has all been a bit of a shock. I'm sorry. I'm supposed to be helping you get better, not burdening you with past tales of woe. But I didn't want you thinking badly of your stepmother. Esmie is one of the most compassionate people I've met – and she's loved you deeply, right from when you were a baby staying in her house at Taha.' He gave a sad smile. 'In those first days after Harold died, your parents lodged with me here, but you stayed on with Esmie. Your mother said it was because a crusty old bachelor like me wouldn't want a crying infant in the house, but we all knew that it was really because you brought such comfort to Esmie's broken heart.'

Andrew's insides twisted. For an instant he remembered what it was like to love his Meemee deeply.

'I'll see you at breakfast,' said Bannerman, moving past him.

Suddenly Andrew asked, 'Which house was the Guthries'?'

'Number Ten, The Lines. Just five houses down the street and around the corner from here.'

Andrew nodded. 'Goodnight, Padre.'

'Goodnight, Andrew. Sleep well.'

Andrew spent most of the following day in bed. He felt listless and his headache had returned. He lay in the dark of the shuttered room trying to rid his mind of conflicting thoughts about his parents and their short-lived marriage. Had his mother really had an affair with Dickie? Was Mamma, in fact, rushing off to be with Dickie when she was kidnapped? Why had Esmie not done more to keep an eye on her friend?

Then Andrew reminded himself that Esmie would most probably have been nursing at the mission and that was why his mother had spent so much time round at the padre's bungalow. And where was he, baby Andrew, during all this? He found it hard to banish the image of Esmie cradling him and tending to his needs while his mother, restless and distracted and perhaps in love with a man who was not his father, plotted to escape and leave him behind.

He drifted into fitful sleep with troubling dreams that vanished when he awoke. Manek came in often, persisting in his attempts to get his master to drink tea and nimbu panis sent in by the padre.

On the third day, feeling stronger, Andrew forced himself up and into uniform. He had lain in bed dwelling on destructive thoughts for too long. He was a soldier who was neglecting his duties while his comrades toiled without him in the summer heat, facing daily dangers. His continued anger at his parents and stepmother seemed petty and self-indulgent.

Andrew rose too late to see the padre at breakfast. Afterwards he determined to see how far he could walk before the heat grew too oppressive. Out of curiosity, he set off down the dusty street lined with bleached wooden bungalows neatly fenced off by hedges of thorn and trim beds of pink and red flowers. In a few minutes he was standing outside Number Ten.

It was set further back from the road than the padre's house and a vine grew along the faded green veranda. A huge mulberry tree half-obscured the dwelling and a monotonous insistent call of a solitary bird pierced the air. Andrew stood hesitating at the gate, wondering whether to go any further. As he reached for the latch, a dog rushed from under the veranda steps and began barking at him.

An ayah came onto the veranda to see what had disturbed the dog. She leaned down and lifted up a small girl, pointing to the soldier at the gate.

Andrew waved. The girl, with round pink cheeks under a yellow bonnet, waved back. With a frisson, Andrew knew he had been there before. Esmie's words came back to him. *'You had an ayah called Sarah but she left us to get married when you were three. After that, Karo helped me. You and Gabina used to run around together, thick as thieves!'*

According to his father, Gabina was to be ayah to the new Lomax baby. How their lives had diverged since he had taken that fateful voyage to Scotland! Gabina had remained closer to his own family in India than he had. Although he had stopped playing with the Pathan girl once he was old enough to go to school, Andrew remembered her as a cheerful companion.

He stepped away from the gate. The small girl was still waving at him from the veranda. As Andrew gave a final wave and walked away, he thought about Belle. Perhaps he cared more about his half-sister than he liked to admit.

When Bannerman returned for afternoon tea, Andrew was already packed. He told his host of his intention to return to the barracks.

'I'm very grateful for the billet you've given me,' Andrew said. 'It's been the lap of luxury compared to being in camp. I can't thank you enough. I hope you'll forgive the harsh things I said while I've been out of sorts.'

'Dear lad!' Bannerman clapped him on the shoulder. 'It's been a pleasure having you here and keeping me company. And I'm the one who should be apologising. Perhaps I was a bit too frank with you about your mother's behaviour at the time of the kidnapping – I know it was a shock to hear it – and Lydia was acting out of character. She was under a lot of mental strain. She couldn't really cope with India. Some British never get used to life here. She can't be blamed for that. The point I was trying to make was that none of it was Esmie's fault.'

Andrew nodded. With difficulty, he asked, 'I wonder, before I go, whether you could tell me where the British cemetery is? Where Dr Guthrie is buried.'

'Of course,' the padre agreed at once. 'I'll take you there myself. Let's have tea first and then I'll drive you round. It's too far to walk in the heat.'

As the sun lost its strength, Bannerman led Andrew under a simple archway proclaiming 'Taha British Cemetery' and then inside a brick-built enclosure. They walked past neat lines of military graves to an area at the far wall where the gravestones were rather haphazardly dotted across the scorched grass, some shaded by feathery trees.

The padre stopped in front of a carved headstone, dappled in late-afternoon light. Someone still tended the grave; the ground around it was greener and obviously watered.

IN FONDEST MEMORY OF DR HAROLD GUTHRIE, BORN JANUARY 1886, DIED OCTOBER 1920. DEARLY BELOVED HUSBAND OF ESMIE MCBRIDE. TILL WE MEET AGAIN, MAY GOD HOLD YOU IN THE PALM OF HIS HAND.

He felt sad and deeply moved by the tender inscription. How wrong he had been to doubt that Esmie had loved Harold. His mother had implied that Esmie had married the doctor merely as a way of getting to India to be near Tom. But this elegant gravestone suggested otherwise – as did the fact that Esmie and his father had brought him all the way to Taha to visit the burial site when he was a small boy.

Andrew asked, 'Do you look after the grave, Padre?'

Bannerman shook his head. 'Malik does. Esmie asked him to do so and Malik would have done anything for the Guthries.'

Andrew nodded. He gazed beyond the cemetery to where the sun was dipping behind the rugged mountains and turning the sky a deep rose pink. Someone went by singing a devotional song in Urdu. Standing in this peaceful place, it was hard to imagine that there was so much conflict going on in the world. For a moment, he closed his eyes, breathed in the soft evening smells and listened to the unseen singer until he'd passed and the song died away.

That's when it came to him: the memory of standing here holding someone's hand – most probably his father's. Andrew breathed deeply, trying to remember more. The sound of hymn-singing; a woman's sweet voice. He recalled looking up through the bare branches of a tree and marvelling at the clearness of dazzlingly white-capped mountains that looked like they were just beyond the cemetery wall.

'That way lies Afghanistan, Andy.' His father's voice. The squeeze of a hand.

Andrew felt overwhelmed by another wave of sadness. It hadn't been his father's hand; it had been a woman's – his Meemee's. He'd squeezed it back because he'd understood that she was sad and had wanted to comfort her.

Bowing his head, Andrew blinked away the tears that had begun to form and said a silent prayer for the brave doctor – and for Esmie.

He cleared his throat. 'Thank you for bringing me here, Padre.'

Then, with the old man's hand resting on Andrew's shoulder, they retreated down the path together.

Chapter 46

'Look!' Esmie exclaimed. 'She's trying to crawl.'

At the sound of Esmie's excited cry, Stella glanced out of the open office window. Belle was lying on her tummy in the playpen, which Tom had placed under the apple tree outside his studio so he could watch her while he painted. The baby was rocking back and forth trying to move. Tom came out to look.

He laughed. 'She's like a wee caterpillar, except she's going backwards!'

Esmie beamed. 'What a clever girl.'

Stella clenched her hands. It took all her willpower not to rush outside, scoop Belle up in her arms and smother her with congratulatory kisses. Instead she watched while Esmie leaned into the pen and patted the baby's back.

After a few more attempts at moving on her tummy, Belle gave a whimper of protest. Tom reached in and sat her up. At five months, her little girl was sturdy with chubby legs and could sit for several minutes without toppling over on her side. Belle waved a hand at Tom. He pretended to bite it, making animal noises. She giggled. To Stella it was the sweetest sound in the world; it left her breathless every time Belle laughed.

Over the summer, Stella had watched her daughter grow into a sunny-natured baby with tufts of light brown hair and a heart-shaped face with a delicate chin and large blue eyes above plumpish cheeks. Her skin had a more ivory tinge than Stella's – the only tell-tale sign of her Anglo-Indian heritage. Guests commented how like the baby was to Esmie, though Stella couldn't see any similarity.

'Those beautiful blue eyes!' Mrs Pennock, a policeman's wife, had cried. 'So like yours, Mrs Lomax.'

But to Stella, the deep blue irises were the same sapphire blue as Hugh's. When Belle gazed back at her, Stella would experience a heaviness in her chest of both longing and regret. Each evening she allowed herself a few minutes with her daughter, playing with her before Gabina took her away for a bath. She knew that by the end of the month she would be returning to Rawalpindi and would not see Belle until the following hot season.

The thought of being separated from her was like a physical pain, as if weights had been pressed on her heart. She would miss eight months of Belle's growing up; she wouldn't be there for her first birthday in March, and by May her daughter might be walking and saying her first words. Stella knew how thrilled Esmie would be to hear Belle say 'Ma-ma' for the first time.

Stella's eyes smarted. Esmie loved Belle like her own daughter – as Stella had hoped she would – and Stella wondered if sometimes Esmie forgot that she wasn't the baby's real mother. It was Tom who often looked guiltily at Stella when she visited the annex and was quick to hand over Belle for a cuddle. But then Tom knew what it was like to lose a baby girl and perhaps he viewed the situation differently. Even though it had been Stella's choice to give up Belle, both she and Tom had suffered a loss that could not be put into words.

As Stella watched now, Tom lifted Belle from the playpen and raised her up high. Belle shrieked with alarm and laughter. Tom did it again, pretending to drop her on the way down and then cuddling her to his chest.

'Tom, don't!' Esmie laughed in mock admonition, moving closer.

Tom put his arm about his wife and held them both. He kissed Esmie's head and then Belle's.

Blinded by tears, Stella turned away from the window and went back to her paperwork.

One afternoon a few days later, her brother Jimmy rang from The Raj Hotel with a message for Stella. The line was crackly and she had to press the receiver to her ear to hear him.

'What's that about Mrs Shankley?' she asked anxiously.

Jimmy shouted down the phone, 'She had a fall a week ago and hasn't got out of bed since. She's failing fast . . . Asking to see you . . . Might not be long in this . . .' His words broke up again. Stella didn't know if he'd said that the old missionary wouldn't be long in the hotel, or in the world.

'Oh, that's terrible!' Stella said in distress.

'Will you come?' Jimmy bellowed. '. . . agitated . . . keeps saying your name.'

'Yes, of course I'll come,' said Stella at once.

As soon as the Lomaxes heard about Winfred Shankley's request they were supportive.

'Of course you must go,' said Esmie. 'Don't wait till the end of the month – she might not last. Jimmy wouldn't have rung if it wasn't urgent.'

Within two days, travel arrangements had been made for four days' time.

Those final days in Gulmarg were precious and bittersweet for Stella. She went more often to the annex to look in on Belle and Gabina. The ayah was quick to hand Belle into her arms.

On the final morning, Stella slipped out of the hotel before dawn and went around to the annex and Belle's room. The baby was stirring and Gabina was heating up a bottle of milk. Stella didn't need to ask; the ayah handed over the bottle.

'I have to sort some of the baby's laundry, Stella-Mem',' she said, and left the room.

Stella sat in the nursing chair where she had first suckled Belle and fed the bottle to the baby. Belle fixed her with a trusting look in her blue eyes as she gulped the milk and wrapped her small fist around Stella's finger. It always amazed Stella how strong a grip her daughter had.

'I have to go away for a while,' Stella spoke softly to her. 'I don't want to leave you – I'll never truly leave you, my darling girl – as you'll always be in my heart. And Mummy Esmie and Ayah Gabina will look after you for me – and Daddy Tom will play with you. You bring them such joy, my little one – you have no idea how much.'

Stella cradled the baby tightly and kissed the top of her head. Belle paused from her sucking and her face creased in a milky smile. It took Stella's breath away. A sob rose in her chest. She sat the baby up and rubbed her back, trying to keep her tears at bay. How could she possibly leave her? It felt as if her heart was shattering into a thousand pieces.

Stella wiped at the tears streaming down her face and continued the bottle-feeding. Eventually, Belle pushed the bottle away and Stella put it down, carrying the baby to the window.

'Look, the sun's coming up over the mountains, Belle. It's the most beautiful sight in the world. You're very lucky to live in such a place. Every morning at sunrise I'll think of you here and send you a morning prayer full of love.'

Stella gave Belle a long tender kiss on her cheek, breathing in her warm milky smell and committing to memory the softness of her baby skin and the loving look in her beautiful eyes.

'No one will love you as much as I do, my precious one! If, someday, you ever discover the truth, I hope you will come to realise that I did it to give you the best life I could. And that it was the hardest thing that I've ever done in my life!'

Gabina returned. Stella took a deep breath and handed Belle over to her ayah. She resisted the urge to hang onto Belle and cover her in more kisses, fearful that the longer she held her the more impossible it would be to let go.

Gabina said quietly, 'We will look after her well, Stella-Mem'.'

Stella nodded and gave a tearful smile. 'Thank you,' she said hoarsely. 'I know you will.'

She hurried from the room and out of the annex. The air was cool and sweet from a heavy dew. The sky over the Himalayas was turning pale gold as the sun's rays poured over the ridge tops, flooding the valley with dawn light. How could the day be so beautiful when her heart was breaking?

Stella wiped her tear-stained face. She must not show her misery. This was the path she had chosen for herself and her daughter. She must be brave for them both – and make the most of a life without Belle.

Chapter 47

Winifred Shankley rallied when Stella returned to the hotel in Rawalpindi. For a while, Stella managed to coax her out of bed and to sit in the courtyard in the shade of the jacaranda. Stella would read to her or simply sit and hold her hand while the old woman dozed.

Stella was shocked by how much the missionary had aged in the sixteen months she'd been away. Winifred was painfully thin and frail and her back was so bent that she was forced to look at the floor when she walked. But mostly she sat in her wheelchair and talked about her family as if they were present, although Stella knew all her relatives had died long ago.

'You won't go away again, will you?' Winifred fretted.

'No, Mrs S, I won't,' Stella promised, squeezing her hand gently.

'I missed you, dearie.'

'And I missed you. But you had my cousin Lucy looking after you well. Yvonne said you got on together like a house on fire.'

'That other girl was nice,' Winifred admitted. 'And I don't want to complain but you and I are like old friends, aren't we?'

Stella smiled. 'Yes, we are, Mrs S. The best of friends.'

Stella resumed her work for the WAC and was thankful that they accepted her reason for being away in Gulmarg for so long. When she wasn't working at the hotel or doing voluntary service, Stella began making soft furnishings out of old curtains, trousers and jackets as well as offcuts of sari material from the bazaar. She sewed on sequins and buttons and made cushion covers, bedspreads and bags.

Myrtle was full of admiration. 'I never thought you could be so good with a needle and thread, Stella. You should set up your own business.'

'Maybe someday,' she answered. 'But not while we're in danger of being invaded by the Japanese. I can't think beyond helping as much as I can with the WAC.'

Stella was glad that she could please her mother after the disappointment of her not being successfully married. She had told no one about Hugh already having a wife – she didn't want their pity or to be the focus of Pindi gossip – but had simply said that they had fallen out of love and that Hugh had left India.

Every day she was tempted to ring Gulmarg and ask for news of Belle, longing to hear her gurgling voice down the telephone wire. But she resisted. She had received two letters from Esmie with news – in October Belle was red-cheeked and teething – and recently she'd started to crawl. Stella appreciated these tantalising snippets of news but suspected Esmie did not write more often for fear of upsetting her.

She found it very hard to visit Ada. While Stella had been away, her cousin had given birth to a baby girl called June – named after the month in which she'd been born – who was now five months old. It was the age Belle had been when Stella had last seen her.

She had met Ada on a couple of occasions, but not with the baby. Eventually, in early November, Stella forced herself to visit. She went round to Lalkutri one afternoon, still dressed in her uniform.

To watch baby June sitting propped on cushions waving a rattle and giving gummy smiles was purgatory for Stella. June looked nothing like Belle; she had a shock of dark hair kept in place by mother-of-pearl hair slides and solemn brown eyes framed by dark lashes. But her gestures and smiles made Stella's heart ache.

'You can hold her,' Ada encouraged. 'She won't cry.'

Stella steeled herself to take the proffered baby and sit her on her knee. Her powdery baby smell nearly made Stella sob out loud. She masked it with a cough and handed her back. 'Sorry, don't want to give her my cold.' Stella fumbled quickly in her handbag and blew her nose.

It was almost preferable to have Ada bombard her with questions about Hugh than to have June in her arms.

'I don't understand why you aren't prepared to wait for Mr Keating,' said Ada. 'Surely he'll come back to India as soon as he can? He has a good job in Calcutta.'

'I don't know if he will,' said Stella, 'but even if he does, I no longer love him.'

'Does he have someone else?' Ada guessed. 'Have you found out he's cheated? Is that it?'

Stella decided that was as near the truth as she was prepared to admit. 'Yes, he was unfaithful to me.'

'I knew it! What a swine.'

By the time Stella left, Ada had convinced herself that she had always known Hugh was a bad one and that she would do her best to find Stella a good husband from among Clive's friends.

Stella laughed and hugged her friend. 'I don't need a matchmaker, thank you all the same.'

'I think you've proved that you do,' Ada retorted.

'Leave Stella alone,' said Clive, picking up June, who had started to grizzle. 'She can make up her own mind.'

'I'm really quite happy being fancy-free,' said Stella.

'But I want you to get married and have a baby like me,' Ada persisted. 'So we can be mothers together.'

Stella's throat tightened. She tried not to gasp for breath. 'Maybe one day.' She kissed her cousin and Clive on their cheeks and left quickly.

Walking home in the mellow sunshine, she pondered the future. It was already the start of the cold season and soon the usual round of social events would begin in this army town – perhaps even more feverishly, given that the war front had come to India. The parade grounds and streets of the cantonment rang to the sound of troops being drilled and there were more regiments than ever passing through Rawalpindi.

She wondered if Andrew's battalion would be given leave from the frontier. The Lomaxes had received a note from him shortly before Stella left for Rawalpindi, saying that he'd had a touch of fever but was now 'right as rain'. He'd met one of their old friends in Taha, a Scottish padre that Esmie had talked about with fondness. Esmie had also been encouraged that the message had been addressed to them both. Stella had been too distracted at the thought of leaving Belle to dwell on Andrew's letter but thinking about him now, she realised how much it would lift her spirits to see him again.

She admired Andrew for joining up and following where his conscience led him. She determined that whatever she did next with her life, she would do something brave to atone for her abandoning of Belle. Perhaps she would volunteer for general service with the WAC rather than local. The thought of leaving Pindi and going somewhere totally unknown on her own was in a way terrifying. Yet the more she thought about it, the keener she was to put all her effort into war work, as Andrew was doing.

She could type fast and do bookkeeping, arrange diaries and take minutes of meetings. She would get Jimmy to teach her to drive. Then she could offer herself as a secretary-cum-driver to the forces or any of the branches of the civil service.

By the time she arrived back at the Raj, Stella was feeling optimistic that she could do something useful. If she couldn't be Belle's mother, she would be the best auxiliary corps woman she could be.

Chapter 48

As soon as Stella entered the hotel lobby, she could sense the excitement among the residents.

Jimmy, hovering like an eager impresario, caught sight of his sister and beckoned her over.

'Stella! Come, come! We have a very special surprise guest.'

At the mention of her name, the visitor leapt to his feet and swung round. He was so tall that he had to duck beneath the dim light-fitting that hung overhead. He came towards her.

Stella's heart thumped in shock. For a dizzying moment she thought it was Tom. But this man was too young to be the captain and he was broader in the shoulders.

He gave a tentative smile. 'Stella, you haven't changed a bit – apart from the uniform.'

Stella found her voice. 'Andrew?'

He gave a bashful laugh. 'Yes. It's been a long time.'

She felt a surge of happiness and excitement that immediately seemed to leave her speechless. Of course he wasn't the boy that she had left behind at Ebbsmouth all those years ago, but she was taken aback by this tall handsome military man who was a stranger, and yet with the lively eyes and the generous smile that were so dearly familiar to her.

He held out his hand. Ignoring it, Stella threw her arms around him and cried, 'Oh, Andrew! It's so good to see you!'

After a moment's hesitation, she felt his arms go around her and they hugged tightly. Stella's head only came up to his chest and for a few seconds she rested it there, her eyes flooding with tears. It was the most comforting feeling in the world to be held by her childhood friend.

'Bravo!' cried Ansom. 'Old friends reunited, eh?'

Andrew kissed her lightly on the head, and she felt a ripple of delight and comfort. Then they were breaking away.

'It's so strange,' said Stella, wiping at her eyes. 'I was just thinking of you as I walked back from Ada's. There were Scottish soldiers drilling at the Victoria Barracks.'

'The Borderers are there too,' said Andrew. 'We're in transit.'

Stella gave him an anxious look. 'Where are you going next?'

'Can't say for sure.'

He stepped aside for her to go first in joining the others. Stella had the impression he knew more than he was allowed to say. It worried her that he might be going east to fight the Japanese.

'Sit down with us, Stella,' said Hester. 'You deserve a break, and it's not often we get our darling Andrew with us, is it?'

Stella saw Jimmy nod in agreement, so she ordered a nimbu pani, noticing that Andrew had also chosen the lemon drink rather than a whisky. She listened to the men speculating about the war.

Stella sipped her drink and watched Andrew as he fielded their questions, making light of the frontier skirmishes he'd been involved in. Again, he reminded her of a younger Tom in his self-deprecating manner, deep voice and easy laughter. She longed to speak to him alone and have the chance to talk about family issues.

All too soon he was draining his drink and standing up. 'I'm sorry to have to leave such delightful company, but I'm expected in the mess in half an hour.'

Stella followed him to the door, her pulse beginning to race. 'When do you leave?'

He gave her a regretful look. 'The day after tomorrow.'

She swallowed. 'So, they're giving you no time to visit Gulmarg.'

He shook his head, his expression sad. 'But perhaps we could meet again before I go?'

'I'd like that,' she agreed quickly. 'Can you come to the hotel for a meal?'

He hesitated. 'Why don't we meet for a morning ride like old times? More chance to talk.' He smiled as he glanced at the chattering residents.

'I haven't had a pony for years,' said Stella with a wry look. 'But I'm prepared to race you on my bicycle.'

Andrew grinned. 'I'll borrow a bike so you have half a chance of keeping up with me.'

Stella laughed. 'The challenge is on!'

'Tomorrow at dawn?' he suggested.

'I'll see you then,' Stella agreed.

Andrew nodded and, putting on his cap, strode out of the hotel. He turned at the top of the path and waved. Stella waved back and then went inside. She couldn't believe how in such a short time she had gone from feeling so desolate to being uplifted by a new vitality and hope.

Andrew could settle to nothing. He was distracted at dinner and took a late walk up the Mall with half a mind to call in at the Raj, but turned back. He could hardly contain his impatience to see Stella again, yet guilt made him retreat to the barracks. Just before leaving Razmak, he'd received a long newsy letter from Felicity – the first one for weeks – and he knew he should be spending the evening writing back to his fiancée.

He stood smoking and looking up at the inky night sky. The stars were obscured by hazy smoke from fires. He had grown used to seeing the glittering galaxy overhead in the rarefied air of the frontier mountains. In a couple of days, he would be far from this northern region and into unknown territory. Andrew regretted that he hadn't been able to go to Kashmir and make his peace with his father and Esmie – to meet his half-sister. How he longed to be reunited with them and show them that they were loved. It was possible that he might never get the chance to do so now.

Seeing Stella again after all these years had brought back to him how much he still cherished this place and its people. The minute he caught sight of her – her heart-shaped face flushed from her walk and her stylish fair hair rippling over her shoulders – it was like a punch in the guts. All the yearning for India and for his family here – for Stella – which he'd buried so deep for so long had come surging back.

He had dreamt of putting his arms about her, but hadn't expected her to welcome him so enthusiastically. Yet, he should have known that Stella would not hold any grudges against him for how he had behaved in the past; she was as engaging and warm-hearted as he'd remembered. And as attractive. Perhaps her face had aged subtly – there were lines across her forehead and the girlish plumpness had gone, leaving her cheekbones more prominent. At thirty, she now had the face and figure of a beautiful woman.

He ground out his cigarette and thrust his hands in his pockets. How hard he'd found it, when she'd been in his arms, not to tilt her chin up and kiss her on the lips. She would have been shocked and maybe a little offended. But he hadn't been able to resist brushing her hair with a kiss. Even that, he thought, had probably gone too far. She had pulled away from him.

Andrew sighed. He could hardly wait for the morning to see her again and yet was already dreading a final farewell.

Stella was up and ready before the dawn broke. She slipped out of the family bungalow before anyone was awake and wheeled her bicycle round the side of the hotel. The air was sharp and she stood, muffled in jacket, scarf and woollen beret, blowing into her hands to warm them up. From the direction of Saddar Bazaar, she heard the muezzin's call to prayer. It was echoed by another call to the faithful from further away.

A short time later, she heard the soft tinkle of a bicycle bell and Andrew appeared out of the semi-darkness. She felt so nervous and yet excited that she was trembling slightly, although she said to herself it must be the cold. She pushed her bicycle up the path to meet him. Their breath rose in clouds as they greeted each another.

Without another word, they set off down deserted Nichol Road, cycling side by side. Turning into Dalhousie Road they soon reached the Mall. As they rode down it, Stella saw the first flush of dawn seeping into the sky above the distant Himalayan foothills. Behind them, stars were still out and the ghostly sliver of a crescent moon hung low over the city.

The trees along the Mall were almost bare, save for a few leaves that began to turn golden in the rising sun. Stella could have ridden for much longer, but she was aware that their time together was brief and so she pulled ahead.

'Race you to the cricket pavilion!' she shouted.

She pedalled faster and veered left towards the cricket ground. Along the cinder track she heard Andrew gaining on her. They arrived at the pavilion in a dead heat and dismounted laughing. There wasn't a soul around.

'Lost your touch, Master Andrew,' she teased, panting for breath. 'Too many mess dinners?'

'Just being gentlemanly towards my old nanny,' he quipped back.

They mounted the steps to the veranda.

'The bench is damp,' said Stella.

'Allow me,' said Andrew, pulling out a blanket from a duffel bag he'd been carrying. He spread it on the bench.

Stella raised her eyebrows in surprise. 'Very organised.'

'Always be prepared – that's what the army teaches us.'

They both sat down. Andrew pulled out his cigarettes and offered her one.

'No thanks, I still don't smoke. Though all the girls at the office seem to have taken it up.'

She watched him light up and saw his hands tremble. Was he as nervous as she was or was he just cold? He inhaled deeply and blew out smoke.

'So, where do we start?' he asked, eyeing her.

She wondered if he realised just how good-looking he was. His blue eyes were startling in his lean suntanned face. His dark hair was cut severely short around the sides and yet it still grew in unruly tufts on top that only hair oil would be able to control.

'Tell me about Scotland,' she said, feeling disconcerted suddenly by her attraction towards him. 'What news of Tibby – and your mother and grandmother?'

'The post is slow – as you probably know – but it sounds like they're all bearing up.'

'Your father said you were worried about your grandmamma losing her memory.'

Andrew nodded. 'I think my mother finds it very trying. Her life is taken up with looking after her.'

'That must be exhausting for both of them. Old Mrs Templeton was so sweet to me.'

'I feel guilty not being at home to help,' Andrew confided. 'But goodness knows when this war will end. My greatest fear is that by the time I do get back to Scotland, she might not be . . .'

Stella quickly squeezed his arm. 'You mustn't think like that. Mrs Templeton is physically fit, isn't she?'

'Yes, I suppose so.'

'You must miss Scotland,' said Stella.

'I do.' He drew hard on his cigarette.

'And your fiancée, of course. Tell me about her?'

Andrew looked away, his colour deepening. 'Felicity is a great girl. She speaks her mind and does what she wants. She's pretty and makes me laugh.'

'It must be so hard being separated from her,' said Stella, feeling a pang of sympathy.

'Yes.' He nodded. 'I haven't seen her for a year now.'

He carried on smoking. They both sat in silence as the light inched through the trees beyond the boundary and stole across the grass.

'I'm very sorry that Hugh treated you so badly,' Andrew said quietly. 'Dad told me what happened. I feel awful for ever having put you in touch with him again. If only I hadn't bumped into him in Edinburgh . . .'

Stella brushed his hand with hers.

'It's not your fault. I was foolish about Hugh. I wanted to believe in this big romantic idea that he was the only one for me – I was so wrapped up in the thought of being in love that I never really stopped to question what sort of man he was.' She sighed. 'There were signs if I'd been looking for them. He only turned up when it suited him and hardly ever wrote – he'd just appear and expect me to drop everything. And then on his final leave before going to Singapore – I thought he was being romantic and wanted to spend every last minute with me, but all he really wanted was—' She broke off, blushing, and turned away from his pitying look.

Andrew extinguished his cigarette and took her hand. His touch was warm and comforting around her cold fingers.

'He was a fool,' Andrew said firmly. 'Don't blame yourself for falling for his lies. If my father's hunch is right, you're not the only one Hugh Keating has tricked into believing he's someone he's not.'

Stella gave him a teary smile. 'Oh, Andrew, you've always managed to make me feel better about myself. I can see you're still just as kind. Your Felicity is a lucky woman.'

Andrew sat back, looking slightly embarrassed by her praise of him. After a moment he said, 'That card you sent me – what did you mean about wanting to explain about Dad and Esmie and my half-sister?'

Stella tensed at his sudden mention of Belle. She now regretted sending the message. She suddenly realised it would be wrong of her to tell him the secret she shared with the Lomaxes without their agreement. If the arrangement was to work then the fewer people who knew the truth about the baby's origins, the better. But should she tell Andrew now? Didn't he have a right to know?

She decided to be cautious. 'We all felt bad about not telling you sooner about the baby. But it was late into the pregnancy before we were sure – before Esmie was sure. Your dad wanted to tell you in person. I'm so sorry you had to hear about Belle from my mother. She'd only just been told and was overexcited. It's no excuse, but no one planned it that way or wanted to upset you.'

She regarded Andrew warily and saw the struggle in his tight expression. Eventually he let out a long sigh and met her look.

'It doesn't matter now. I admit it was a shock to hear about the baby and I suppose I felt a bit pushed out, but I've had time to get used to the idea of a sister.' He gave a rueful smile. 'Tell me what she's like.'

Stella felt her eyes prickle with tears. 'She's beautiful – with big blue eyes and brown hair – and she's sunny-natured – always laughing. She loves being sung to and she has the strongest grip. I had to tie my hair up to stop her pulling out handfuls! She wasn't crawling when I left but she is now. And Esmie thinks there's a tooth coming through.'

Andrew's smile broadened. 'Sounds like you were a wee bit smitten with my new sister.'

Stella swallowed a sob and nodded, turning away to look at the sunrise. She didn't trust herself to speak.

After a pause, Andrew said reflectively, 'I met a friend of my parents in Taha – a Reverend Bannerman – a wonderful old man. I recuperated at his house after I'd been ill in July. He told me things that made me rethink how I feel about Dad and Esmie. I heard quite a different side to the story about my mother's kidnap from Taha. Apparently, I was there too.'

'Go on,' Stella encouraged.

'Mamma was having an affair with Dickie Mason – or so the gossip went. I'm not really concerned about that – she must have had her reasons and I know my father wasn't the easiest man to live with – but I never knew about Esmie's part in rescuing Mamma. Did you ever hear anything about it?'

Stella nodded. 'Yes, I remember the fuss at the time. Even though my mother thought the incident too upsetting and hid the local newspaper from me and Jimmy, the baroness let us read her copy. It said how your mother had been snatched by Pathans and held for ransom and how she'd been rescued by Esmie. "Plucky Scotch nurse saves beautiful young Englishwoman," it said, or something along those lines. Baroness Cussack will probably still have the cutting.'

Andrew shook his head in disbelief. 'Imagine the army and the police asking such a thing of Esmie? Sending a lone woman into tribal territory with just a mullah and a couple of local guards. According to Bannerman, my father insisted on going too but could do little to help. It was Esmie who took all the risk . . .' Andrew stopped and gave her a pained look. 'I feel terrible for thinking the worst of Esmie and I wish I could see her to say sorry. I've been so cruel and childish towards her over the years and she never deserved it.'

Stella was joyful at his admission. 'She'll be so happy if you did tell her that. She's never stopped loving you, Andy. Apart from your father, there's no one Esmie loves more.'

His mouth twisted. 'Not even the perfect Belle?'

Stella was silent.

Beyond the cricket pitch, the town was stirring with early traffic; horses trotted by pulling milk carts; an army truck trundled past belching blue smoke into the chilly air.

Stella knew their time was running out. In a short while she should be returning to the hotel to help get Mrs Shankley washed and encourage her to eat some breakfast, even though she had no appetite these days. For the past week Stella hadn't even been able to coax her out of bed or to get dressed.

'Do you know where you're being posted?' she asked.

He met her look. 'Most likely down to the Burma border.'

Impulsively, she grabbed his arm. 'You will take very good care, won't you, Andy? Don't go trying to be ridiculously brave.'

He covered her hand with his. 'Don't worry – I just give the orders.'

She smiled. 'I know that's not true. I'm very proud of you. We all are.'

Andrew's eyes glinted. 'Thank you, Stella. That means a lot.'

For a long moment they held each other's look. Stella felt her heart brimming with affection. She glanced down at their hands touching; it was such a comforting feeling. She ran the tips of her fingers over his.

'You still bite your nails,' she said.

'Habit,' Andrew admitted.

Stella said, 'They're not as bad as they used to be though.'

'I remember how you would sometimes try and kiss them better,' he said wryly.

She raised his hand and gently kissed his fingertips. 'That better?'

'Much.'

She saw the glint of emotion in his eyes and swiftly let go her hold.

Andrew cleared his throat. 'Will you give my love to Dad and Esmie?' he asked. 'Tell them I'm sorry I didn't get to see them before leaving the Punjab.'

'Of course I will.'

'Are they happy, Stella?' he asked abruptly. 'With the new baby?'

'Very,' Stella said truthfully. 'They adore her – and your father has started painting again. That's always a sign that he's in good spirits.'

'I'm glad,' Andrew said, smiling wistfully. 'I hope one day I'll meet my sister.'

She leaned towards him and lightly kissed his cheek. As she brushed against him, she was aware of his unshaven chin. It gave her the same frisson she'd experienced the day before when he'd kissed her hair. Quickly she stood up.

'Let me ride back with you,' Andrew said.

'No, it's the wrong direction for you,' Stella replied, 'and you'll only slow me down.'

Andrew laughed. 'Oh, Stella, I've missed your teasing.'

Hastily, she pushed off and pedalled hard. To linger would be too distressing and she didn't dare look back. She had waited over nine years to see Andrew again and their time together had been so tantalisingly brief. She had forgotten just how much she cared for him. The tears came, and a confusing mix of sadness and yearning pressed on her chest. Stella sent up a prayer that she would see him again, safe and unharmed.

Chapter 49

A week after Andrew left Rawalpindi, Stella entered Winifred Shankley's room and knew something was wrong. There was no reply to her morning greeting. The old woman lay still and when Stella approached, she didn't move. But leaning over Winifred, she could hear her shallow breathing.

'Mrs S, are you all right?' Stella smoothed back wispy white hair from the missionary's brow.

Winifred's eyes flickered open. Her expression was confused. She didn't answer; her hand fumbled for Stella's and tried to hold it, but her thin fingers were too weak. Stella sat on the bed and, lifting Winifred's hand to her lips, kissed it. Winifred smiled and closed her eyes. Her rapid shallow breathing continued. A lump formed in Stella's throat; instinctively she knew that her old friend's life was finally ebbing away.

'Would you like me to sing to you?' Stella asked gently.

Winifred gave the slightest of nods. Stella began singing the missionary's favourite hymn, 'There is a Green Hill Far Away'.

As she sang, the old woman's face relaxed and her breathing grew calmer. Stella wondered if she should go for help and get Jimmy to call the doctor, but when she tried to draw away, Winifred's fingers fluttered in agitation. So, Stella stayed and kept on singing hymns while stroking the missionary's brow.

Abruptly, Winifred's breathing changed. It grew deep and ragged, and she gasped as a bronchial, rattling noise sounded in her chest.

In alarm, Stella broke off singing. 'Mrs S?'

Winifred's eyes opened wide. She saw Stella leaning over her and smiled. 'Glory to God!' Then she closed her eyes again.

Stella bent down and kissed her tenderly on the forehead. 'Glory to God, Mrs S,' she whispered.

A few minutes later, Winifred Shankley stopped breathing.

Mrs Shankley's death spurred on Stella to volunteer for general service with the WAC. By December, news was seeping out that Indian and British forces were engaged in battle with the Japanese in the Arakan, a coastal area inside Burma close to Chittagong in East Bengal. She didn't know for sure, but it was likely that Andrew was involved in the fighting. While she worried about him, it made her the more determined to do her bit.

'I'm spending most of my time volunteering as it is,' she explained to her mother. 'And there's no reason why a single woman like me shouldn't be prepared to go where I'm most needed.'

'What about next season?' her mother questioned. 'Won't the Lomaxes expect you to help at The Raj-in-the-Hills?'

Stella felt a now familiar feeling of anxiety and sadness at the mention of the Lomaxes. 'Not if I'm volunteering full-time in general service. I've written to explain.'

In some ways, it would be easier not to return to Gulmarg and be confronted with seeing Belle every day while not being able to mother her. Going to work somewhere with no associations with Belle or the Lomaxes would be easier in the long run.

After that, things moved swiftly. By mid-December she had been given her posting. Stella was slightly stunned to find she was being sent to New Delhi as secretary to a conservator of forests who had been seconded to the Defence Department as an inspector of gun carriages. It sounded a very responsible position, on top of which Delhi lay over four hundred miles and a long train journey away.

'His name's Major Maclagan,' Stella told her family, 'and he used to work in Lahore before the war, so at least we'll be able to talk about the Punjab. He's going to be away in Bombay for Christmas, so they've agreed I can spend Christmas here and then travel down to Delhi before the end of the year.'

'What does inspecting gun carriages mean?' Yvonne asked curiously.

Stella shrugged. 'Something to do with the timber used to make them, I think. I don't imagine I'll need to know more than how to spell the names of the trees used.'

'Well, you'll be good at that,' said Jimmy. 'You've always been happiest among the trees and plants of Kashmir, haven't you?'

Stella gave him a grateful look. 'I'm going to miss you all so much though.'

'We'll miss you too,' said Yvonne with a sad smile. 'But it won't be forever.'

On Boxing Day, the Duboises went round to Auntie Rose and Uncle Toby's flat in Lalkutri for the traditional Dixon all-day party. There was a false heartiness to the Dixons' welcome and Stella knew it was because they were trying to mask their worry over their eldest son Rick, who was rumoured to be flying military supplies over the Arakan.

'They say that the British are getting bogged down in the jungle,' said Clive, 'and that only the Indian Air Force is saving them from defeat.'

'I don't know where you get such tales from,' Auntie Rose exclaimed to her son-in-law. 'That's anti-British propaganda.'

'Yes,' Auntie Lucinda agreed. 'I'd heard the Japanese pilots are so short-sighted they need three pairs of spectacles to see. So fit young men like Rick will defeat them every time.'

Cousin Sigmund snorted in disbelief. 'Auntie! That's nonsense. The Japs have proved themselves deadly in the air from China to Burma.'

'Let's not argue today,' Ada intervened. 'Stella will be leaving us soon too, so let's just be happy the rest of us are all here together.'

Stella hid her concern at Clive's gloomy words – she too had picked up rumours from a WAC friend who worked in the telegraph exchange that the conflict in the Arakan was not going well.

But there was no point in dwelling on it. This would be her last family party for the foreseeable future and she was going to make the most of it. She went to chat to her cousin Lucy who was hopeful that Monty might get leave soon; she hadn't seen her fiancé for over a year and a half.

'But his last letter hinted he'd soon be leaving the desert behind,' Lucy said, her eyes shining. 'I just want him home long enough to get married!'

'I'm sure he will if he possibly can,' said Stella with a smile of reassurance.

Stella was distracted from their conversation by baby June, who was red-cheeked and grizzling. Bracing herself, she went over and took her from Ada's arms.

'She's teething,' said Ada, 'and keeping us up all night.'

'Party girl,' said Stella, smiling.

She settled the fretful infant in the crook of her arm and pressed the knuckle of her little finger between June's hot gums. June bit down with surprising strength. Stella's chest tightened to think of Esmie or Gabina doing the same for Belle. She walked around the room, bouncing her gently in her arms and whispering rhymes in her ear while all around them was chatter and laughter.

Gradually the baby's whimpering eased and her eyelids grew heavy. Stella was struck by how long and beautiful her eyelashes were against her creamy skin. She bent and kissed June's hot cheek and then handed her back to Ada.

The cousins exchanged a long look.

'You're a natural mother,' said Ada with a quizzical smile.

Stella felt herself blushing. 'Plenty of practice with my nephew,' she answered.

A moment later, Sigmund was thrusting a drink into her hand and asking her about Andrew.

'You know he came round here when he passed through Pindi in April?'

'No, I didn't,' Stella said, her pulse beginning to thump at the sudden mention of his name.

'It was like we'd never been apart,' said her cousin. 'He was just the same.'

'Yes,' Stella agreed. 'He's as friendly as ever. I saw him in November.'

'So he's left the North West Frontier?'

Stella nodded. 'I think he's down in Chittagong – maybe the Arakan.'

Sigmund pulled a face. 'Let's hope not.' He must have sensed her anxiety. 'Even if he is, Andrew can take care of himself – he always could.'

'Yes, let's hope so,' said Stella, sending up a prayer to keep him safe, wherever he was.

When it was time to go, the Duboises – merry with good food and drink – clattered down the outside steps to the street below, waving and shouting their thanks.

'Merry Christmas again, everyone!' Jimmy called out.

'Good luck, Stella!' shouted Sigmund.

'Bring back a handsome officer!' Ada teased.

Stella laughed. Her throat constricted with emotion at the sight of her relatives leaning over the balcony and grinning. She had no idea when she would see them again.

'Goodbye!' she called back.

As they walked home, a few snowflakes fluttered around them and they bent their heads into the raw night wind. Myrtle and Yvonne walked ahead, pushing a sleeping Charles in his pram. Stella linked her arm through Jimmy's.

'Dad would have enjoyed today,' she said wistfully.

He squeezed her arm. 'He'll have been hosting a pukka party wherever he's gone.'

Stella smiled. 'Yes, he will.'

Jimmy added, 'There's no need to worry about Ma – I'll look after her.'

'I know.' She kissed his cheek.

'What was that for?'

'Because Pa would have been so proud of you – and so am I.'

'Stop being sentimental!' He laughed and then kissed her back.

Chapter 50

New Delhi, January 1943

On the dot of half past seven in the morning, Major Maclagan breezed into the small, cramped office that had been lent to his operation by the Director of Armaments. Stella was already at work, knowing how enthusiastic her new boss was for punctuality.

'Morning, Miss Dubois!'

'Good morning, Major. There's tea in the pot, sir. Would you like some?'

'Aye, don't mind if I do,' he said, rubbing his hands. 'It's a raw day.'

Taking his coat and military cap, Stella hung them on the stand by the door and then proceeded to pour out tea into his favourite large china cup while her boss sat down to work. She had never known anyone who drank as much tea as he did – gallons of it – and he was happiest drinking it lukewarm, well stewed and with three heaps of sugar.

As she placed it before him, he asked, 'I hope you're settling in well, lassie?'

'Yes, thank you, Major.' Stella smiled. 'My room at the YWCA is quite comfortable and I can cycle easily to work – thanks to you finding me that bicycle.'

Stella wondered if she sometimes chattered on too much to the major – her mother had warned her against it – but he was an easy man to talk to as long as it didn't interfere with work.

She was beginning to get to grips with her duties: hours of typing up his half-illegible notes on timber supply, sending letters, wiring telegrams and making sure he had his lecture notes for training ordnance officers in timber duties.

She typed letters about grades of timber and rough planking to meet the demand for air screws for the ever-expanding Indian Air Force. She wrote on Maclagan's behalf to sawmill suppliers in Calcutta, timber merchants in Bombay and workshops making rifles in Jubbulpore. She took minutes on meetings about plywood pontoons and whether tent pegs could be made from teak scraps.

Her boss, a gaunt-faced wiry Scottish veteran of the Great War, worked himself tirelessly on behalf of the military forces and expected Stella to do the same. They worked twelve-hour days and he was single-minded in his efforts to deliver what was needed, from ammunition boxes and flexible duckboards to radio towers and flying boats.

At first Stella had been wary of his brusque manner. In her first week he had lost his temper with a junior officer for allowing shoddy work to pass inspection in a factory making tent poles.

'We can't afford sloppiness,' he had explained to a startled Stella. 'If the timber is bad quality or the machinery is not properly maintained, then the products will be rejected. It costs us all a lot more in the long run. Better to find a substitute such as bamboo than accept dud wood.'

But she soon grew to realise that under his gruff exterior he was a compassionate man who was missing his wife and family. He had a photograph on his desk of a smiling woman with her arms around a lanky serious-faced boy and a grinning younger girl with curly hair.

'Margo went back home in the summer of '39,' he confided to Stella one evening when they'd been working extra late. He looked exhausted after a particularly stressful day attempting to persuade the North East Railways to prioritise the transporting of bamboo to Calcutta. 'She went home to settle our son into school and when war broke out decided to stay – didn't want to risk the children being torpedoed on the way back out.'

Stella was aghast. 'You haven't seen them for three and a half years, sir?'

He shook his head, his brown eyes glinting with tears.

'That must be very hard for you both,' said Stella, 'and for the children.'

He took a moment to compose himself. 'Some have it worse,' said Maclagan. 'At least they're all still alive and relatively safe. They're living near Inverness with Margo's mother and loving the outdoor life.'

It made her think of the Lomaxes being separated from Andrew for far longer and how that had taken its toll on them all.

Stella sympathised. She was doing the same; driving herself hard at the office so that she lessened the time she had to dwell on what Belle might be doing. She knew that her boss appreciated her work ethic and sometimes apologised for keeping her so late at headquarters.

'Do you have a young man waiting for you somewhere, Miss Dubois?' he suddenly asked.

Stella blushed. 'No, not now. I was engaged for a while but it ended . . .'

'I'm sorry,' said the major. 'Was he killed in action?'

'No, nothing like that. It turned out he was already married.'

He stopped for moment and stared at her, and Stella wondered why on earth she'd told him. Perhaps because he'd been so ready to confide in her. He wasn't the buttoned-up military man that others took him for.

'Well, you're better off without such a scoundrel,' he answered. 'Somewhere, Miss Dubois, there will be a man worthy of you. Don't you dare settle for less.'

He went swiftly to his desk and from the large bottom drawer pulled out a bottle of sweet sherry. He poured a little into two tea cups and handed her one, saying, 'It's medicinal. Drink it, lassie.'

Despite not liking sweet sherry, Stella was touched by his concern.

He raised his cup. 'To reunions with loved ones!'

'That I can drink to,' said Stella with a grateful smile, and clinked his cup.

At times, Major Maclagan had to go away on business, visiting saw-mills in Calcutta or inspecting armaments at the gun carriage factory in Jubbulpore. Stella would arrange his travel and accommodation as best she could, and deal with telephone calls, letters and telegrams in his absence.

'You'll have a bit of respite while I'm away,' he said with a smile. 'Make sure you play some tennis or socialise with your fellow clerks.'

But Stella found that time hung heavy on her hands while he was gone and looked for extra jobs to do, helping out at the WVS canteen rather than going back early to her digs. Yet she was thankful that Maclagan was away in early March on Belle's first birthday. Stella found the day excruciatingly difficult. She couldn't settle to typing or even the simplest of filing jobs. She made excuses to a deputy assistant about being unwell and retreated to the YWCA.

She spent the rest of the day stitching flowers onto a sunhat for Belle and crying over the one photograph she carried everywhere. It was of her daughter sitting propped on a pile of cushions in the hotel garden at Gulmarg, looking wide-eyed at the camera, her mouth a little blurred as she was on the point of smiling.

Stella had already sent a birthday card with some money for the Lomaxes to buy clothes or something practical for the girl. Then, as evening descended, she decided to write a letter to her daughter that she never intended to send, but wrote simply to ease the pain of separation.

> *My darling Belle,*
>
> *Today is your first birthday and a year since you came into my life like a fierce flame – brightening my existence and at the same time burning a hole in my heart as I knew I wasn't able to keep you. I wonder what you are doing on this special day? I imagine the Lomaxes are spoiling you with jam sandwiches and cake. Perhaps Gabina has taken you for a walk through the village in your pram – but no, there will still be snow on the paths so maybe Mr Lomax has put you on his shoulders and carried you to see the first spring blossom? I can just see you riding high like a chubby little goddess, your cheeks red in the cold! Do you wear the knitted outfit I sent or have you already outgrown it?*
>
> *I feel so desolate that I can't see you changing day by day – you are no longer a baby – and I know from Esmie that you are beginning to point to things and babble as if you are carrying on a conversation.*
>
> *But what keeps me going is knowing that you are being cared for by people who love you almost as*

much as I do. One day, I will hold you in my arms
again and kiss your soft hair – that day will not come
soon enough – and even though you will never be
truly mine again I will be happy for any involvement
in your growing up. I can no more stop loving you
than stop breathing.

> *Happy birthday my precious girl!*
> *With all the love in the world,*
> *Your adoring Mummy xxxxxxx*

After the anniversary passed, Stella settled to her job more easily
and with a renewed determination to do her best for the major. The
news on the Burma Front was grim, and for the umpteenth time
Stella worried over Andrew and whether he was involved.

'There's going to be a lot of reorganisation,' Maclagan pre-
dicted. 'General Slim is being put in charge of rebuilding the 14th
Army – and there's talk of a new command being set up to coordinate all the forces in the east against the Japs. The Americans are
insisting on more being done to help them support the Chinese
resistance.'

'Is that why there are so many Americans passing through
Delhi?' asked Stella.

'Aye, they're heading for Calcutta and the air bases in Assam,'
said the major.

In May, as the temperature climbed and Delhi became unbearable in the pre-monsoon heat, the major went to a conference in
Baroda to speak on soil erosion – his area of expertise – and came
back dispirited at the lack of enthusiasm for his suggestions. She
knew that his greatest passion was the forestry work that he'd had

to give up while he was seconded to the army for the duration of the war.

'Perhaps people don't have the energy to think beyond war work at the moment,' Stella suggested. 'One day, they'll be more grateful for your ideas, sir.'

He brightened. 'Thank you, Miss Dubois. You're a great tonic to my flagging spirits at times. I love the optimism of the young.'

She ordered up a jug of lime juice and for a few minutes the major relaxed while she distracted him with talk about The Raj Hotel and its eccentric long-time residents. He too enjoyed reminiscing about his early days in the Punjab, and Stella knew that his love of the region had been one of the reasons he'd chosen a secretary from Rawalpindi, so they would have something in common.

'I must say I envy you all those summers you worked in Gulmarg. Never got that far into the mountains myself,' he admitted. 'But one day I'd like to take Margo there – when she comes back . . .'

Stella saw sadness cloud his eyes and said quickly, 'I'm sure the Lomaxes would give you a great welcome if you stayed at The Raj-in-the-Hills, sir. There's no more beautiful spot in the world.'

She felt such longing for the place. She would never be able to tell her employer that the main reason for this was her baby daughter, whom she missed every day of her life. Despite starting afresh in a city hundreds of miles away, her yearning seemed to grow stronger rather than diminish as time went by.

As spring turned into summer, as the days grew ever steamier and it seemed there was no relief to be had, Stella grew to regret that she hadn't taken any leave and gone back to the mountains. The monsoon arrived with a torrential downpour that turned the baked roads to muddy ponds. Greenery sprouted from gutters and ditches, roofs leaked and children shrieked with joy as they splashed each other with tin bowls of water.

Then a letter came that made Stella thankful that she hadn't gone away as it would have lain unread until her return.

'It's from Andrew Lomax!' She couldn't hide her euphoria at hearing from him at long last.

'The young officer from the Borderers you've talked about?' Maclagan asked.

'Yes, my childhood friend.' Stella tore the single sheet of thin paper from its envelope and read it eagerly.

'Is he well?' the major asked.

Stella swallowed, her pulse thumping in relief. 'Yes – thank you. He's in Chota Nagpur on jungle training. Where is that exactly?'

'West Bengal way,' said Maclagan. 'Covers a large area between there and Bihar. That'll be General Slim getting them in shape for Burma.' Quickly, he added, 'Not that young Lomax will necessarily be sent there.'

Stella was touched at his attempt to reassure her.

She reread the short note – written on a scrap of paper that looked torn from the back of a book. It was breezy and affectionate yet told her little.

> *. . . I got your nice letter from Delhi and it means a lot that you think of me. But there's no need to worry, I'm still in one piece and fit as a fiddle. It's horribly hot and sticky here in Chota Nagpur. My poor friend John Grant (one of the best officers I've ever served with) got a dose of malaria and has been shipped off to the hills to recuperate. I would give my eye-teeth to be in Gulmarg right now or swimming in Dal Lake. Is Delhi like a furnace too? Or maybe*

you've been allowed to escape to the mountains by
your taskmaster of a boss?

I often think of our morning together in Pindi –
I'm deeply grateful I had the chance to see you before
going on active service. I know I've always been a
hopeless pen-pal but please keep writing to me all the
same. You have no idea how much it brightens up my
day to get a letter from you.

Love from Andrew xx

Stella gazed at the final line. Was it just a casual signing off or was it indicating something stronger? What did the two kisses mean? She quickly folded the letter; she was reading more into things than she should. It was just Andrew being typically friendly. He was engaged to another woman and had probably never thought of her romantically at all.

Ridiculous as it seemed, she realised that that brief time seeing him in Rawalpindi as a grown man had stirred deep feelings in her that she didn't think she'd ever feel again after Hugh.

'Are you all right, Miss Dubois?' Maclagan asked her quizzically.

Stella shoved the letter in her pocket. 'Yes,' she said a little breathlessly. 'I'm fine, thanks.'

She went swiftly to her typewriter and forced her mind back on her work.

Chapter 51

Two weeks later, the major came into the office brisker than Stella had seen him for a while.

'I'm being sent up to the Forest Institute at Dehradun to run some tests and I'll take the opportunity to check on some of the plantations while I'm up there.'

Stella felt a pang of envy; Dehradun was on the fringe of the Himalayan foothills. 'Very good, sir. What would you like me to do while you're away? I could prepare some material for the next inspection at Jubbulpore.'

His gaunt face lit in a tired smile. 'You're coming with me. And there's to be no argument. I can't possibly manage all that typing and letter-writing without you.'

Stella let out a squeal of delight. 'Wonderful! Thank you, sir.'

'Good,' he replied. 'We leave in two days' time. See if you can book us onto the night express – it'll be slightly less unbearable than travelling during the day.'

Three nights later, Stella and the major were boarding a crowded train heading north to Dehradun. Because of the lack of billets, they had to share a carriage together, which was also occupied by two middle-aged men dressed in a uniform that Stella didn't recognise. They stood up and bowed politely. To her amazement, they turned out to be Italians. Maclagan, finding a common language with them in French, discovered they were veterans of the Italia Redenta.

'They've lived in China and the Far East since the end of the Great War,' Maclagan relayed the conversation to Stella. 'Quite remarkable. If I understand correctly, they came from Trieste, which used to be part of the Austro-Hungarian Empire, and were taken prisoner by Tsarist Russians. I don't think they've ever been back to Italy – but they certainly don't approve of Mussolini and his thugs.'

The smaller one, with a glistening bald head, pulled a face at the mention of the dictator's name and drew his hand across his throat in a cutting gesture. He laughed at Stella's alarmed expression.

'What on earth are they doing in India?' she asked.

'They're with the Free French. Got out of Indo-China, where they were road engineers, and have offered their expertise. They're on their way to the army training camp at Roorkee. They're very excited about the recent news that the Allies have landed in Sicily.'

The larger Italian nodded enthusiastically at the major's words. 'Fight for Italia – for freedom – it begins!'

Stella smiled at them and gave a thumbs-up gesture, astonished and impressed by their tale. It brought home to her how this war had tipped so many lives upside down right across the world. She shared out their picnic of tinned cheese, biscuits and bananas with the men, and then settled down to try and sleep in the stuffy carriage.

She dozed off to the sound of one of the Italians humming under his breath. In the early hours of the morning she was vaguely aware of the train shunting to a stop, but fell back asleep. It seemed moments later when the major was gently shaking her shoulder.

'Time to get off,' he said. 'We're at Dehradun.'

Stella looked around but their travelling companions had gone.

'Got off at Roorkee,' said Maclagan.

Stella had the strange sensation that she'd dreamt the whole episode of the itinerant Italians who had left their homes during the Great War and had been wandering the east ever since.

Stella was awe-struck by the size and setting of the Forest Institute. By travelling just three miles, they had left behind the noisy bustling streets around Dehradun's railway station and entered an oasis of lush green lawns and trees dominated by a sprawling college of red brick and gleaming white pillars. Some of the lawns had been dug up and planted with wheat, a tell-tale sign of the war.

'It looks like the viceroy's palace in New Delhi,' Stella exclaimed. 'Apart from those mountains!' She gasped at the sight of the Himalayan foothills looming behind, a shimmering blue in the heat.

'Aye,' said Maclagan with a wistful look. 'Margo and I were lucky enough to live here for two years while I taught at the college.' Then he said more briskly, 'Come on, they might still be serving breakfast at the Cranstons' bungalow.'

The major had arranged the accommodation for this trip. He would be lodging with the principal while Stella was given a room in the household of one of the instructors, Mr Cranston. The major introduced Stella to the instructor's wife, a petite dark-haired woman. 'I'll leave you to settle in,' said Maclagan, 'and you can join me at the institute in an hour.'

Mrs Cranston welcomed Stella in with an excited flutter of hands. 'Very pleased to meet you, Miss Dubois! How was your journey? I bet Delhi was roasting.'

Stella could tell at once by her looks and pronounced sing-song accent that she was Anglo-Indian, and it made her think fondly of her mother.

'It's very good of you to have me to stay,' she answered.

'Not at all,' said Mrs Cranston with a kindly smile, and she ushered her into the dining room.

The next four days were spent at the college while Maclagan oversaw the testing of long lengths of Sitka spruce for use in aircraft. Stella observed the operations in a vast godown stacked with planks and smelling of pine resin. It made her yearn for the mountains and she was impatient for the second half of their trip, which would take them north to Mussoorie and beyond.

It was still hot in Dehradun, which was only twelve hundred feet above sea level, and Stella was thankful to retreat into one of the cool, high-ceilinged wood-panelled rooms of the college to type up the major's findings. The place was busy with uniformed men from the different forces, all channelling their efforts into practical solutions for the never-ending demands of the war machine.

Stella searched the faces of those in khaki in the unlikely hope that Andrew might suddenly be among them. There was no reason that she could think of that would bring him to the Forest Institute, but she found increasingly now that she just couldn't get him out of her mind.

At the end of the week, the major borrowed a car from the college and they set off in a heavy downpour for Mussoorie. The mountains had disappeared behind a curtain of grey cloud, but Stella's excitement wasn't dimmed as they left the flat green acres around the institute and headed for the tree-covered hills.

The higher the car climbed, the more the roads twisted around hairpin bends. When the rain eased, Stella stuck her head out of the window and breathed in the sweet scent of rain-soaked ferns and pine needles.

'This reminds me of Murree and the road to Kashmir,' Stella said, and then realised she had tears on her cheeks. Self-consciously, she wiped her face with her handkerchief. 'The cold air's making my eyes water.'

Maclagan gave her a look of understanding. 'It reminds me of Murree too. For you, it must feel like going home.'

Suddenly unable to speak, Stella nodded and gave a tearful smile.

Chapter 52

Stella was overwhelmed by a feeling of familiarity as she walked with her employer in the evening light along the Mall, which was busy with rickshaws and people strolling. Red tin rooftops of houses and hotels nestled among the trees along the steep ridge of the hill station, and the balconied buildings of the main street leading towards the parish church could have been those of Murree.

As the light waned, the mountains behind emerged out of the mist, glowing pink. The banks of cloud sank below the town and obscured the valley where Dehradun lay.

'It's like living above the clouds,' Stella said, gazing in awe at the scene. 'Quite magical.'

They stood leaning on one of the ornate railings watching as the town went into shadow and the sun caught them in its final rays, illuminating their faces. Any moment now, they would be in darkness and the air would turn delightfully chilly.

'Stella?'

Startled by the voice, she turned sideways but couldn't see the man clearly. He was an indistinct outline in the sunset. She shaded her eyes. He came towards her. Her heart knocked against her chest.

'Stella, it *is* you!'

She gasped. 'Andrew? W-what are you doing here?'

He grinned down at her. 'I was going to ask you the same question.'

She wanted to throw her arms around him but felt inhibited by the major's presence. 'This is Major Maclagan. I'm with him on timber business.' She tried to keep her voice from trembling. 'Major, this is my friend Andrew Lomax.'

'Ah, the brave young officer from the Borderers! Miss Dubois has told me all about you.'

As the men shook hands, Andrew looked a little quizzically at Stella. 'I don't know what Stella's been telling you, but she's prone to exaggeration,' he quipped.

The major laughed. 'Tell me,' he said, 'what brings you here?'

'A week of leave,' Andrew explained. 'A friend of mine is recovering from malaria here and wanted some company. And I couldn't resist a trip to the mountains.'

'Isn't it so like Murree?' Stella exclaimed. She was breathless at standing so close to him.

Andrew's eyes shone.

'And where is your friend?' Maclagan asked.

'He's back at the boarding house,' said Andrew. 'He's almost fully recovered – I left him playing chess with a Welsh gunner.'

'Perhaps I could treat you both to dinner tomorrow night? We're paying guests at St Mary's Lodge and the food is plain but plentiful.'

'That would be very kind,' said Andrew. 'I accept on behalf of us both.'

Stella was thrilled. It was like an unexpected gift. They had so much catching up to do since they'd both left Rawalpindi.

The sun set and lights came on along the Mall.

'I think we should head back to the lodge,' said Maclagan. 'I want to be up early to go to the deodar plantation.'

Stella hoped Andrew might walk with them but it appeared his boarding house was in the other direction, so in frustration, she said goodbye and watched him walk away.

Although Stella enjoyed the next day tramping beneath the towering deodar trees helping the major take measurements, she couldn't wait for the evening and seeing Andrew again. She took care to style her hair and put on some lipstick, and then decided at the last minute to rub her lips clean. She felt ashamed of trying to make herself attractive to a man who was already engaged.

The two officers arrived promptly at six and were served sherry in the airy hallway before being ushered into the communal dining room. Andrew's friend, John Grant, was an amiable man with well-groomed reddish hair and moustache, though his skin was still sallow from his bout of fever.

They all shared a long table with the other lodgers. Stella, who was sitting between the major and John Grant, had little opportunity to talk to Andrew, who sat on the major's other side and was monopolised by the matronly wife of an army doctor. Stella chatted to Grant about Scotland. He was from an army family and he talked with affection about his parents and an older sister called Jeanie whom he obviously missed.

'But the army's like family too,' John said with a smile. 'It's amazing how quickly you grow close to men you rely on to keep you alive. Lomax is like a brother to me now.'

Afterwards they were served tea in the sitting room.

'I hear you enjoy a game of chess, Lieutenant Grant?' said the major.

'The game of kings,' replied John with a ready nod.

They retired to a corner table and set up the chess pieces, continuing their conversation about deodar trees and mountain flora.

'Let's leave them to it,' said Andrew. 'Would you like to go onto the veranda and catch the sunset?'

'I'd love to,' Stella said, and she walked ahead, her heart hammering.

The lodge veranda had an elevated view over the Mall and the town below. A handful of other residents were already there so they moved to the far railing.

'It's clearer this evening,' said Stella, breathing in the scent of roses and sweet peas that wafted up from the pocket-size garden that clung to the hillside below. 'We'll get a view of Dehradun.'

Andrew lit up a cigarette and leaned on the balcony, scrutinising her. 'So why did you decide to leave Pindi?'

She gave him a wry look. 'It was partly your fault.'

His dark eyebrows rose. 'My fault?'

'That last time we met – it made me think. You were heading off to fight and I was still doing little more than filing a few memos. I needed to do something more worthwhile for the war effort – not as much as you were doing, but at least something.'

'Well, I had no idea.' Andrew blew out smoke. 'I don't think I've ever inspired anyone to do anything before – least of all you.'

Stella laughed and nudged him. 'Don't let it swell your head too much. It wasn't the only reason.'

Andrew grinned. 'Tell me about Delhi and your job.'

Stella talked about her work for the major.

'Now your turn,' she said. 'Did you see combat in the Arakan? Only tell me what you're allowed to, but don't just say it was all okay because I know from the major that it wasn't.'

Andrew ground out his cigarette and glanced around. He lowered his voice. 'It was a disaster. We were totally unprepared for the conditions – our sappers tried their best to lay roads and get our vehicles moving but it was hopeless in all that hilly jungle. And we didn't have the supply lines – we'd have been finished off if we hadn't retreated. The only thing that saved us was that the enemy were struggling to get supplies in too. We've had a reprieve – but only a temporary one.'

'So how soon will you be going back there?' Stella asked anxiously.

Andrew shrugged. 'We're certainly training for jungle warfare now. The enemy aren't going to give up the prize of India easily. It could be as early as the cold season.'

Stella tried not to show how upset the thought made her. She turned and watched the sun set over the plain, obscuring Dehradun in a hazy golden dust. Searching for a lighter topic she asked, 'Any word from Scotland? I miss hearing Tibby's news to your father.'

Andrew hesitated and then said, 'Grandmamma passed away in April.'

Stella put a hand on his arm. 'Andy, I'm so sorry. I didn't know.'

He nodded. 'She caught a cold which turned into pneumonia. Mamma said that right at the end her mind cleared and apparently she asked for me – wanted me to help her down to the flower room so she could arrange a bouquet as an engagement present. Mamma had to remind her I was in India. After that, she didn't try to get out of bed. My mother said it was very peaceful at the end.'

Andrew held her look and for a moment said nothing.

'What will your mother do now?' Stella asked. 'Will she stay on in the big house alone?'

'She says she wants to keep it ready for when I return,' said Andrew, turning away to study the view. 'In case Felicity and I want to start married life there.'

Stella felt hollow at this reminder that Andrew had a life back in Scotland that she would never be a part of.

'Of course,' she murmured. 'That's thoughtful of your mother.'

439

'Mamma hates being on her own,' said Andrew. 'Though I can't quite see her living under the same roof as Felicity – or vice versa.'

'Do they not see eye to eye?' Stella asked.

He pulled a rueful expression. 'You know my mother – she likes to be the queen bee and my fiancée is showing all the signs of being the same. Mind you,' Andrew added, 'Dickie Mason has been visiting more frequently since Grandmamma's funeral which is making Mamma happy. I'm thankful for that. Makes me feel less guilty that I'm not there to comfort her.'

Stella said, 'It must be very difficult for you to be away from home for so long.'

He gave her a strange look. 'I'm beginning to wonder—'

'Lomax!' They were interrupted by a cry from John Grant. 'I need a dram. The major got to checkmate before I'd hardly made a move.'

Behind him, Major Maclagan chuckled. 'You must still be a little light-headed from the malaria, Lieutenant. I have to take advantage while I can.'

They settled into wicker chairs and summoned drinks from the bearer.

John said, 'The major has very kindly asked us if we'd like to accompany him up to Chakrata tomorrow and stay for a couple of days.'

'Really?' Andrew's eyes widened in surprise.

The major nodded. 'Your friend has shown such an interest in my work and I could show him around the spruce and fir plantations.'

'I must say, I'm very keen,' said John. 'And we don't have to travel back to Chota Nagpur till the end of the week.'

'If you're feeling strong enough?' Andrew queried.

'Feeling tip-top, Lomax.'

Andrew glanced at Stella and she smiled in encouragement, willing him to accept. She held her breath.

'Then yes,' Andrew agreed. 'I can't think of a more pleasant way to spend the rest of my leave.'

The resthouse at Chakrata was a simple whitewashed bungalow with blue wooden shutters and a tin roof, but with a breathtaking view through a break in the fir trees to far snow-peaked mountains. The slope in front was white with marguerites.

'Margo and I sledged here before the war,' Maclagan reminisced.

Stella saw Andrew's expression of longing. 'Does it make you think of Gulmarg?' she asked.

Andrew nodded and Stella saw sadness well up in his eyes before he turned away from her.

That afternoon, the major hired local ponies for them all and a couple of hillsmen with mules to carry and cook their food and bring back any timber samples he wanted taking from the forests.

After a short explore around the nearby deodar forest, they retired to the bungalow for an early supper of rice and curried fowl, tinned pears and fruit cake, washed down with a local milk drink called lassi. By lamplight, Maclagan and Grant settled down to a game of chess and a tot of whisky while Andrew wrote home. Stella would have liked to talk further with Andrew but didn't want to interrupt his letter-writing and so took herself off to bed, falling asleep to the murmur of the men's voices.

Andrew got up from the table, abandoning the half-written letter to his mother.

'Just going for a breath of air before turning in,' he told the chess players.

The air was cool and smelt of the forest. The mountain peaks looked ethereal in the moonlight. The Himalayas – how he had yearned for them and was ecstatic to be finally among them. With soft lamplight spilling out of the whitewashed bungalow, he was transported back to the Gulmarg of his childhood. What a happy childhood it had been. In the clarity of the mountains, Andrew realised how much he had missed India and his family here: his dad, his Meemee . . . and Stella.

He couldn't write a letter home feeling as he did now; it would have been too full of his joy at being back in the foothills of the Himalayas and in Stella's company. Whatever he'd written he wouldn't have been able to hide those feelings, and his mother would undoubtedly have guessed at the source of his happiness. She would probably have been upset and jealous too – and perhaps would have told Felicity.

Felicity and his life in Scotland now seemed so remote, so cold and dull, whereas the mountains and forests of India heightened his senses, making him feel alive and full of energy – and dangerously in love.

He looked at the bungalow and the curtained room where Stella was sleeping. The shock and delight of coming across her in Mussoorie – her beautiful face lit up in the sunset – had made him realise how foolish he had been to dismiss his feelings for her as just a boyhood crush. They went far deeper. Did she guess at them at all? And if so, what did he mean to her? He could tell that she enjoyed his company too – but then they had always got on well and perhaps it meant she would always just see him as no more than a good friend.

He felt weighed down with guilt. He must be careful not to do anything rash that would hurt either his fiancée or Stella.

442

Chapter 53

The next two days were spent riding through the forests and along ridges that gave spectacular glimpses of the mountains. Stella relished this chance to ride again.

Whenever they broke from the cover of the forests, the sun was intense and they would picnic by rivers or streams, pulling off their shoes and cooling their feet in the icy water. Stella noticed how Andrew encouraged John to chat to her and repeat anecdotes about their army life. John was an amusing and genial man, but it was Andrew's company that she craved. She longed to have him to herself so that they could chat freely, but Andrew appeared to be avoiding such opportunities. It frustrated her. Then she chided herself for having such thoughts. No doubt he was missing Felicity, which was just as it should be.

'Is there anywhere to swim around here?' asked John on their penultimate day. 'My friend Lomax likes nothing better than hurling himself into cold water.'

'You can swim at Tiger Fall,' said the major. 'We must make sure you have the opportunity before you leave.'

But on the third and final day, they woke to thick mist.

'Can't see an inch in front of us,' said Maclagan in frustration. 'No point going far today.'

Stella got down to typing up the major's notes while the young men played chess and looked distractedly out of the window. The mist cleared, but rain came on and drummed on the tin roof, making it impossible to have a conversation. When it finally eased, the major said, 'I want to go and see the felling contractor at the next village. Does anyone want to come with me?'

'Yes, I will,' said John, eager to get out.

'How far is Tiger Fall?' Andrew asked.

'Half an hour's ride,' said Maclagan. 'You could easily do it and be back for tea. Take one of the local syces to show you the way.'

'Stella.' Andrew turned to her. 'Do you want a swim?'

Her interest quickened, but she looked to her boss. 'Do you need me, sir, or can I go swimming?'

'Of course you must go,' said Maclagan. 'If anyone deserves an afternoon off it's you, lassie.'

Stella could hardly contain her excitement as she and Andrew set off on ponies behind a local hillsman riding a mule that was carrying their swimming towels and a tiffin basket of provisions. Wisps of mist hung in the trees like giant cobwebs and the branches overhead dripped onto them, soaking their shirts and topees. But it was warm and by the time they had reached the ravine, the sun was breaking through.

They dismounted and stepped towards where the syce was pointing across large boulders that were steaming in the sudden sunshine. Stella could see a stream bubbling and frothing between the rocks and a vertical cliff towering above that was festooned in creepers and overhanging bushes of vivid green hues. They could hear the waterfall thundering nearby but couldn't see it.

Andrew held out his hand. 'It looks slippy.'

Stella took his hand and they scrambled over the rocks. They rounded a stony outcrop and abruptly the ravine opened into a sheltered grotto of ferns and foliage. A wall of water cascaded down the cliff face and drummed into a large pool of grey-green water.

Andrew gave a whoop of delight and pulled Stella onto a sunny ledge of beige rock. At once, he stripped off down to his underpants and plunged in. He came up bellowing at the cold and flicking water from his hair.

'Come on, Dubois, it's wonderful!'

Stella laughed. With a pang, it reminded her of the times they had swum together in Kashmir, diving off the baroness's shikara into the Dal Lake. She swiftly undressed – she'd put on her costume under her clothes at the bungalow – and jumped in after him.

'Oh, it's freezing!' she shrieked, splashing about.

Andrew swam towards the waterfall and dived through the spray, leaping out of the water and disappearing under again. Stella climbed out and sat on the sunny ledge watching him. Although the water had come up to her chest, when Andrew stood it hardly came beyond his waist. She couldn't help noticing the dark hairs on his broad chest and navel and the tautness of his muscled arms. He was wearing something around his neck that looked like a small ivory head.

He caught her staring.

'I was wondering what you had round your neck?' she said, blushing.

'It's Ganesh.' He fingered the head. 'A good luck charm from Dawan – belonged to his father. It's to keep me safe.'

'I'm glad to see it's working,' said Stella.

He looked askance at her and then grinned. 'Why have you got out so soon? You used to tease me about not staying in long enough.'

'I've grown soft in Delhi.'

He swam over to her. 'Oh, have you now? Well, there's only one remedy.'

'Which is?'

And without warning he grabbed her round the waist and pulled her into the pool.

Stella gasped and grabbed at him to stop herself pitching backwards. They both went under. Stella came up spluttering and coughing, her hair steaked across her face. Andrew was laughing. She splashed at him. He dived off and she went after him, throwing water in his face whenever he stopped to look round. They continued their water fight until she was breathless and panting.

'Stop,' she cried.

'Does that mean I win?' he asked, a wide smile across his tanned face.

'Maybe.'

He stood over her. 'I've waited a long time to hear an admission of defeat from Stella Dubois.'

He looked both boyish and virile and Stella felt her heart suddenly ache for him. In that moment as they looked at each other, half-teasingly, half with deep affection, she realised how utterly she had fallen in love with him. She had always loved Andrew – but until recently she hadn't been *in* love with him. The truth of it winded her and made her desolate. She looked away.

'Hey, Stella, what's wrong? I'm only joking.'

She felt treacherous tears brimming. 'I know you are . . .'

He took her gently by the arms. 'What is it?'

His tender touch was too much for her. 'I'm sorry. I'm just worried about you going off to Burma soon. I really care about you, Andy.' She started to cry.

For a moment, he stared at her in bewilderment and then he was pulling her into his arms. 'Oh, Stella. Don't be upset.' He stroked her hair.

She leaned against him, overwhelmed by the feel of his skin against her cheek.

Andrew slackened his hold. 'Stella,' he said quietly, 'I care for you too. I always have done.'

They held each other's gaze. Andrew pushed wet strands of hair away from her face. The feel of his fingers sent a ripple of desire through her. The next moment he was bending towards her, cupping her face in his hands, his lips close to hers. She didn't know if she made the first move or he did, but suddenly they were kissing. She was rocked by the taste and feel of his firm lips. Instantly, she was opening her mouth wider and kissing him eagerly.

Seconds later they were breaking apart.

'Sorry,' Andrew said, 'I shouldn't have . . .'

'No, I'm sorry,' Stella said in confusion. 'It was wrong of me. I don't know what I was thinking.'

She turned and began clambering out of the pool. How could she have allowed herself to kiss him when she knew he was engaged to Felicity? She was behaving no better than Hugh in letting her desire get the better of her. She knew that if Andrew had carried on, she would have willing given herself to him, without a second thought for the promises he had made to the Douglas girl.

Stella felt sick with wanting him and self-disgust. She snatched up her clothes and headed back to the picnic spot. Andrew followed after her but kept his distance. They returned downstream to the syce who had tiffin ready for them on a picnic blanket. Stella towelled off and put her clothes back on over her damp costume.

They hardly said a word as they sat eating. Andrew chatted to the hillsman in faltering Hindustani. They didn't linger and remounted their ponies as soon as the picnic was packed away.

Andrew struggled to say something. 'Stella, I don't know what happened just now but—'

'Don't worry,' she interrupted, engulfed in shame. 'It was entirely my fault for getting emotional. You were just trying to comfort me, I understand that. Please don't think badly of me – I would never try to come between you and Felicity. You won't mention it to anyone, will you?'

His blue eyes looked so sad that she could hardly bear to look at him. She had ruined something between them today and she feared it would never be quite the same again.

'I won't say anything,' Andrew said, his expression tightening.

Stella kicked her pony into a trot and led the way back up the path, trying to keep down the sob that rose in her throat.

Chapter 54

The relentless, energy-sapping heat and humidity of the monsoon season was abating and the temperature in the office was once again bearable under the ceiling fans. In the evenings, there was even a welcome breeze as Stella cycled home in the dark an hour after sundown.

There was a heightened atmosphere about the city. Earlier in the month, Lord Louis Mountbatten had arrived to take up his position as Supreme Allied Commander of South East Asia – his brief to coordinate all three forces across the region. The organisation was soon known simply as SEAC and having it based in New Delhi seemed to have infused the officers and civil servants with a revived energy and sense of purpose.

Major Maclagan grew more optimistic. 'With the good news about Italy siding with the Allies, it looks like the tide is turning in Europe,' he said. 'And we're finally getting the reinforcements we need out here.'

Stella knew that his spirits were also buoyed up by relief that his family in Britain were safer, with the danger of invasion over and their chances of being bombed having lessened too.

New Delhi was full of military personnel – Indian, British, American and African – in transit to postings further east. They filled the canteens and the clubs and then moved on. When some of the other clerks at the YWCA asked Stella to join them at club dances, she declined, saying she was too tired or had letters to write. After a while, they stopped asking.

Major Maclagan drove himself as hard as ever and Stella was happy to work long hours too, for it took her mind off thinking about Belle growing up without her – and stopped her dwelling on her feelings for Andrew.

Yet when the night came and she had solitary hours in her room, she couldn't prevent her thoughts turning to Andrew and their brief time together in the hills. Those days in Mussoorie and Chakrata when they had been constantly in each other's company seemed dreamlike. She had never been so happy – and yet it had all changed after that fateful kiss at Tiger Fall.

Stella lingered over the details of her memory of what had happened – so brief and yet so intense and passionate. Who had instigated it? And who had drawn back first? She had never been sure. It was as if both of them had felt it the most natural gesture – that the pony trek and the swim had been leading up to such a moment. She was convinced she had seen the love in Andrew's eyes – the same love that had stirred inside her.

Yet they had pulled apart almost as quickly as they'd come together, both taken by surprise at the ferocity of the kiss. Stella still blushed with shame at the thought of how she had so easily embraced another woman's fiancé. For all that she loved Andrew, she should never have allowed it to happen.

Andrew obviously felt the same too. He had been silent on the ride back to the forest bungalow and had made sure that they were never alone again. Any subsequent conversation had been in the presence of either John or the major. The following morning, they had left the lush meadows around Chakrata and returned to Mussoorie. A day later, Andrew and John had departed on an early train south and she hadn't seen him again.

Back in a sweltering Delhi, Stella had written to Andrew.

> . . . I can't say it enough, how sorry I am about the incident at the waterfall. It should never have happened. I feel it has spoilt things between us and that's the last thing I want. I hope we can still stay friends. Once this war is over – and I believe one day we will win – you can return to Scotland and Felicity knowing that you did nothing wrong and that I wish you well in your future together. Please forgive my moment of weakness and don't think of it again.

Stella had eventually had a postcard from Andrew of some temple in Ranchi. It made no mention of the kiss at Tiger Fall or her apology. It told her that John Grant was fully recovered and that it was probably thanks to the fresh air and exercise in the hills, which they had both enjoyed. He sent his greetings to the major and wished her well in her work. He had signed it from 'your friend, Andrew'.

There had been no kisses this time and the words sounded so final that Stella doubted he was going to write to her again. With that in mind, she hadn't written since. Yet, it didn't stop her thinking about him constantly and wondering where he was.

November came and the mornings grew pleasantly chilly, but the major's workload increased even more. SEAC were demanding camping tables and packing cases of which there were acute shortages. The RAF needed lightweight containers and Stella sent a flurry of telegrams to a supplier of Kashmir willow baskets, who was inflating his prices.

Meetings ran on late into the evening to resolve which department had the priority in requisitioning wood products. There were endless discussions about tent poles, for which there was a constant need, and about trying to source bamboo from depots all over India.

In December, the major made a hasty trip to Calcutta to oversee the transfer of a shipment of Masonite hardboard for the manufacture of amphibious handcarts. He returned shocked by what he had seen on the city's streets.

'I knew that the Bengal rice harvest had failed,' he said, his look harrowed, 'but not that there was such famine. Everywhere . . . people like skeletons begging. I've never seen anything like it. Terrible, absolutely terrible . . .'

He was subdued for several days and Stella knew he was dwelling on the horrors he had witnessed. She was at a loss as to what to do, overwhelmed by the scale of the distress that the major had described. No one else at her hostel wanted to talk about it.

As Christmas approached, Stella sent an extravagant parcel of clothes for Belle, along with a cardboard picture book and a pull-along wooden mouse. They cost a small fortune to post but shopping for her daughter gave her a bittersweet enjoyment.

She sent cards to the Lomaxes, to her mother and family in Rawalpindi – and to Andrew. She wasn't sure when he would receive it. He might already be back at the front in the Arakan or at some other point along the hundreds of miles of the India-Burma border. But she knew that any post received on active service would be good for morale.

On Christmas Day, hearing that she was going to be on her own, the major invited her to lunch with him.

'I find it difficult without Margo and the children at such a time and don't really want to play happy families with kind friends, so you'd be doing me a great favour, Miss Dubois.'

He took her to a Chinese restaurant, the Cathay, as a complete change from canteen food, and they laughed self-consciously at their attempts to master chopsticks.

'You're missing him, aren't you?' Maclagan startled her with the question. 'Your young Lomax.'

Stella sipped her fruit juice and tried to make light of it. 'He's not my young Lomax, I'm afraid. Already spoken for.'

'Nevertheless,' he answered, 'it was apparent to me – and to Lieutenant Grant – that he has a deep affection for you.'

Stella's insides knotted. 'He might have done,' she admitted. 'But not as much as I do for him. And I don't think he does now.'

'Why do you say that?'

Stella blushed. 'I embarrassed him – that trip to Tiger Fall – I got a bit too emotional and kissed him. We both knew it was a mistake as soon as it happened. But what upsets me the most is that I've spoilt our friendship because of it. We've always been the best of friends and now he doesn't even want to write to me – and I can't blame him.' She put her hands to her burning cheeks. 'I don't know why I'm telling you all this – not very professional of me!'

The major gave her a smile of sympathy. 'I'm sorry, I shouldn't have pried in the first place. I'm supposed to be giving you a day of good cheer, not making you sad over Lomax.'

'You're not making me sad,' said Stella, picking up her chopsticks again. 'It's a lovely meal, thank you.'

453

'Good,' said Maclagan. 'Eat as much as you can but leave space for pudding. I know just the place for jalebi when we're done here. The old jalebi-wallah in Chandni Chawk has been selling the most delicious syrupy sweets in Delhi since Queen Victoria's day.'

Stella smiled. 'Well, if they're better than the ones Felix makes at the Raj-in-the-Hills, I'll be impressed.'

Maclagan chuckled. 'Felix sounds like a man after my own heart.'

Chapter 55

As the New Year approached, Stella wondered how best to get through the festivities without dwelling on the family celebrations at The Raj Hotel. The major was being invited to a dinner party and dance at the club.

'Go out with your friends,' he urged. 'Have a bit of fun, Miss Dubois. I shan't be expecting you in the office tomorrow.'

So, when her office colleagues asked her to go along to a buffet supper at a friend of a friend's house, Stella accepted.

Stella enjoyed the party far more than she thought she would. Perhaps she had been wrong to hide away for months and not socialise. She was naturally gregarious and enjoyed being in company. Her guilt over Andrew had knocked her self-confidence but she was determined to have fun this New Year's Eve.

It was held in an apartment in New Delhi belonging to a couple called Mitchell. Drink flowed and the atmosphere grew raucous. Some naval officers organised them into a series of chaotic games. Ordering Mrs Mitchell to find scarves and napkins for blindfolds, they divided people into two competing lines.

Amid shrieks of laughter and shouts of encouragement, oranges were passed around. Stella found herself being grappled by an American who took the opportunity to kiss her roundly on the mouth.

'Sweetest fruit I ever tasted, yes ma'am!'

She pulled off her blindfold, dug her nails into the squashed orange and sent juice spirting into his eyes. He staggered out of the line laughing.

One of the sailors pulled her to the side. 'You're disqualified, miss. Your punishment is to dance with me later.'

Stella watched in amusement as the game descended into chaos and ended with a heap of bodies on the floor and no winners.

The next game they played was attempting to blow eggshells from one wine glass to the next. This was hampered by people removing their glass to drink or dropping eggshells on the floor.

Eventually, Mr Mitchell stood on a chair and announced it was eleven o'clock and time they all went on to the dance.

The dance was in a club that admitted well-to-do Indians as well as Anglo-Indians like Stella – young women who were filling clerical posts and volunteering for war work.

The dance floor was packed and the band played so loudly that Stella had to shout to be heard over the music. Gerald, the sub-lieutenant who had disqualified her from the game with the orange, grabbed her hand and pulled her into a quickstep.

They danced together for two more dances and then he pushed a way through the crowd to a table and found her a seat.

'It's nearly midnight,' he said. 'I need to get us drinks to toast the New Year. Back in a minute.'

Stella sat back, catching her breath. She was having more fun than she'd imagined. Her partner for the evening seemed pleasant enough. Before being conscripted, Gerald had worked in a bank in Dorset, or maybe Devon – it had been too noisy to hear. He was on his way to join a new ship in Ceylon – his previous one had been torpedoed and he'd been rescued from the sea. He seemed determined to enjoy the evening's merriment.

'Well, blow me down! If it isn't Stella Dubois!'

A woman's voice made her swivel in her chair. At first, she had no idea who the woman with the permed blonde hair and bright-red lipstick was, but then she recognised the high-pitched laugh.

'Moira Jessop?' Stella stood up, recognising her chaperone from the voyage to Britain over a decade ago.

'The very same!' Moira grinned and held out her arms.

Stella gave her a hug. 'It's wonderful to see you,' she said enthusiastically. 'Blonde hair suits you – and that permanent wave. You look so sophisticated.'

Moira patted her groomed hair and smiled. 'Thank you, sweetie. And you look as pretty as ever. I always envied you your green cat's eyes.' She plonked herself down in the seat next to Stella, fanning herself with a gaudy pink fan. 'Who are you with? Is it that navy lad going off to the bar? He's a bit of a dish.'

'I'm not really with him as such . . .'

'Tell me, what are you doing in Delhi?'

'I'm with the WAC working for a Major Maclagan,' said Stella. 'He's in charge of the timber supply to the forces.'

'Heavens, that sounds boring.'

'It's actually quite interesting.' Stella smiled. 'And he's a very nice man who's missing his family in Britain.'

Moira arched her brows. 'Are you having an affair with him, poor lonely man?'

'Certainly not!' Stella went red.

Moira burst out laughing. 'Oh, Stella, you're still as sweet as ever.' She seized Stella's left hand. 'Still not married, I see.'

'No, what about you?'

Moira pulled off her evening glove and waggled a ringed finger. 'Hooked one in the end.' She grinned. 'Never thought I'd end up back in India, but my husband's job is here – well, Calcutta – but we thought it safer if me and the sprog came to Delhi, just in case of the Japs.'

'You have a child?' Stella asked, her heart skipping a beat.

'Yes, a boy – Jonathan – he's just over a year old. Think he's going to be a holy terror, just like his dad.' She laughed. 'You might remember him.'

Stella looked at her, bemused. 'Who? Your husband?'

'Yes, he was on the SS *Rajputana*. In fact, I think he had a bit of a thing for you at the time. Hugh – Hugh Keating. We met in South Africa of all places. I was out there nannying and he was a refugee from Singapore. Isn't it strange how life works out?'

Stella was stunned. She stared at Moira, not quite believing what she'd heard. 'Hugh?' she said incredulously. 'That's not possible . . .'

'I know it sounds outlandish,' said Moira, 'but we did have a bit of a fling on the boat after you'd left. We saw each other for a while, but then he came back out here and we lost touch. When we met again in Cape Town – well, the spark was still there.' She leaned towards Stella and whispered, 'Between you and me, we jumped the gun a bit. Jonathan arrived six months after we got married. Still' – she laughed – 'no one cares about things like that when there's a war on, do they?'

Stella suddenly found it hard to breathe and it was almost as if the room around Moira, sat in front of her, her mouth still moving, had begun to spin. Hugh couldn't possibly be married to Moira. It didn't make sense. For a wild moment, she wondered if Moira was talking about a different Hugh, but then realised how ridiculous that was. There was only one Hugh Keating, only one man who had stolen her heart and then betrayed her.

She felt clammy and sick. She couldn't speak.

'Are you feeling okay?' Moira asked. 'Had a few too many cocktails, eh?'

Stella nodded, bile rising in her throat.

'Oh, look, here he comes with the drinks!' Moira said, waving. 'Hughie, over here. You'll never guess who I've found!'

Stella thought she would faint. Limping slightly and coming towards her, followed by a waiter bearing a tray of cocktails, was Hugh. He was dressed immaculately in a modern dinner suit, his wavy hair a little more receding than before but his face still handsome. The smile on his face froze as he caught sight of Stella. They stared at each other.

'It's Stella,' said Moira. 'Don't you recognise her? Stella Dubois from the SS *Rajputana*.'

Hugh recovered quickly. 'Stella! What a surprise! How very nice to meet you again.' He held out his hand.

Somehow, Stella managed a brief handshake and found her voice. 'Hugh, this certainly is unexpected. Moira tells me you're married – and with a son. Congratulations.'

Seeing him and speaking to him was purgatory, but she had a flicker of satisfaction in seeing him redden and stutter in reply.

'Y-yes . . . th-thank you.'

He sat down beside Moira and started issuing orders to the waiter. 'Give one to the other memsahib too.'

'Not for me, thank you,' said Stella coolly. His discomfort at the situation was giving her strength. 'Gerald is getting me a drink.' She eyed him. 'So, Hugh, what have you been doing since we last met?'

He seemed flummoxed by the question. 'Well, let me see. After a visit home to Dublin I – er – stayed in Britain for a while in '33.'

'Seeing me,' said Moira, with a wink.

Hugh ploughed on. 'Then I went back out to India.'

'To Quetta?' Stella asked.

'Er – no—'

'You couldn't go back there, could you, Hughie?' Moira laughed. 'Not after being shot in the leg by that cuckolded army officer.' She put a gloved hand on Hugh's arm. 'He was a terrible one for the ladies in his bachelor days – but I've always found a bad boy irresistible.'

Stella hid her astonishment. To think how, on the steamer, he had filled Andrew's head with boastful stories. At least he looked embarrassed now.

'Oh, so you left the Agricultural Service?' Stella feigned surprise, enjoying seeing him squirm. Hugh nodded.

'He went to work for McSween and Watson in Calcutta,' Moira answered for him. 'He's done very well. In charge of the whole operation in northern India.'

Stella couldn't resist asking, 'So has Mr Lamont retired?'

Hugh looked at her, sheer panic written across his face.

'Did you know Lamont?' Moira asked in surprise.

'As a passing acquaintance,' Stella said.

'Well, what a small world,' said Moira. 'But that's India for you.'

'Yes, isn't it?' Stella gave Hugh a meaningful look. She turned to Moira. 'Well done you, for being the woman to tame the wild bachelor boy at last.'

'Yes.' Moira grinned. 'Probably because I knew him so well. I wasn't going to fall for that old trick of his for getting out of marriage.'

Stella tensed. 'And what trick was that?'

'Ladies—' Hugh tried to interrupt.

Moira gave a tipsy laugh. 'Pretending that he's already married.'

'Oh?'

Moira leaned towards Stella and in a stage whisper said, 'But I knew from his sister that that was a little fib. Hugh's never been

460

married before.' She sat back. 'Anyway, Hughie and I are made for each other, aren't we, darling?'

'Match made in heaven,' said Hugh, avoiding Stella's look.

At that moment, Gerald returned, having secured a couple of drinks. She saw Hugh visibly relax. There were quick introductions and then the band leader announced the countdown to midnight. They stood up and joined in the loud chanting.

'Ten, nine, eight, seven, six, five, four, three, two, one! Happy New Year!'

Stella knocked back the whisky that Gerald had bought her and then took his hand. 'Let's dance.'

'Great idea,' Gerald agreed.

Stella was trembling all over from the shock encounter with Hugh but took deep breaths as they pushed their way through the melee and began to dance. As she did the foxtrot with the sailor, she tried to absorb all that she had heard.

Her head spun with Moira's words: '. . . *that old trick of his for getting out of marriage . . . pretending that he's already married.'* The letter Hugh had written from Singapore promising to return and marry her once he'd divorced his wife in Ireland had been a double deceit: not only had he never intended marrying her but there had never been another wife.

Stella calculated that at the time Belle was born, Hugh must already have been having an affair with Moira in South Africa. He would never have returned to be with her. Jonathan might already have been conceived before Belle had taken her first breath.

How had she ever fallen for such a man? He was undoubtedly charming, but he was also self-centred and callously manipulative. He had played with her affections, and then used and discarded her.

Stella's shock was turning to seething anger. She was filled with a sudden urge to march up to the Keatings and let rip. She was almost choking with fury.

461

'Are you okay?' Gerald asked. 'You're shaking like a leaf.'

'Do you mind if we go somewhere else?'

He gave her a quizzical look. 'You don't want to stay with your friends?'

Stella was frank. 'No, I can't stand that man.'

'Then I don't mind,' he said with a reassuring smile.

Stella went quickly back to the table and snatched up her handbag and jacket.

'You're not going?' Moira asked.

'Yes,' said Stella.

'But you can't! We've so much to talk about. You haven't told me anything about your life. You simply must stay—'

'Don't badger Stella,' Hugh interrupted his wife. 'Let her go and enjoy her evening with her young man.' And then he winked.

It was too much for Stella. 'You don't need me here to tell you how I've been, Moira. You can just ask Hugh.'

'What do you mean?'

'Ask him about my life at The Raj Hotel – he's been there often enough – and ask him about the week he spent with me up in Gulmarg before he disappeared off to Singapore.'

Moira looked at Hugh, baffled. 'Hugh?'

Flustered, he tried to laugh it off. 'I've no idea what she means.'

'Really?' Stella challenged. 'Then you have a very short memory. Because I remember it all too clearly. The last time I saw you, you'd just bought me a sapphire engagement ring. Don't you remember that, Hugh?'

He was no longer smiling. Stella could see fear in his expression and it made her feel complete disdain. She was sorely tempted to tell Moira about Belle but stopped herself. She wanted to protect her daughter from any association with this contemptible man.

Instead she said, 'But you're welcome to him, Moira. And I hope you give him hell if he so much as looks at another woman.'

462

Linking her arm through Gerald's, Stella made swiftly for the entrance, leaving Moira berating a downcast-looking Hugh.

Outside, Gerald gave her an admiring look. 'Well, you certainly told him where to go.'

Feeling relief and exhilaration, Stella asked, 'Do you like jalebi? I know this amazing place in the old Delhi bazaar.'

'Well, I've no idea what jalebi is,' he admitted, 'but I'm willing to try.'

'They're delicious and ridiculously sweet,' said Stella with a smile, 'and just the way to celebrate the start of 1944.'

Chapter 56

Mayu Range, Burma, January 1944

Andrew sat smoking on a camp chair, a sketch book in his lap. He'd begun drawing again for the first time since leaving Ebbsmouth and wished he could talk to Dawan about it. His latest pencil sketches were of the coastal strip of Burma that they had been patrolling since December. First, he'd drawn a man in a lungi cycling along a network of paths between rice fields, holding an umbrella against the sun, then a fishing boat with a pointed prow that reminded him of the shikaras on Dal Lake and, finally, a village of thatched-roofed bamboo houses.

They didn't convey the vivid colours of the emerald paddy fields, khaki-green fishing pools or the piercing blue of the sky. Dawan would probably call them 'wishy-washy' but they kept Andrew absorbed in the tense hours between patrols and skirmishes with the enemy.

He'd found drawing had been the saving of his sanity in the hard months of training after his leave in the hills in July. His encounter with Stella had left him in turmoil and he'd welcomed the 'toughening up' that their commander ordered. They'd undertaken gruelling route marches through dense jungle in broiling heat and relentless monsoon rain. They'd crossed swollen rivers, stripped naked and carrying their kit on their heads, while dislodged stones whipped their flesh and shingle cut their feet. They'd tried out new machinery, taught mules to cross rivers and shared wet rations crawling with weevils.

Andrew's muscles had ached and his legs had become like iron rods, but it had stopped his feverish thoughts. Blistered, soaked, hungry, caked in mud and with only a sodden groundsheet to sleep on, Andrew had welcomed the exhaustion that delivered him into dreamless sleep.

They'd carried out mock skirmishes against West African troops who had neatly ambushed them and captured their weapons. But they had quickly learnt how to march in silence and to track through jungle without leaving detritus to betray where they'd been.

Their commander told them bluntly, 'We've failed in the past because our enemy has proved the master of jungle warfare – infiltrating and encircling us and cutting off our line of command. We have to be just as cunning in the jungle – and to help us will be the RAF and our allies in the air.'

Their superior liked to quote the charismatic Brigadier Wingate whose guerrilla force, the Chindits, had been dropped behind Japanese lines and supplied by courageous airmen: *'Have no Lines of Communication on the jungle floor. Bring in the goods, like Father Christmas, down the chimney.'*

Before leaving for the front, John had been promoted to captain and Andrew to first lieutenant.

Sitting in the sunshine in the shelter of a scrub-covered slope in Burma, with the new year just a few days old, Andrew found himself reflecting once more on his feelings for Stella.

He had been electrified by her kiss at Tiger Fall. It had nearly felled him. Just beforehand, she'd started to cry and said how she cared for him. He'd hugged her and the feel of her wonderful body pressed against his was like sweet torture. He remembered pushing aside her straggly wet hair and touching her face – that beautiful face he had loved for as long as he could remember – and knowing that he wanted to kiss her.

But it was Stella who had kissed him – and with a passion that had shocked and excited him. It was a moment he had dreamt of for years and yet as soon as it had happened, they had both sprung apart as if they knew it shouldn't have. Within seconds he was feeling remorse and she was reminding him about his fiancée – apologising – which had just compounded his feeling of guilt towards Felicity.

At the same time, he'd wanted to tell Stella how he felt about her and how he knew he should regret what he'd just done, but didn't. She hadn't allowed him to speak and had fled. Nothing he'd done with Felicity had ever affected him in the way that brief embrace with Stella had.

All the way back to Chota Nagpur, Andrew had agonised over what to do. Did it mean that Stella really loved him too? Not just in the way of good friends but with physical desire, like he did? He had been on the point of writing to her several times to make his feelings plain and then she had written to him. Her words had been devastating – she'd regretted the kiss, and didn't want to come between him and Felicity.

It had filled Andrew with renewed shame over his fiancée and he'd buried his feelings for Stella by writing a long letter to Felicity instead. He was still mortified that it was Stella who had reminded him of the right thing to do. When the war was over, and if he came through it unscathed, he would return to Scotland and pick up his old life there.

'Penny for your thoughts, Lomax?' John interrupted his tortured pondering. 'You're not going to the gallows yet.'

Andrew gave a wry smile and stubbed out his cigarette. 'I'm just thinking what an idiot I've been.'

John gave an enquiring look. 'Anything in particular?'

Andrew took off his bush hat and rubbed his temples. 'Over women.'

'Ah,' John said, sitting down beside him. 'Is this anything to do with the lovely Miss Dubois?'

Andrew shot him a look. 'How did you know?'

'Because you've been pining ever since we left Mussoorie, Lomax.' John clapped a hand on his shoulder. 'And that Christmas card Stella sent you is falling apart from being read so much. Besides, you never talk about your fiancée in Scotland any more. It's obvious to me who you're in love with.'

'But Felicity. I feel so guilty . . .'

'When was the last time she wrote to you?' John pointed out.

'She's never been great at letter-writing – neither of us has. That's not a good excuse for letting her down.'

John said, 'We're on the eve of battle. It might all be academic in a few days' time. But for what it's worth, I'd write to Stella and tell her how you really feel. Write to the fiancée too.' His look turned grim. 'Write to them both while you can.'

Before the sun set that evening, Andrew wrote a letter to Stella. For months he had been torn by mixed feelings, but once he finally put pen to paper, he found what he had to say came easily.

As night fell and they bunkered down, alert to attack under cover of darkness, Andrew gave the letter to John.

'Grant,' he said. 'If anything happens to me and I don't make it through, will you make sure Stella gets this, please?'

John gave him a long enquiring look. 'Don't you want to send it anyway?'

Andrew shook his head. 'I don't want to force anything on her that she doesn't want. If I survive, then I must pluck up the courage to tell her in person.'

'Of course, Lomax.' John nodded and, taking the letter, put it safely in his leather attaché case.

Chapter 57

That day, the Borderers fought their way over the Ngakyedauk Pass – the 'Okeydoke' pass as the Tommies and Jocks had soon named it – to arrive at Sinzweya, the hastily defended administration area at the east end of the pass. With characteristic speed and stealth, the Japanese had slipped through the front lines of XV Corps' forward divisions, encircled them and routed the headquarters of 7th Indian Division. Everyone had been taken by surprise.

After the Allies' successful capture of the small port of Maungdaw in January, Andrew's platoon of Borderers had been protecting the doggedly courageous Indian sappers from sniper fire as they'd blasted and widened the pass. But suddenly, the attack they had been expecting from the enemy had come from the north and west – the opposite direction from where the Japanese army lay – and also over the Mayu Range by a seemingly impossible route.

By nightfall the Scottish soldiers reached Sinzweya, which in the past twenty-four hours had become the de facto headquarters for the 7th Division. Troops from the surrounding area, hastily ordered to defend the new HQ, had been struggling in all day. In the fading light, Andrew could see it was a clearing of small fields among hilly, tree-covered slopes, barely half a mile wide.

It was a chaos of milling soldiers running at the double with equipment, hauling artillery and ammunition boxes and digging trenches, while enemy guns fired on them sporadically from the surrounding hills. British tanks were rolling in from the pass behind them. Officers bellowed orders as dressing stations were swiftly set up in dugouts with makeshift bamboo coverings. Ammunition dumps were being piled up at the foot of a central hillock.

With urgency, John Grant was soon detailing their men to dig in. He relayed the stark position to Andrew. 'We're completely cut off from the supply route along the coast but we're to defend the 'admin box' until reinforcements arrive. There's to be no retreat.'

'Let's hope Wingate's Father Christmas comes dropping parcels from the sky,' said Andrew with gallows humour.

That night, as they continued to dig slit trenches, set up gun placements and lay barbed wire, the enemy attacked the perimeter. In the pitch dark, Andrew heard strange animal and bird noises followed by bursts of rifle fire. Only then did he realise the jungle calls were the enemy signalling to each other. Grenades exploded and briefly lit up the conflict. The bitter smell of cordite filled his nostrils and he gritted his teeth at the screams from nearby wounded. All night, they took it in turns to man the posts and open fire on the sounds in the bush.

As day dawned, the attackers crept back to their dugouts in the surrounding hills and a ferocious barrage of shelling began. The Indian and British artillery fired back and the screeching of jungle animals was drowned out by the scream of mortars while the hills reverberated to the pounding of guns.

Then the skies overhead filled with dogfights. Squadrons of Japanese Zeros engaged in battle with Spitfires and Hurricanes. Astonishingly, during these fierce fights, the Dakotas of Troop Carrier Command flew in and dropped vital supplies of food, ammunition and fuel. Andrew watched in awe as the pilots came in low over the Range, almost brushing the jungle canopy to drop their loads by parachute.

Andrew and his platoon gave covering fire as men rushed to retrieve the supplies and carry them to the central dumps. All day, the supply planes kept up their courageous missions.

Amid the noise and danger, the cooks and orderlies managed miraculously to produce meals of rice and tinned meat, and a plum duff pudding made of fruit cake mashed up with crushed biscuits and chocolate.

Andrew found himself squatting on his haunches next to a young moustachioed risaldar who'd been helping organise some sepoys in the human chain retrieving the dropped supplies. He looked about the same age as himself.

'I recognise your insignia, Risaldar,' said Andrew, speaking to him in Urdu. 'You're with the Peshawar Rifles.'

The Indian officer nodded. 'Yes, sahib. My family have served with the Rifles for three generations.'

Andrew smiled. 'Mine have too.'

The risaldar's eyes widened in surprise. 'Then I am very honoured to meet you, sahib.'

'What's your name and where do you come from?' Andrew asked.

'Mohammed Ali Khan, sahib. I'm from Gardan in the North West Frontier.'

'I was stationed at the Frontier when I was first posted out here,' said Andrew.

'You did not want to join the regiment of your ancestors, sahib?' he asked.

Andrew hesitated. 'No, I decided to join a Scottish one.'

'And, sahib, may I respectfully ask your name?'

'Lomax,' Andrew answered. 'Lieutenant Lomax.'

The young officer's face broke into a broad smile. 'Lomax! That name is talked of with honour in my family.'

'Really?' Andrew grinned with delight.

'Yes, sahib. My grandfather Tor Khan served with a Captain Lomax on the Frontier and in Mesopotamia. Perhaps your grandfather? He spoke most highly of him.'

Andrew's smiled faded. 'It can't have been my grandfather. He was retired by then.' He felt a familiar tension at the thought of his father's career ending in disgrace. The young man would hardly be talking about Tom. Why had he risked a conversation with a Peshawar Rifles officer?

'Then your father was in Mesopotamia?' Khan persisted.

Andrew nodded. 'But I don't think your grandfather can mean him. I'm afraid my father let down the regiment and had to be court-martialled. He's a good man but cracked under pressure – war affects some men like that.'

Mohammed Ali Khan looked at him, puzzled. 'No, no. Captain Thomas Lomax was a hero. My grandfather says Lomax Sahib was a lion among men. He risked court-martial to save the life of a sepoy.'

'Saved a sepoy?' Andrew repeated in confusion.

The risaldar nodded. 'One of our kin. He had fought all through the war. Very brave man. But he went mad and threw away his rifle. Lomax Sahib refused to allow a firing squad.'

Andrew stared at him. 'Are you saying that my father was court-martialled for refusing to execute one of his own men?'

'Yes, sahib. Thanks to Captain Lomax my kinsman was spared.'

Andrew's chest tightened. Why had his father never spoken of this? All these years he had been led to believe that his father – when put to the test – had been weak and cowardly. But here was a Pathan warrior – one of the fabled Peshawar Riflemen – who had grown up hearing about the gallantry of Captain Lomax.

Andrew put a hand on the officer's shoulder. 'Thank you for telling me that, Risaldar Khan. That means a great deal to me.'

Khan put his hand to his breast. 'I am greatly honoured to meet you, Lieutenant Lomax.'

'And I you.' Andrew smiled. 'Please convey greetings from my father to your grandfather when you next see him.'

Minutes later, they were on their feet and back to their duties. Andrew was shaken by the encounter. He'd never thought to challenge the slurs on his father's character that he had heard in his childhood. They had just sat within him, all these years, part of his thinking about who his father really was. In a large part, he had to admit, he'd been influenced by his mother's jaundiced opinion about her former husband. But as a youth he'd been desperate to win her love and was prepared to believe whatever she told him.

Yet it seemed that the truth was that his dad had shown true courage in standing up for one of his men, even when his own nerves were shattered and he must have known the punishment would be severe. His admiration for his father soared, and Andrew vowed that if he survived this battle, he would make it up to him for all the wasted years of misunderstanding.

Further air drops came in the afternoon, which Andrew and all of the men were grateful for. Then, just as the light was beginning to wane, there was an enormous explosion in the heart of the camp by Ammunition Hill. Andrew, two hundred yards away, felt the heat of the blast and staggered back as earth and metal fragments rained down. Thick black smoke filled the air and sucked out the oxygen in his lungs. Coughing, he got up and ran to help. An ammo dump had taken a direct hit.

As others rushed to try and put out the fire, Andrew ordered a detachment of his men to help with bamboo stretchers to seek out the wounded in the billowing smoke. The screams of the victims filled the air and the smell of charred flesh was nauseating. They ran back and forth, ferrying the injured to casualty dressing stations.

To Andrew's horror, he saw that one of the wounded was Mohammed Ali Khan. His hands and half his face were burnt and blood was seeping from a chest wound. Instantly, Andrew ripped off his shirt and stuffed it over the wound to staunch the blood. As he was stretchered, Andrew ran along beside the risaldar, encouraging him.

'You're in good hands, Khan. Don't worry, we'll soon have you patched up.'

The young officer gritted his teeth stoically, though Andrew could tell he was in agony. He fixed his gaze on Andrew as he spoke, though his eyes were glazing over with shock and pain.

At the dressing station it was pandemonium. Doctors were rushing about assessing the casualties and shouting for assistance. Orderlies followed with bandages and pain relief. Andrew stayed with the risaldar until he was carried further into the makeshift hospital dugout and out of sight.

As the light drained away beyond Mayu Range, the guns that had pounded the Admin Box all day fell silent. Andrew knew it was only a temporary reprieve – the night patrols harrying their perimeter would pour down the surrounding slopes under cover of dark and attempt to breach their defences.

Andrew retreated to a bamboo bivouac under a tree, lay down half-clothed and fell into exhausted sleep.

Andrew was shaken awake by Corporal Mackenzie. 'Sir! Sorry to wake you, sir, but Captain Grant is asking for you.'

The sky was a pre-dawn grey through the bamboo fronds. Andrew stirred, stiff and aching, unable to believe he had slept untroubled for so long.

He found Grant near the mess tent, clutching a tin mug of tea. John handed it to him. 'Have a slurp.'

'Thanks.' Andrew took it and drank the tepid tea thirstily.

John said in a low voice, 'You'll hear about this officially soon, but there was a raid on the main dressing station last night.'

'The one near the perimeter?' Andrew gasped. It was where they'd taken the casualties from the ammo dump explosion.

'Enemy broke through and temporarily captured the hospital.' Andrew saw the harrowed look on John's face as he ploughed on. 'They bayonetted the patients and shot the medical staff.'

'God in heaven!' Andrew cried.

John's face was taut with suppressed anger as he nodded. 'A handful managed to escape – the less injured ones. I don't know if your young risaldar friend was among the lucky few.'

Andrew covered his face with his hands. 'I should have stayed awake. I should have been there!'

'You couldn't have stopped it,' said John. 'They were overrun. But you can help now with the burials. Take a few men and report to Major Swinson. Some of our boys were among the injured taken there yesterday too.'

The grim task of identifying the butchered patients and burying them in hastily dug graves away from the trenches went on all morning under renewed enemy shelling. Three young Borderers were among the dead – men whose families John would have to write to, relaying the news they would have been dreading. And they retrieved the mutilated body of Mohammed Ali Khan.

Andrew had hardly known the young risaldar but had made an instant connection with him over their shared family history with the Rifles. If it hadn't been for their chance meeting, Andrew would have lived on in ignorance about his father's quiet bravery. Mohammed Ali Khan had given him a precious gift and he determined he would write in person to his grandfather, Tor Khan, and tell him of the risaldar's courage.

The killing of defenceless doctors and patients had a huge effect on the morale of the troops. Fuelled by outrage and a desire for revenge, they redoubled their efforts to defend the 'box' and inflict as many casualties on the enemy as they could.

Day after day, they withstood a relentless barrage from heavy guns, machine guns and mortar fire, while planes strafed them from above. Close to the perimeter they fought with rifles and hand grenades as a fusillade of bullets whistled overhead. The jungle clearing and surrounding hillsides were burnt and scarred by battle, looking as if fire and locusts had swept through the land. At times, in the ferocity of attacks on their posts, the Borderers fought in hand-to-hand combat, repelling the enemy with bayonets and pistols. They took many casualties.

At night, soldiers from the rebel Indian National Army, fighting alongside the Japanese, crept down to the perimeter and taunted the Indians inside the 'box' to turn on their British oppressors and desert. None of them did.

Then, a week after they had first regrouped at Admin Box, on the night of the fourteenth, the Japanese army made an all-out attack. In the confusion of darkness and dense smoke, they broke through the defence of guns, barbed wire and soldiers and by morning had succeeded in taking command of a hill on the perimeter.

But the next day, the Allied troops, supported by tanks of the 25th Dragoons, retook the hill with heavy loss of life.

Andrew and John took it in turns to take command of the unit. Their existence was one of fierce fighting, hastily eaten meals and snatched sleep in the bottom of a trench, hardly aware of the rats that scuttled around them. They had brief conversations.

'If it wasn't for the tanks,' said John, 'we'd have been overrun days ago.'

'And the air drops,' said Andrew. 'Those pilots and air crew deserve bloody medals for what they do.'

'Aye,' John agreed. 'The High Command had a stroke of genius on that one.'

Andrew rubbed his tired eyes and scratched his bearded chin. He looked at his friend in admiration. 'And I don't know how you manage to keep shaving in these conditions. You look ready for dinner in the mess.'

John laughed and took another bite of dry biscuit. 'I'm dreaming of the day we're dining in the mess in Delhi together, Lomax. It'll not be long.'

Andrew gave him a grateful smile. His fellow officer had a knack of raising morale with his encouraging words and cool head. John Grant was unflappable and Andrew strove to follow his example.

As the battle for Admin Box entered its third week, they began to notice changes. The Zeros that had inflicted damage from the air were no longer seen racing out of the blue sky; only their own Spitfires and transport planes were in evidence.

The ground attacks became more sporadic and the tanks that drove counter-offensives at enemy dugouts were being met with less resistance.

John relayed the latest intelligence to Andrew.

'They're not being resupplied like we are,' he said with grim satisfaction. 'They reckon Colonel Tanahashi and his men are running out of ammo – and rations. And what's more,' said John, excitement in his voice, 'relief is on its way.'

Exhausted and battle-weary though he was, Andrew was exhilarated by the news. He felt heady with relief. This was the first time the combined Indian and British armies had stood their ground and defeated the Japanese forces. It would be a huge blow to the enemy and their plan of invading India.

As the friends stood up in the trench, Andrew clasped John's shoulder. 'That is bloody good news, Captain Grant! It calls for a celebration. I'm off up the trench to swop my chocolate ration for some cigarettes.'

John laughed and clapped him on the back. They began to move off. A few paces along the trench, Andrew heard a grunt behind him. He turned around to see John looking at him with surprise on his face. The next moment, there was a whistling sound and a mortar shell exploded on the lip of the trench.

Andrew hardly had time to push his friend out of the way when he was thrown into the air. Something hard slammed into his head. An unbearable noise rang in his ears. Everything went dark. He had a split-second vision of diving into Dal Lake. Stella was already in the water grinning at him. *'I'm here with you.'* Were the words his or Stella's? Then he knew nothing more.

Chapter 58

New Delhi, March 1944

Major Maclagan had been away all week on another frantic chase around Northern India for tent poles, visiting sawmills and harassing suppliers to speed up their operations.

Stella was thankful for his return so that they could now discuss the latest developments on the Burma Front. Her emotions had see-sawed throughout February as bad news was followed by more hopeful reports.

Tales of incredible courage and sacrifice were seeping out as it became clearer by the day that the Indian and British forces had held out against huge odds and had not been annihilated. Not only had they repulsed the Japanese brigades but they had gone on the offensive, capturing border territory along the coastal strip.

'I wonder if Andrew and Captain Grant are among them?' Stella fretted. 'I wish I knew.'

'No news from his parents while I've been away?' asked her boss.

Stella shook her head. She hadn't heard from them since February when Esmie had sent her a joyful but emotional letter telling how Andrew had written to her on the eve of battle.

. . . He said he was truly sorry that he had wasted so much time being angry with me and that I'd never deserved to be treated so cruelly. He was full of remorse about it – dear Andy! – and he asked for my forgiveness. I can't tell you how many tears I've shed since the letter came – tears of relief but also regret. I should have made more effort to win him back too. Oh, Stella, I long for the day when I can throw my arms around our dear boy and hug him tight. We're so anxious about him, knowing he is in the Arakan – or so he tells us in a coded way, referring to his 'friends' the mosquitoes and leeches – and also how there are fishing boats that look like shikaras . . .

Stella was thrilled for Esmie that Andrew had finally offered an olive branch. How she wished she too had received a letter from Andrew to comfort her with loving words. But none had come.

Then she thought how unfair she was being to him. He had obviously reached the same conclusion as she had, that their romantic embrace at Tiger Fall had been an aberration – a moment of madness brought on by the magical setting – and one that should never be repeated. Stella had come to terms with the reality that Andrew belonged to Felicity Douglas. Her greatest wish was that he would come through the conflict in one piece and have a long life ahead of him back in Scotland.

Maclagan tried to cheer her. 'Miss Dubois, it may be trite to say that no news is good news, but it's true. You must take heart from that.'

As winter came to an end, Stella threw herself into long hours at work despite the rising temperature and being hampered by the choking dust that managed to get into everything from the typewriter keys to her shoes. She received a cheery letter from Gerald, the sub-lieutenant she'd met at New Year. In return, she sent him a parcel of jalebi, for which he'd discovered a passion, and hoped that they wouldn't congeal into a sticky mess by the time they arrived at whatever port he docked at next.

Stella avoided all contact with the Keatings, resisting Moira's attempts to meet up for lunch. The only thing she would never regret about her time with Hugh was being able to bring Belle into the world. Despite the agony of separation from her daughter, she could not imagine a time without her. From Esmie's occasional letters, Stella knew that her girl was growing up healthy and loved in the hills of Kashmir.

As the heat of Delhi intensified, Stella turned her thoughts to escaping the city and the impending monsoon for a short break in the hills. She would ask Maclagan for a couple of weeks' leave. In the past she had resisted his attempts to make her take holiday, saying she would only do so when he did. But she had missed Belle's second birthday and increasingly longed to see her again – however briefly – and witness for herself that her daughter was happy.

The day after her boss had granted her request for leave, a letter came for Stella in the office dak. It was in an official buff envelope. Intrigued, Stella took it to her desk and slit it open with a letter knife. Inside was another envelope. Her heart leapt to see Andrew's writing on it: addressed to her, care of the New Delhi office address. With trembling fingers, she pulled out the letter and read. Puzzled, she saw it was dated in January.

My dearest Stella,

I'm in camp sitting watching a glorious sunset over the Bay of Bengal – it's worth the irritation of moskies to see it. I enclose a sketch, though the pencil doesn't do the colours justice. I've taken up drawing again since we last met – I must say that it helps take my mind off things in these worrying times – and it's also been a distraction from examining my heart.

Tonight, though, my good friend Grant has impressed on me that time is running out to let my feelings be known, as we will soon be in the fray once more.

Stella, you have been in my life for as long as I can remember – my good friend, my playmate, my confidante, my rival in sport, my nanny! No, that last one was just to tease you. I have never ever thought of you in that way, despite what my mother would wish. Because men don't fall in love with their nannies – and Stella, I have been in love with you all my life.

I have never loved anyone as strongly as I love you – not even my parents – and I'm ashamed to say, certainly not my poor fiancée.

In the early days, when we went to Scotland together, it was still a boy's infatuation – a schoolboy crush. I pined for days after you left and only really started being happy again after I went to boarding school and made new friends.

But growing into manhood and meeting other girls, I couldn't help comparing each one of them against my ideal of womanhood, which was you, Stella. Not in a million years would I have told

Felicity this, but when I first saw her, I was struck by how her fair hair and pretty eyes reminded me of you. I was drawn to her because in a very small way it was like having a glimpse of you. I'm not proud of that, Stella, and I don't think that's why I asked her to marry me, but I wish you to know that the only woman I've ever really wanted is you.

Seeing you again in India has only confirmed my feelings. I can't tell you how much your kiss at Tiger Fall meant to me. Every time I think of it, I am filled with hunger for you and wish that I could hold you in my arms one more time.

But if you are reading this now, then that longed-for embrace is never to be. I am giving this letter to John for safekeeping and to be sent to you only in the event of my not surviving the battle ahead.

My darling Stella, I had wanted to say these things to you in person – would have done, had I come through this war. But at least I have been able to put my true feelings in writing and hope you aren't too embarrassed by my outpouring. I kiss you across the miles, my dearest heart.

My love forever,
Your Andy xxxxx

Stella's hands shook as she pored over the letter and stared at the neat sketch of fishing boats in shadow. She was too overcome to speak. Never in her wildest dreams had she imagined that Andrew had harboured such deep and lasting love for her. Her chest ached with yearning for him and yet she was paralysed by a sudden numbness. Surely he could not be dead? It was impossible to imagine that such a vibrantly alive man as Andrew could no longer be living somewhere on this earth. Would she not have heard from the Lomaxes if such a dreadful thing had happened?

But the letter told her it was true. Captain Grant would only have sent it if Andrew had been killed. Her darling Andy! How could she bear it?

Stella doubled over, clutching her stomach as if she'd been gored, and let out a howl.

'My dear Miss Dubois!' Maclagan came rushing over from his desk in concern. 'Whatever is the matter?'

Though she could barely breathe, Stella managed to say, 'It's fr-from A-Andrew. He's d-dead . . .!'

She reached out to the major and burying her head in his shoulder, wept uncontrollably.

Chapter 59

The only thought that kept Stella from succumbing totally to her grief was that she must get to Kashmir. Like a lifeline, she clung onto the idea of being with Belle and the Lomaxes.

Major Maclagan swiftly made arrangements for her to travel.

'Of course you must go and be with Andrew's parents,' he encouraged. 'They will want to be with you too, I'm sure of it.'

He insisted on going with her as far as Srinagar. 'I'll book the train to Jammu and then we'll hire a car. I don't like to think of you travelling on your own in such distress, Miss Dubois. And I can do battle over those packing cases and baskets while I'm in the Kashmir capital.'

Stella was deeply grateful for the care he was taking of her. She had no words to describe the darkness that had descended on her since Andrew's letter had come. Even the grief she had felt for her father did not come close to the acute pain she was experiencing now.

She sent a telegram to the Lomaxes to say she was coming, and the next day, she and the major boarded an overcrowded train to the north.

She recalled little of the train journey, only that it was stuffy and hot and the major did his best to coax her to eat and drink.

'Can't have you arriving dehydrated and ill, Miss Dubois.'

Her appetite had gone but she drank the tea he proffered. As the train rattled on, all she could do was fix her mind on seeing Belle – her sapphire-eyed child – whom she had been parted from for nearly two years. What would she look like now? Would she remind her painfully of Hugh or would there be a likeness to her, Stella? Her heart ached to think that Belle would not know her at all; she would be a stranger coming to visit. Esmie would probably introduce her as Auntie Stella. But she could put up with the distress of that as long as she could see and touch and speak to her daughter. It was the one thing that gave her the will to carry on when she felt as if part of her had died with Andrew.

They arrived in the town of Jammu at dawn. A peach haze covered the River Tawi and the plain, and obscured the surrounding hills. By the time the major had negotiated a hire car and they were leaving the busy station, the mist was beginning to clear. Numbly, Stella sat in the passenger seat and gazed at the receding view of the pink fort and the glinting domes of temples and mosques.

Soon the road was taking them upwards into the hills; its twisting and turning made Stella queasy, so she closed her eyes and tried to sleep. She was awoken by the car abruptly stopping. All around were icy-white mountain ranges standing boldly against an azure sky.

Stella gasped. 'Are we in Kashmir?'

'Yes.' Maclagan smiled. 'You've been asleep for hours. I didn't like to stop.'

'I'm so sorry,' said Stella. 'You must be exhausted.'

'I'll be glad to stretch my legs,' he said wryly.

As soon as Stella stepped out of the car, she was hit by the cool freshness of the air. Thick clumps of snow still clung to the side of the road, but all around she could hear the sound of ice melting and streams gurgling.

They were on the edge of a town on a small plateau, surrounded by fresh green fields and orchards. Stella gasped at the sight of apple and cherry blossom like puffs of cloud enveloping the branches.

'It's so beautiful!' she murmured. 'Where are we?'

'It's called Islamabad. They say some Mughal governor once built a garden here.'

Stella breathed in deeply. She had forgotten quite how entrancing Kashmir could be. If anywhere could soothe her bruised heart then it was here: the balm of sweet-scented air, the April blossom and the awe-inspiring jagged peaks of the Himalayas.

By late afternoon, they were driving along the straight road of the Vale of Kashmir with its long avenue of tall poplars and reaching the customs post on the outskirts of Srinagar. Half an hour later the major was parking up outside the elegant Nedous Hotel where he'd booked them in for the night.

Stella was impatient to reach Gulmarg, but realised that it would soon be getting dark and it was still a two-hour drive away. She had insisted to Maclagan that she would make her own way the following day and that he wasn't to go further out of his way to take her there.

'I'll get a lift onwards in one of the traders' vans,' she'd said. 'There'll be plenty of traffic with businesses getting ready for the season.'

What she hadn't told him was that the road might not yet be fully open after the winter snowfalls. It was still nearly a month before the hotel would be up and running for the hot season. The baroness would not be at her houseboat yet, although the town was already busy with military personnel on leave. At the sight of men in uniform, Stella experienced a fresh wave of grief for Andrew. She could only imagine what depths of despair Tom and Esmie must be feeling. God forbid that such a loss would turn Tom suicidal.

She went for a walk to view Dal Lake as the weakening sun sank behind the mountains and spilled golden light over its glassy surface. Across the lake, the vivid green trees of the former Mughal gardens formed perfect reflections in the water. A shikara laden with fodder glided by.

Stella's eyes stung with tears at the memory of swimming there with Andrew long ago, diving off the baroness's shikara into the cold water. One day, she would teach Belle to swim and bring her to the lake.

Suddenly Stella was comforted by her surroundings; it was as if she could feel Andrew's presence with her, urging her to be strong.

'Andy . . .!' She breathed out his name, blinded by tears.

She would make sure that her girl would grow up with the same zest for life and love of this place as Andy. Painful as that thought was, it also brought her solace. She turned back, curbing her impatience to be reunited with her daughter.

At the hotel, the major had got chatting to a fellow forester who was driving up to Gulmarg the following day.

'He's happy to give you a lift,' said Maclagan. 'And it would put my mind at rest to know you weren't attempting the journey on some unreliable cart or lorry.'

'That's very kind.' Stella accepted readily.

She slept little and was up and packed before dawn. She grew tearful as she said goodbye to the major.

'You've been so good to me, sir. I couldn't have got through these past few days without you.'

He patted her hand. 'Not at all. You're to take as much time with the Lomaxes as you need,' he insisted. 'I'll muddle along fine. Good luck, Miss Dubois.'

'Thank you,' Stella said huskily.

Half an hour later, she was waving goodbye and leaving Srinagar in the forester's car.

Stella spent most of the drive in silence. She stared out of the window at the spectacular mountain views as the car bumped over icy ruts on the winding road up to Gulmarg.

Her heart pounded faster the nearer they drew to the mountain resort. When the cluster of chalets and hotels appeared, Stella's vision blurred with fresh tears. The receding snow and the sprinkling of spring flowers across the marg reminded her poignantly of the weeks she'd spent here after giving birth to Belle.

Stella thanked and parted from the forester at the foot of the settlement where he was meeting a colleague. Glad that she had packed stout walking shoes despite the Delhi heat, she swung her canvas bag over her shoulder and trudged up the soggy paths through the village.

The Raj-in-the-Hills came into view. Stella halted, panting for breath. It all looked dearly familiar: the green corrugated roof and the sweep of veranda that was still shuttered and awaiting the summer guests. The lawns and rockery were emerging from the snow in a flurry of alpine flowers. It made Stella think of John Grant and how she had encouraged him to visit Gulmarg. When she felt stronger, she would write to him and thank him for sending on

Andrew's letter – and tell him how she would treasure it till the end of her days.

There appeared to be no one about, so Stella made her way around the side of the hotel to the annex. Tom's studio looked locked up – the door bolted and the windows shuttered – but there was no surprise in that. Would he ever paint again after losing his beloved son? As she rounded the corner, she saw movement on the annex veranda.

A small child, dressed in a pale-blue knitted jacket and tartan skirt, was pushing a wooden toy at the top of the steps. Stella's heart missed a beat. It was the toy mouse that she'd sent as a Christmas present. Pulse racing, Stella walked forward. As she reached the steps, the infant looked up and stopped her playing. She observed Stella with large blue eyes full of curiosity. Stella was winded by their similarity to Hugh's. But then the impression passed, and she saw that the girl had the same-shaped face as hers with a delicate chin and cupid-bow lips. Stella's throat was so tight that she couldn't speak. She stood rooted to the spot, swallowing hard.

'Hello, lady,' the girl said unexpectedly.

Stella gulped back a sob. 'Hello. You must be Belle.'

'Me, Belle,' the girl agreed.

At once a woman appeared out of the shadowed veranda and grabbed Belle's hand to stop her toppling off the steps.

It was Gabina. She gasped in surprise. 'Stella-Mem'!'

Stella mounted the steps. 'Hello, Gabina. Didn't you get my telegram?'

'No,' the ayah answered. 'But please, come, come. Lomax Memsahib will be so happy to see you. It's been too long, Stella-Mem'!'

They hugged. Belle clung to Gabina's salwar kameez and stared up at Stella.

'Who lady?' she asked.

Gabina and Stella exchanged looks. Quickly Gabina said, 'This is your Auntie Stella.'

'Auntie S'ella,' the girl repeated.

Stella crouched down and smiled, drinking in the sight of her daughter after all this time. She noticed that the colour of her hair had lightened to a pale brown. It was wavy, just like Myrtle's.

Stella touched her jacket lightly with a finger. 'I sent you this for Christmas. It suits you. And I'm glad to see you like your wooden mouse.'

Belle suddenly remembered she'd been playing and rushed to pick up the thick string of the toy. She began tugging it across the veranda, where it bumped off the furniture and overturned. Stella hurried to help right it.

'What does the mouse say?' Stella asked. 'Squeak, squeak!'

Belle gave a smile of delight. 'Squeak, squeak,' she imitated.

They laughed and made mouse noises at each other. Stella had to resist pulling the girl into a hug; she didn't want to alarm her. She could hardly believe she was right there beside her.

A voice made her jump. 'Stella? Can it be you?' Standing up, she saw Esmie in the doorway.

'How wonderful!' cried Esmie, holding out her arms.

Stella stumbled towards her, suddenly on the verge of tears. 'Esmie, I had to come!'

Esmie enveloped her in a warm hug. Stella burst out crying.

'Oh, lassie,' Esmie crooned, stroking her hair. 'I'm so glad you did.'

Stella stood clinging onto the older woman and sobbed into her shoulder.

Esmie said gently, 'It must be very emotional, seeing Belle again?'

Stella made a supreme effort to stop weeping. She broke away and fumbled for a handkerchief. Glancing round, she saw Belle had retreated to Gabina and was watching her warily.

'Yes, it is.' Stella was frank. 'I've missed her so much. But that's not why I've come. I sent a telegram. Gabina said you didn't get it.'

'No,' said Esmie. 'When did you send it?'

'Three days ago.'

'Ah, well. Things are less reliable these days – the war has other priorities.'

With a leaden heart, Stella said, 'As soon as I heard about Andrew, I knew I had to be with you.'

Esmie was startled. 'So, you've heard?' she asked.

With fresh tears welling, Stella nodded. 'I – I got a letter . . . from Andrew.'

'You did?' Esmie steered her into a chair. 'It's been such a terrible time, hasn't it?'

Stella blew her nose. 'How is Mr Lomax? He must be distraught.'

Esmie sat down beside her. 'He couldn't bear to wait around here. He's gone to be with Andrew.'

It was distressing to think of Tom, half out of his mind with grief, rushing off to find Andrew's grave. How very cruel for him to have lost his only son to war as well as his only daughter at birth.

'Life is so unfair!' Stella cried. 'I can't believe how strong you are being.'

Esmie gave a puzzled smile. 'I know it's very worrying, but at least we still have him. There's every hope.'

Confused, Stella met her look. 'You mean we still have Mr Lomax?'

Esmie frowned. 'No, I mean we still have Andrew.'

Stella felt faint. 'I don't understand. Andrew is d-dead. I had his letter from Captain Grant – to be sent if he didn't survive . . .'

492

Esmie looked baffled and then grabbed her hand. 'No! He's not dead. It's Captain Grant who died. There must have been a mix-up about the letter.'

'Not dead?' Stella whispered. 'Andrew's not dead?'

'Oh, poor lassie! No wonder you're in such a state.' Esmie squeezed her hand. 'Andrew was wounded in battle but he's still alive. He was taken to hospital in Comilla – near Calcutta – and that's where Tom's gone.'

Stella staggered to the veranda rail. She leaned over and vomited into the half-frozen rose bush below. Her head spun, and then her knees buckled with the shock and she gripped the rail to stop herself collapsing. A moment later, she felt Esmie's hands holding her up.

'There, there, my poor lamb,' she said. 'I'm so sorry you've had to suffer over this misunderstanding. I was waiting to write to you until I had better news from Tom. But Andy's still alive and – God willing – he'll recover and Tom will bring him home. We must hope for the best. Don't cry, Stella.'

Stella gave a sob of relief. Just then, she felt a soft patting on her stockinged leg. She looked down to see Belle staring up at her with solemn eyes.

'Don't cry, S'ella,' Belle repeated, 'don't cry.'

Later, after Esmie had ordered up fresh tea and toast, they sat in the annex sitting room while Gabina took Belle for a short walk.

Esmie told Stella all she knew. 'According to Andrew's superior, Major Swinson, poor Captain Grant was shot dead by a sniper and Andrew was injured in a mortar attack – just when they thought the battle was over. Your letter from Andrew must have been sent when someone went through the captain's effects, but Andrew

493

wouldn't have been there to stop it. By then he was being airlifted out of the Arakan to hospital.'

'How bad is he?' Stella asked anxiously.

'He suffered head injuries and he's lost the sight in one eye.' Esmie spoke calmly but Stella could see by her drawn features that the worry had taken its toll. 'They hope the sight loss might be temporary, but he was weakened by a bout of fever in Comilla. That's why Tom felt he had to be with him. His latest telegram was much more hopeful.'

Esmie drew it from a pocket and showed it to Stella: *Fever passed and Andrew stronger – STOP – Injuries healing but concern over sight – STOP – Humour intact*

Stella handed it back with an anxious smile.

'We must pray his sight recovers,' said Esmie, her expression pained. 'I'm just thankful that Tom is with him.'

Stella was still shaking from the shock of discovering Andrew was still alive and hearing of the death of his friend John.

'Dear Captain Grant,' Stella said. 'He was such a nice man. Andrew will be very upset at his death.'

'You met him in Mussoorie, didn't you?' said Esmie. 'I remember you mentioning him in a letter – though you never told us much about it. I was so envious of you seeing Andrew.'

Stella gave her a guilty look. 'Yes, I'm sorry. At the time . . . well, it didn't go well with Andrew.'

'Oh dear. What happened?'

Stella began unburdening herself to Esmie – there was no better listener than the Scottish nurse. She told her everything about the intense few days in Mussoorie and Chakrata.

'I thought I'd spoilt it all by kissing him at Tiger Fall,' she confessed. 'I felt terrible for doing it but the truth is I'd fallen completely in love with him. We didn't keep in touch after that. I accepted that he'd chosen Felicity and was resigned to not seeing him again. But then his letter came.'

Stella trembled. 'It was a declaration of love – he said he'd always been in love with me. Oh, Esmie, it was the most wonderful letter but it broke me in pieces because I thought he was dead! I was in hell thinking I'd never see him again or have the chance to tell him that I felt the same.'

Esmie touched Stella's shoulder. 'But he's not dead, and you will have the chance to tell him – if that's how you truly feel.'

'Yes!' Stella was choked. She wiped at her eyes. 'And yet . . .'

'What?' Esmie asked. 'Tell me.'

'He wrote that letter in January, never intending to send it,' Stella said. 'I don't doubt it's from the heart but it was only to be a message from beyond the grave.'

'What are you saying?'

'That he might feel differently now. Even though he loves me, he might still care for Felicity too – enough to feel he has to honour his promise to marry her. And I wouldn't want to stand in Andrew's way if he does still want to go back to Scotland and his fiancée.'

Esmie sighed. 'I don't know what is in Andrew's mind – neither of us do. But we'll face it together, lassie. All I want just now is to get him safely home.'

Stella smiled and squeezed her hand. 'So do I.'

Just at that moment, Gabina returned with Belle. The little girl bowled in, cheeks pink with running around, and thrust a posy of wild flowers at Esmie.

'Meemee, flowers!'

Esmie gasped in delight. 'Thank you, wee lamb. They're lovely. Can I give some to Stella? She loves flowers too.'

The girl looked at Stella, assessing her, and then nodded. She grabbed at the posy, pulling a couple of heads off the daisies, and thrust them at Stella. 'This for you.'

'Thank you, Belle.' She couldn't resist touching her daughter's cheek. The skin was soft and warm, just as she'd remembered it.

The girl turned and skipped off to join Gabina.

Stella looked at Esmie. 'She calls you Meemee,' she said quietly.

Esmie nodded. 'I didn't feel it was right that she called me Mummy or Mamma. Tom and I both agreed that I should be her Meemee.'

Stella smiled. 'Just like you are for Andrew.'

'Yes, just like.' Esmie smiled back.

Chapter 60

To keep their frantic minds occupied, Esmie and Stella threw their energies into preparing the hotel for the season. Stella wrote to Major Maclagan telling him the wonderful news about Andrew's survival and asking permission to stay until after her friend's return to Gulmarg. While she awaited his reply, she busied herself with the myriad jobs that she knew so well. A week later a letter came from the major, joyful at her news and telling her to stay as long as needs be; he would find a temporary secretary in the meantime.

While Stella had sleepless nights worrying over Andrew and wondering if they could possibly have a future together – daring to hope that they might – she found huge comfort in being with Belle. Each day she grew to know her daughter better and relished playing with her. For the first few days, the girl was a little shy of her and would hover around Gabina or Esmie, peering at Stella in curiosity.

But soon she was running up to Stella when she caught sight of her, shouting, 'Auntie S'ella! Come on!'

Stella would thrill at the sound of her excited cry and the way the small girl took her by the hand and led her to see a snail on the garden wall or to play with the wooden mouse.

She thought her heart would burst the first time Belle climbed onto her lap and relaxed against her. Stella sang her nursery rhymes and they did hand claps together. She didn't want to think beyond the present or having to return to Delhi without her daughter. As the snowline receded and the margs burst into full flower, she determined to enjoy this gift of time with Belle in this heavenly spot.

Halfway through May, Esmie heard from Tom. Andrew was being discharged from hospital and sent on leave. If all went to plan, they would be back in Gulmarg by the end of the week.

That Friday, Stella thought how Gulmarg was looking at its most beautiful for Andrew's return. Was he already in Srinagar? What was he feeling? This would be his first time back in Kashmir since he left as a thirteen-year-old – it would be a very emotional moment for him.

Or would his thoughts already be racing to Scotland and a life post-war? She had no idea if Andrew's injuries would prevent him from staying in the army. She knew how important his army career was to him and worried at what losing it would mean. Stella pushed away troubling thoughts; the main thing was that he was safe and alive and coming back to his family.

Stella looked at Belle's animated face as the girl babbled and chased after butterflies. How she hoped that Andrew would accept the girl as part of his family.

She found the wait unbearable. Only playing with Belle kept her mind half-occupied, but after the girl had had her tea and Gabina had taken her for a bath before bed, there were still two hours of daylight left – and no arrival from Srinagar.

'If you don't mind, I think I'll go for an evening walk,' she said to Esmie.

Every time she tried to imagine what meeting Andrew would be like, she was struck by the thought that if she was nervous, then

Esmie would be doubly so. Stella thought it might be best if Esmie saw Andrew on her own when he first returned.

'You won't go far, will you?' Esmie asked anxiously. 'And not into the woods. A bear was seen up by the Gujjars' huts a few days ago.'

Stella smiled at her concern. 'I promise not to go into the woods. I'll just circle the golf course and the village. Watch the sunset.'

After wandering aimlessly around the settlement, Stella, still restless, retraced her steps to the high marg. It would only become dangerous after dark and from there she would see the sunset at its best.

Reaching the open meadow, she sank down against a log to regain her breath. The light over the mountains grew mellow; birds called in the surrounding trees. Stella closed her eyes and relaxed. She dozed.

Stella came fully awake. Some noise had disturbed her. In alarm, she looked around. She was in shade and the air was chilly. The sunset was now a fiery orange over the snowy peaks. It must be minutes away from darkness.

She heard it again. Someone calling her name. It sounded like Tom. Stella scrambled to her feet and peered down the slope. In the dusk, a tall figure was making a slow winding progress uphill from the back of the hotel.

He stopped and called out. 'Stella!'

Her heart knocked in her chest. 'Andrew?' she shouted back.

The man waved.

Stella started running downhill, slipping and scrabbling on the dampening grass. Moments later she arrived breathless in front of Andrew. His forehead and one eye were bandaged. He held out his arms.

'Oh, Andrew!' she cried, hugging him tight. He winced and she pulled away. 'Sorry, does that hurt you?'

'I can bear it,' he said with a grimace.

'How are you?' Stella couldn't think of anything to say that would be adequate in the light of what he'd suffered.

'Getting better,' he said.

She sensed a reserve in him, neither of them knowing quite what the situation was between them.

'Your poor eye.' She reached up and gently touched his bandage. 'Though you look very piratical in that eye patch.' As soon as she'd said it, she regretted the remark. It sounded so flippant. 'Sorry, I don't mean to make light of your injuries.'

He smiled. 'Don't be. It's refreshing after all the earnest faces and comments. People mean well but . . .' His breathing was laboured.

'Oh dear,' said Stella. 'I've made you come out searching when you should be resting. Let's get you back.'

'Stella,' he said, 'can we sit somewhere for a minute?'

'Of course.'

He had suddenly sounded so serious, and as they made their way down the slope to the top of the hotel garden, she felt deeply anxious.

Sitting down on a bench, Andrew sighed. Stella wondered if he too was thinking of the last time they had sat there together – just before taking the fateful trip to Scotland – when he had poured out his troubles to her. Once again, she waited breathlessly for him to tell her what was in his heart. Stella watched the final rays of sun light up his features. He had lost weight. His face was thinner and scored with new lines of pain.

Quietly, she said, 'I'm so very sorry about the loss of John Grant. He was a fine man.'

He nodded and she saw him swallow hard.

After a moment, he turned to look at her directly. 'I know from Esmie that you got my letter. It was in John's attaché case. It shouldn't have been sent.'

Stella's insides clenched. 'I know that, Andrew. And I know it must be awkward for you now. I won't hold you to any of it. It's Felicity that you're—'

'Stella,' Andrew interrupted. 'I don't regret anything I wrote in that letter. I only regret that you didn't hear it from me in person – that you had to suffer the anxiety of thinking I was dead.'

Stella said with vehemence, 'Oh, Andrew, it was far more than anxiety. I thought my world had ended when that letter came. It was such a wonderful letter – I had no idea you felt that strongly – and I was so desolate to think I would never be able to tell you . . .'

'Tell me what?' Andrew seized her hand.

Tears brimmed in her eyes. 'That I loved you as much as you said you loved me.'

Andrew clutched her hand harder. 'And do you still feel that way? Because I do.'

'Yes, Andy,' she said, 'very much.'

He pulled her towards him and their arms went around each other. She laid her head against his chest and for a long while they just held one another. Part of Stella never wanted the moment to end, but she also felt she had to know right then what the future meant for them.

She sat back. 'But, Andrew, what about Felicity? I don't want you breaking your promise to her because of what I feel for you.'

'I won't be,' he said.

Stella tensed, bracing herself for the worst. 'Oh, I see . . .'

'I got a letter from Mamma while I was in hospital. It gave me two bits of news – one of them being that Felicity got married to a colonel in the Scots Guards over a month ago.'

Stella looked at him aghast. 'Never?'

Andrew smiled again. 'I should have known she wouldn't have the patience to wait for me. With Flis-Tish it's always been a case of "out of sight – out of mind".'

'I'm sorry,' said Stella, shocked by the fact that Felicity had left it to Lydia to break the news to Andrew.

'I'm not,' he said. 'When I wrote that letter to you, I also wrote to Felicity breaking off our engagement. You see, she had every right to do what she did – although I suspect the colonel had probably been courting her for months anyway.'

Stella gazed at him and gently touched his face. 'I'm glad for her – and I'm glad for us.'

Andrew looked at her intently. 'Will you marry me, Stella?'

Stella felt a surge of happiness well up inside. 'Oh, Andy, yes,' she gasped. 'Yes, a hundred times over!'

They reached for each other and kissed each other fiercely. Stella felt the same passion that had coursed through her at Tiger Fall and yet this time there was no guilty pulling apart. They loved each other equally and Andrew's eager kiss showed that their desire was mutual. When they broke from their embrace, they both were breathless and then grinning.

Not quite believing what was happening, Stella pressed herself against his chest. 'What was your mother's other news?'

Andrew gave a grunt of amusement. 'Another wedding,' he said. 'Marriage seems to be in the air.'

'Who?' she asked. 'Do I know them?'

'Yes, it's Mamma. Dickie finally proposed.'

'Really?' Stella exclaimed.

'Yes, she sounds very happy about it. Was apologising about not waiting till I got home but said at their age they wanted to get on with it.'

'And are you pleased?' Stella asked.

'Very,' Andrew admitted. 'It makes me less guilty about not rushing back to Scotland.'

Stella eyed him. 'So, where do you plan to live?'

'*We*, Stella,' he remarked. 'Where do *we* plan to live. I've been talking things over with Dad. I may not be fit enough to return to the brigade for a while. But if – *once* – this war is won, I want to be wherever you'll be happiest. I shan't stay in the army – I want us never to be parted again. I just want to be with you, Stella, living and working alongside you. Maybe at the Raj in Pindi – or here in Gulmarg. I know this place is very special to us both.'

Stella was tearful at his tender words. 'Yes, it is.'

She felt overwhelmed at the thought. Not only would they be living in the place they loved best, helping Tom and Esmie, but it would mean she would never be parted from Belle. Then anxiety over her secret weighed on her anew. The burden of it was suffocating. Andrew deserved to know the truth. Yet she dreaded telling him, in case he thought less of her for giving up her child.

'Andy' – she hesitated – 'there's something I have to tell you. It might make you think differently about me. But I can't have secrets from you.' A minute ago she had felt that her happiness would never end, but now she needed to steel herself to say the words that she felt might bring that happiness crashing down. 'You see, it's about Belle . . . She's not who you think she is—'

'Stella.' He stopped her. 'I know about Belle.'

Stella was startled. 'How can you?'

'Dad told me.'

Stella put a hand to her mouth and smothered a cry. 'Then you know who the real mother and father are?' she croaked.

'Yes.'

'You must think me such a coward,' Stella whispered, 'giving up my daughter and making your father and Esmie take her.'

Andrew tilted her chin towards him. 'Stella, look at me. I don't think there's a cowardly bone in your body. You were put in an impossible position by that awful Keating. He's the coward. I don't blame you for what you did.'

'Thank you,' Stella said, shaking with relief.

He wiped at her tears with his thumb and kissed her.

'I looked in on Belle as she was sleeping,' he said, his voice tender. 'She's so obviously your daughter.'

Stella gave a teary smile. 'Do you think so?'

'Yes, I do,' he said. 'She's beautiful. And if I'm honest, it makes it easier for me too.'

'In what way?'

'To love her. I understand now why my father and Meemee couldn't tell me about her earlier. I don't have to get used to her being a sister – but I could get used to her being a daughter.'

Stella gasped. 'What are you saying?'

'That once we're married, Belle can live with us as our child.'

Stella clung to him. 'You'd be prepared to do that for me? To take on another man's child – even Hugh's?'

'Of course,' Andrew insisted. 'Belle is your daughter – she's never been, and never will be, Hugh's.'

Stella stifled a sob. 'What about your father and Esmie?'

'They won't stand in our way,' he said. 'They'll be nearby, and they only want what is best for Belle – and for us.'

Stella put her hands around his face and kissed him tenderly on the lips. 'I didn't think I could love you any more than I already do.' She smiled.

Andrew smiled back, and then he was kissing her again with such warmth that she knew, whatever the future brought, they would face it together – always.

Epilogue

Bright autumnal sun filtered through the yellowing leaves of the trees in the British cemetery. Behind the brick walls of the tranquil compound, the stark mountains of the Khyber Pass stood like sentries at attention. As they walked along the path, Stella saw fresh military graves in gleaming white stone and sent up a silent prayer for the bereaved families.

Andrew squeezed her hand. He always seemed to know what she was thinking; he had a gift for empathy. They'd been married for over a year now – the war had been over for nearly three months – and every day she gave thanks that he had been spared.

He'd been invalided out of the army because of his partial sight and they were planning their future between the two Raj Hotels. But The Raj-in-the-Hills was now closed for the cold season and the whole Lomax family would soon be embarking on a voyage back to Scotland for the winter. While Stella relished the thought of seeing Tibby again, she was in some trepidation about meeting Lydia, who had been less than enthusiastic about having Stella as a daughter-in-law. But she would face that encounter with Andrew at her side.

Before the sea journey, Tom and Esmie had decided on this pilgrimage to Peshawar. Although not far from Rawalpindi, Stella had never been to this border town – part ancient trading post of the Pathans, part British army cantonment – on the route to Afghanistan.

Belle broke away from Andrew's other hand and skipped ahead, catching up with Tom and Esmie.

'Wait for me, Meemee!'

Stella turned to Andrew. 'Are you okay?'

He nodded. 'Yes, I want to do this.'

She leaned up and kissed his lips. 'I love you very much.'

He looked back at her adoringly. She had long got used to him wearing an eye patch over his sightless eye; to her it was part of his charm. Everything about him made her happy.

They caught up with the others. Belle was running around restlessly and jumping on and off a low border of bricks around a graveside.

Stella went to her daughter and whispered, 'Why don't you pick some of those wild flowers under the trees for Granddad Tom – to cheer him up?'

'Is Granddad Tom sad?' she asked, her sweet face frowning.

'A little bit.'

'Why is he sad, Mummy?'

'Because he's come to say goodbye to his baby daughter, Amelia,' Stella explained. 'She died a long time ago and is buried here.'

'Like your dog Frisky was buried at Gulmarg?' Belle asked.

'Yes, like that.'

Belle dashed off. 'Back in a minute!'

Stella exchanged amused looks with Andrew. At three and a half, the energetic Belle kept them busy all day long, as well as entertained with her chatter and observations.

They joined Tom and Esmie who were standing in quiet contemplation over two graves: one for Tom's first wife, Mary, and the second for their infant daughter.

Stella read the inscription on the first headstone.

IN LOVING MEMORY OF MARY MAXWELL LOMAX, DEARLY BELOVED WIFE OF CAPTAIN T. LOMAX OF THE PESHAWAR RIFLES, BORN 2ND JANUARY 1888, DIED 5TH JANUARY 1913. ERECTED BY HER SORROWING HUSBAND.

'O FOR THE TOUCH OF A VANISHED HAND, AND THE SOUND OF A VOICE THAT IS STILL.'

Stella had a pang of pity as she watched Tom struggle not to weep. But it was the second grave that tore at her heart.

IN MEMORY OF AMELIA MARY, INFANT DAUGHTER OF CAPTAIN T. LOMAX. BORN 5TH JANUARY 1913, LIVED FOUR DAYS.

'MY FLESH SHALL REST IN LOVE. SAFE IN THE ARMS OF JESUS. OF SUCH IS THE KINGDOM OF HEAVEN.'

Seeing the desolate, loving words, Stella understood for the first time just how much of a burden Tom must have carried for so long – grief that he had bottled up and refused to speak about. Only Esmie, patient and caring over many years, had been able to break through Tom's reserve and show him that he was allowed to grieve for his lost wife and child – owed it to them to acknowledge their existence and pay tribute to their short lives.

Esmie handed Tom a bunch of white chrysanthemums. He placed them on Mary's grave, crouching down to touch the stone.

He rested his hand there a moment. When he stood up, Esmie put her arms around her husband and hugged him in comfort.

Stella turned to Andrew. 'Are you ready?'

He nodded, clutching the second bouquet that Esmie had just passed to him. Andrew stepped over to the baby's grave and spoke in a clear voice.

'Amelia, today I meet you for the first time. All I know about you is that you fought to hang onto life for four days. We don't know what you looked like. Perhaps you and I might have looked alike. I wish I'd got to know you – my big sister.'

He cleared his throat and glanced at Stella. She gave him a nod of encouragement.

'But what I do know,' he carried on, 'is that you were greatly loved. Your dad – *our* dad – has never stopped loving you and never will. Because we Lomaxes are loyal to those we love.' He turned to his father. 'Let's lay the flowers together, Dad.'

Tom stepped towards him and, shoulder to shoulder, they bent and laid the flowers at Amelia's stone. As they stood back up, Tom said hoarsely, 'Thank you, Andy.'

Abruptly, Tom grabbed Andrew in a fierce hug and began to weep.

Stella exchanged an emotional look with Esmie and went to hold her hand.

Just then, Belle came tearing back, waving a ragged bunch of weeds.

'Look, I've got this for you, Granddad!'

Tom let go of Andrew and wiped his eyes quickly with the heels of his hands. He took the proffered grasses.

'Thank you, Belle. They're the best bunch of flowers I've ever been given.'

Belle looked at him in disbelief and laughed. 'Silly Granddad! It's not flowers, it's grass.'

Tom smiled. 'Well, it's the best grass I've ever been given.'

Belle nodded, seemingly satisfied with this. She skipped up to Stella and slipped her hand in hers.

'Mummy, can we go now?'

Smiling at her daughter, she bent down and kissed the top of her head. 'Yes, darling.'

Belle reached up to Andrew to take her other hand. 'Come on, Daddy, we can go.'

Stella's heart was brimming with such fierce love for them both that she couldn't speak. She and Andrew grinned at each other over the girl's head. Then, swinging their daughter between them, they headed for the cemetery gates and into full sunshine.

GLOSSARY

ayah	nurse or nanny
box-wallah	person in trade
burra	big, most important
chaprassy	messenger
chota hazri	breakfast
chota peg	small alcoholic drink/sundowner
chowkidar	watchman, gatekeeper, doorman
dak	mail/post
jalebi	syrupy Indian sweets
mali	gardener
marg	meadow

memsahib	a polite title or form of address for a woman
mofussil	countryside
nimbu pani	lemon/lime drink
sahib	a polite title or form of address for a man
sepoy	Indian soldier
shikar	hunting
shikara	small open boat found on Dal Lake, Kashmir
syce	groom/stable boy
tonga	two-wheeled, horse-drawn carriage
topee	sunhat

ACKNOWLEDGMENTS

In researching this novel (as with *The Emerald Affair*), I would like to acknowledge Ali Khan's wonderful history book on Rawalpindi: *Rawul Pindee: The Raj Years*. I hope, one day, to be able to meet Ali and Ayesha in person.

I wish to express my huge gratitude to those who have worked so hard on my behalf during these unprecedented and difficult times of a worldwide pandemic. Thank you, as ever, to my champion editor, Sammia Hamer and to structural editor, Mike Jones, for his very great care and guidance in shaping this novel. Much appreciated. Also, many thanks to Jill Sawyer for her expert touch at the copyediting stage, to Gill Harvey for her sensitive and careful proofreading and to Plum5 Limited for a gorgeous, evocative cover.

ABOUT THE AUTHOR

Janet MacLeod Trotter is the author of numerous bestselling and acclaimed novels, including *The Hungry Hills*, which was nominated for the *Sunday Times* Young Writer of the Year Award, *The Tea Planter's Daughter*, which was nominated for the Romantic Novelists' Association Novel of the Year Award, and *In the Far Pashmina Mountains*, which was shortlisted for the RNA Historical Romance of the Year Award. Much informed by her own experiences, MacLeod Trotter was raised in the north-east of England by Scottish parents and travelled in India as a young woman. She now divides her time between Northumberland and the Isle of Skye. Find out more about the author and her novels at www.janetmacleodtrotter.com.

Printed in Great Britain
by Amazon